THE RAVENSWOOD WITCH

JENNI KEER

Boldwood

First published in Great Britain in 2024 by Boldwood Books Ltd.

Copyright © Jenni Keer, 2024

Cover Design by Alexandra Allden

Cover Illustration: Shutterstock

The moral right of Jenni Keer to be identified as the author of this work has been asserted in accordance with the Copyright, Designs and Patents Act 1988.

All rights reserved. No part of this book may be reproduced in any form or by any electronic or mechanical means, including information storage and retrieval systems, without written permission from the author, except for the use of brief quotations in a book review.

This book is a work of fiction and, except in the case of historical fact, any resemblance to actual persons, living or dead, is purely coincidental.

Every effort has been made to obtain the necessary permissions with reference to copyright material, both illustrative and quoted. We apologise for any omissions in this respect and will be pleased to make the appropriate acknowledgements in any future edition.

A CIP catalogue record for this book is available from the British Library.

Paperback ISBN 978-1-78513-979-6

Large Print ISBN 978-1-78513-980-2

Hardback ISBN 978-1-78513-978-9

Ebook ISBN 978-1-78513-981-9

Kindle ISBN 978-1-78513-982-6

Audio CD ISBN 978-1-78513-973-4

MP3 CD ISBN 978-1-78513-974-1

Digital audio download ISBN 978-1-78513-977-2

Boldwood Books Ltd
23 Bowerdean Street
London SW6 3TN
www.boldwoodbooks.com

Sharon – this one is for you.
Absolutely not a reader, yet you always read my books,
because that's what friends do...

1

1885

Her heart was pounding and her breaths were raspy in her throat. She was beyond exhausted and had to rest for a moment, steadying herself by placing her hand on a rough gatepost and bending forward to stop herself being sick. It was only then she noticed the jagged scarlet scratches across her fingers where she had pushed the hanging brambles away from her face in her flight. Her terror was such that she hadn't even felt the sharp thorns tear at her skin. How had it come to this? That she should be a fugitive, running from everything she knew?

She dared not stop for long because they were after her, fully aware that she was heading for the ferry, and the horses' pounding hooves were much faster than her shaking legs. An earlier thunderstorm had left the dirt paths and grass banks slippery and wet, and she worried that she would lose her footing in her bone-weary state. Glancing over her shoulder, she saw the gold and copper hues of the rising sun blurring into the deep indigo of night. Dawn was breaking, and soon the blanket of black that had afforded her a degree of cover as she'd raced along the stony tracks and scrambled through the bushy undergrowth would be gone.

Her eyes desperately scanned the riverbanks ahead, searching for the craft that would convey her across the water to Manbury. There, she would catch a train to London; the anonymity of a large city might offer her safety, even though she knew that the few shillings she had wouldn't last long. The coins jangled in her pocket, weighing heavier than they should because they were ill-gotten gains. Her heart beat faster in her chest, weighing heavier than *it* should because it was broken. But it was her soul that weighed the most, for she'd sold it to the Devil.

She forced herself onwards and hurried around the bend in the road, finally spotting a small wooden boat in the distance, moored to a jetty that jutted out into the dark water. Relief flooded through her. It was on her side of the river and would surely set off as soon as she passed the ferryman some of her precious coins. She started to scamper down the stony track that curled towards the river, just as the bulky figure of a man stood up from the steep bank and collided with her.

Unaware of each other until the moment of impact, they became a twisted knot of limbs as they tried to anchor themselves and avoid tumbling to the ground. Inevitably, they toppled backwards as one. Her foot was caught under his leg and there was an unpleasant crunch as the weight of him snapped her ankle.

The pain was intense, and she let out a scream.

'Where the hell did you spring from?' he snapped, and then realised she was crying. 'Damn and blast. I could do without an injured girl on my hands, especially as I seem to have done the damage. But you appeared from nowhere.' He slid his body from hers, briefly wincing as he clutched at his shoulder.

'I'm sure my ankle is broken.' Her sobs came thick and fast. Everything was ruined. She knew enough to know it wouldn't bear her weight and would take weeks to heal. Even if she could somehow hobble to the boat, going any distance beyond that was impossible now. She was done for. They would catch her and she would have to face the consequences of everything that she'd left behind. It was almost certain that she would be hanged.

She noticed his pained expression as he clutched at his arm again.

'Are *you* injured?' she asked. 'Your shoulder…'

'It's not connected to the fall.' He brushed her concern aside, and his brow furrowed as he bent towards her feet to look at her ankle. 'But kind of you to ask.'

She closed her eyes for a moment, the tears still falling. They would certainly catch up with her now. There was nothing for it but to surrender to the inevitable and await her fate. Using a grubby hand to wipe away her tears, she noticed the man's pocket watch had fallen to the soft soil in the tumble. She reached for it but as she turned it over, she saw that the glass had cracked.

'Oh no, your beautiful watch,' she said. 'I'm so sorry. What have I done?'

'What have *you* done? What have *I* done, more's the point. Here you are, likely with a broken ankle, and yet you are concerned about my timepiece. Watches can be mended.'

'So can ankles,' she pointed out, shifting her position slightly, but the pain was too much and she let out a cry.

'Besides, I have long since given up worrying about material possessions. It's people who matter in this world.'

His words brought home to her how totally alone she was. No one would want anything to do with her now. Daniel was dead and she was ultimately responsible. Her body crumpled like a deflating hot air balloon and any remaining fight was expelled with one long, defeated exhalation of breath.

'For goodness' sake, don't faint on me.' He got to his feet using his uninjured arm and leaned over her. 'Let's see if you can stand.'

His large frame made her feel vulnerable, but she gripped his spade-like hand as he heaved her up onto her good leg. The moment she rested her injured foot on the ground, she felt a searing-hot pain. Further tears spilled from her lower lids – partly the excruciating agony and partly the futility of her desperate situation.

'And now you're crying.' His eyes rolled to the heavens. 'I'm not used to the tears of women – they make me uncomfortable.'

'But I must catch the ferry,' she tried to explain, casting glances towards the jetty in the distance. 'It's imperative that I get to London.' She felt giddy and the concerned face of the man before her began to blur as she felt her body sway.

'This is not good,' he muttered to himself. 'I'm taking you to the house.'

'No, I...' But he wasn't asking her permission. The man slipped one arm around her waist and the other under her slender legs, scooping her up and holding her close to his chest. She could smell the sweat of physical exertion and an earthy fustiness coming from his clothing. There were smears of soil across his shirt and forehead, but he was too smartly dressed to be a farm labourer, and too well-spoken, yet he had the look, scent and build of a man who had already been several hours toiling on the land – which made no sense at this early hour.

There was a decidedly unstable moment as he struggled back up to the path, his feet slipping on the wet bank, and she thought they were destined to fall back towards the river again. She might be slight, and he was built like a Shire horse, but by holding her, he had no free hand to steady himself as he attempted to mount the steep incline. He stumbled a couple of times as clumps of soil skittered downhill, but he managed to keep them both upright.

Too weary to do anything other than lie in his arms, she resigned herself to her fate. This complete stranger was in charge and she had no fight left. He was taking her somewhere, regardless of her protestations, and what he chose to do with her when he got her there was out of her control. She was the cornered rat at the back of the barn, who knew the farmer was about to put a swift end to everything with the sharp edge of a shovel. Although a rat would fly at his attacker and fight to the last. But she was no rat.

The approaching rumble of hooves was almost a welcome sound after her two days of flight.

'I am undone,' she whispered, and let her head fall against his neck and her eyes close.

'Hey! You there,' a voice called.

'How can I help you, constable?' the man holding her asked.

'Hand the woman over, there's a good chap.' The trotting came to a halt. 'Goodness, what have you done to her? Has she fainted?'

'Broken her ankle, I fear.'

Her eyes were open again now as she accepted this was the end, and she saw the younger of the two men dismount and walk towards them both.

'This is the woman. I'm sure of it,' he said to his colleague. 'I can take her now.'

Her rescuer looked down at her face and she was sure he could read all the misery and guilt written across it. There was no need for words and no plea of innocence she could utter, because she had done bad things and felt that God was entitled to condemn her. Their eyes met and held, and if her emotions were clear from her expression, so were his. It was as if they shared a brief moment of understanding, both sensing the pain and weariness of the other. The silence lasted longer than it should have done, and the officer gave a small cough to remind them both that he was waiting.

'I don't understand. What on earth do you want with my wife?' He kept his focus on her as he spoke to the policemen.

She scrunched up her eyes in confusion. Had the stranger just told the officer that she was his *wife*? A nauseous feeling washed over her, as the unrelenting throbs of pain made it difficult to focus.

'This woman is not your wife.'

'Are you accusing me of lying?' he challenged, and he changed from the concerned gentleman of before to someone bristling with irritation. 'I think I damn well know my own wife. We've been married for nearly ten years.'

'Of course, Mr Greybourne,' said the older gentleman from his mount. 'But the fugitive was of similar appearance. Slim and with pale yellow hair. She was last seen in a long grey cotton dress, asking about the Manbury ferry. You can't blame us for the assumption.'

'Fugitive?' he enquired.

'Yes, wanted for murder.'

There was an almost imperceptible clench of his square jaw as he absorbed the information.

'I've been out here by the river since first light and I've seen no one of that description come past.'

'Apart from your wife,' the constable said, raising an eyebrow.

'Apart from my wife,' the man repeated.

The older policeman tugged at the reins and the horse lumbered forward a couple of paces, enabling him to inspect the woman in Mr Greybourne's arms.

'Luna Greybourne. Well, well, I don't think I've set eyes on you for nearly seven years. Not close up, at least.' He peered down quizzically at her pale face and frowned. 'You look different to how I remember. Smaller somehow.'

'But, as you all know,' Mr Greybourne reminded the men, 'my wife has been unwell for a very long time.'

'Indeed.' There was an awkward pause.

'So, do please excuse me. I must take her to Mrs Webber, who will know what to do with the ankle, and perhaps have a sedative to ease the pain.'

'Of course.' The younger policeman stepped aside, and the older gentleman doffed his hat.

'If you see anything—'

'I'll be sure to let you know.' He turned towards the house and paused. 'We did hear someone running, not ten minutes since, when we were down at the water's edge. I thought it was children playing but could it have been your runaway?'

The older man nodded. 'Sounds possible. Indebted to you. Come on, Jones, let's not dawdle. Time is of the essence. We don't want her getting on that ferry without us and crossing to the other side.'

The men rode away and the thudding hooves grew fainter, as Mr Greybourne began to walk back up the very path she had run down only minutes before.

'Don't be alarmed. I'm taking you to my home. I fear more rain is on its way and we would both do well to retreat inside. I will not harm you and, if you cause me no trouble, I will keep you safe until your injuries have healed. I shall ask only once and I promise not to pry into your personal business any further, but I should like to know your name, at least?'

She lifted her eyes slowly, taking in his broad shoulders, his square jaw and unshaven skin, until finally their gazes met for a second time. His eyes were as world-weary as her own and dark circles shadowed the sockets. Her chest heaved and she refused to break the questioning stare. A whole minute went by as she contemplated the bleakness of her situation, and then she made a decision, right there on the banks of the river in the cool morning sun. She could never return to her old life and here he was, offering her an alternative – an escape. She would be a fool not to embrace his audacious lie. It offered the possibility of sanctuary, even if only temporarily.

'I'm Luna Greybourne,' she said, raising one eyebrow and challenging him to disagree. 'Your wife.'

2

As she was carried back up the dirt track that ran alongside the winding banks of the river Bran, a large, whitewashed house loomed into view – tall yet crooked, like an old man bending over a cane. Separate from the village she'd run from, it stood alone in the landscape. There had been no other dwellings for over a mile, and it was entirely possible this one was uninhabited. Surely this was not where he was taking her?

To her surprise, Mr Greybourne paused at the gate. The property had a neglected look about it, despite the beautiful meadow of waist-high spring flowers that stretched between the house and the river. Tiny dots of colour bobbed in the breeze and a freshly scythed path cut through the long grasses to the front door, where a solitary clump of butter-coloured daffodils drew the eye. But the building was in a poor state; black mould ran from the corners of the windowsills like tears, and paint peeled from the pretty fascias and gables. Beyond its angular silhouette was the thick backdrop of dense woodland. It was as though the house had crawled from the darkness of the trees and collapsed as soon as it had ventured into the daylight.

Something black shifted in the corner of her peripheral vision and she looked across to the letter box mounted on the opposite gatepost. Her head jerked back in horror. The dead body of a raven, almost the size of a small cat, hung by its feet, nails through both legs and each wing fanned out to the side, catching the breeze like lacy black sails. The creature had a broken neck, its head at a strange angle, as a steady drip of tiny pearls fell from the glistening corpse. As Mr Greybourne pushed the heavy gate open with his good shoulder and took them both through, she leaned closer out of morbid curiosity and then pulled back in shock when she realised that the glistening pearls were maggots. They were writhing around in the nearly empty chest cavity and falling to the ground in search of further food. Had she anything in her stomach, she might have been sick, but she hadn't eaten for two days.

He followed her eyes and his face set into a severe frown.

'Apologies. I haven't had the chance to deal with that yet.'

Had he killed the poor creature? she wondered, and displayed the corpse in such an abhorrent manner? Was it a deterrent to others of his kind? A warning to stay away? And then she noticed the house name carved along the top rail of the gate – Ravenswood. The dead bird and the thick web of trees behind the house almost made the sign superfluous, but the realisation that *this* was their intended destination made the fine hairs on her arms ripple in alarm. She had been warned about this place the previous evening, when she'd spoken briefly to a tinker in the nearby village of Little Doubton. He'd been sitting outside his caravan and hammering a pot into shape on his large steel anvil when she'd asked how best to cross the river.

'The ferry is just past Ravenswood,' the old man had said. 'But don't you be going anywhere near that house and take care to steer well clear of those woods, too. 'Specially at night,' he'd stressed. 'You don't want to be coming across the Ravenswood Witch. Evil, she is. She cursed old Mother Selwood and the poor woman was only able to utter gibberish, her mind completely deranged, until she died three weeks later.'

Dead ravens and witch-inhabited woods. The thought of some evil old crone wandering about casting spells just a short distance away made her shudder in the stranger's wide arms as he strode up the path, carrying her as though she weighed nothing.

Instead of entering through the main door, he took her to the back of the house and into an ill-lit and surprisingly empty kitchen. There were very few pots or utensils about, the dresser was almost bare of crockery and there was sparse furniture for such a big room. In the shadow of the oppressive woods behind the house, it was a gloomy space, but she could feel the heat of the range and there was the comforting aroma of baking bread.

'I think her ankle is broken,' Mr Greybourne said. 'I need your help.'

A middle-aged woman jumped to her feet, holding a half-plucked duck. Tiny downy feathers floated in the air, dancing in the shafts of low light that cut across the lofty room, as she lumped the bird onto a thick wooden board and wiped her hands on her stained apron. Her face was round and ruddy, and when she began to speak, it was apparent that she was missing several teeth.

'Who is she?' the woman asked, hastening towards the dresser cupboard and taking out a small wooden box, which, when opened, contained an assortment of lotions and potions.

'If anyone asks, you will say that this is Luna, returned to us in time for tomorrow's visit. Is that not fortuitous? After all those days hiding out in the woods.'

'Luna, be damned,' a gruff voice came from a dark corner, but the newcomer could not see who had spoken.

There was a prolonged silence as Mr Greybourne and the older lady looked at each other, almost as if they, too, were having a telepathic conversation.

'Luna. Of course. Very good, sir,' the woman concurred. 'And how did this regrettable injury happen?'

'I was washing my hands down by the river and she collided with me as I mounted the bank, entangling herself in my long limbs on the way down. Unfortunately, I landed across her ankle.'

'I'm certain that it's broken,' the injured girl said, wincing from the pain as Mr Greybourne lowered her gently into the older lady's recently vacated chair. He immediately flexed his sore shoulder, before fetching a small pine footstool and lifting her damaged foot onto it.

'Our trusted housekeeper, Mrs Webber, will know what needs to be done.'

He has kind eyes, she thought, as he spoke – dark, and definitely troubled, but kind.

'If the bone is broken then you'll need to send for Doctor Gardener.' Mrs Webber approached Luna and knelt on the floor beside her to assess the damage.

'I'd rather not. We no longer have a good relationship with him, as you know.' He began to pace up and down in front of them both, rubbing his chin with his hand. 'You've always managed Luna's injuries so well in the past, without the need for outside interference or intrusive questions. Can you not tend to it yourself?'

'Yes,' the false Luna hastily agreed, wondering if she could hide out here until she had recovered enough to be on her way again, despite the tinker's warnings. For the moment, she was safe and being cared for. These people might even see their way to feed her. 'It would be best not to involve the doctor if you think we could manage the break.'

And then she wondered what ailments and injuries had previously befallen Mrs Greybourne that required such ongoing attentions. More confusingly, where was the woman whom she'd so unexpectedly replaced? Still hiding in the woods? Perhaps she'd also been cursed by the Ravenswood Witch and was lying under a tree, mumbling nonsense and unable to move.

The housekeeper carefully removed the young woman's soggy, mud-encrusted boot and began to feel the ankle, but the pain was so intense that the stranger thought she might pass out.

'A clean break, I think. Jed – cut me a piece of stiff leather and I'll bind it up. And grab the brandy bottle, for goodness' sake, sir. I think she's about to faint.'

There was a grumble from the shadows, undoubtedly Jed, followed by the scrape of chair legs across the wide flagstones. Moments later, there was the sound of a distant door being slammed.

The older woman handed Mr Greybourne a large bunch of keys. He strode over to a padlocked corner cupboard and took out a thick green stoppered bottle, pouring a small measure into a glass tumbler and passing it to his housekeeper. She put it to the younger woman's lips and persuaded her to take a sip. It was unpleasant and made her cough, but she felt the warmth of it slide down her chest and further dull her already woolly senses. The kindly lady rubbed her back and gave her a largely toothless smile.

'The leather splint will hopefully stop her moving the ankle whilst it heals. I'll wrap a bandage around the injury, and then we'll need to keep the foot elevated, but this is going to require a substantial period of bed rest. Where shall we put the poor mite?'

'I shall take her to my bedroom.'

The older woman gave a little gasp.

'We currently have no other rooms that are habitable,' he pointed out. 'Although, I will of course sleep on the chair so as not to disturb her or risk jarring the injury.'

'Very well, sir. Do I need to lock her in?'

The surprise nature of this question alarmed the imposter. Was she to be kept prisoner here? What had she allowed herself to become part of? All at once, she had the weirdest sensation that she was falling – her stomach was plummeting and her chest rolling, even though she was securely seated on the chair. Her vision started to cloud over and she couldn't keep her head upright.

'All the colour has drained from her face and her eyes have gone mighty strange, sir,' the housekeeper said. 'What do I call her? Madam? Miss?'

'I thought I'd made myself perfectly clear. If anyone asks, most especially our imminent visitor, she is your mistress. They are similar enough. I have no other name for her so I suggest we consider her as such for the time being. Oh dear, I think she's going... Luna? Luna? Luna?'

She felt her head get heavy and thought for a moment she might be about to bring the brandy back up, but as she finally succumbed to the fainting that had hovered around her since her injury, she echoed the name out loud.

'Luna,' she affirmed. Mr Greybourne had suggested she bore a similarity to his absent wife and had resolutely stated to the constable that it was Luna he held in his arms. With nothing to lose, she decided to let it be so. It was as good a name as any and she would happily claim it if it meant these people would tend to her and conceal her from the police.

The thought of a real bed alone was worth the pain, and almost enough to dispel her disquiet regarding the nearby witch. She had not slept properly since the nightmare of two days ago, but she could remain at Ravenswood as Luna Greybourne – he had promised her that, if only until her injury had healed.

And as she slipped into unconsciousness, she let her old life slip away, too.

3

The false Luna awoke some time later in a large four-poster bed. It took her a while to remember the events of that morning, work out where she was, and recall that she had willingly stepped into the shoes of another woman.

Despite the sunshine outside, the room was draughty and a fusty smell lingered in the air. The wallpapers were faded and the furniture dusty and dull. Hardly any light came through the rain-speckled windowpanes, obscured as they were by lofty, waving trees. An unsettling silence hung heavy. She couldn't hear any of the sounds one might expect in a busy household: the chatter of servants going about their daily tasks or the scampering of feet, as they hurried along corridors with hot water jugs and chamber pots.

It took her a few moments to notice the man seated in the far corner, his head in his hands, unaware that she was awake. There was an open book resting across the arm of his chair, and she studied him for a while, his large fingers rubbing at his temples and the occasional deep sigh punctuating the silence, like a worn pair of bellows expelling their last puffs of air.

This was the person who had simultaneously foiled her escape plans by accidentally immobilising her, and then offered her refuge – perhaps to offset his guilt. She was at the crumbling and isolated house on the edge of the woods, and he was Mr Greybourne.

From out of nowhere, the sash window that had been open a couple of inches to allow the room to air, dropped suddenly and inexplicably, with a loud bang. He jolted and knocked the book from where it was balanced. It landed with a thud and he hastily retrieved it, before placing it on the small tripod table beside him.

'Ah, you're awake. You have slept for most of the morning and through a very noisy rainstorm. April is certainly living up to its reputation.' He jumped to his feet and came to her side.

She winced in pain and tried to shuffle up the bed but this only agitated her ankle further.

'Is there anything I can do?' he asked, rubbing his large hands together, anxious to assist her. Still not dressed in the smart attire she would expect of a man who owned such a sizeable property, he continued to resemble a labourer. His shirt sleeves were rolled up to the elbows, and he was in woollen trousers, with a small blue neckerchief under his collar.

'Can you please pull me up to a sitting position?' She was grateful for his practical offer of help, but he was alarmed by her words.

'You *want* me to touch you?'

She took a moment to reflect that two strangers unchaperoned in a bedroom, one male and the other female, was verging on scandalous. But then it hadn't been her idea to come to this house, or indeed to place herself in his bed. She saw him chew at his bottom lip as he contemplated her request. He hesitated a fraction before placing his hands under her armpits, gently heaving her slim body towards the headboard.

As he hoisted her into position, she noticed for the first time that she was wearing a voluminous white cotton nightgown. He followed her concerned eyes and colour flooded to his cheeks.

'Mrs Webber bound your ankle and saw to your night attire. If you suspect that I have done anything untoward, you are quite wrong,' he snapped.

His eyes narrowed and she felt momentarily guilty, because it had crossed her mind that he had brought her to Ravenswood for nefarious purposes. Hadn't she learned the hard way that some men believed women were put on this earth purely to service them and their carnal desires?

'I'd like you to eat something,' he said, clearly keen to move the conversation on. 'Could we tempt you with some soup? I fear you were in quite a state of distress before the accident and a hearty meal and a period of rest will help. I feel responsible for your broken ankle and am anxious to make amends.'

He paused, took a step backwards, and sat gingerly on the foot of the bed, trying not to crowd her. But he was nervous. She could sense it.

'The thing is, there is a clerk from the solicitor's due at the house tomorrow,' he continued. 'We have a visit every year, to ask my wife questions about her health and general well-being, and to ensure the terms of her inheritance are continuing to be met. As you may appreciate, it is a meeting I had every reason to suspect would end in disaster but perhaps, with our unexpected encounter, it might have a more... positive outcome. It's not the same gentleman as last time, which is rather fortuitous – they seem to get through these junior clerks quite quickly – but the young man will need to establish that Luna is fit and well...' He looked down at the mound of quilt that concealed her legs. 'Or more accurately, *alive*, in order for her annual allowance to continue...'

So, this was about money, she finally realised. This was why he had claimed her so impetuously down by the riverbank. She was a convenient puppet in a theatrical production where he wished her to play the part of his wife in order for him to continue to draw income from the estate of some relative or other benefactor of Mrs Greybourne. His generosity had more mercenary motives than she'd hoped. At least she'd not been kidnapped to be abused or assaulted. But where was his wife? Rather careless to mislay a whole person. And at what point would she be returning?

'Do you think I am up to it?' she whispered.

He considered her question, rubbing his chin with his hand as he studied her face. 'Yes, I have a feeling you will do admirably.'

She'd already decided that it would suit her purposes to assume the identity of another for a while, but how on earth would she pass herself off as someone she had never met and knew nothing about?

'But I won't press you too much on the matter immediately. Instead, I will go to the kitchens and fetch you up a tray of food. You look half-starved.'

'Can you not ring for someone?' she asked, pointing to the bell pulls either side of the bed. The house was huge and must surely have a complement of staff. It seemed silly for him, the master of the house, to be fetching her something to eat.

'Not since the wires were severed.' He shrugged, as she contemplated his choice of adjective. Not damaged or broken, but *severed*. A malicious and deliberate act.

At that moment, her empty stomach growled and he smiled.

'Food is the priority,' he said, rising to his feet. 'Mrs Webber's cooking is truly atrocious but I'll wager, like me, you are not in a position to care.'

'Thank you... erm... Mr Greybourne.'

'You must call me Marcus,' he supplied. 'And the servants have been instructed to call you Mrs Greybourne, especially as you seem so reluctant to divulge your true identity.' He immediately put his hands up as if to deflect any defence of her actions that she might offer. 'I don't say that to enquire into your secrets, nor am I passing any judgement on the accusations made against you by those we encountered by the river. I have learned the bitter lesson that life is not black and white. We are none of us truly one thing or the other, but shades of everything in between.'

Did he have dark secrets too? she wondered. Was he not willing to condemn her because he had also done things worthy of condemnation? She'd certainly done a wicked thing and was only glad her parents were not around to witness how far she had fallen into the bowels of hell. But the truth of the matter was, desperate people would always be driven to commit desperate acts through desperate circumstances. He appeared to understand this, and she felt reassured. She would be Luna for him because he had been a saviour for her at the moment when her whole life could so easily have spiralled even further, and perhaps irrevocably, out of her control.

'I *am* Luna Greybourne,' she said, confirming the decision she'd already made as she'd passed out in the kitchen, but on this occasion meeting and holding his eye. 'But my recent accident has left me confused and forgetful. I will need your help to regain my memory.'

A sigh of relief escaped his lips as he nodded his gratitude.

'We have the whole afternoon ahead of us,' he said, and walked to the half-open door, which she belatedly noticed had a large key on the inside, and a padlock hanging from the outside. Having made the decision to follow through with the ridiculous pantomime that she was his wife, there was still something about this house and its occupants that unnerved her. Had she leapt from the spitting frying pan and into the raging fire?

As he left, gently closing the bedroom door behind him, she put her hand to her throat in an attempt to stem her rising emotions, only to realise that she was still wearing her small coral pendant – a painful reminder of the life she had run from. It was not a piece of great value, but it was what it represented that angered her so. Gripping the thin chain with determined fingers, she ripped it from her neck and flung it across the room in her fury. It was supposed to ward off evil and ensure good health, but had failed her on both counts. She could not bear to have it around her neck one moment longer.

Overcome, she allowed her head to fall back onto the feather pillows behind her, her heart heavy and her emotional and physical pain so overwhelming, she didn't know which one would break her first. In a few short months, her whole world had changed; she had gone from moderately content, to wishing she were dead. The man she loved had died and her heart had been ripped in two. Slowly, her eyes focused on the panelled canopy above her head, frowning at the scratches and deep marks she could see gouged into the oak – her attention drawn to one in particular.

She couldn't be absolutely certain, but the large pentagram directly above her head appeared to be upside down. And, if that were the case, it was not the protective sign of life favoured by pagans, or representative of the five wounds of Christ within Christianity, but instead confirmation of her worst fears. It was a disturbing indication that Devil worship was being practised in this house.

* * *

Mrs Webber came upstairs a little while later and presented her with a bowl of watery beef soup and a slice of thick bread, spread with lard and rosemary. She forced the barely palatable food down, fondly remembering the culinary expertise of Mrs Banbury, the cook at Church View – that woman had been a wonder with a piece of brisket and could whisk up a béchamel sauce with her eyes closed.

The housekeeper fussed about, plumping the pillows, tucking in her sheets and tidying up the gloomy and largely masculine space. She took a dusting cloth from her apron pocket and flicked it over the surfaces, and the girl in the bed wondered why the household staff had not kept the master bedroom in better order.

At one time, the colourful tapestry bed canopy, rich mahogany Georgian furniture and thick Persian rugs across the floor would have made this a most opulent bedroom, but the neglected nature of everything tainted it all. Dark green, flocked wallpapers and poor natural light made her feel as though the walls were pressing in on her. As grateful as she was for the food and shelter, she had the uneasy sensation that the house was as much of a prison as the one she'd striven so hard to avoid.

'You poor child,' Mrs Webber said, scooping up the broken pendant from the floor and placing it on the dressing table. 'Taking such a tumble and having that great lump of a man fall on your leg. And now stuck here with us on the edge of nowhere, when surely there must be folks desperately missing you back home.'

It was not phrased as a question but Luna knew she was enquiring about her circumstances.

'There is no one. This is my home now. You are my family.'

'Lovely thought, to be sure, but I wouldn't wish living here on anyone. We need to get you well again and on your way as soon as we can. Before bad things happen.'

The older woman's concerns mirrored her own but she had struck a deal with Marcus and intended to honour it, wherever the real Luna might be and whatever dark arts were being practised inside the house.

'Your master needs me to be Luna Greybourne and so, for the duration of my stay, that's who I intend to be.'

The housekeeper shook her head in resignation.

'So I was told, and I heartily disapprove, even though I would not dare go against Mr Greybourne.' She cast an anxious glance at the bedroom door and lowered her voice. 'But if you're staying here, you'll need protecting. Have you not seen the markings? We're being watched by the spirits of the dead.'

The housekeeper pointed to a small evil eye above the curtains that Luna hadn't noticed – a painted black circle with thick lines radiating from the outer oval. After rummaging in her pockets, Mrs Webber passed over a small wooden cross bound with red thread.

'There's a wickedness within this house, on the Greybourne lands, and even in our village. It's like Ravenswood has pulled in all the dark forces for miles around – a terrifying whirlwind sucking everything that is monstrous into its eye. Mutilated livestock keeps being found on the fields, sicknesses break out for no reason, and the dead come back to haunt us. Keep the charm about your person at all times. It's rowan,' the older woman explained. 'Wards off witches and malevolent spirits.'

Where were these malevolent spirits? And how would she even know if she was in the presence of a witch? She was curious and reached out to grip Mrs Webber's sleeve, hoping she might supply some direct answers. 'An Irish tinker in Little Doubton told me that a witch lived in your woods. Is she the person you are trying to protect me from?'

Was there an old crone lurking in the thicket of trees that stretched beyond Ravenswood? Someone who would curse all she came across? Perhaps this witch was even connected to the mysterious disappearance of the mistress of the house and was in league with Mr Greybourne?

Mrs Webber narrowed her eyes and chewed at her bottom lip with her remaining top tooth before answering.

'There ain't no old crone living in the woods. Quite the opposite; the Ravenswood Witch is young and beautiful, but she's a cruel one, with a beastly temper and not of her right mind... You, Luna Greybourne, are the witch.'

4

The shock of the housekeeper's announcement caused a sudden coldness to pierce the imposter's very core. She couldn't believe that she'd assumed the identity of a woman who, according to the tinker, was widely regarded as a witch. A woman who had cursed another and brought about her death. Not quite sure where she stood on matters relating to the supernatural, she had always been one to err on the side of caution. She covered mirrors after a death to prevent the departed becoming trapped inside the glass and threw spilled salt over her left shoulder to avoid bad luck, but had not given much thought to those individuals who claimed to harness supernatural powers – for good or ill.

Before she had the opportunity to question Mrs Webber further, Marcus returned upstairs and the false Luna surreptitiously slid the rowan cross under her pillows.

'Ah, you have eaten something.' He glanced at the tray of food. 'Excellent. I've come to take you to the drawing room as I'm sure you would welcome a cheerier aspect now that the sun has been bold enough to show her face. Besides, we need to talk and I feel uncomfortable doing so whilst you are reclining in a bed.'

Talking was certainly the order of the day, and her first question would be the allegations of witchcraft against his wife. If she was lurking in the woods, was it feasible to continue this charade? And if she wasn't, then where was she? Because it would not be wise to anger such a woman, especially one given to cursing those who crossed her.

After some further fussing from the housekeeper, Luna was gently swept up into Mr Greybourne's arms and taken down the wide staircase.

'Excuse the startling embellishments,' he said, avoiding her eye but clearly aware she was horrified by the décor around her.

The bedroom may have been shabby, but the walls of the hall and staircase were defaced to a horrific degree. The wallpapers were shredded, and she recognised several further marks associated with dark magic: alchemical symbols for sulphur and brimstone, another large black outline of an eye, and reddish-brown writing in foot-high letters declared 'ROT IN HELL'. She didn't want to contemplate what might have been used to write these words, but she suspected blood or, at the very least, something deliberately chosen to resemble it.

'I've been working hard to remove them. Most of these remaining daubs and unpleasant scribblings should be gone by nightfall,' he said, in an attempt to reassure her.

As he carried her through to the drawing room, she noticed another large padlock hanging from the outside of the door, and a number of strong bolts on the inside – much like in the bedchamber. She shuddered. Was it to keep someone out or lock someone in? Her relief at being cared for and fed was quickly becoming the fear she might end up as some satanic sacrifice. Would the Ravenswood Witch come for her and carve her beating heart from her chest in order to cast a demonic spell? She'd read about such things in the newspapers and sensationalist novelettes, although more often in relation to the alleged cannibalistic practices on the African continent, rather than being conducted at quiet English riverside dwellings.

It then crossed her mind that Marcus might be in league with his wife. Did he procure young women for her Devil-worshipping rituals? Collide with unsuspecting individuals on deserted riverside paths, immobilise them and take them to Ravenswood under the pretence of being a caring stranger? Because if the large and powerful Mr Greybourne was also a practitioner of black magic then she stood no chance of out-hobbling him, never mind out-running him.

He carefully lowered her onto a chaise longue, rubbing again at his sore shoulder after he'd deposited her. She cursed her broken ankle. If only she had been paying more attention on the riverbank she could be on her way to London by now, far from those who were hunting her and would see her hanged, and not beholden to strangers who clearly had dark secrets.

Mrs Webber briefly reappeared with a blanket for her legs and a preparation of laudanum to relieve her ongoing pain, but the offered medication troubled her. She'd eaten the food presented to her without question, but it suddenly occurred to her that it might suit them to have her drugged and incapacitated. She knew nothing about these people but was fully aware that padlocks, satanic symbolism and associated wood-roaming witches were not to be found in most respectable households. The intense throbbing of her injury, however, was her immediate concern so she reached for the glass.

Marcus frowned.

'Please be mindful that this contains opium,' he said. 'Only have what you need. It's dangerous stuff.'

Perhaps she was not to be a sacrifice after all, or he would be encouraging her to drink the sweet-smelling but bitter-tasting opiate in order to bend her to his will. She scolded herself for allowing her silly imagination to run away with her. He'd been nothing but kind to her from their first encounter, genuinely mindful of her frail state and keen to aid her recovery, even though there were some pressing matters he had not addressed.

'Is witchcraft practised in and around Ravenswood?' She finally found the courage to voice her concerns. 'The words on the walls by the stairs...'

His jaw clenched and his eyes grew dark.

'It is all a nonsense performed by deluded individuals who either wish to control others or justify malicious behaviour. I do not and have never tolerated such foolishness in this house. If someone chooses to paint strange symbols on a wall, chant gibberish around a bonfire, or imbibe herbs and other concoctions under the delusion that they have supernatural gifts, then more fool them. What you see about you now is a remnant of the past that I am working hard to erase.'

'But the Ravenswood Witch—' she began.

'I promise that she is no threat to us. Let that be enough.'

What on earth did that mean? That she was locked up? That she had been sent far away? Or even that she was dead? But Marcus moved the conversation on, obviously feeling that particular topic had been adequately dealt with. He was telling her that the witch was delusional – that the sorcery was not real. So, who did she believe? A gossipy Irish tinker, or the kind and earnest man who had spent the day overseeing her care?

'I want to familiarise you with the drawing room, since Mr Meyer is due tomorrow at ten o'clock and it would not be appropriate to conduct the interview upstairs.' Marcus settled himself in a nearby chair, as she looked about her and noticed how cluttered the room was. It had every sort of furniture dotted about, from ornate mirrors and glazed display cabinets to practical items, such as a table where one might eat a meal – but very little floor space.

A small fire was crackling and spitting in the grate, doing its best to bring cheer to a cheerless room on such a changeable April day. She could see outside to the meadow that she'd been carried through that morning, and beyond that she glimpsed the river Bran. These windows were south-facing, and the strong beams of sunshine that fell across the multitude of objects scattered around the room promised that the world outside was bright and inviting, even if the house was not.

'When he arrives, we shall partially draw the curtains and explain to him that you are suffering from a headache.'

'Yes,' she agreed, realising he was providing a convincing excuse for poor light, which would limit any chance of their deception being discovered. 'And, as you said to the policemen, I have been unwell for so many years.'

He frowned at her wholehearted adoption of her role as his wife when they were the only two people in the room, but she would play her part earnestly and fully, to be certain there was no chance of her forgetting the charade. Besides, she had no choice but to remain at

Ravenswood. If she could be of use to him whilst she was incapacitated, he might think kindly of her. But she would be gone from here as soon as humanly possible.

She belatedly caught sight of a wedding photograph of a much younger Marcus Greybourne and his wife on the circular table beside her. He noticed her interest in the item.

'Ah, yes, this will not stand up to close scrutiny.' The image might lack colour, but Luna's pale eyes were apparent, unlike hers, which, despite her fair hair, were hazel.

He reached over to the table and picked it up, his thumb caressing the glass.

'Such a deceptively promising start to my marriage. My father-in-law was already quite sick by then, but the weather was kind to us. We married in the Little Doubton parish church, as my bride had a somewhat strained relationship with the vicar from her home town. There was an arch of moss and summer flowers across the lychgate, and rose petals were strewn in our path as we walked to the carriage. I laid on wedding celebrations here at the house, inviting a handful of curious locals, keen to meet the new mistress of Ravenswood. It was a happy day and I foolishly believed myself in love. But over the ensuing years, she changed beyond comprehension.'

'Yes,' she agreed. 'I have altered considerably...'

His brows knitted together as he recognised her stubborn insistence to play her part. He met and held her gaze. 'You don't have to do this.'

'If I trust you, will you trust me?' she asked, wanting to be as honest as possible. 'Know that I have done a bad thing but that I am a good person. Believe that I will do you no harm, if you promise that I am safe here for a short while.'

They exchanged a long and searching look, as though they could find the truth in each other's eyes. She had believed in another once before and been brutally betrayed, so this was a huge leap of faith on her part. Marcus Greybourne appeared genuine but could she still trust her judgement?

He lowered his voice, almost to a whisper.

'If I ask nothing of your past, could you really be her? Wholly and completely, until you are well enough to leave? Accepting that there are things I equally am unwilling to share?'

Her chest felt tight and her whole body flushed under his questioning stare but she nodded her agreement. Seemingly satisfied, he rose to his feet and picked up the photograph. Sliding the black velvet backpiece upwards, he removed the image and placed the empty frame in the deep drawer of a bow-fronted sideboard, before walking to the fireplace, and allowing the print to fall from his hand into the dancing flames. There was a sudden moment of combustion as the fire engulfed the paper. A hiss from the all-devouring fingers of orange and red, and it was gone... The woman in the photograph was no more.

'Then, *Luna*, shall we focus on the impending visit?'

There was a startling secondary roar from the fire, even though the paper print had long since been reduced to ash and there was nothing further to ignite beyond the solid logs that had been burning quietly for some time. She shuddered. It was as if the universe knew that the woman claiming to be Luna Greybourne – with her broken ankle stretched out before her on the chaise – was an imposter.

Marcus returned to the high-backed chair, filling the narrow seat and reminding her that he cut a bulky figure.

'When Mr Meyer arrives, it might be a good idea to apologise for your behaviour on the previous visit. You were quite rude to the gentleman they sent last time.' He sounded compassionate rather than accusatory, but was clearly uncomfortable addressing this prior encounter. His wife was obviously a difficult woman.

'My health was poor,' she said confidently, leaning forward in her seat and fussing with the nightgown and blankets. 'And I've been feeling so much better of late – despite the ankle.'

'Yes,' Marcus agreed. 'The change in you has been quite remarkable.' There was a further moment when their eyes met and held again – a tacit acknowledgement of everything that was happening.

'If Mr Meyer is satisfied that all is well – that *you* are well,' he clarified, 'then your recuperation may continue at Ravenswood, even though I am going away for a few weeks.'

He was giving her permission to remain at the house, even after she had served his immediate needs, which was a kindness. She would be an inconvenience to the staff and a drain on his resources, but then perhaps she was doing enough by securing this money for him and it was his way of saying thank you.

'Away?'

'I've not been able to travel much in recent years beyond Little Doubton village, or occasional trips across the river into Manbury, and my business affairs have suffered as a result. If the funds are released, as I hope, then I must at least attempt to reverse my fortunes. The care of my wife... *your* care has long been my priority. You have been suffering from a disturbing malady of the mind, but I would like to think that you will give the Webbers no trouble whilst I'm gone.'

She nodded her understanding.

'You *can* trust me in your absence. I owe you a great debt and will not let you down.' She hoped he could hear the honesty in her voice.

He nodded. He trusted her enough, it seemed.

'Then I shall leave you in peace for a while,' he said, and began to roll his shirt sleeves up to his elbows, revealing his strong tanned forearms. 'I have some redecorating to do.'

5

ELOISE – THE PREVIOUS YEAR

Eloise knew she was lucky to have such kind and devoted parents. They had married for love, neither having come from a social class wealthy enough to have had their marriages arranged, and this love had endured. The only sadness that David and Freda Haughton bore was that they had been blessed with just the one child. But Eloise carried the secret joy that her father loved her as much as, or maybe even more than, he loved his wife.

As the proud owner of a small shoe factory on the outskirts of town, he would often return from a long day's work, having stopped off to buy her a length of pretty ribbon or colourful paper dolls for her scrap albums. On one occasion he even came home with a new bonnet for her. But there was, he said, no present he could possibly buy that would ever compare to the beauty of his daughter.

It wasn't strictly true, and she knew it. Despite her fair hair, she did not possess remarkable eyes or an enchanting almond-shaped face. She had neither the height nor the grace to catch a man's eye, and was not captivating enough to stand out from the crowd. There were no floods of suitors banging down their door, merely a few interested parties that her father did not deem good enough for his precious only child. But she was bright and managed quite well in life, smiling when she needed to, and she had a gift of saying the right thing to people, which generally endeared her to them.

However, everything changed quite dramatically for the Haughton family, and certainly with regard to Eloise's marriage prospects, when she turned twenty and her father rather unexpectedly inherited a fortune of some considerable size. A distant relative died childless and, as one of the few males in his family line – and the only one with a sensible head on him – he was named as the sole beneficiary in the will.

Overnight, she became one of the most attractive young ladies in her neighbourhood, and even more so when that neighbourhood changed. The Haughtons went from moderately well off, renting a townhouse on the outskirts of Branchester, to remarkably wealthy, enabling her father to purchase a large Georgian property in the countryside, as befitted their newfound status. From employing merely a cook and a maid-of-all-work, the family now boasted a staff of eight. Young Eloise even had her own girl, Rose, who helped her to arrange her fair hair into glamorous curls and squeeze into the multitude of fashionable dresses that her father paid for without a second thought.

Generally a content young lady, she became increasingly restless and unhappy. This was largely due to the sedate nature of rural life, which curtailed her trips to the theatre and limited her social circle. And that's where all the trouble began. Because suddenly her world became more focused. Everything, from her friendships to the activities she undertook, centred around the small, albeit pleasant, village of Lowbridge. Adding to her frustrations, she was also wrestling with a whole gamut of new emotions that she had no idea how to navigate, including, for the first time in her life, her father saying no to her.

Because Eloise Haughton fell in love and, conveniently forgetting that he had been permitted to choose *his* own bride, her father decided that the young man in question was unsuitable. His only daughter, with a promised dowry of not inconsequential size, could do better.

But she was used to getting what she wanted and set about doing exactly that.

* * *

'Has a new family moved in across the green?' Eloise asked her mother, as she sat in the window seat of their morning room, looking across their driveway and out into the village.

The Haughtons' house stood in the centre of Lowbridge, taller and grander than all the buildings in the immediate vicinity, save the church. The small school and several modest dwellings encircled the village green, along with a run of smart tied cottages, which housed workers from the Lowbridge estate. It was these cottages that had been her focus for much of the morning.

'A Mr Thornbury and his son,' her mother replied from across the room. 'The wife died unexpectedly a couple of years ago and the father moved here to be near his sister, I understand. Men do so struggle with household management and often require the overseeing eye of a female. And with no daughter, I assume he is more than happy to defer household decisions to his next closest female relative.'

They had been there barely three months themselves, arriving at the tail end of a bitter and unforgiving winter, but were now nicely settled. Her father, in particular, was enjoying the weekly games of cricket that took place not one hundred yards from his house, and his wife had ingratiated herself with Lady Fletcher, the owner of Lowbridge Hall – by far the grandest house for miles around, but set apart from the village. Consequently, her mother now behaved as though she were part of the landed gentry.

'Mr Thornbury senior has secured an undergardener job at the estate, and I believe the cottage came with the job.'

'Shall I ask Cook to make them a cake and we can take it over?' Eloise suggested, embracing the largesse that the vicar often reminded his congregation came with wealth and privilege. 'They will be overwhelmed and exhausted by the move and will appreciate such a gift.'

'A kind thought, dear,' her mother agreed.

Kindness was part of her motivation, but curiosity was certainly another. Eloise had seen a strapping young man busying himself in and out of the end cottage for the last hour. Dark-haired and unusually tall, he had a flopping fringe, which he continually swiped at with a free hand. Was he the son of the grieving Mr Thornbury? She was keen to find out.

After asking Cook to bake a fruit loaf, Eloise continued to watch the comings and goings from her bedroom, which gave her a clearer vantage point. A heavily laden Pickfords wagon appeared during the course of the day, stuffed to capacity with furniture, rolled rugs and a lifetime of possessions. These were duly unloaded by two older men in woollen caps, and she watched, utterly fascinated by the endless stream of chattels that came from the interior of the vehicle – far more than she ever could have conceived fitted into such a compact space. It was rather like the knotted string of silk handkerchiefs she had once witnessed being pulled from the sleeve of a touring magician.

As the last box was carried inside, and the wagon trundled away, Eloise decided that the floppy-haired young man must surely be in need of refreshments by now. He had worked tirelessly for the last two hours.

And she had just the thing.

* * *

'Welcome to Lowbridge. I am Freda Haughton and this is my daughter, Eloise.'

Her mother presented the delicious-smelling cake as Eloise noted with satisfaction that the young man who had opened the door was indeed handsome, even more so close up.

'We have brought you a little something for your afternoon tea. Consider it a welcome gift to enjoy in your new home.'

He had an open book in his hands and hastily turned down the corner of the page before placing it on a side table and accepting the cake. Eloise noticed her mother's unease at spoiling a book so.

'Thank you. I'm Daniel Thornbury.' The young man nodded, unable to do anything other than dip his head now that both hands were engaged in the receipt of a large tin. 'Please, step inside and let me introduce you to my father.'

The pair ducked under the low lintel of the cottage and entered an exceedingly small front room, where an older gentleman leapt to his feet as the necessary introductions were made.

Eloise's mother looked at the grubby appendage that was offered to her and wrinkled up her nose. It was truly the hand of a working man: rough skin covered in callouses, with a crescent of soil under each nail.

'Ladies, please take a seat,' Mr Thornbury senior said.

Mother and daughter looked to the low upholstered chairs with not an antimacassar in sight, and both noticed the worn arms and faded fabric.

'How kind, but really we can't stop,' her mother said. Eloise, however, was torn; her new dress was of salmon-coloured silk with a delicate lace trim. It was immaculate and she wanted to keep it that way, yet part of her also wanted to stay because she was close enough to the smiling Daniel to detect the lingering aroma of tobacco, and the unnervingly masculine smell made her knees weak and her breath catch in her throat.

'Shall we see you at church on Sunday?' she asked, thinking that more salubrious surroundings might be preferable in her efforts to impress.

'Not for me, I'm afraid,' said the father. 'I don't much see eye to eye with the big fella since he took my Dora and was hardly an admirer before. I'm not even sure there is a God. Religion is just a convenient way of keeping the poor in their place. Seven days to create the world – ha, a likely story. Because to my mind, he didn't do a particularly great job. But then that's what happens when you rush things. Like to take my time, me. Think things over. Consider all me options.'

Her mother tried to hide her shock at being in the company of an atheist but Eloise saw the alarm in her eyes. God was paramount in all things – after Lady Fletcher, that is.

'Have you no thoughts of marrying again, Mr Thornbury? Have someone to cook for you and keep the house in order?' Eloise said. *And who might instruct you better to keep your fingernails clean,* she thought.

Mr Thornbury sighed. 'Well, I don't know about that. I loved my Dora but she could be a dreadful nag. Maybe you're right; two years is a long time to be clambering into an empty bed, with no one there to warm you up. I don't half miss the cuddles and the jiggling about.' He grinned at the ladies.

Eloise glanced at her mother who looked horrified by the notion, staring at Mr Thornbury as though he were something unpleasant she'd just stepped in.

The older man shrugged. 'It's just one of those things I haven't got around to yet.'

'I imagine he's got at least another two-score years on this earth, so plenty of time to consider his options,' Daniel said, under his breath, and rolled his eyes. She chanced a slight smile and Daniel winked in return.

And that was all it took for her to fall head over cream-leather heels in love.

* * *

'And how is the prettiest girl in the whole of Christendom?' her father asked later that day, kissing his daughter's forehead, having returned from a trip to his Branchester factory.

'We visited the Thornburys.' Eloise was still fizzing from the visit.

He looked blank.

'No one of note, dear,' her mother ventured, unpicking a crooked stitch from a small, embroidered tobacco pouch she was making for her husband now that she was a lady of leisure. The project, however, was not going well. 'Father and son who have just moved into the village.'

'Ah, but from the animated look on your face, I suspect there is something you're not telling me, Eloise. Was the young man handsome? Something has certainly perked up my darling daughter. You've been moping about of late but there is much more colour about your cheeks than when I left this morning.'

Her mother huffed from her seat by the fire, and her father walked over to his wife, absent-mindedly placing his hand on her shoulder. She turned her head to drop the smallest of kisses on his fingers before looking up to his face and Eloise wished, not for the first time, that she had someone who looked at her like that.

'The son was easy on the eye, to be sure, but Eloise can banish any thoughts of that nature. We shan't be mixing with them beyond crossing paths about the village. The son is a factory worker in the city, and the father is an unabashed heathen.' Her mother shuddered. Factory work and a lack of religion were clearly things to be ashamed of.

She'd become increasingly judicious over who she deemed suitable acquaintances in the few short months of acquiring their inherited wealth. Shop people and those in industry had been good enough for her before. She'd even tried to persuade her husband to sell the shoe-making business, wanting to sever their association with trade, but the factory had been started by David Haughton's father, and he claimed it was in his blood. Eloise did not share her mother's newfound snobbery. Yes, she had money and status now, but did not mind mixing with those who did not. Much to her own surprise, it turned out that she was driven by something more primal: her emotions.

She would ignore her mother's instructions because Daniel had stirred something in her. The attraction was intense, and she'd not felt like this about any of the young men who had come into her world since their altered fortunes. All she had to do was work on her father, because he always let her have what she wanted... Eventually.

6

Marcus and Luna sat together in the drawing room the following morning. He'd spent much of the previous afternoon sharing various details of his life with her: his upbringing and schooling, along with the importance of Ravenswood to the Greybourne family. The facts, if not the emotions, pertaining to his marriage were covered, but he avoided eye contact as he talked of the real Luna's misguided supernatural practices, blaming her ill health and associated delusions.

The whole situation remained utterly bewildering. This man had declared *her* to be Mrs Greybourne to help her evade the law and allow him to imminently claim an ongoing inheritance payment, but the woman was nowhere to be seen and no one seemed unduly concerned. It also transpired that his wife was known to the locals as the Ravenswood Witch and, whilst such accusations were not as perilous as in centuries gone by, it was still a dangerous position for her to put herself in – particularly if the woman was anywhere nearby. It was not wise to annoy someone who professed to have magical powers, even if, as Marcus insisted, they were only in his wife's head.

'The clerk from the solicitor's has arrived, sir. Shall I show him in?' Mrs Webber enquired.

The fun and games were to begin and the imposter had a very important role to play. *I am Luna Greybourne,* she repeated in her head, *and I must convince the visiting gentleman that this is so.*

The housekeeper announced Mr Meyer – a young fellow with a serious face and a nervous manner. Marcus directed him to a seat as the guest cast anxious eyes at Luna. He removed a pair of spectacles from his breast pocket and took a small bundle of papers from his leather case, balancing them on his knees, unsure of quite how to proceed.

'I don't wish to take up too much of your time, Mr Greybourne, but the terms of the allowance state that a representative of Crooker and Fairbrother must establish that your wife is alive and flourishing on a yearly basis in order for the monies to continue to be paid.'

'Absolutely. My wife and I are perfectly happy with this arrangement. We have nothing to hide.'

The clerk gave a curt nod and returned his focus to the documents before him.

'It says in my notes that Mr Buckle was concerned about your health last year, Mrs Greybourne. You were restless and erm, challenging.' He coughed, clearly paraphrasing whatever had been written.

'I was unforgivably rude, as I recall,' Luna said, looking up to Marcus and receiving a grateful glance in return. Encouraged, she continued, '... For which I apologise unreservedly. I've been unwell for several years, and I know my poor health has been of immense concern to my husband, but I do feel we have turned a corner. Despite my unfortunate broken ankle, I hope you can see I am much improved.'

The visitor peered at her through his spectacles.

'I didn't conduct the last interview, so it is difficult for me to comment. To my thinking you are unnaturally pale, although my colleague noted that you were practically skin and bone on the previous visit and you do appear to have regained some weight.'

'And her mind is much more settled,' Mr Greybourne said, walking over to her and standing protectively behind her chair. She felt him place a hand on her shoulder and the warmth of it surprised her. Without thinking, she reached her own hand up to cover his and felt him freeze for the smallest of moments. She squeezed his fingers and then turned her head to place her lips on his warm knuckles, dropping a gentle kiss there. It was what people in love did. She had witnessed it on so many occasions. But Marcus slid his hand away almost immediately, as though she'd burned his flesh with that simple act.

'My husband has been very kind and most attentive, nursing me back to health.' She tilted her head back up to meet his eye. 'I couldn't have got through this last year without you, darling,' she said.

Both men frowned. She noticed her husband's first and then turned back to Mr Meyer, who was frantically scribbling notes with a confused concertinaing of his brow. Had she said something wrong?

There followed a few straightforward questions about how she spent her days, and enquiries as to any ailments she'd had in the previous twelve months, but nothing too taxing. At no point did the young clerk question her identity, and he seemed largely content, if somewhat surprised, by her health and eloquence. He shuffled his papers together and she began to worry that he would be suspicious of such a dramatic recovery. After Mrs Webber's shock announcement, she had quizzed the housekeeper further and discovered that the woman she was claiming to be was wholly responsible for the destruction of Ravenswood – from the scribbling on the walls to the smashed and broken furniture. Mrs Greybourne, it seemed, was not of sound mind, and she felt she should address this.

'Please don't think some miraculous cure has been found,' Luna said. 'There are still days when I am not as in control as I would like. I continue to have melancholy periods and dark thoughts. But I no longer have the overwhelming urge to destroy or to lash out at others. I think it was the opium in the laudanum,' she finished, thinking back to Marcus's concern over her taking the medicine. 'And I no longer rely on it as much as I once did.'

'Yes, that might explain the improvement. And it has certainly been a pleasant surprise to see you so calm and approachable today.' He seemed satisfied and slid everything back into his case. 'I think I am done here, although I must speak to the staff before I go, as is detailed in the terms of the inheritance agreement. It does rather appear though, according to these reports, that you have fewer staff with every passing year.' He raised one eyebrow.

'Only Mr and Mrs Webber remain now,' Marcus confirmed, 'but then our wants and needs are simple, and my finances have been somewhat strained...'

'Indeed,' Mr Meyer agreed, as Luna contemplated the startling news that this huge house was run by only two people. No wonder she hadn't seen any other servants – there weren't any.

'They have been with me for several years now, and will give a good account of Luna's recovery, I am sure. My wife's improvement of late owes a great deal to my housekeeper's kind ministrations.'

Mr Meyer nodded, gathered up his briefcase, and Marcus gave him directions to the kitchens.

'Did I speak out of turn?' Luna asked, as soon as they were alone. 'When I thanked you for your kindness?'

'Not at all, although it has been a long time since anyone has called me darling. Perhaps the solicitor was surprised that we seemed so close after reading the report from the last Crooker and Fairbrother visit. I know I was.'

'Sorry. I was overly familiar. I should have been more guarded.'

The pain from her ankle was starting to cause quite severe discomfort as the laudanum was wearing off, and she felt agitated. Why had she started this stupid game? She was fumbling around in the dark trying to make sense of this confusing and slightly scary situation that she'd landed in, but she felt like a meteor falling from the skies onto a planet where it did not belong.

'Don't apologise. You did splendidly, and I'm more than happy for you to continue with the endearments.' He looked her squarely in the eye. 'I liked it.'

Her heart rate accelerated at his words. The nightmare of only a few short days ago had almost drowned her in a torrent of devastating emotions, but her current situation was proving equally frightening. Part of that fear was the peculiar things this man was doing to her insides. There was a teetering anxiety, not that he would harm her, but that he would continue to be kind and she would not want to leave, because when your whole world had been destroyed, you clung to any small fragment of solid ground.

Marcus walked over to the window and looked out across the meadow that he had carried her through only the day before. A few minutes of silence passed between them but, considering the man was a relative stranger, she didn't feel uncomfortable. They were lost in their own troubles, but lost together.

He finally spoke. 'The hedgerows and riverbanks are bursting with colour this time of year, but our garden is sadly lacking. I was digging new beds down by the gate yesterday when you happened upon me, because the meadow is the only place on the Ravenswood lands that the flora seems to flourish now. The columbine, cow parsley and lady's smock rise up with the long grasses every year regardless of neglect, but I long to return the gardens to the glory days of my father. I hope to acquire some cowslips and primroses this autumn so that, next spring, Ravenswood will be dappled with the bold yellow of sunshine.'

Luna had followed the patches of gold that he spoke of as she'd run along the shimmering silver ribbon of the river Bran from Lowbridge. The colours had cheered her desperate spirits as she scampered through the wet landscape as though her feet were on fire, afraid to stop. She'd felt far safer in amongst the violets and periwinkles two nights ago, resting in the dense undergrowth, than she'd ever felt in the streets of Branchester at night as a child, even with her father beside her.

'A woman I love very much gave me an appreciation of gardening many years ago,' he continued, 'and particularly the cultivation of flowers. She taught me their names and instructed me in their care.' He immediately pulled his lips taut, regretting his openness and embarrassed by his admission. 'You must think it's a silly interest for a man.'

'Not at all,' she said, noticing he'd said *love*, in the present tense, meaning Luna was still alive somewhere. She had visions of the pair of them as newlyweds tending to the gardens, before the poor woman became addicted to the opiates and her behaviour spiralled out of control.

Mr Webber entered, dipping his head in deference to his master, but scowling at Luna. He was carrying a large basket of logs and began to stack them on the hearth. The presence of servants, Luna knew well, did not and should not interrupt the activities of those they served, but they were both conscious that they were no longer alone.

'I heard my first cuckoo down by the river this morning,' Marcus said, walking over to join her. 'It's a good luck omen, as you know, and my sombre spirits of late are lifting. Along with my plans to redecorate, I might fell some of the trees at the back of the house to give the north-facing rooms more light. So much has been neglected hereabouts, and for so many years.' He swung to face her. 'Do you have a favourite flower?'

'I know very little about the tending of a garden because I grew up in the city.' Worried then that she was slipping from her role, especially as the manservant was present, she hesitated. Giving him information about her past was not wise. 'Besides, you know I have not been well enough to care about such things and am content to leave such matters entirely to you.' After all, this was not her house or her business.

Marcus nodded. The pantomime, it seemed, was in full swing.

'Well, I've always had a soft spot for roses, so I've instructed Mr Webber to purchase some bushes from Manbury this afternoon. I should like to get them planted by the gate before I leave, in the hope they'll be in bloom when I return. Before we know it, summer will be here, but I shall be sad to miss the interweaving of these two life-giving seasons,' he continued. 'I have never thought of January as the start of the New Year. For me, it has always been the spring when everything begins to grow anew. Now, more than ever, April shall be my beginning.'

She wondered how long he imagined she would stay for. It was only her intention to heal from the ankle injury and then she would be on her way. The house was unsettling. Mrs Webber's shocking revelation that Marcus's wife was a witch, coupled with her own firm belief that her old life would catch up with her eventually, meant this couldn't be a permanent solution to her troubles. He seemed nice enough and she didn't want him tarred with her very dirty brush. Besides, she could only be Luna Greybourne until the real Luna reappeared to depose her, or someone crept from the woodwork of her past to reveal her true identity. It was a risky game, one to be played for a short while only, because they would surely be exposed soon by a relative, a neighbour, or even a visiting tradesman.

As if he could read her thoughts, the conversation circled back to his wife.

'It's been hard caring for Luna... for you.' He hastily corrected himself. 'Many things have suffered as a result – not least the deterioration of the house. It's why we need your inheritance payment so badly. I'm sorry to have put you through that again, but I'm hoping with your greatly improved health, you will now refrain from destroying any repairs that I undertake and sabotaging my planting. It has been quite fruitless in the past to attempt any restoration, when you've suffered from such wild and unpredictable paroxysms.'

She nodded. He was confirming Mrs Webber's assertions that Luna had been responsible for the destruction she could see thereabouts and that Marcus had been fighting a losing battle in his attempts to keep the house in a habitable state. Such a pity, as she could imagine Ravenswood being an impressive residence in its day. The Greybournes had clearly been a family of note, and these spacious rooms and wide hallways should be bustling with life and busy servants. Instead, it was an empty shell, with the echoes of unhappiness and despair bouncing off the defaced walls.

'I should check on Mr Meyer. He must have all the information he needs by now,' Marcus said, and then turned his attention to the manservant. 'Has he interviewed you, Webber?'

'Yes, sir, and I spoke as I was told.'

Mr Greybourne looked at the wooden clock on the mantel and Luna belatedly realised the glass was missing. Something else his temperamental wife had damaged? But she felt emboldened by their friendly conversation earlier and ventured to try her hand at being mistress of the house. What might a wife do on a sunny April afternoon with her husband?

'Please also ask Mrs Webber if she might bring us both afternoon tea. I should like very much for you to sit with me a while. We can look out over the front meadow and discuss your plans for the gardens further.'

Marcus looked as though she'd requested he strip naked and dance a jig, but he rallied quickly.

'That would be... really quite lovely,' he said.

7

The first thing that struck Luna as her sleeping brain floated back to consciousness the following morning was that, even though her eyes remained closed, she was being watched. The second thing was how much her ankle still hurt.

As she scanned the room, the concerned face of Marcus Greybourne, who had pulled up a chair at the bottom of the bed, was indeed entirely focused on her.

They had spent the previous afternoon drinking tea, until Mr Webber had returned from Manbury with the eagerly awaited rose bushes. She had then watched Marcus through the window for quite some time as he busied himself planting the shrubs and tidying the front gardens beyond the meadow. So driven was he by his tasks that he'd excused himself from dinner and it was Mr Webber who returned her to the bedrooms at nightfall, and his kindly wife who had helped her undress.

'Good morning,' Marcus said. His tone was brisk but not unfriendly. 'Mr Meyer has already sent a letter in the first post assuring me all is well so I'm leaving shortly for London, but didn't want to go without saying goodbye and passing on a few instructions.'

'Because you're worried what I might get up to whilst you're away?' She shuffled up the bed.

Her pretend husband's sleeves were rolled to the elbows again and his forehead was damp with sweat. He was certainly not a man afraid to get his hands dirty and had clearly been busy already that morning. She looked to the bedside clock and was chastised by its vertical hands for sleeping until almost midday. Not used to such decadence, she could only assume the laudanum was making her drowsy.

'Believe me,' he said, wiping his face with a large handkerchief from his pocket, 'if you had lived my life for the last few years you would realise that there is very little left in this world that would distress me.'

'Because I've been such a handful since our marriage?' she asked, remembering her role as his wife of nearly ten years, and knowing that she could remain at Ravenswood, safe from inquisitive officers of the law, as long as she perpetuated this myth.

'My marriage has certainly seen some difficult times but an opportunity to make a potentially lucrative investment has been presented to me and I have to at least try to head off what I sadly believe is inevitable.'

She nodded her understanding and settled herself against the pillows, the pentagram once again catching her eye.

'Should I be concerned by these markings?' she asked, pointing to the scratches in the wood, and he ducked his head under the canopy of the four-poster.

'I'd forgotten about those but pay them no heed. Sometimes, when you live with things for long enough you don't see them any more. I'll instruct Mr Webber to deal with them later today. You will, at least, find the staircase much improved. I have washed the walls and Mrs Webber has been airing the upstairs rooms to rid them of some of the more fetid odours.'

Luna shivered. What had gone on in this house before her arrival?

Marcus noticed her worried expression. 'I hope you are sensible enough to know that superstition and dark magic are silly nonsense. It is only real – only has power over you – when you believe it. The marks mean nothing. A scratched shape in a panel can't harm you.'

She frowned but nodded mutely, certain there was more to this world than the tangible. She had witnessed inexplicable and other-worldly phenomena with her own eyes at the Branchester music hall: an Indian princess levitating above a chair as a hoop was passed over her body, and a woman in a wooden box sawn in half. She also knew people who had successfully spoken to long-dead relatives with the assistance of a medium, and these spiritualists had provided information that only the deceased could possibly know. Even the cook at Lowbridge was convinced her nephew had been born with webbed feet after his father had been cursed by a gypsy. Would Marcus think her silly for admitting such? Mrs Webber clearly believed in the forces of good and evil. Her gift of the rowan cross proved that.

'On to practical matters,' Marcus said, 'and the reason I am rather inappropriately loitering at the foot of your bed—'

'You are the master of the house. I think you are entitled to loiter wherever you so wish.'

She had merely stated a fact but his eyes dipped and the merest hint of pink swept across his cheeks as he considered that there were other implications attached to her words.

He cleared his throat.

'As I said previously, you must run the household whilst I'm absent, particularly as we've established that you are not in a position to leave. There is no one else and it would be odd for the mistress of the house to take orders from the servants. You have given me no trouble thus far and were extremely helpful yesterday, so I shall send you back some money as soon as I can to this end.'

She was horrified. 'What am I to do with this money?'

'Don't look so alarmed. I will send detailed instructions regarding how it is to be spent, as the Webbers cannot read or write; but I don't want you exerting yourself. You've clearly suffered quite the ordeal and are still lacking colour.'

She nodded her understanding, even though she was bewildered by this sudden responsibility. He must truly have no other options.

'I should also like you to oversee the manservant as he continues to repair some of the damage that the house has suffered in recent years. I'll engage some tradesmen to undertake the tasks Mr Webber cannot manage alone, and you may set about making whatever small improvements you wish, as I'm certain you have a far better eye for fabrics and furnishings than I do. I can even arrange for some catalogues to be sent to the house.' He paused and narrowed his eyes. 'I can trust you, can't I?'

The question was not whether she would select curtains that wouldn't clash with the wallpapers, or fritter away the money on exorbitant and unnecessary luxuries; he was asking whether he could trust her, full stop. He'd heard the older police officer say she was wanted for murder and she'd seen his brief but shocked reaction at the time. And yet, he was prepared to leave her in sole charge of his household. His need for money must be very great, as must his certainty that his real wife would not return to expose them both.

She nodded.

'I only ask two things of you: that you are to have nothing to do with the local folk healer – a Mr Findlay, who peddles nonsense and fear – and that you stay away from the attics. They are out of bounds for everyone but me, as the items I have stored up there are of an intensely personal nature – not that you are sufficiently mobile to climb the steep stairs. Other than that, you may treat Ravenswood as your home. I shall ask Mrs Webber to focus on feeding you up and getting your strength back, as you won't be putting weight on that foot for some time. Her husband may be somewhat taciturn but he is tall and wiry, and can easily carry you downstairs each morning so you are not shut in this gloomy bedroom.'

If he recognised it was gloomy, she wondered why he hadn't moved the bed to the other side of the house, with the brighter southern view.

'May I be allowed to sit outside, if the weather is pleasant?' Spring was in full swing and she wished to be part of the wide-open spaces, glorious scents, vivid colours and clean air.

'Naturally, my wife should not have to ask my permission for such a thing. Embrace your role as mistress whilst I am gone and try not to behave like a timid mouse, afraid of her own shadow. There are sadly an awful lot of shadows at Ravenswood so you will have to be strong.'

Becoming his wife meant more responsibility than she'd anticipated, but in for a penny... She'd made her comfortable bed and must now lie in it.

'You can rely on Mrs Webber...' Was the implication that Mr Webber was not so favoured? '...but do not get drawn into her superstitious nonsense. I shall be gone for four or five weeks and we can assess our... domestic arrangement upon my return.'

He was reminding her that when her ankle had healed, she must be on her way. Her stay at Ravenswood was merely a temporary respite, but she was grateful. In the meantime, she would do her best not to let him down, whether there were evil spirits lurking and witchy goings-on or not.

* * *

Mrs Webber came to her room a little while later with a breakfast of devilled kidneys. She informed her that Marcus had now left for the Manbury ferry, and was then hoping to catch the train to London, much as Luna herself had been planning to before the unfortunate collision.

'He looked every inch the gentleman in his freshly pressed suit, but I watched him walk through the meadow, shoulders stooped and head hung low,' she said. 'Poor man. Breaks my heart to see him so downcast. You'd better not cause him no trouble – he's had a lifetime of that.' She shook her head. 'I can't deny I find it odd that he left a stranger in charge. Sometimes I wonder if he's as mad as his wife.'

'I *am* his wife,' Luna gently corrected. 'And I will do my very best to run Ravenswood in his absence.' The older woman nodded and kept her tongue. 'You have all been very kind to me and I intend to repay that kindness. With your guidance and expertise, between us I'm certain we can manage.'

Somewhat mollified, Mrs Webber left her to her breakfast, but the overuse of butter and spices quite turned Luna's stomach. Marcus was correct: cooking was not the woman's forte. Perhaps one of her first purchases as mistress of the house should be a copy of *Beeton's Household Management*; the recipes were badly needed by her cook, and the information regarding the responsibilities involved in running a large house would be invaluable for herself.

Mr Webber came to fetch Luna downstairs as the clock struck ten. He was a more angular man than his master and not so gentle with his handling of her. There was also an unpleasant smell of stale alcohol and dead animals about him. Because the weather had much improved since the recent storms, she asked to be taken outside, not wanting to remain in that gloomy house for the entirety of the day.

Born a city girl, it was only in the last year that she had come to love and appreciate the countryside. She now knew what it was to spend a glorious summer afternoon sitting in the shade of a large elm, watching twenty-two men play a friendly game of cricket on a village green. There were, of course, parks and bodies of water in the city, but the air never had that fresh grassy smell, and the river Bran, so much closer to the factories, kicked out a foul stench in the warmer weather. You may know your immediate neighbours, but you could walk a hundred yards from your house and, swallowed up by the bustle of a busy city, not recognise a single soul. It was the main reason London had so appealed to her – the anonymity both a blessing and a curse.

Mr Webber grunted his agreement, obviously reluctant to execute the ridiculous pantomime that a complete stranger could step into Luna Greybourne's shoes. He informed her there was a long wooden bench at the front of the house where she might enjoy looking out across the meadow. He took her out through the kitchens and the contrast in light was almost blinding.

Now that she wasn't running for her life, she could see that Little Doubton and the Ravenswood estate were set in a shallow valley, with gently sloping chalk hills running up either side of the river. The landscape was largely one of open fields, dotted with clusters of trees, and criss-crossed with verdant hedgerows.

As he lowered Luna onto the bench, Mrs Webber came running towards them.

'Jedidiah! You'll never believe it. I got me one still alive! Everything's gonna be all right, after all.'

Mr Webber, whose Christian name was apparently Jedidiah, looked up as his wife stopped before them both cradling a fair-sized bulge in her pinny, with a wide, mostly toothless grin across her face. There was something concealed in the folds as she held the hem to her waist like a hammock.

'You never found a raven?' His face was a mixture of disbelief and curiosity.

'I took some of them empty wooden crates out to the old Dutch barn, now that the master is starting to get the valuables down from the attics. I was tucking 'em behind them mouldy bales of straw when I saw it. Caught in one of them traps and it must have been there a couple of days. Thought it was dead at first but then I saw it twitch. I used a garden fork and managed to lever open them evil metal jaws and get it out.'

'Bloody miracle it's survived, then. If it happened when she did for all the others, it's been three days.'

'Language!' the housekeeper chastised. 'Not in front of the mistress.'

He rolled his eyes and made no apology. 'Bring it 'ere then and let me see proper.'

'She don't want to see a half-dead bird, but if you come to the kitchens with me, you can give me a hand. Think it's broke its leg, never mind being half-starved.'

'No, I want to see,' Luna said, curious that some poor creature was injured and possibly in pain. There might be something she could do to help.

Mrs Webber pulled back a corner of the apron to reveal the iridescent black feathers and smooth head of the largest member of the corvid family, with that unmistakable bluish sheen to the plumage and the shaggy ruff of feathers around its throat. The pale grey eyelids were closed and the bird wasn't moving.

'Looks dead to me.' Mr Webber was dismissive of his wife's find. 'And if it ain't, I can easily put it out of its misery.' He shrugged, clearly not caring either way.

Perhaps aware of its imminent demise, the bird flicked open an eye, but only briefly, as if the exertion was too much.

'No! Don't you see? Everything is going to be all right. If we can save the bird, we can save Ravenswood.'

Luna looked blankly at the animated housekeeper, who cradled the bundle closer, as her plump cheeks lifted in excitement. 'Legend says that if the ravens leave the woods, the house of Greybourne will fall,' she explained. 'That vile witch of a wife... I mean, the birds were murdered by... erm, we thought they was all dead,' the older woman said.

Was Marcus's real wife responsible for the inhumane animal trap? And had she nailed the other raven to the gatepost? Luna shivered. The housekeeper was right; the woman she was claiming to be was an unpleasant and cruel person.

'I'm in two minds.' Mr Webber shook his head and rubbed at his unshaven chin. 'P'raps it might be better if I just wrung its—'

'No!' the women exclaimed, simultaneously.

'If you would be so kind as to bring me a strip of bandage and a small splint, a dish of water and something I might try to feed it,' Luna said. 'Perhaps some bread soaked in milk?' She shuffled herself more upright on the bench, feeling a renewed energy. She had a purpose, at last.

'I'll sort the leg,' Mr Webber grunted, reluctantly. 'Done it before with chickens...' He gave Luna a piercing glare, before dropping his eyes to her own damaged ankle. '*And* suspicious strangers who happened across our land out of nowhere. I'll bring it back when I'm done and you can play nursemaid. You've got nothing else to fill your time, so you might as well make yourself useful.'

He followed his wife and they disappeared around the back of the house, with Luna acknowledging the gruff manservant didn't like her very much. If she were a bolder person, she might have reprimanded him for speaking to his mistress with such disrespect, but she was not that brave, and with every day that she remained at this house, her fear was increasing.

* * *

Luna's focus on the half-dead raven over the following couple of hours helped her to forget her pain to some degree. And took her mind off the dark goings-on at Ravenswood.

Mr Webber dealt efficiently with its leg and, using a glass pipette from the medicine chest, Luna was able to get some water into the bird. It remained wrapped in the apron to begin with, and she gently laid it across her lap as she tried to get it to eat a few morsels of food from some tarnished sugar tongs the housekeeper had found, but it wasn't interested. The water made a difference, however, and she was rewarded by a few more flutterings of the one eye that was visible.

Quietly content, watching the occasional traveller and trader pass along the riverbank and take the ferry over the water, Luna spent a pleasant afternoon talking to the injured bird. It was a one-sided conversation but she prattled on, glad of the company, and occasionally checking her charge hadn't passed away.

Until the horrific events of that week, her days had always been so busy. A steady stream of callers came and went from Church View and the occasional visits from the young Mr Thornbury had brightened her days. The thought of Daniel made her heart heavy and she blinked away building tears. She mustn't dwell too much on his death or it would break her completely. It had been such a muddle of misunderstandings, lies and uncontrollable jealousy. An innocent man had died, never part of the plan, and she would have to live with her role in all that had happened for the remainder of her life.

By the afternoon, the bird had opened its eyes and was now upright, even if it was not moving much, and she was cautiously optimistic about its recovery. They had both suffered at the hands of another and it made her sympathy for the creature even greater.

The pair were carried inside by Mr Webber as the temperature began to drop, and he was none too pleased when Luna asked if she might have one of the crates from the barn to keep the bird in her room for the night. He grunted rather than replying but did as he was asked, as well as informing her that the creature was male. Luna consequently decided, should the raven survive until morning, she would give him a name, even if, like hers, it was only a temporary one.

Eventually, the sky outside filled with wide slashes of plum and apricot, and the sun began to sink down to the west, finally dipping below the treetops, which were silhouetted black against the colourful backdrop.

Thankful for any small moments of joy, she reflected that she had never witnessed such a dramatic sunset in the city. She had experienced both rural and urban living in her short life and knew which she preferred. Her plan had been to make for London, but God had other ideas and she must enjoy this period of unexpected respite whilst it lasted. Her stay at Ravenswood may only be for a short while but she was safe for the moment. From the police, if not the Devil.

8

During the night, Luna was woken by the sound of footsteps. At first, she thought they were from the corridor, but they were followed by a thump on the ceiling and she realised that there was a person in the attic rooms above. Mr and Mrs Webber had quarters off the kitchens, and would be tucked up in their beds by now. There were no other servants. Or so she'd thought.

Did Ravenswood have another inhabitant? Surely the housekeeper would have mentioned it. Either Mrs Webber didn't know there was someone up there, or didn't want Luna to know. She couldn't even get out of bed to investigate. It made her realise how vulnerable she was – an injured girl in an unsettling house in the middle of nowhere, unable to flee if she was attacked.

Then she rationalised the noises. The Webbers were likely looking for something – they had mentioned Marcus was bringing valuables down, possibly items kept out of the way of his destructive wife. It was a strange activity to be undertaking in the middle of the night though, and she decided to question them about it in the morning.

She leaned over to check the bird in the crate, strangely comforted that there was another living soul in the room with her. He was still alive but moving very little. The attic was now silent and she began to wonder if she'd imagined the sounds. As she struggled to get back to sleep, she played a hundred things over in her head: from the awfulness of recent events at Lowbridge, to the secrets of this place and her desperate hope that the injured creature was on the mend.

Amongst these troubled thoughts, she remembered that the city of Branchester had got its name from the Celtic word for raven. Indeed, there had been an alarming proliferation of them in this part of the country during medieval times. Once viewed as a pest, and blamed for killing livestock and spreading the plague, they had been ruthlessly persecuted and numbers had declined in recent times. But through the city name, the river and even the house she now found herself in, their legacy remained. It struck her as a perfect name for her charge and so, like the river that flowed forty miles from the once raven-troubled city and out to the sea, she called him Bran.

The next morning, Luna was delighted to find the bird upright in the crate and encouraged when he began to take small morsels of hard-boiled egg from the tongs. Like her, he could not bear weight on his broken leg, but he seemed brighter and she had every reason to hope that he might make a full recovery. She was content chattering away to him, convinced he was listening as he tipped his lustrous head to one side, until Mrs Webber arrived with her cheery, toothless smile to help her dress.

'Is there someone sleeping in the attics?' she asked. 'I heard noises during the night.'

The housekeeper shook her head. 'I can assure you that it's only the three of us here, now that the master no longer has dogs, so I'm reckoning it was squirrels or rats.' She seemed definite in her assertion.

'But I heard footsteps,' Luna persisted and the older woman frowned and clutched at a small crucifix she had about her neck.

'The spirits have many ways of making their presence known. I've heard tell of knocking, vivid smells, the caress of a hand or even objects flying across a room. Perhaps she's up there, searching for something, unable to move on.' Mrs Webber didn't need to specify who she was referring to, and her comments suggested she thought her former mistress was dead – which was not a pleasant notion.

They were interrupted by a knock at the bedroom door and Mr Webber appeared. He informed Luna that she had a visitor and immediately her chest flooded with panic. Had someone from Lowbridge tracked her down? Or was the constable back to arrest her for murder and cart her to Branchester gaol?

'Don't look so alarmed. I've asked my good friend Mr Findlay to call, but it's imperative that the master doesn't hear of this visit,' Mrs Webber said, straightening the bedcovers and folding up the borrowed nightgown. Luna was back in the dress she had arrived in, now washed and pressed by the housekeeper. 'Whilst my loyalty to Mr Greybourne is absolute, he has funny ideas about the poor chap. He refuses to have him in the house because his ways aren't the ways of science, but I can assure you, he is a wonder. Cured a young boy of his strange fits. Helps me with headaches and even pulled out several of my teeth when they were... damaged. I've been taking the mistress to visit him in secret since he moved into Honeysuckle Cottage, and he can help that ankle of yours to heal faster – I just know he can.'

Luna's unease was apparent on her face. Marcus had expressly asked her to have nothing to do with the man, and he would immediately know her as the fraud she was, but the housekeeper put a hand on her arm to offer reassurance.

'He knows the situation. Don't worry, *Mrs Greybourne*, our secrets are safe with him.'

Her husband grunted again before scooping his temporary mistress up, ignoring the flapping wings and squawks from Bran, and carrying her from the room. The bird clearly didn't like the manservant, but then, as Webber lumped her down the stairs, she acknowledged she didn't much like him either.

* * *

Mr Findlay was quite the sight to behold. Although his hair was almost white, the face beneath was not that of an old man – quite the opposite. He was, she thought, perhaps fifty, or a little younger. He was small of stature and dressed in a rainbow of colours: a silk cravat of tangerine, bright-green trousers, and a brocade waistcoat of lemon yellow, with a sprig of dried lavender in his buttonhole. His face was round and cheerful, and a small black leather medicine bag sat by his feet.

He stood up as she entered and introduced himself, informing her that he lived just upriver of Ravenswood, beyond the ferry, barely five minutes from them. Luna was comforted to know the house was not as isolated as she'd first thought. He told her that he was what people called a cunning man, or folk healer, and that he had kept Mr and Mrs Webber safe with an array of charms and potions when Luna had been lost to her own mind. Marcus, she knew, didn't hold with anything magical or not of this world, although she wasn't quite sure where she stood on such matters herself. She had a tendency to be too trusting – her willingness to throw herself into this whole charade had demonstrated that. If someone stated a thing as fact and had an earnest look about their face, she was inclined to believe them.

Her guest leaned forward for a slice of fruit loaf, took a small bite and wrinkled up his nose. The cake and the plate were discreetly placed on the floor just as a terrible rumpus drifted down the stairs. It was Bran, cawing and calling, and Mr Webber's agitated tones could be heard chastising the creature. He must have managed to flap himself out of the crate.

'What on earth is that hullabaloo?' Mr Findlay asked, nodding a grateful thanks as his teacup was topped up, and then chuckling to himself. 'Are you shortly to open a zoo here at Ravenswood?'

'I'll see what the fuss is about, madam, and shut the bird in your room,' the older lady said, and bobbed her head before departing.

'It's a raven from the woods,' Luna explained as Mrs Webber scuttled away. 'He is recuperating in a crate upstairs and I suspect his agitation is because Mr Webber is painting one of the bedrooms. The bird has not taken to him.' Despite the manservant splinting Bran's broken leg, it was almost as if he knew Mr Webber's initial suggestion had been to wring his neck.

The surprise on Mr Findlay's face was immediate. 'That one should have survived!' He put his teacup down and clasped his hands together in delight. The apples of his cheeks flushed pink with joy, and then he leaned forward with an earnest look about his bright-blue eyes. 'Mrs Webber told me about the despicable slaughter of the birds after a particularly distressing period of melancholy that Luna... you suffered. It is *imperative* that your husband ensures a colony of ravens remains to protect the woods, despite his failure to recognise the danger of the black arts.'

The cook had obviously filled their visitor in on all the goings-on at Ravenswood and, though he might address her as such, he knew perfectly well she was not who she claimed to be. If he'd been attending to Mrs Greybourne in private, he would be one of the very few people who had seen her close up in recent years.

'However,' he said, 'I am here to assist with your broken ankle and do not wish to outstay my welcome.' He reached for his bag and produced a small ceramic pot with a square of cloth secured around the rim with string. 'I have prepared for you a healing ointment that will speed up the knitting of the bone. Apply it twice a day, morning and evening, gently over the damaged area.'

Luna took the offered item and lifted it to her nose. She couldn't bring herself to criticise the gift but it had the faint smell of dung. Mr Findlay noticed her expression.

'Ah, yes, the comfrey has a very distinctive odour.' He grinned. 'This preparation also includes the bark of white oak, ground black walnut leaf, wormwood and lobelia... amongst other things. And I passed some freshly picked comfrey leaves to your housekeeper upon my arrival with detailed instructions for a tea that will also aid your recovery.'

He reached out for her elevated leg, meeting her eye and asking, 'May I?'

She nodded as he laid his hands gently on her swollen ankle, mumbling soft words under his breath. The heat from his touch was immediately soothing.

'Do not mind me, Mrs Greybourne.' He looked up to meet her eye and smiled. 'A simple charm as old as the chalk in the nearby hills. My magic, such as it is, is benevolent. A counter to the maleficence of others. I appreciate that your husband does not take kindly to me and gives no credence to the supernatural, but please trust me.'

'I'm not quite sure what to think.' She hesitated. 'My husband said that magic is only real if you believe in it.'

'He's wrong. There are many dark forces at work within our world and to dismiss them is foolhardy. When evil triumphs over good, it is not because the good has failed, but that the evil was stronger. And that is often down to calling on powers that are not of this realm.' He reached for her hand. 'I have been working hard to thwart *your* magic for a long time.'

She was momentarily thrown by his words until she realised he was talking of Marcus's wife. By being this woman, she had to accept the previous actions of the Ravenswood Witch would now be attributed to her.

'The people of the village often come to me after your careless curses and vindictive actions: failed harvests, sick livestock and babies born with deformities because you held grudges against the families. I could not save Mother Selwood, but I have kept the Webbers safe. There are undoubtedly wicked things going on hereabouts and those you think you can trust are the most likely to betray you.'

This struck a chord with Luna, who had been too trusting before. Ultimately, it had been her undoing. She nodded.

'Be warned, my dear, we often decide someone is wholesome and good because this is how they present themselves to the outside world. The benevolent vicar, who gives of his time to minister to the needs of his congregation, but who hides disturbing secrets... Or the innately good people forced to do wicked things. Maybe, a man who has care of someone who is unspeakably cruel to him, for example, who might be driven to commit a crime deserving of the noose.'

He paused to let his words sink in and she wondered if he was referring to Marcus. Did Mr Findlay know what had happened to the real Luna? And if so, was he suggesting her husband had done away with her in his desperation? Even though she barely knew Marcus, she couldn't believe that he was capable of such an act.

'Many people in this world have two faces. Perhaps even you?' Her visitor raised both eyebrows and lowered his voice, before gently patting her knee. 'We both know that you are not Luna, but rest assured that I will happily play along. Evil things happened around your predecessor and she was not kind to her husband. He strikes me as a good man who needs someone to love, and to love him in return, and I think that someone might be you.'

Uncomfortable at the romantic advice being offered by a stranger, she shook her head. 'I have no idea what you're talking about, Mr Findlay. You have tended to me in the past, and I appreciate that you are taking the time to help with my broken ankle now. I love my husband and I regret my previous unacceptable behaviour.'

He gave a slow nod of resignation.

'I see you are set on this pantomime, yet you hardly know the man that you claim you are married to. My divination cards foretold of your arrival, and they also tell me that you will have an important role to play in Mr Greybourne's life for many years to come. No matter, stick to your story, but be assured that love will find you. I know these things.'

He patted her knee a second time, in the way an adult might patronise a child's stories of make-believe. Love had already found her and then she'd lost it. Her heart was not ready to be given to another.

Humming a merry tune to himself, Mr Findlay offered to pour her a further cup of tea but she shook her head, so he filled his own cup, not offended by her play-acting, and settling back in the chair with a smile.

'You must come and visit me at Honeysuckle Cottage when your ankle is better. Eventually Mr Greybourne will realise I am not the enemy that he supposes but, until that day, I should like to see you from time to time to reassure myself that you are safe. I am usually to be found at home preparing my medicines and you would be most welcome.'

'Could you not come again whilst my husband is still away?' She liked this friendly but curious man, and it had been refreshing to talk to someone other than the housekeeper and the grunting manservant.

'I have been forbidden to step on Greybourne lands and I should not have come this time, but Mrs Webber was insistent. In his ignorance, your husband has taken against me, but I respect him for all that. He did his best for his wife, never leaving her to the care of others, often shadowing her day and night to keep her from harm, and even following her into the woods. But everyone has their breaking point and I suspect she pushed him to his. I understand she has not been seen for days and yet he hastily instates a replacement. I can only hope that wherever she is now, she has found peace.'

As if in answer to his speculating, the low flames in the grate surged forward and there was a roar as they lurched into the room. If Luna had been killed, she reflected, it seemed most unlikely that she would contentedly move on. Not when there was an imposter living her life, and she had her own death yet to avenge.

9

ELOISE

'What do you know of cricket, Rose?' Eloise asked.

Her young maid had been an age sectioning and plaiting her long blonde hair, skilfully pinning an expensive false piece to the back of her head to create the highly fashionable style so popular in the big cities, but probably wasted on the rural folk of Lowbridge.

'Very little,' Rose replied, finishing the arrangement with a decorative tortoiseshell comb.

Eloise reached for her small coral pendant and fastened it around her neck. It was an inexpensive item that she'd purchased long before her family's change in fortunes, amused by its supposed ability to bring good luck. It had certainly done its job, although she wasn't entirely convinced that a piece of some long-dead sea creature was responsible for their newfound wealth. Her mother would tut, wondering why her daughter insisted on wearing such a tawdry item, but Eloise like the colour.

'Apparently the village has a team and they are playing the neighbouring parish next Saturday afternoon. I know little of the game myself, but Father informs me that a man defends some sticks in the ground with a bat, as a cork ball covered in leather is hurled in his direction.'

'I'm sure it's somewhat more involved than that,' her maid said, smiling.

'I thought I might watch so perhaps you'd kindly look out an appropriate summer dress for the occasion? Father always says autumn shades reflect in my eyes and make them shine like freshly fallen conkers, but June is surely a month for soft pinks and sky blues. Something in a pastel colour would be perfect.' She paused. 'Do you think the young Mr Thornbury will be asked to play?'

'I'm not sure, but I can enquire. The vicar, who I understand captains the team, is not enamoured of the Thornburys after the young man told him that those who attend church and boast of their good works are often the least compassionate and most dishonest people he knows.'

'I, for one, admire his refreshing honesty. We all know that the grocer makes a huge show of what he puts in the collection plate, but Cook is convinced that the finest-quality flour that he charges double for, comes from the same sack as the standard flour.'

Eloise was fascinated by the stir the new arrivals were causing in the village. That they openly challenged the church, an institution she herself long felt was a hotbed of hypocrisy, was incredibly brave and rather thrilling. Daniel Thornbury had also confronted the schoolmaster over the man's firm belief in the absolute obedience of children, insisting instead that it was vital for them to question and challenge. And she had been at the village May Day celebrations and overheard his conversation in the presence of Lord and Lady Fletcher about privilege and entitlement, quoting Plato, of all people.

He was clearly an intelligent man who was fighting a society that only gave opportunities to those born into the right families. In fact, she'd been so intrigued by the philosophies and ideas he talked of that she'd read up about the social reformer Robert Owen after Daniel had mentioned his name in a conversation about the duty of employers to their staff. It was rather eye-opening how he'd transformed the lives of the villagers at New Lanark with his belief that happier workers were more productive. When her father came across her flicking through such books in his study, he was pleasantly surprised. The thing of it was, she'd always been bright, but had never bothered to apply herself before.

However, Eloise's opinions did not always align with those of the young Mr Thornbury. He talked of abolishing the monarchy and she quite liked Queen Victoria. And she noticed that his advocating of equal rights for all didn't always extend to the gentler sex. His vision of an ideal world involved the redistribution of wealth so that everyone had an equal share, and there was a small part of her that, having come so late as a family to their personal fortune and seeing how much easier it made life for her hard-working father, she would rather like to hang on to it. She might not agree with *everything* he stood for, but for the first time since moving to Lowbridge, Eloise was engaged and felt passionately about all manner of things – including Daniel.

* * *

The Saturday of the match, Eloise looked out across the village green as a well-turned-out older chap in a cloth cap walked back and forth with a garden roller. Swallows were darting about in the skies above Lowbridge, a sure sign summer had arrived. She flung open her small casement window and the scent from the bed of white stocks beneath her drifted into the room; the day promised sunshine and joy – both of which it delivered.

The first of the strawberries had been picked from the gardens, enough for one small bowlful, which her parents graciously allowed her to have in its entirety. She then spent her morning getting ready, giddy with anticipation.

But when the housekeeper informed Eloise that the match was shortly to begin, her mother cried off, claiming a headache, and her father had already left for London, having been invited to spend the evening at a gentleman's club. Still not having made a great many friends, and certainly none of her own age, she requested Rose accompany her, to give her someone to talk to, if nothing else.

They laid out a blanket in front of the Thornburys' cottage, under the shade of an old elm, but she was disappointed that Daniel and his father were nowhere to be seen. With neither girl understanding the rules of the game, the match dragged. After the loud crack of the bat making contact with the hard ball, there was always a polite ripple of applause. She clapped when the people around her clapped, but she had little interest in two men running back and forth in a tiny rectangle of grass.

After the first innings, they queued up for a plate of dainty sandwiches and slivers of fruit cake, all being served in a marquee set up on a lawn behind the church.

'I thought you said Daniel Thornbury was coming, but I can't see him anywhere.' Eloise had hoped to impress him with her reading.

'That's what I was told, miss. But perhaps he is not a man who honours his word. He seems earnest in his beliefs but frivolous in his pursuits. I've heard talk that he regularly swims in the Bran...' she lowered her voice, '...in nothing but what the good Lord brought him into this world wearing.'

Eloise blushed at the thought of the unclothed body of the young man in question, removing her gloves as she was handed a plate. She tried to clear her mind of the alarming vision by changing the subject.

'I really don't think I can sit through several more hours of this stupid game. Let's have our afternoon tea and then return home.'

After consuming more cake than was good for them, the pair headed back to the green and were surprised to encounter the object of Eloise's affections, sitting on a bench underneath an ancient yew, at the front of the church. He had his nose in a book and did not look up, even when she stopped directly in front of him, her shadow falling across the pages.

'Mr Thornbury,' she said, in mock severity. 'I didn't think to find you in a churchyard, of all places. I thought you and God were not on speaking terms.'

'I'm here for the shade, not the religion.' He met her eye but there was no smile to match her own. He also did not immediately jump to his feet as most gentlemen would, and instead returned to his reading.

'Not for the cricket? I was expecting to see you out on the field,' she said, frustrated at his reluctance to engage in conversation.

'I've been asked, because I'm young and they are desperate, but I've barely been here a month. Not really a game for the likes of me; it's a sport for the entitled. Saturated with tradition, full of unnecessary theatrics and ridiculous language, and with so many interruptions that it fails to adequately hold my attention. I'm far happier improving my knowledge than my spin bowl.'

'I quite agree. One can learn so much from a book. I have recently ordered some of Robert Owen's essays from the public library in Branchester, in a bid to expand my limited, and rather privileged, horizons.'

Daniel closed his book and studied her face as he finally got to his feet. 'You know of Owen?'

She nodded. 'Interesting man who certainly practised what he preached,' she said, feeling confident that she had hooked her fish. 'He was to be admired. And if you would care to join us as the match resumes, we can continue this most interesting discussion.'

'May I be excused now, miss?' Rose's anxious eyes met her own. She was not comfortable in the presence of Mr Thornbury and Eloise understood – she felt quite nervous of him herself.

'Of course.' She smiled at the kind girl who always did as she was bid without complaint.

Daniel was persuaded to join her on the blanket as the second innings began. There was no denying he was handsome, if a little rough around the edges. His calloused hands alone were proof of an honest day's work, and she rather liked that. He wasn't stuffy and formal, but open and relaxed. And, as it turned out, had the same lack of regard for the silly game they were watching as she did. Their conversation was animated and informative, and had absolutely nothing to do with cricket.

The Fletchers wandered past, attending the game in their capacity as village squire and squire's wife, and stopped to speak to them, or rather to Eloise. They had been slow to make associations with her family, having learned that the Haughtons' wealth was a more recent acquisition, but remained keen to be seen as benevolent landowners. Lady Fletcher was also possibly flattered by her mother's fawning attentions, and saw it as her duty to save young Miss Haughton from a situation she did not require saving from.

'Miss Haughton, you must sit with us. We insist,' Lady Fletcher said, looking down her nose at Daniel, who had got to his feet as they had approached. 'I'm sure this young man won't mind if I steal you to discuss the upcoming rota for the church flowers.'

'Not a bit,' Daniel said. Her companion was already making moves to leave, and Eloise was a little disappointed that he was so indifferent to her company. 'I've seen enough of the game, and Milton's ideas regarding free will are calling me.' He reached down to collect his volume from the grass. 'I only popped out for the fresh air and to ascertain the score for Father, who is feeling under the weather today.'

'Do pass on our regards.' Lady Fletcher dug particularly deep for her manners. 'And how are you and your father settling in to your... small cottage?'

'Small suits us. It has two bedrooms and there are two of us. I have never aspired to live in a large house with more bedrooms than occupants.'

'Ah, a liberal?' Lord Fletcher spoke for the first time. 'Or perhaps a revolutionary?'

Daniel shrugged. 'Better to fight for a world where every man has equal opportunities and rights, than to sit back and accept a world where it is only the accident of your birth that determines your worth.'

It was all said without malice, Eloise noticed. He was stating facts and expressing his opinions with the most disarming smile across his face.

'Well, really...' Lady Fletcher blushed a deep pink. 'Miss Haughton?' She stuck out her arm to allow the younger woman to step with her away from this indelicate conversation, and Eloise hardly felt she could refuse.

Daniel bowed deferentially as they took their leave and, as she dared a backwards glance, she was jerked back in line by her irate companion.

10

After the departure of Mr Findlay, heavy clouds drifted from the west and settled overhead, casting the landscape in a theatrical light. Another storm was imminent and Luna asked if she might be carried through to join the Webbers in the kitchens. The drawing room unnerved her, even though she knew she was being silly by imagining the ghost of Marcus's wife to be loitering in the fireplace. She had no proof that Luna was dead but had the inexplicable feeling that the house, or someone within it, was watching her, and she didn't like it. Prickles dashed across her skin when she was alone and she occasionally caught fragmented whispers and couldn't be certain if they were real or imagined.

Mr Webber didn't like the mistress of the house being seated in what he considered the servants' domain and grumbled about being watched, but his wife seemed happy to have someone to chat to. It also gave Luna the opportunity to make delicate suggestions with regard to improved food preparation and for her to observe how the household was run – which was rather haphazardly, as it turned out.

It was interesting watching the pair of them go about their tasks, the manservant sneering every time he so much as looked at his wife. There was no love there, to be sure, yet, despite wearing his contempt for the world permanently across his face, Luna thought he was still quite an attractive man for his age, with strong features and chocolate-brown eyes. She could imagine he had been quite the catch for Mrs Webber back in the day.

She asked if Bran might be brought downstairs, and was heartened to see him cautiously hopping about on his good leg across the flagstone floor, holding the other off the ground. The raven and the manservant kept to opposite corners of the large room though, she noticed.

She decided to quiz the couple about the Greybourne legend and the housekeeper confirmed that ravens had lived in the nearby woods for hundreds of years. When a holy well had been dug there by the nearby Cistercian monks in medieval times, the people of Little Doubton came to associate these curious and intelligent birds with the protection of this precious water source, even though those further afield persecuted them as harbingers of bad luck and death.

'There's a well in the woods at the back of the house?' Luna said, somewhat surprised as the river was so close.

'Yes, but it don't have water in it no more,' Mr Webber muttered from his dark corner, the smell of damp soil and cheap brandy quite obvious when he came in for his lunch. The rain was now beating against the windowpanes like a thousand tiny stampeding horses. 'Dried up donkey's years ago. But I don't know what all the fuss was about. It's hardly like we're miles from water.' He echoed her own thoughts, as he struck a match and began to puff on an old clay pipe.

'Ignore him,' his wife said. 'He knows this was different. Pure. Came from under them hills and had magical properties. Some old monk in the thirteen hundreds was told in a vision to dig in a particular spot, and he happened upon this underground spring that fed into the Bran. Special water, it was. My grandmother remembers it curing a man of blindness.'

Luna was amazed that the water was so powerful it could make a man see again.

'Part of the abbey lands back then, but then fat old King Henry sold it off and all's left is ruins. You can still see some of the abbey walls when you walk into Doubton.'

'Problem is...' Mr Webber leaned forward in his chair so that his face loomed from the shadows, '...there be darker folk wanting that water –

Devil-worshippers an' such, who do their ill-wishing at the well.' He spoke slowly and deliberately, like someone relaying a ghost story to children. If he'd wanted to scare Luna, it worked, as a distant rumble of thunder added to the eerie atmosphere. 'They travelled from miles around to gather at the witching hour and called on evil spirits in them woods. You won't find no one out after dark on All Hallows' Eve in these parts, coz that's when he's summoned up through the well and walks through the village, collecting the restless souls of them that can't move on.'

'Who?' she asked, suspecting she knew the answer.

'The Devil,' Mr Webber whispered and then, noticing her horrified expression and trembling hands, he laughed out loud. 'You're as bad as the missus. Look at yer both. Faces as pale as milk.'

He'd taken far too much pleasure in scaring them and she felt increasingly uncomfortable in his presence, even though Bran had flown to her side when the talk had turned to Devil worship and tortured souls unable to leave this realm.

Not long afterwards, Luna overheard the pair of them whispering in the scullery. Mrs Webber reminded her husband that he might well tell everyone to stay inside when the Devil was walking, yet she knew damn well he went out himself last All Hallows' Eve. He told her to mind her own goddamn business, and Luna heard a scuffle of feet followed by a yelp from his wife, suggesting the man was not averse to lashing out when riled. Suddenly the kitchens no longer seemed an appealing option and she didn't ask to sit with them again.

* * *

Every morning after that, Mr Webber carried her straight to the drawing room and Bran hopped slowly along behind them, not wanting to lose sight of the woman to whom he owed his recovery. He was now happier out of the crate and spent most of his time flapping between the windowsill and the top of her high-backed armchair. When he spread his obsidian-black wings wide, she was astounded by the size of him. It was obvious that the bird had become attached to her, even though he was growing increasingly pushy, nudging her hand when she had the effrontery to stop petting his soft black head. But at his most content, he would make a delightful low gurgling sound, and she liked his company, feeling safer with him beside her.

'I asked my husband to make you these,' Mrs Webber said, passing over a pair of rough-hewn crutches. 'They ain't nothing special and, despite the bit of padding I've wrapped around the crosspiece, you won't be able to use them for long, but if you promise not to put any weight on that foot, you can at least get about now.'

Luna was moved by the woman's kindness but also delighted to have more independence and not be totally reliant on the housekeeper's gruff husband to carry her about. Thoughts of leaving were never far from her mind, so the quicker she could become mobile, the quicker she could cross the river and start a new life in London. Her nights had been increasingly troubled by imagined voices, whispering to her that she was not wanted, although with all she'd been through recently, these cruel tricks of the mind were not a surprise.

'How thoughtful. This will allow me to explore the house and see where I could make improvements. Mr Greybourne mentioned sending me some catalogues and I would like to be of service whilst he is absent.'

The housekeeper raised an eyebrow. 'Be prepared, is all I'm saying, coz you ain't going to like what you find...'

In the few days since she'd been at the house, the only rooms Luna had seen were the kitchen, drawing room, and the gloomy bedroom, yet the property was sizeable and she was keen to explore – if only because she was so terribly bored.

The crutches were heavy and awkward, but she was able to hobble around the ground floor, only to find Mrs Webber was right; she was met with sights she couldn't even begin to understand. Despite Marcus's best efforts before he'd left for London, she found room after room lying empty and in various states of disrepair. Walls were covered in writing; dark and jagged words repeated over and over, barely decipherable but largely threatening, and all the rooms had a black eye painted somewhere on the wall, much like the one in her bedroom, as if to remind anyone entering that they were being watched. There were disturbing scratch marks around the bottom of the doors, as though someone or something had tried to claw their way out, and debris lay in every corner, swept to one side, but she recognised chair legs and broken china amongst the litter.

More alarmingly, there were several dark scorch marks in the floorboards, charred and black, where small fires had clearly been lit, and the floor of the library was covered in the same symbols and markings that she'd seen on the bed canopy. A huge sweeping chalk circle took up the central space, with melted pillar candles dotted at regular intervals, and animal bones (at least, she hoped they were animal bones) laid out in strange patterns in the gaps between.

Luna felt sick. Weird things had been going on in this house and this room was the most unsettling of all. As she turned to go, she noticed a dirty mattress and a small hoop-backed chair in the window, with one grey blanket thrown haphazardly across the makeshift bed. Was this where his wife had slept? She felt incredulous. Mrs Greybourne had been treated no better than an animal.

Mr Findlay may have claimed her husband was kind to his former wife, but he had not been privy to these rooms, and she started to wonder if Marcus was one of the 'wholesome and good' people that the cunning man had warned her about…

11

Two weeks into her stay and Luna had received several letters from Marcus. The first one contained news that his business contacts were proving useful, but it also included several packets of flower seeds and instructions for Mr Webber to plant them in the greenhouse. The next two contained moderate sums of money. She was asked to pass a certain amount over to Mrs Webber in order to run the household, and was told anything remaining she could spend at her discretion...

> *It belatedly occurred to me that you might need clothing and other articles for your toilette, although anything suitable you find about the house you may use. I shall trust you won't just take the enclosed money and run into the sunset – or should I say, limp...*

She couldn't help but smile.

All the letters had started 'My dearest wife', and had finished 'Your husband, Marcus', which reassured her that they were both continuing in their agreed roles. If anyone came looking for her, the household would swear to her being Mrs Greybourne, but she would be gone long before he returned to Ravenswood, with no need for the sham marriage to continue in person.

Bran was now hopping quite freely about the house, his head jutting forward with each step, and his body lopsided as he tentatively used the splinted leg. Mrs Webber tutted about having a live bird in the area where she prepared food but, from her two visits to the kitchens, Luna knew hygiene standards were somewhat lax, as dead birds abandoned on the refectory table and attracting flies were apparently fine.

As time went on, wherever Luna was to be found, Bran was usually not far behind. They presented quite a comical sight: a slender young woman hunched over a pair of crude crutches, hopping along, as a jet-black raven waddled unevenly beside her.

'Are you kissing me?' she would ask, as he rubbed his soft, feathered head against her own, and decided that perhaps he was. She had, after all, saved his life.

But he was a wilful creature, stroppy and demanding one minute, placid and gentle the next, and the wild animal in him remained. On days when the weather was sufficiently pleasant for her to sit outside, he would stretch out his wings and soar up into the blue, disappearing for increasingly longer spells of time. Mr Webber often reported seeing him circling above the woods, yet he always returned to Luna.

'It's strange how he's attached himself to you,' Mrs Webber said, bringing the luncheon tray and shooing the raven away from the food. The soup, which was of indeterminable ingredients, was steaming hot, so Luna stirred it as the older woman talked. 'But the master will be pleased we've saved a bird. Not because he's superstitious about the curse, more that he's the sentimental sort. It's why he insists on remaining in this dilapidated shell of a house; his grandfather built it and that means a lot to him. And it's why he stuck with her... you,' she hastily corrected herself. 'Duty and honour.' She shook her head.

Whilst she appreciated the housekeeper's support of her assumed role, Luna decided it was time to find out what Mrs Greybourne had subjected her husband to, particularly should she be put in the position again where an outsider was being asked to believe she was responsible for the past actions of his wife.

'What really happened here?' she asked. 'What was Luna like?'

The housekeeper cast wary eyes about the room and one hand

clutched the thin silver crucifix about her neck. She lowered her voice to barely a whisper.

'She had the most startling eyes of pale grey. Like an angel, she were, with a halo of yellow hair about her head. But she weren't no messenger of God.' Mrs Webber shuddered. 'Men were always drawn to her like bees to a honeypot, even my Jed. And when she did all that naked prancing about by the well, young men from the village would try to cop an eyeful by skirting around the edge of the woods. They started the rumours and she lapped it up, taking an unhealthy interest in the dead and the occult – happy to be called a witch. Sad, really.' She sighed. 'Last time I set eyes on her, she were reduced to a pitiful sack of bones.'

Luna was unsettled. Was it worse if the woman was dead or alive? Because she certainly didn't want to encounter her either way.

'Everything he loved, she destroyed,' the housekeeper continued. 'Heirlooms that had been in the family generations. She threw much of the porcelain and dinnerware at him and smashed up the furniture. Two years ago, when her condition was becoming unmanageable, she took all them books from the library and started an enormous bonfire out the back. It's a miracle the whole of the wood didn't go up. Poor Mr Greybourne managed to get the blaze under control, but you can't replace a collection like that. He went on a terrible rampage that night, doing a fair bit of damage of his own. He don't know that I saw him growling and smashing his fists into the wall, but I did.'

Marcus had a temper then, Luna noted.

'Was it because she was so destructive that you put bolts on the doors?' It finally occurred to her that they were to keep the woman out, not lock her in.

'Saved what possessions he could – you can't set fire to the silverware – hid what he could in the attic and gathered what remained of the furniture in the drawing room, just so's he'd got a place he was safe. Locked her out if he was elsewhere, and himself in when she got too violent. Jed and I have locks on our rooms, too, though it weren't largely us she wanted to hurt.'

Again, her eyes darted about as though she was afraid they might be overheard. It was becoming obvious that she was intimidated by her husband – maybe she didn't want him to know that she was talking about such matters. Or perhaps she thought the Ravenswood Witch was listening.

'She tried to kill him several times. Attempted to strangle him whilst he was sleeping and set fire to his bed; that's when he added the locks.'

The revelations were becoming increasingly disturbing and it confirmed Luna's decision to leave as soon as her ankle was strong enough, even though she had begrudgingly accepted that there was another magic at play. She could feel it wrap its gentle arms about her – a kindness from the housekeeper, and even from Marcus himself, along with the protection that Bran offered. There were two forces toying with her: good and evil. It was as if both wanted to weave their spell about her and anchor her to Ravenswood for entirely different reasons.

'And he never locked her up?'

Mrs Webber shook her head. 'Not once. Remember him saying she was like a wild cat – "trap her and she'll become even more savage". Always insisted she was free but that she was his responsibility and, as she became more unmanageable, his life became more focused on her, with little time for anything else.'

So, Marcus had spent the last few years looking after his increasingly unstable wife, helpless as she destroyed everything that was precious to him, and living with the stigma that he was married to a witch. No wonder he was occasionally driven to moments of rage. Her heart went out to him; he had suffered, as she had, at the hand of another. Perhaps it was a good thing he thought witchcraft was all poppycock; his pragmatism probably saved his sanity.

'Where is she?' It was the question she needed answering the most, but she had promised Marcus she would not pry into his past if he did not pry into hers.

'I wish I knew. She went off into them woods and for all I know, she's still out there. I get this queer feeling sometimes, like she's watching me, so p'raps it's best we talk of other things; I don't want none of her cursing.'

The woman was genuinely distressed so Luna changed the subject as she tore a corner from her bread and tossed it to the floor for Bran.

'I appreciate the undergarments you found me, and the nightgown...'

She had discovered that the reason her nightwear was so voluminous was that Mrs Webber had supplied one of her own the day Marcus had brought her to the house. 'But is there a wardrobe of clothes I might use?' she asked, aware Marcus had precious little money for that end. She only had the dress she had arrived at Ravenswood wearing, even though Mrs Webber had washed it that first evening, but it was in desperate need of repair; the hems particularly frayed from scrambling through undergrowth to evade capture by the constable.

'Not much that is suitable. Your predecessor tended to wear things that were... unconventional – draped herself in bed sheets and curtains. Most of the nicest gowns were shredded in a mad rampage, but there might be something locked in the attics.'

Luna really had destroyed everything in this house. From defacing the walls to ripping up her own dresses, the woman had run wild.

'Perhaps you would be so kind as to bring me what remains, and I'll see whether I can cobble together something serviceable. Is there a sewing box I can use?'

'Not any more. The pins were used for... other purposes and the pretty rosewood sewing table that belonged to Mr Greybourne's mother was destroyed.' She didn't need to say by whom.

'I'll make something from the curtains, if I have to, but I must have at least one other dress.'

'Jedidiah goes into the village tomorrow to pick up groceries and the like. Shall I get him to stop at the haberdashers and buy some pins, needles and coloured threads from Mrs Cole?'

Luna nodded. She didn't like the idea of spending Marcus's money unless necessary – it seemed he had precious little of it – but she could hardly live in the same dress until either she was well enough to leave, or he returned next month, regardless of how few visitors he professed would call. After all, she'd already entertained one unexpected gentleman caller.

'That would be most kind. Thank you.'

* * *

Later that evening, as she readied for bed, she used the crutches to manoeuvre herself over to the large wardrobe that stood near the door. In his letter, Marcus had said she could use anything in the house she could find, and she wondered if there might be something suitable still hung inside, but it only contained those clothes of his that he had not taken away with him. This was, as she suspected, no longer a bedroom the Greybournes shared, but instead his alone – perhaps his only real place of sanctuary.

Her mind wrestled with all the revelations of the day, as her heart wrestled with conflicting emotions. Perhaps she should stay until his return. It would be the polite thing to do. But as she went to close the wardrobe door, she noticed a run of words scratched into the wood, jagged and rough, haunting and alarmingly prophetic, making her reassess her decision of moments earlier.

She is coming.
She will replace me.
She must die…

12

Mrs Webber told Luna that Bran was now well enough to be set free, insisting he was 'too flappy' for her liking and belonged in the wild. The bones of birds healed faster than those of people and, when the splint was finally removed from his leg, her sour-faced husband took him to the edge of the woods and left him there. Three times, the raven reappeared at Ravenswood until Mr Webber resorted to leaving him with a feast of fruit and chicken carcasses deep in the dense thicket of trees, returning to the house and closing all the doors and windows.

That night, Luna woke to a tapping sound. Petrified that the Ravenswood Witch or her spirit was attempting to break in and fulfil the frightening prophecy in the wardrobe, she bravely struggled over to the windowpanes in the dark, only to see the black beads of the raven's serious eyes staring in. She pulled up the sash and he hopped over the sill. Perhaps he simply couldn't bear to return permanently to the woods now that none of his kind were left. So, instead of fighting it, Luna decided to let him come and go as he pleased from then on.

Over the following week, there was quite the to-do when several items went missing from the house: the silver sugar tongs, the milk money, a writing quill, a tiny wooden snuff box, and even her broken coral pendant – not that she cared for it any more. Suspicious of the manservant, who was often lurking in rooms he had no reason to be in, Luna was relieved not to have made accusations when many of them, although not all, turned up in the Dutch barn. The crate used for the raven's recuperation had been returned there recently, and the roaming bird had stolen the objects and tucked them into the folds of the blanket inside.

Bran became increasingly chatty as his health improved, corvids being excellent mimics. He had a surprising number of words and phrases in his vocabulary – from a 'Hello, there' and 'Go away', to her favourite: 'Nice bit of pie'. She felt comforted with him around, even though he was a food thief – eating anything and everything, from biscuits left out on a tea plate, to a large spider that foolishly wandered across the wooden floor in his path.

On May Eve, Mrs Webber busied herself with various traditions that she insisted were essential for the protection of all at the house. Much like All Hallows' Eve, it was a night for supernatural encounters, or rather, the avoidance of them. Evil spirits were particularly active on this night of the year, she told the younger woman, as she hung birch and cowslips above the doors to banish the witches.

After the unsettling discovery of the words in the wardrobe, Luna was more than happy for her housekeeper to do whatever she felt necessary to keep the household safe. The woman went about her strange rituals, as Luna sat by the fire altering a terribly outdated dress that had been found in the attics – although Mrs Webber had grumbled that the master, who must have been looking for something quite specific before he left for London, had left the wooden trunks in a terrible state.

'Witchcraft has been practised in these parts for hundreds of years,' she said. 'One legend says that blindfolded villagers chose pebbles from a basket and whomsoever picked the pebble with the Devil's mark was sacrificed down the well to appease him for another year.'

'This is nonsense, surely?' Luna said, carefully pinning two pieces of fabric together. 'Thousands of years ago, maybe, but not since the digging of the well. We are a civilised people, not a nation of savages.'

Mr Webber grunted from where he was damping down the drawing room fire for the night. 'The master may think it's a load of old claptrap,' he said, 'but I've seen things. He laughs at the tales told by the villagers and says it's just stories spun to terrify the children, but who's been skinning them poor lambs up on the top field and gutting neighbourhood cats? The postmaster found one practically inside out in his yard.'

Luna was far from a child but was becoming increasingly terrified, nonetheless. Being informed of such things on the night that the housekeeper was doing everything in her power to prevent ghostly apparitions and vengeful forces from entering the house was hardly conducive to sleep. Mr Findlay had raised the possibility that Marcus's wife was dead, but Luna wasn't convinced that ghosts could skin cats. If the Ravenswood Witch was still alive, could *she* be responsible for this cruelty? Wandering around Little Doubton and performing horrific rituals under the cover of darkness?

Mrs Webber drew the heavy curtains and began extinguishing the lamps.

'Don't forget, we saw a woman driven to madness by it all. Once Satan got his claws in, even poor Mr Findlay couldn't save her. I don't know why I stay here, really I don't. This house and its secrets will be the death of me.'

It was time to turn in and Bran flew to Mrs Webber's shoulder, content to be carried up the stairs in this manner, as Luna got up on her crutches and made her way into the hall.

'Curse you,' Bran muttered as Mr Webber passed by them all on his way back to the kitchens.

'Pay the bird no heed, mistress. He's picked up such things from hearing them in the woods,' the housekeeper said.

Or perhaps he is simply an astute judge of character, thought Luna, but she kept this to herself.

As the older woman helped her to undress a little while later, she noticed a run of bluish-purple bruises along the housekeeper's forearms. They exchanged a look.

'It's only when he drinks,' she mumbled, and Luna reflected sadly that the man smelled of drink from dawn to dusk. 'Besides,' she said, as though she were merely talking about a grumpy child throwing a tantrum, 'a nice bit of pie always calms him down again.'

Bran flew up to the window ledge and began flapping his wings and squawking into the night. Mrs Webber, more mobile than Luna, walked over to see what the bird was making so much fuss about.

'Jed.' She shook her head and reached into her apron pocket, pulling out a rowan cross and holding it close to her chest. 'I can't protect him when he leaves the house. Always out in them woods, but foolish beyond measure to do so on May Eve. The boundary between this world and the next is at its thinnest and beings not of this realm will be walking about tonight.'

'Please close the window. Bran will have to stay inside until the morning,' Luna said, wondering why the manservant should be heading out in the forest after proclaiming there was so much evil about. Was he going to the well to witness the gathering of witches? Or maybe even join them? Were the sorcerers and malevolent spirits already creeping through the trees and heading to Ravenswood to cast spells and utter curses? And would a few branches and some wilting yellow woodland flowers really keep them out?

After the woman had left, Luna couldn't stop her imagination from running amok and Bran was as unsettled as her. The creaks and groans of the house seemed louder that night as she lay back in the oversized bed, thankful that the disturbing symbols and marks on the canopy had been removed.

There was a sudden drop in temperature as a cold chill circled the room, and she shuffled up the bed, clutching the counterpane to her chest. Glancing nervously about, she caught a pale shape in the window to her left. Bran began to flap his wings in an agitated manner from his perch on the back of the bedroom chair.

'Curse you! Curse you!' he screeched.

Her heart stopped.

A face.

She sat bolt upright but the image was no longer there. She recognised her own stupidity; it must have been the reflection of the candle in the glass. And yet she felt that Bran had seen it too...

'The magic is only real if you believe,' she repeated. Marcus would be disappointed that she was allowing her mind to play such laughable tricks. If only Mrs Webber hadn't put such silly notions in her head.

She climbed back under the covers, only to become aware of the bitter smell of smoke. How strange. The housekeeper would not be cooking at this hour. Bran started to flap madly about the room.

'Hello there! Hello there!' he squawked, homing in on something at the foot of her bed.

Luna manoeuvred herself upright again, only to see a wisp of pale grey floating up from the floor and realise her counterpane was on fire. She hobbled over to the pitcher on the washstand and quickly extinguished the flame. How had that happened? She'd not taken the candle to that part of the room. Her eyes scanned the shadows again but saw nothing.

Her protector flew to the bed, settling by her feet.

'All's well,' Bran squawked, over and over, and she wondered if these were the words Marcus had repeated to his distressed wife in his attempts to soothe her, but she felt far from soothed – someone or something had tried to set her bed on fire, and the words of the prophecy returned to her: *she must die*.

She finally fell asleep dreaming of a coven of witches dancing through the woods, with Luna at the head, as they slit the throats of innocent children and posted their lifeless bodies down the abandoned well.

* * *

As the calendar flipped over to May, Beltane heralded the arrival of summer, and the yellow, blue and purple palette of early spring blooms bled into the softer pinks and bright reds of the coming season. A cherry tree growing to one side of the house was a veritable cascade of vibrant watermelon and rose quartz; this display inspired Luna to ask Mr Webber to dig some flower beds in preparation for the seedlings he was growing for Marcus's return. The man grumbled at being given more to do, but did as he was bid. If only she could be of more practical help. Her ankle was healing at an astonishing rate, thanks to Mr Findlay, but she was still limited as to the activities she could undertake.

The first week of the month was exceptionally warm and she was once again able to spend time outside. This also suited Bran, who was gliding and somersaulting above her head, the black fingers of his wingtips clearly visible, and the only soaring silhouette in an otherwise strangely birdless sky.

It was glorious to inhale air that was so fresh and clean because, despite everyone's best efforts, the house still had a lingering smell of damp and the bitter tang of smoke from the open fires. She spotted the rose bush that Marcus had planted by the gate and made slow but steady progress down the meadow path to check that it was being cared for, knowing he would be upset to find it neglected in his absence. As she approached, she saw it was dotted with small green rosebuds, slits of creamy white showing where the petals were waiting to burst through.

She looked across to the bank where she'd collided with him back in April. Given everything that she'd been through recently, it was nothing short of miraculous that she was living this life: mistress of a household, fed, watered and sleeping in a comfortable bed. And all because they'd both been so preoccupied in that one moment that they hadn't seen the other.

As she looked over to the river, the banks a lush green and the shimmering water reflecting the clear blue sky, she heard gruff voices floating down the track. Encumbered by her walking aids, she could not move out of view fast enough, and a small group of men approached, clearly on their way to the ferry. She remembered Mrs Webber talking about the hiring fair in Manbury and guessed that they were from the village, heading to the town in search of employment.

The loud chatter died down when they spotted her by the gate, and she caught snippets of what they were saying as they advanced.

'...That's her. Don't let her catch your eye.'

'You sure?' a questioning voice asked.

'Yeah, Ned saw her prancing about naked in them woods that run up the hill, didn't ya?'

'Wasn't looking at her face, if I'm honest.' A ripple of laughter broke out.

'Who else would it be, y'fool? Besides, Jedidiah's been saying she's out in daylight now and calmed down a bit.'

'Blimey, don't think I've seen her in years – not close up, at any rate.'

As they drew level to the gate, she decided to brazen it out.

'Hello, gentlemen,' she said. 'Lovely morning.'

'Dirty witch,' an older man said, avoiding her eye, and then spat on the ground.

One or two of them doffed their caps, perhaps out of embarrassment, but she kept her head high as they passed by, fighting back her tears at being treated so.

The contented feeling of only moments before was lost and she suddenly felt desperately alone. Even Bran was nowhere to be seen, doubtless bothering Mrs Webber for scraps. She'd thought being someone else for a while might solve her problems, but what she hadn't counted on was being someone hardly anybody liked.

She remembered Mr Findlay's invitation to call on him at any time. Other than Mrs Webber, he was the only kindly soul nearby, and she could do with a hearty dose of kindly right now. It was taking all her strength not to cry at the way the men had spoken to her, so she waited until she saw the ferry take them over to Manbury before wrestling with the gate and heading down the winding track to Honeysuckle Cottage. Her housekeeper had told her his property was hidden by the curve of the river and barely a quarter of a mile from them.

The path was uneven and had a loose gravelly surface, which increased the possibility of her slipping. Another broken bone would be catastrophic and further delay her leaving, so she made certain to rest at regular intervals. Soon, however, she spied a charming whitewashed thatched cottage in the distance, nestled in a cluster of trees.

As she approached, she could see that the small but fragrant garden was well-tended and positively overflowing with plants of all descriptions. Many were unfamiliar to her but she felt certain most were planted for their healing properties. The sweet trill of turtle doves drifted down from the purple splendour of the copper beech, as she entered through a gate in the glorious hawthorn hedging, white with May blossom.

She quickly spotted Mr Findlay in his garden, kneeling on a cushion and tending to a herb border. Hints of mint and rosemary were carried from the breeze that danced over the river and up the banks to the house. Even the water had lost the unpleasant stench of effluent and death that swirled up from its muddy depths in the city.

'Mrs Greybourne,' he exclaimed, when he heard the squeak of the wooden gate. 'What an absolute delight. The ankle must be much improved for you to undertake such a walk. How marvellous.'

On this occasion he was wearing a battered maroon bowler hat – perhaps to shield his head from the sun – with a black-and-brown striped pheasant feather poking out from the band. He came to her side and slipped his hand under her elbow to take her weight. She was grateful as the crutches were digging into her armpits and causing her increasing discomfort.

'Come inside and rest awhile. I might be able to rustle up a herbal tea that will aid your recovery even further... if you are prepared to risk the wrath of your husband, that is.'

He helped her step over a high stone threshold and into the cottage, the interior of which was gloomy due to the poor light. The space was undivided, an open fire on one side with a high-backed bench and fireside rocking chair in front. Low, wide beams were hung with bunches of drying herbs, and slender shelves lined the walls, full of stone jars and glass bottles, with labels proclaiming lavender oil, dried eyebright and ground horsetail.

A huge refectory table stood in the centre of the room, covered in further glass vessels, small brass weighing scales, and a round-bottomed flask standing on a metal tripod over a small paraffin burner. *Culpeper's Complete Herbal* sat on the corner of the table closest to her. There was a strong aroma of exotic spices and woodsmoke, and it was clear that Mr Findlay's life was devoted to the preparation and packaging of his cures and charms.

He saw her eyes alight on a sturdy locked trunk next to a small bookcase.

'Ah, those powders and potions that are dangerous in the wrong hands,' he explained. 'Poisonous berries, rare spices and delicate scientific instruments that cost me dearly. They are locked up as I have been the target of thieves and accused of all sorts by non-believers. So frustrating that I am revered when ailments are cured and misfortunes are reversed, and vilified when they are not – but many things are beyond my control, such as the failure of a harvest. Occasionally, I too have been labelled a witch.' He shrugged.

She knew from her own experience that people were quick to judge, and it appeared he'd been bundled up in the dark accusations levelled against Luna, when all he'd done was try to help.

'Despite Mr Greybourne's insistence that I stayed away from his wife on pain of death, she would seek me out, and I was attempting to alleviate some of her mental suffering. She felt uncomfortable that Marcus could issue such violent threats, but his belief that magic is nonsense was as strong as Luna's conviction that it was not.' His visitor did not bother to repeat the false assertion that she was Luna. 'Unfortunately, the woman was... unpredictable and did not always follow my instructions, but I helped where I could, as I am helping you now.'

'I suffered similar judgements this very morning from passing villagers,' she said, as he helped her to the fireside bench, humming to himself, and slid a small three-legged stool out for her foot.

A cast-iron kettle was already hanging above the flames, and he unhooked two pottery mugs from the mantel, setting them on the hearth stones, before embarking on the preparation of the promised tea.

'Pay them no heed. They simply don't understand the difference between confused and delusional individuals, and the very real threats from realms outside our own.'

'Then you do believe that evil forces exist? You believe in magic?'

'Do *you* believe in God, Mrs Greybourne? In the miracles talked of in the Bible? That Jesus rose from the dead?'

'Of course.'

'Then you already believe in magic, and there must be darkness to counteract the light. One cannot exist without the other. We pray to summon the help of the Lord in times of crisis. Do you not think there are those praying to His nemesis? However much we might wish this were not the case.'

There was a pause as she contemplated his words. He poured the infusion through a strainer and stirred in some honey, before changing the subject.

'Hibiscus, chamomile and the red clover flowers – all will help with the further healing of your bones. I had quite the reputation in my beloved Amesbury for healing, and I drew on the strength of the nearby Stonehenge megaliths. I was sad to leave such a sacred place, but my cards told me that there was a time coming when my gifts would be needed here. And it is not so very far away, only thirty miles or so, should I wish to visit old friends.'

He handed her a small mug half-full of a floral-smelling tea. She put it to her lips and took a sip as he studied her face.

'Who are you?' he asked. 'I mean, who are you *really*, my dear?'

The drink wasn't unpleasant, helped by the sweetness of the honey, so she took another mouthful.

'Luna Greybourne,' she said with conviction.

Mr Findlay nodded, perhaps with a grudging respect that she still could not be persuaded to stray from her story. He took a seat in the rocking chair opposite, and they talked for a while of gardens and the delights of countryside living. It felt good to be in the company of someone other than a grunting man, an anxious woman or a temperamental bird.

Eventually, she moved to take her leave.

'I've prepared some comfrey and arnica poultices for you. Mrs Webber knows how to apply them.'

'What do I owe you? She can drop off your fee.'

'Nothing. Your company has been payment enough. I should very much like us to be friends and want you to know that you can call on me should you ever be in need. I am not welcome at Ravenswood, but you are always welcome here, any time of the day or night. Whenever you feel in danger.'

'Why would I be in danger?' she asked, wondering if he might suggest the floating spirits and roaming witches Mrs Webber seemed so keen to protect herself from, but he had something altogether more tangible in mind.

'Oh, my dear child,' he said, leaning closer, his face etched with concern. 'Because the woman you claim to be, for reasons that are not mine to question, has simply disappeared from the face of the earth. I have consulted the cards and spoken with the departed, and am utterly convinced that she has been murdered, even if I do not know for certain by whom.'

13

Despite Mr Findlay's shocking assertion that Marcus's wife had been killed, Luna began to embrace her role as mistress of Ravenswood. Previously, she had merely observed the running of Church View, aware that she would only be in charge of a household should she marry. Was it really just one month ago that she'd left that life behind?

Marcus wrote to her again and reported that his investments were proving more fruitful than he'd anticipated. He included further instructions for the Webbers and requested that she undertook the less physical tasks, such as choosing which rooms to place the salvageable furniture in, and ordering essential missing crockery and glassware through the enclosed catalogues. She was only too happy to oblige, recognising that it would be nice for him to return and find the place more homely, even if she had gone by that point. Luna still felt uneasy at the house, and often sensed she was being watched, even though all traces of the evil eyes had been removed. Could there possibly be someone else at Ravenswood? The noises in the attic had never been satisfactorily resolved, and the smoking bedspread incident preyed on her mind. A fire did not start by itself.

Her suspicions were further aroused when Mrs Webber asked for the grocery allowance to be raised. Luna had questioned this, as she doubted that she ate as much as Marcus, so couldn't understand why they were getting through more food. But the housekeeper claimed that it was Bran – a creature with a veritable bottomless pit for a stomach – who was to blame. Knowing that he often stole from her own plate, she acknowledged that he did always seem to be eating and paid the grocer's increased bill.

One night, she had quite the fright when she was woken by a clear voice proclaiming, 'Go away.' Scrabbling for a weapon to defend herself with, and panicking that someone had entered her bedroom, she was relieved to see Bran perched on the open window ledge. Realising this sound had got her attention, he woke her up with the same cry three nights running, but by the third, she just rolled over and muttered, 'No, *you* go away,' back to him, as she stuffed her head deep into her feather pillows.

Further to Marcus's written request, and with the grunting help of Mr Webber, who'd made enquiries in the village, a Mr Kelling and his son were employed to rehang wallpapers in the entrance hall and up the stairs. It required particularly long ladders and two persons, whereas the other rooms, Marcus felt he might tackle himself upon his return.

The Kellings duly arrived early one morning, a large number of pale blue floral William Morris rolls that Luna had selected having been delivered directly. Mr Webber had spent a day preparing the walls to a height he could manage, so the Kellings' first task was to strip the remaining papers from the ceilings down, before they could begin to hang the new. They shuffled in with buckets, brushes and scrapers, but the way the adolescent lad behaved when Luna was in their vicinity was disconcerting: his eyes fixed on her face, and his body facing her at all times, as though he expected her to cast an evil spell or summon the Devil at any moment.

'You *are* going to pay me proper at the end of this, right?' Mr Kelling asked, as a brush clunked into the tin bucket at his feet. Bran had swooped in from the drawing room and landed on the newel post at the bottom of the stairs, ever curious as to what was going on.

'Of course.'

'Coz I need the money.'

'Rest assured, my husband has sent me the agreed sum.'

The man shuffled from foot to foot, building up to something.

'And get rid of the bird. I don't like it. Its beady little eyes are following me, like it knows stuff I don't want it knowing.'

Truth be told, she often felt the same. Bran's eyes would look deep into her own, his head tipped to one side as if to indicate he was waiting for further elucidation, and she wondered if he knew what she had done in her most desperate moments. If so, did he judge her actions?

'It should be in the woods,' the older man mumbled. 'Ain't right, flapping about the house, trailing around after you like a dog.'

'We have tried.' Luna was indignant. 'He's free to come and go.'

'Well, maybe if you didn't spoil him with treats an' such he wouldn't be so inclined to linger.'

It was true that she now kept a small pot of dried fruit near her chair for her feathered friend, but it was not the hope of a sugary morsel that bound Bran to her. It was something deeper. Besides, Mr Webber had told her that the ravens had never strayed from the grounds in all his fifty-two years of living in Little Doubton. They were on the Greybourne coat of arms, he pointed out, and showed Luna a small yellow shield with three black ravens and a circle of oak leaves above the doorway in the entrance hall. These magnificent corvids were a fundamental part of the Ravenswood estate, and not just because they were part of the name.

She left Mr Kelling to his work and asked her housekeeper to keep the men supplied with mugs of tea. To give them their due, the pair worked quickly and efficiently, but she suspected this was because the faster they worked, the sooner they could leave the unsettling house, and by nightfall of the third day they were finished. The hall looked so much brighter and more welcoming, and she was pleased that her choice of colour had lifted the gloomy space.

She handed over payment, which was almost snatched from her hand to be counted.

'You're not like I thought you'd be.' He looked up from the handful of coins.

'What do you mean?'

''Spected you to be more wild and crazy. No offence, Mrs Greybourne, but there's a reason you don't get many visitors and the villagers steer clear.'

She rolled out the story that Marcus had fed the young clerk. 'I've been unwell. A malady of the mind. But I can assure you I am much improved.'

The young lad skipped down the staircase with the last of their tools. From nowhere, Bran appeared and began to flap around him, squawking, and trying to peck at his top pocket.

'Get 'im off me,' he cried, waving his arms about and trying to swipe the enormous raven away, but both bird and boy were becoming increasingly agitated.

'Don't hurt him.' Luna was quick to put herself between Mr Kelling's son and her beloved raven, fearing Bran might be injured by the bucket Kelling junior was now brandishing.

'Curse you! Curse you!' Bran screeched and started pecking violently at his clothing.

The boy immediately fell to his knees, arms raised to shield his face, and head turned away.

'Here, have it back. It's just a stupid spoon. You've got loads.' He pulled a silver spoon from his jacket and threw it across the floor. 'Undo the raven's curse, you evil witch. Undo it. You don't want two deaths on your hands. Was Mother Selwood not enough for you?'

'What have you done, son?' his father asked, shock across his face, as the offending item clattered into the skirting board.

'I'm not a witch,' Luna tried to explain. 'I do not cast ill-wishes.'

But, having clambered to his feet, the boy was gone from the house faster than a rabbit bolting for its burrow. Mr Kelling gathered up the last of his brushes and left almost as promptly.

'Witch,' he mumbled under his breath as he threw his tools on the back of his cart. 'You and your familiar need locking up.'

14

ELOISE

It is an acknowledged truth that when you are denied a thing, it becomes all the more imperative to have it. Cook batting your hand away as you reach for a freshly baked biscuit because their vanilla butteriness makes you salivate. Your mother refusing to allow you a dog because it will inevitably leave hair and muddy paw prints on the expensive, upholstered furniture. Or your father insisting that the handsome and outspoken man that you have developed strong feelings for is not a suitable match.

Eloise wanted Daniel Thornbury because his obvious intelligence and strong desire to self-educate intrigued her. She was also attracted to his handsome features and the broad, muscular torso that resulted from the physical work he undertook. But she wanted him most of all because he appeared completely indifferent to her.

He may have been a lowly factory worker but there was something about the way that he said what he thought, particularly to people whose station in life might be considered above his, that made him appear powerful. Mrs Banbury said the father was not much better and had argued publicly with the vicar, which was not a wise move, regardless of your stance on the existence of God. The vicar had the ear of the Fletchers, and the Fletchers employed him. Eloise sympathised with the Thornburys, however, as someone who had increasingly strong opinions on various subjects herself. The difference was, she knew when to bite her tongue. She also knew, if she wanted to attract the attentions of young Daniel, that it would take time and she would have to be patient.

One glorious summer evening, she spotted him walking across the green with something rolled up under his right arm. Thrilled at this serendipitous encounter, she called a cheery hello and waved, expecting him to respond. But he didn't walk across the grass to talk to her, or even wave back. She felt slighted. Manners dictated that he should at least reply. There was merely a dip of the head in acknowledgement and then he went on his way.

It was three weeks before she encountered him again. That was the problem with people who worked for a living; they were always, well, working. But one sticky August Sunday, she left church early, feigning a headache because she was bored by the hypocrisy of the vicar's preaching. As she slipped through the gothic oak door, she saw Daniel walking towards Cotton Lane – a small road that led out of the village. She followed, curious as to where he was heading, and even more so when he entered the grove of decades-old sweet chestnuts that bordered the Bran. The grove led nowhere, as the only way to cross the river was the low Norman stone bridge that had given the village its name, half a mile eastwards.

Her steps were tentative as she picked her way through the knee-high bracken and leafy branch-strewn mulch of the woodland floor. The tree canopies were dense with leaves and covered in clusters of the bright-green prickly fruits, but Daniel was nowhere to be seen. Had he veered off on some path she'd overlooked? Or had his long strides simply outpaced her?

'What *do* you think you're doing?'

The voice, loud and clear, came from the heavens, and she briefly wondered if God Himself was speaking to her. Her own thoughts had been along similar lines. What was she doing? Tracking him like a hound after the fox, when surely it should be the young man pursuing her.

'...Because, if I was to hazard a guess, I'd say you were spying on me.'

She looked up and was startled to see a pair of worn leather boots and two long legs swinging ten feet above her head. He was a grown man of perhaps twenty-five and yet was sitting on a wide bough of the sweet chestnut like a boy. It was a further example of him doing exactly what pleased him, without worrying about convention or the opinions of others, and this thrilled her.

'Not at all.' Her face flushed hot and she tried to regain some composure. 'I'm taking a stroll through the grove, hoping the fresh air will relieve the headache brought on by this morning's ponderous sermon. But I should like to know what *you* think you're doing?' She flung his initial question to her back at him.

'Climbing a tree because it offers me a splendid view of the surrounding landscape. I feel like a king, sitting up here and surveying the land. It also reminds me that man did not create the world and nor does he own it. Such a view is humbling and empowering. Not that you would understand.'

'Why? Because you think I wouldn't join you, or that I lack the imagination to contemplate anything beyond my own existence?'

'Have you *ever* climbed a tree?' He looked faintly amused and this both excited and annoyed her. She hadn't, but would not admit as much to him.

'I hope the bough has room for two.' She hitched up the front of her skirts, tucking the hem into her waistband and scandalously exposing her white woollen stockings. She placed her right foot on the lowest limb and heaved herself up. This particular tree had two low, wide branches fanning out from either side of the trunk, and then further boughs at convenient intervals, each one as thick as a man's leg, making it a perfect choice for climbing. But it was useless. She was not, and had never been, a tomboy. She stepped back onto the ground and accepted defeat.

'You're an interesting girl, Eloise. You have spirit, and I admire that, but suspect you're one of those girls who likes the idea of not conforming until it comes to taking action. You wanted to stay and talk to me at the cricket match back in May but couldn't be seen to slight Lady Fletcher. Tell me, was her conversation so much more engaging than mine?'

He was quite correct; she had done as Lady Fletcher insisted because everyone had been watching, and her mother would never have forgiven her had she not. But she didn't want to discuss her failings; she wanted to climb the tree and show him that she was indeed spirited.

'It would be manageable if I didn't have these stupid skirts and petticoats. I'm of a mind to remove the lot just to prove that I can climb this ridiculous tree.' She moved to unbutton the back of the skirt.

Daniel's face became more serious.

'Oh no you don't, missy.' He slid both feet onto a lower branch, twisted his body around to hug the massive trunk, and dropped to the ground beside her, scooping up what she could now see was a rolled-up linen towel. 'It's all right for you, but if anyone happens upon us and you're in a state of undress, it will be me who gets blamed and shamed. Girls like yourself don't think through the consequences of your rash actions.'

'Someone wears a chip on his shoulder,' she muttered. He definitely displayed an antagonistic attitude towards anyone who had more in life than him.

'And I suppose you'll be the one to knock it off?' he challenged. 'You strike me as spoiling to do battle.'

His face was inches from hers and the blood racing through her veins was making her feel giddy. What was it about this young man that had her all of a tither? Had a lifetime of unconditional adoration from her father given her a desire to seek out love that was more of a challenge? The tobacco smell, combined with his considerable height advantage, sent an unexpected flush of heat through her body.

Overcome with recklessness, she leaned forward and clasped her arms about his neck, jerking him towards her and tilting her lips up to brush her mouth briefly against his. She felt him tense immediately and he raced for her wrists, snatching them apart and holding her hands firmly away from his face. His expression was dark and his tone severe – which only served to arouse her further.

'I'm not interested in your games, Eloise. Don't you know that it is the gentleman who courts the lady. Not that your behaviour today is that of a lady. Go back home to your parents. You don't need to climb trees to feel like royalty, because they already treat you as such.'

He shook his head as he dropped her hands, turned from her and walked away.

But she'd read enough romance novels to know that there was always a clash between hero and heroine: a locking of horns before their true feelings were acknowledged. He liked her; she was certain of it. He admired her spirit; she was surely like no other girl he had encountered. All in all, she was an attractive proposition. It only remained for her to get him to admit it.

* * *

'Eloise, we need to have words.'

She stepped into the dining room and her father's face wrinkled into a frown. He placed his newspaper on the breakfast table, and she was alarmed by the tone of his voice. He rarely got cross with her and she couldn't think what she'd done to rattle him so, until she saw her mother's flared nostrils and red cheeks. Something had upset her mother and her father had been ordered to deal with it.

'You were seen with the Thornbury son in the sweet chestnut grove after you left church yesterday.'

She slid into the chair opposite his and reached for a slice of freshly toasted bread.

'I don't know what you mean. I came straight back after the service.'

'You were seen,' he reiterated. 'And I distinctly remember you returning with dirt on the hem of your skirts.'

'Eloise!' her mother reprimanded.

'We barely exchanged three words—'

'He was holding your hands,' her mother interrupted. 'Do not insult us by pretending the two of you were discussing the weather. This obsession with the young Mr Thornbury has to stop. The man is a progressive, when he is hardly in a position to voice his extreme views. I will not have your head filled with silly notions about the equality of all when we are in the process of elevating ourselves above such people.'

Eloise had never been one for book learning until she'd met Daniel but now that she had begun to study the subject, she understood the hypocrisy of her parents' views. They had moaned when they had been the ones affected, but their good fortune had apparently rendered their previous beliefs redundant.

'You are not to encourage him, do you hear? I don't want you mixing with his sort, and if I find out you've disobeyed me, I shall make it known that he has been forcing his inappropriate attentions upon my daughter.'

Eloise scraped a curl of butter across her toast and bit at her lip.

She felt bad for her actions in the grove. Her behaviour had been unacceptable and she had acted impetuously. Daniel had been right – he had been blamed when she knew that the attentions had come entirely from her.

15

After the hasty departure of the Kellings, Luna asked her housekeeper what she knew about the death of Mother Selwood. The protracted demise of this unfortunate woman had now been mentioned to her several times.

'From what my husband says, Mrs Greybourne cursed her by the well one night, although he's always been a bit cagey about what *he* was doing out there at such an hour.' She rolled her eyes. 'Apparently, the old woman fell to the ground, muttering gibberish and clutching at her head. He scooped her up and brought her to the house but there was little I could do, and she became sicker and sicker, until she died three weeks later.'

No wonder Mr Kelling's poor son had been so wary of Luna. The Ravenswood Witch had a fearsome reputation.

'This was years ago, mind, just after we started working here. My Jed'd had a bit of trouble with the law. I know he ain't always been a good man but he had no reason to lie about this. I even consulted Mr Findlay, but the Selwood woman was beyond help.' The housekeeper adjusted her bosom and sighed. 'I was always a lot more wary of my mistress after that and was all for handing my notice in, but I was *persuaded* by my husband into staying.'

Luna didn't want to contemplate what the persuasion might have involved.

'What did this woman do to justify being cursed?'

Mrs Webber shrugged. 'Apparently, she looked at Mrs Greybourne wrong. It didn't take much to set the mistress off.'

Bran flew from his new favourite perch – an empty ceramic jardinière stand – and landed on the back of her chair, dipping his head. She rubbed her forehead against his. It was an intimate gesture they had developed and which she thought of as their kiss. She had been without physical contact for too long, and it was one of the reasons she was so conflicted about her current situation; the house unnerved her and she was desperate to escape, but at the same time, she was being looked after and experiencing genuine care from Mrs Webber, Mr Findlay and even Bran. She wanted to leave and to stay all at once.

This inner turmoil was brought home to her by a seemingly minor incident later that day. She was alone in the drawing room, still an oppressive space, with its heavy velvet curtains and proliferation of possessions that held no memories or special meaning for her, but which shouted that she did not belong. Alone with her thoughts, she heard a delicate, almost indiscernible flapping in the room, and knew this was no stroppy raven wanting her attention. Her eye was drawn to the windows where something considerably smaller than Bran was repeatedly beating its beautiful but fragile wings against the windowpane.

She pulled herself up onto one of the crutches and made her way over to investigate. It was a butterfly trapped on her side of the glass – a large white. The stark chalky purity of it contrasted with the inky smudges and matching black dots on its wingtips, reminding her that dark and light were so often found together. It struck her then that, however much she would like to believe herself a good person, she too had inky smudges that she would carry with her always. She felt sympathy for the creature, knowing it did not belong at the house any more than she did. If she stood by and did nothing, it would damage itself in its desperate desire to be outside. Lifting up the lower sash, she allowed the insect its freedom, watching it zig-zag into the sunshine, navigating an uncertain path towards the enticing aromas and hypnotic colours of the meadow ahead.

Satisfied, she returned to her chair, only for Bran to swoop into the room not long after she settled. As he landed on the floor at her feet, she saw the broken, milky wings crushed in that lethal beak of his. He dropped his prize to the floor and toyed with it, shunting it backwards and forwards, before scooping it up again, throwing back his head and swallowing it whole.

Stunned, Luna sat open-mouthed. The butterfly had not stood a chance from the moment it had strayed into the house. It would have undoubtedly suffered a drawn-out death away from its natural environment, yet it had escaped and still met a brutal end.

And as the sun went down on another bewildering day, she wondered if her options were similarly ill-fated.

* * *

Luna hadn't mentioned Bran to Marcus in the month since he'd been gone, having responded on a couple of occasions to his correspondence by taking the addresses from the top of his letters. Instead, she kept strictly to matters relating to the running of the household, feeling she didn't know him well enough to witter on about more frivolous matters, such as nursing a wild bird back to health. And, of course, knowing that relations between the two men were strained, she made absolutely no mention of Mr Findlay, even though his ministrations had undoubtedly accelerated the healing of her ankle.

Worried that the locals might seek revenge for the assumed cursing of the Kelling boy, she was keen to seek further advice, so decided to visit the cunning man again the following day, taking a small cake she had baked herself as a thank you for all his help. There were a dozen questions rattling around her confused head, and she hoped he might help her to understand more of the mysteries surrounding Ravenswood before Marcus returned and their contact was curtailed.

She waited until Bran was absent from the house, knowing he often became agitated when she approached the boundary of the Greybourne lands. It was almost as if he knew that she'd be ill-treated by outsiders and wanted to spare her that. Mr Findlay was delighted that she'd returned and pleased to see she was no longer reliant on the crutches. He prepared her another healing tea and she noted how much more relaxed she felt at Honeysuckle Cottage with this kindly gentleman. There were no strange whispers in the air or disturbing shadows in the corners. Luna's presence was woven through every part of Ravenswood, but here she felt she'd escaped the woman. Here, she felt safe.

And yet, she was presenting herself as the very person she was trying to be free from.

'Mrs Greybourne, my dear, you look troubled.' He happily accepted her ongoing charade as he cut the cake.

'I have memory issues and there are parts of my life that I am struggling to recall,' she explained, as she took a small slice.

'Would these be the parts before you broke your ankle?' He chuckled to himself as he settled into the chair opposite her.

'Mrs Webber said you have long since tended to me, even though my husband is unaware of your care, and I wonder if I had confided in you at all?'

'You were quite deluded back then,' he said, deciding to play along on this occasion, 'and thought you could summon Satan himself. Although quite what you intended to do with him should your nonsense have worked, I'm not sure. Perhaps that is all behind you now.'

'I am certain it is, but I would like to understand why I was so drawn to the woods. Mrs Webber mentioned a well,' she said.

'Indeed. It stands in a clearing, and is fed from a spring somewhere deep underground, but it dried up decades ago and no one knows why. Legend says, "when new life is created at the well, so shall the well come back to life", but I'm not sure anyone really knows what that means. You were very much consumed by the legends and folklore of the Greybourne lands, and were keen for the waters to flow again.'

'Were they really curative, as the legends claim?'

He shrugged. 'They were undoubtedly pure, and as such could be used to heal any flux of the body. Pilgrims walked for hundreds of miles to buy small lead ampullae filled with the holy waters. Over time, however, the site attracted those who practised dark magic. People would utter imprecations at the cursing well, or stick pins into clay poppets to direct evil forces to those they wished harm, leaving the tiny figures at the site. But, should it ever flow again, I would certainly be interested to test its healing capabilities.'

'Is it still visited by those who want to access it for these darker purposes? Witches and the like?' she questioned. 'Because my husband doesn't believe witches are real.' She tried to sound confident with her assertion but failed. 'Are they?'

'If you're asking me whether you are a witch, then the answer is no, but I do believe the well is a magical place and such people exist. When the farmer's wife asks me for a charm to protect against the neighbour who's blighted their crops, even if I am inclined to think the weather is responsible, I will supply the required item – for their peace of mind, if nothing else. But when I look into the eyes of the monster who has ill-used little children, then I know that evil exists, and it frightens me. Have you not felt the overpowering aura in the clearing?'

'I haven't been into the woods,' she admitted. 'I can't bring myself to step foot in them. All that talk of the Devil being summoned makes me quite anxious.'

'Not all magic is bad.' He leaned forward to pat her knee. 'And not every danger we face is other-worldly. Sometimes our greatest threats are more tangible. Mrs Webber has told me that on at least one occasion, Mr Greybourne... your husband... has gone for you, hands around your throat, until she intervened. He has a temper. A calm and measured man, until he is pushed too far, and then he snaps as easily as a dried twig on the forest floor.'

She'd seen herself how quickly his mood could change when the policemen had doubted his word, and knew that he had gone on the rampage the night his wife had destroyed his beloved library.

'Wicked acts aren't always planned,' Findlay continued. 'Mr Webber accidentally killed a man in a bar brawl.'

The surprise on Luna's face led him to explain.

'It happened before I moved here but I understand he spent some time in gaol, and it was widely reported in the papers. He was full of drink and will undoubtedly regret his actions for the remainder of his life. Do you not think your husband might be capable of snapping, too?'

She knew Marcus to be kind, thinking about how he'd taken her in. But was it possible that he'd been pushed to breaking point by a woman he'd given ten years of his life to, only to be met with abuse and disdain?

She shook her head.

'However much damage was done to his beloved Ravenswood, and even after the cruelty he suffered, I can't honestly believe he would be driven to such a violent act.'

'Maybe not, but I am the keeper of many confidences and even the most forgiving of men would struggle to forgive the infidelity of his wife.' The older man raised his eyebrows. 'I think that might drive even a good man to violence...'

16

The news that Mrs Greybourne had been unfaithful was disturbing, upsetting Luna more than it should have done. Poor Marcus. She knew she was getting sucked deeper into the lives of those at Ravenswood, despite her intention to leave as soon as her fake husband returned.

As if summoned by her thoughts, she came across the man himself, striding up the path where they had first met, as she walked back from Mr Findlay's delightful little cottage. It took her by surprise as they had known he was due to return mid-May, but had not had word of a date. This time, however, their encounter was infinitely less fraught. Despite Mr Findlay's warnings, she was pleased to see him and no longer thought of him as a stranger. He looked smart in a new knee-length frock coat, with neatly clipped hair and more colour in his previously pale cheeks. His head jolted backwards as he spotted her approach and he dropped the carpet bag that he was carrying. It took him a moment to recover from his shock.

'The dress,' he said. 'I thought you were... I thought, oh, it doesn't matter what I thought.'

'I altered some garments that Mrs Webber found in the attics,' she hastily explained, belatedly realising that she was wearing one of the few salvageable items of Luna's. With her fair hair, she was similar enough in appearance to the woman she'd replaced for the sight of her to be uncomfortable for him.

She wondered if he was cross with her. Was it time to end their charade? Would he expect her to pack her bag and be gone by nightfall? She should have left before his return, as going would be more awkward now. But then again, *he* had announced to the constable that she was his wife, *he* had corresponded with her as though they were a married couple, and so she would continue in this role until *he* requested otherwise.

'You must have new clothes,' Marcus said, rather sharply. 'I will pay for an entirely fresh wardrobe, especially now the warmer weather is upon us.' He bent down to retrieve the bag. 'You caught me off guard. I wasn't expecting to see you looking so well... or, indeed, out and about. Surely that ankle can't have mended already?'

Not wanting to reveal she was returning from Mr Findlay's, or that the cunning man was the reason for her injury healing so rapidly, she was careful with the truth. 'Mrs Webber has worked wonders,' she said.

'As has her somewhat dubious cooking, by the looks of you.' He took the time to study her properly and she felt unduly scrutinised. 'There is such a healthy glow about your cheeks. You look content, relaxed and...' he paused, '...really quite beautiful.'

Any colour she might have already had deepened further as he paid her this unexpected compliment.

Finally, their eyes locked.

'You stayed.' It wasn't a question.

She smiled. 'And you have returned. We've missed you.' She tried to behave as any good wife might when greeting her husband after a lengthy spell away but, as she said the words, she realised she meant them. He was back now and, although she had done her best in his absence, every troubled ship needed a captain to steer it true.

'There is so much to show you,' she continued, as he swept up his luggage and she looped her arm through his.

They walked up the path together and he continued to glance in her direction, saying nothing as she wittered on about the new wallpapers in the hall, that the garden was coming along nicely, and how most of the furniture had been returned to its appropriate rooms. A tentative smile danced across his lips. She looked up at him to reassure herself that she was absolutely not gazing into the eyes of a killer.

'We have replaced some of the broken crockery and glassware, but please don't think I have been a spendthrift with the money you sent. There is still plenty left, and you might like to use it for new furniture...'

The slowly sinking sun cast a shadow, low and long, before them on the ground. They were as one, she reflected, looking at the shape that started at their feet and stretched up the path ahead. There was not a single patch of sunlight between them. A white butterfly fluttered past their faces, and they watched it settle on the fragrant flowers of the honeysuckle which had woven its creeping stems along the hedgerow. He turned his head to hers, with the same look of wonderment across his face as when he'd regarded her properly only moments before.

'I have missed my beloved house, and the peace and quiet of my woods. It would seem I was right to trust you with their care in my absence. Honestly,' he said, sliding his arm about her waist, and leading her up to the wooden gate, 'this is the first time in years where I can say that I am genuinely pleased to be home.'

17

'I've been catching up with Mrs Webber, and she says only good things.'

Marcus sat back in an upholstered chair and casually threw one wide leg across the other. He looked so content, younger even, in contrast to the troubled man who had left her only a few weeks ago. The housekeeper's cooking had been passable that evening, and the glassless clock struck nine.

'And I can see for myself the improvements you have made to the house,' he continued. 'This room is infinitely more pleasant, without the clutter of so much furniture.'

There was a cooling breeze circling the room, offering some respite from the heat of earlier in the day. The sun was barely visible, just a fiery strip of orange across the hilltops to their right, and the distant chatter of working men returning on the last ferry drifted in from the open window.

'I think Mr Webber is heartily sick of me issuing instructions to him,' Luna said. 'I'm sure he had hoped that in your absence he would not be worked so hard, and I'm afraid I have given him the work of ten men.'

Marcus's delight at the small improvements she'd organised lifted her own spirits. It was a further thank-you gift to him. Her way of giving something back for letting her stay. And with her ankle now nearly back to normal, perhaps her parting gift also.

'Mr Webber, I think you'll find, is grateful to have a job at all, seeing as no one else hereabouts would employ him, and I needed staff. The arrangement suited us both.' Suddenly Marcus's open face became shuttered. A flicker of irritation darted across his brow, and she detected the temper that Mr Findlay had talked of.

She looked across at him and frowned, but he did not elaborate. It was only because of Mr Findlay that she knew of the manservant's criminal past.

'I appreciate that you have had issues finding servants willing to work here with all the accusations of witchcraft.' It was obvious that the dwindling staff over recent years had been because of his wife's behaviour.

'Indeed.' His eyes met hers. 'I know you understand how difficult it has been.'

'And your trip was successful?' she asked, changing the subject.

'Relatively so.' The furrows that had formed momentarily across his brow smoothed out. 'I had hoped to call in on my Great-Aunt Elspeth whilst I was in London, but she was away.'

'I didn't know you had any family remaining.'

'Very little, and that is why she's so precious. She was my grandfather's sister. An opinionated woman who never married. My father said it was because there was not a man brave enough in the whole of England prepared to take her on, but she's long had a soft spot for me and we were quite close when I was a boy. We share a love of the outdoors, and it is she who gave me an appreciation for flowers.'

Luna turned her head towards him, trying not to smile. So, this was where his passion for the garden had come from.

'I was, however, able to invest some of the money that was released and reconnect with fellows I had long since neglected. I feel cautiously optimistic that my fortunes could be on the up, even though I suspect our overly superstitious cook believes that the death of our ravens will spell my downfall.'

'About that...' she began, but Bran, whose timing on this occasion was impeccable, flew down to the open window ledge behind Marcus, his black silhouette outlined against the still-vibrant apricots and crimsons of the glorious sunset. The bird cast a shadow across the faded rug on the floor between them.

Alerted by the flapping wings, Marcus turned, and immediately leapt from his seat. 'My God! One survived.' He turned back to her, his face a curious mixture of shock and delight. 'A raven has survived!'

Bran spread his feather-cloaked wings wide and swept across the room to land on the jardinière stand next to Luna. He tipped his head to meet hers, kissing her in his raven-like way, and Marcus followed his flight, open-mouthed.

'Darling Bran,' she said. 'Where have you been? Look who has come home.' Her eyes returned to the stunned man before her.

'You didn't mention this in your letters,' Marcus said, staring at the bird. 'There is a silly legend that my mother took particularly seriously that says that if the ravens leave the woods, the Greybourne family will fall. I spent so much of my childhood climbing those mighty oaks and losing myself in the mystery of such a magical place – and all the while, knowing those wise birds were standing guard, generation after generation, keeping my birthright safe. I thought they had all been killed, but this is a favourable omen, indeed. My future may yet be secure.'

'I thought you weren't superstitious, so the survival of a raven surely has no bearing on your fortunes or those of the Ravenswood legacy.' Part of her spoke earnestly, but part of her was teasing him, and she felt the tiniest flicker of amusement cross her face.

His eyes crinkled at the corners, acknowledging that he'd been caught out. 'Ah, but many of the superstitions we give credence to originate for eminently logical reasons. Saying "bless you" after a sneeze, when such a symptom might indicate an illness that will take your life. Not walking under a ladder so that you are less likely to have something land on you from above...'

'But a legend predicting the possible fall of your family cannot seriously be tied with such logic to the loyalty of a flock of birds.'

'Ravens are intelligent creatures, and if they leave the woods, it's for a sensible reason. Perhaps plague, pestilence or famine are imminent and the Greybourne family is better off elsewhere.'

Or there is a madwoman frequenting them, with murderous intentions, she considered.

'They didn't *choose* to leave on this occasion,' she pointed out.

'No,' he agreed, his face solemn. 'They did not. So, where did you find this extraordinary fellow?'

Bran hopped over to the small stoneware pot and tried to prise open the lid with his beak, eventually succeeding and helping himself to the juicy currants within. Worried he would overindulge, she sprinkled a few on the hearth and then replaced the lid, but more securely this time. She then told Marcus of the bird's discovery and subsequent recovery, as his face grew increasingly serious.

'Trapped at the back of the barn?' He looked distressed. 'He must have been there for several days. I'll ensure Mrs Webber leaves scraps out for him. We don't want to encourage him into the house.'

Luna said nothing. He would soon realise that they had little choice in the matter.

Bran hopped onto her chair arm and was grumpily pecking at her hand in an attempt to persuade her to feed him further treats.

'He appears to be extremely attached to you,' Marcus noted. 'But please be wary – they are dangerous birds. Highly intelligent but incredibly aggressive at times. They steal eggs from nests and attack livestock in the fields, pecking out the soft eyes of the newborn animals when the mother is at her most vulnerable. Not a creature to be domesticated like a household pet.'

Luna shuddered. This was an unpleasant side to ravens that she didn't want to contemplate.

'Nice bit of pie? Nice bit of pie?' Bran repeated, distracting them from dwelling on his darker qualities. He'd clearly spent too much time around the kitchens of late, and they both smiled at the bird's words.

'He's less dependent on me than he was at first. He returns to the woods at intervals and in this clement weather, I leave windows open for him to come and go.' She was about to speculate as to what they might do to accommodate his visits when autumn came but knew that she would be long gone by then.

There was a moment of awkwardness as they caught each other's eye.

She wanted to tell him how glad she was that he had returned, how handsome he looked in his tailored suit and white starched shirt, and what a pleasant evening she'd had in his company. The two short days they'd spent together before he'd left for London had not been long enough to get to know one another, and yet she already felt as though he was family. Plus, with his return, she was no longer quite so afraid, despite the seed of doubt Findlay had planted.

'Tomorrow we shall head into Little Doubton and order you a new wardrobe. The villagers have not set eyes on the mistress of Ravenswood for many years and need to be reminded of exactly what she looks like.'

'Would that be wise?' she asked. 'I don't think Luna Greybourne is very popular amongst the villagers. I've had encounters along the footpath to the ferry, and Mrs Webber must have mentioned the incident we had with the Kellings.' Added to her unease about how the villagers would treat her, she didn't want him spending money on her when she would shortly be leaving.

'Simple folk have simple ideas. One person cries, "wolf" when he sees a stray dog and everyone believes him. But by confronting the gossip-mongers and being seen to be so healthy, happy and no longer a threat, we can start to address these silly rumours. Let them meet you and they will soon realise you are no witch. I can't hide you away in the house forever.'

It seemed she was not to be packed off to London just yet then.

* * *

For the remainder of the day, Marcus continued the charade that they were man and wife. Unlike the time before his absence, there was not one unguarded moment, one instance when they were truly alone, that he acted as though she were anything other than the woman he'd been married to for almost ten years. Could it simply be that, after so long, he was enjoying a period of domestic contentment, where life was calm and nothing was demanded of him? Surely he was allowed that after everything he'd been through? And she had willingly agreed to be Luna back in April, wholly and completely, until she was well enough to leave, after all. It was a game – of course it was – but one she had to admit she was quite happy playing.

He was obviously in no hurry to send her on her way, but his plan to take her into the village was foolhardy. Why, she asked herself, would he risk letting her face be seen, allow people to ask questions and study her in close proximity, when it increased the risk of their deception being discovered? Prickles of anxiety surfaced. Was he starting to believe their fantasy?

There were a couple of occasions that evening when Marcus approached Luna – to show her something in a catalogue he wanted her opinion on, or pass her a small glass of sherry – when Bran's jealous side came to the fore. He flapped his large wings in irritation and placed himself between the pair of them. As delighted as he was that there was still a raven on the Greybourne lands, she sensed her would-be husband's bubbling irritation.

'Call off your overeager guardian,' he said. 'You are in no danger from me.' But Luna wondered if the bird knew something she didn't as she reluctantly ushered him out into the night.

At the end of a long but pleasant day, they mounted the stairs together in candlelight, the flickering flame casting their shadows onto the walls beside them as they walked along the corridor. The Webbers had long since retired, but it was only as they neared Luna's bedroom that it occurred to her that the sleeping arrangements had not been discussed – Marcus could hardly spend the night on the corner chair. From his correspondence, she had always known he was returning mid-May, although not the exact date. Extra food had been ordered in and his clothes were freshly laundered and pressed in anticipation, but he'd arrived without warning and she'd given no thought to their imminent predicament.

There was only one room on this landing that had a suitable bed, and that was the room Marcus had so generously surrendered to her the day of her fall. She knew from her explorations that there were a couple of broken bed frames at the end of the corridor, but no serviceable mattress, and the only reason his room had survived Luna's violent rages was because in recent years it had been padlocked in the day and bolted from the inside during the night. Luna, she gathered, had been intent on destroying everything that mattered to Marcus – out of spite or madness, she didn't know.

They stood opposite each other outside the door of the master bedroom, and she was aware he was studying her face. For the first time, it occurred to her that his reasons for claiming her as his wife might have more carnal motives. He was a healthy, red-blooded male, after all, who she felt it was likely had been denied any form of marital relations in recent times. Did he expect something else in return for sheltering and feeding her these past weeks?

He reached forward and his hand brushed her cheek. She swallowed hard. Men were all the same: kind words and flattery to get what they wanted, and if you didn't respond to their flowery advances willingly, they would claim their spoils regardless of your cooperation. This she knew.

'May your dreams be filled with love, laughter and hope,' he said.

He leaned forward, and she prepared herself for the kiss of a man claiming his wife, but instead he dropped his lips to the top of her head, in the manner her own father had often kissed her as a child.

'Goodnight, Luna, sweet dreams.' He passed her the candle. 'Take this. I am used to roaming about the house in the dark.'

'Where shall you sleep?' she asked, as his shadowy figure began to retreat down the landing.

'Don't worry about me. These past weeks have afforded me the most peaceful slumbers I've had in years. I could curl up on a linen line and be content. I will only be next door so should you need anything in the night, just shout.'

'But there is no bed.'

He smiled. 'Something I must imminently address, but tonight all I want to do is rest. The travelling has quite exhausted me.'

She slipped into her room and pulled the bolt across the top of the door, paused, and then slid it back again.

As she took the pins from her hair and placed them on the dressing table, she was shocked to notice several words written into the light covering of dust that had settled there. The room was not cleaned as frequently as she would have liked because the lack of staff meant the bedroom was not a priority.

Leave this place or die was clearly visible, even by candlelight, and Luna knew the words had not been there that morning. Who was sending her such an unpleasant message? Mr Webber? His wife? Surely not Marcus – he'd seemed pleased that she was still at Ravenswood. Or had someone else entered the house to warn her off? She used her sleeve to wipe the menacing command away.

There was a flutter of wings and Bran appeared at her open window, hopping over the frame.

'Kiss me?' she asked, as he flew to her side and made the low gurgling sound of contentment.

The bird obliged and rubbed his feathered head against her own before hopping back to the ledge, where he stood like a sentry guarding the woman who had nursed him back to health, his jet-black eyes occasionally blinking as he stared into the dark night and out across the Greybourne lands.

If the Ravenswood Witch really was still out there, she had done Luna no real harm thus far, but had the reappearance of Marcus changed things? Had she written the words in the dust? Her spite had seemingly always been directed towards him and, now that he was preparing to parade an imposter around as his wife, might it fan the flames of her anger? Luna could only hope that between them, Bran and Marcus would keep her safe if there was a vengeful madwoman lurking in the woods. Both had reason to do so; Marcus had suffered at his wife's hand for years and was only now rebuilding his life, and Bran had so nearly been a victim of her vicious cull of the ravens.

She lay back on her bed, looking up to the recently sanded canopy, and felt at peace. And, as sleep took possession of her body, she finally acknowledged that there had been the tiniest flash of disappointment when Marcus had only kissed the top of her head.

18

Bran left Luna in the early hours to do the mysterious things that ravens had to do, and she had struggled to get back to sleep after he'd departed. Marcus's return had upset her routine and caused her to think of Daniel again. He'd been on her mind a lot over the past few weeks. The horrific nature of his death and her role in it would haunt her until the end of her days. She had woken so many times since arriving at the house with her pillows damp from tears and her chest tight with panic. Would she be caught and made to pay for his death? Jostling for attention with all the other worries that Ravenswood had presented her with, she still had not decided whether staying or going would result in the worst fate.

Daniel had been such a surprising young man, not prepared to compromise and convinced of his mission in life. Her ambling mind wandered along a path she had not visited before and she found herself comparing him with Marcus: both tall men but Daniel slender and wiry, whilst Marcus was what her elderly grandmother might have described as 'built like a brick privy'. There was something disconcerting about them both, and yet that was part of the attraction. She was in awe of their different strengths. Daniel had excited her; Marcus offered security and protection – but could she trust him?

In the middle of her restlessness, she heard a door slamming somewhere downstairs, so she slipped out of bed to investigate. Illuminated by a full moon and a clear sky, she saw a shadow slink towards the woods. Too slender to be Marcus, she assumed it was Mr Webber going out again. But what was it about the woods that attracted him at such an ungodly hour?

It was then she saw the corpses of a dozen white butterflies scattered across her bedroom floor. She briefly wondered if Bran had brought them in, but suspected he would have eaten them had he been responsible. It felt as though they'd been left as a warning, particularly as she'd strongly identified with the trapped creature of a few days ago. And yet she was certain that no one had entered the bedroom since she'd retired for the night. No one human, at any rate.

Luna clambered back into bed and it wasn't long before the colours of the day began to seep into the room. The absence of birdsong struck her again. Back at Lowbridge, the robins, blackbirds and thrushes started up the orchestra of twittering voices that announced the dawn. Their cheery chorus was a precursor to the bustle of the household waking up, as they sought out mates and established their hard-won territories. But at Ravenswood, it was as though all the creatures of the earth, save Bran, were giving the woods a wide berth. Was the well a place that drew evil spirits and dark doings? And if so, did the wildlife sense it?

As the daylight slowly filtered into the dark room, she finally drifted off to sleep, eventually waking to the clock on the mantel chiming ten. Embarrassed that Marcus might think she was playing the cosseted mistress of the house, she rose and dressed quickly. Mrs Webber brought a late breakfast into the dining room; she'd recently asked her husband to set up a small drop-leaf table in the window for the mistress, until such time as the room could be furnished properly.

'If that's everything, I'll be off now. The master said I can clear this up later as I've been given a few hours off to visit my sister in Manbury.'

'It's no trouble for me to take my things through to the kitchen when I've finished,' Luna offered, but the housekeeper was having none of it.

'Absolutely not. He'd have my guts for garters if he knew the lady of the house was doing the work of the servants, even though he's doing exactly that as we speak. There was a delivery of paint earlier and he has been in the library since first light.' Mrs Webber chuckled to herself. 'My Jed don't know what's hit him. Lazy bugger can't get away with late starts and sloping off to smoke his pipe no more. Had him working on them floors since daybreak.'

The library was the room that required the most attention and, Luna suspected, where the disturbing ritualistic worship had taken place when unpleasant weather made it impossible to venture into the woods. After her breakfast, she wandered down to see how the men were faring. The scorch marks were paler now where Mr Webber was sanding, and the windows were wide open to let in light and wholesome outside air.

Her heart gave a weird little skip as she stood in the doorway observing the man she called her husband, his shirt sleeves rolled up to his elbows and a smart pair of dark braces on show. He didn't notice her at first and was totally engrossed in sweeping the paintbrush backwards and forwards in those small areas of wall that were not covered by bookcases. The men were mid-conversation but she only caught the tail end of the exchange.

'...She was absolutely distraught and told me, in no uncertain terms, that she wouldn't stay a moment longer if Luna remained.'

Mr Webber's familiar grunt came from the corner. 'Pay her no heed, sir. I'll soon put her straight. We ain't going nowhere without my say-so.'

Luna felt upset that the housekeeper had kept these feelings hidden from her. Why had the older woman pretended to care, offered her talismans and helped her sort a wardrobe, if she didn't want her at the house? Had she merely been fulfilling an unpleasant duty until the return of her master? It wasn't fair to make the Webbers participate in their lies, as it was now obvious that her stay was causing issues. If she remained for much longer, would they also leave, as the other staff had done?

Finally, Marcus saw her lurking in the corridor.

'Ah, darling, there you are. Have you remembered that we are going into Little Doubton today?'

The 'darling' caught her off guard, but then she had addressed him as such in front of Mr Meyer all those weeks ago. She brushed thoughts of Mrs Webber's threats to one side and smiled, trying to match his cheery demeanour with her own.

She nodded.

'Our first port of call will be to Mrs Cole, who runs a haberdashery and undertakes some dressmaking on the side. She is one of the more sensible members of our local community. I also want to place an order with the ironmonger, and make some general enquiries for further staff. We will need at least one maid and a strong lad to help with running the household now that your health has improved so dramatically. I'm hoping if the villagers can see that you are no longer afflicted with such melancholy, and I offer an attractive enough wage, we will get some applicants.'

Melancholy was one way of putting it; total delirium was another. But his plans confirmed that he had no intention of asking her to move on – not yet, at least.

He placed the brush across the small tin bucket of paint and took a handkerchief from his pocket to wipe his brow.

'Let me freshen up and then we can set off, if you think your ankle is up to it? I found an old walking stick of my grandfather's that may help. I'm afraid I had to sell the horses several years ago, but will also be making enquiries about purchasing a well-schooled pony to pull the cart. The stables are perfectly serviceable, and the gig only needs a lick of paint. But, today, I'm afraid our legs will be carrying us to the village.'

'My injury is quite healed,' she insisted, and it was true; her recovery time had been remarkable.

Marcus nodded in acknowledgement and peered at his pocket watch, which she could see had now been repaired.

'Goodness, is that the time? Some of us have been up since dawn.' He gave her a cheeky raise of the eyebrow and she couldn't help but smile for a second time. He was teasing her and it felt the most natural thing in the world.

* * *

They set off a little after ten o'clock. Marcus was full of chatter and high spirits, as they navigated the footpath that followed the gentle curve of the river. Luna, on the other hand, was a bundle of nerves, keeping her head low as they walked companionably together in the rising heat of the day. Although she was miles from Lowbridge and all that had happened there, it was not impossible for someone who knew the truth of her identity to be passing this way. And even if no one from her past life was to be found in Little Doubton that day, there was the equally unpalatable possibility that the villagers really would believe she was Luna, and vilify her for everything Marcus's wife had done and said in the last few years.

Unlike the resigned and world-weary man back at the end of April, her husband was animated and keen to share his detailed plans for restoring the house. It was structurally sound, he stressed, and much of the neglect was superficial; walls could be repapered, floors sanded and possessions replaced. But he was also interested in her opinion. What did she think of Japanese-style furniture? Did she have particular flowers or herbs she wished planted? She gave vague, non-committal answers. It was not her house: not her future.

'Did your parents only have the one child to continue the Greybourne name?' she asked, thinking how Ravenswood depended entirely on him. She was also an only child and it had been lonely growing up without brothers or sisters, but she did not carry the huge weight of responsibility that he bore. Was that why he'd so happily claimed the first replacement wife that had barrelled into him without even checking her credentials? So that he was no longer facing everything alone?

He shrugged. 'What can I say? A miracle child after years of them believing my mother was barren. She was nearly forty when she had me. Although, it is only by luck that I lived to see my seventh birthday.'

'Oh?'

'I've never told anyone this, and I mean *anyone*, but I was larking about in the hayloft, back in the days when we had working stables, and I launched myself onto a pile of hay that the stable hand had thrown down to the floor below. Only the stupid fellow had left an upturned pitchfork on the top, and it had been partially covered by his abandoned jacket…'

Luna gasped.

'Missed me by a fraction of an inch. I lay there for a long time staring at the four long sharp metal tines, all in a row alongside my body. I wasn't allowed in there, you see. And I didn't want the lad getting into trouble; he was always very kind to the lonely little Greybourne heir.'

He put his hand out to help her over a wooden stile and she took it willingly, thrilled that he'd trusted her with information that he'd not told another living soul.

His focus returned to the house.

'I can't tell you how much it means not to be undertaking the renovations at Ravenswood alone. Our most pressing need is obviously for a second bed, which I have now ordered from Maple and Co.' He tapped his jacket pocket, which she knew contained various correspondences, including orders with the seedsmen, and which he intended to post in the village.

'Longer term, I am keen to employ a full household of staff, but they have to trust that they are safe with us, so our gradual reintroduction of you to the villagers is our first step.'

The truth that had been creeping up behind her since his return hit her then – he didn't want her to go – as another more important truth presented itself: she was equally content at Ravenswood. Being married to Marcus Greybourne was a much-preferred option to starting a new life in London with little money, no friends and the very real likelihood of spiralling into poverty and abuse. Making this broken man happy was giving her more joy than she'd felt in a long time. It was important to her that he knew she did not take his kindness for granted.

'I would like to help out more now that my ankle is stronger. I can assist Mrs Webber with simple tasks, like plucking fowl and lighting the range.' But she'd apparently said the wrong thing as his face clouded over.

'No.' He let her hand drop as she stepped onto the dusty path below. 'I will not have the mistress of the house working like a servant.'

'But you've been stripping wallpapers and sanding floors,' she pointed out.

'That's different. This mess is of my making.' He set his eyes to the path ahead and groaned. 'My folly was to fall for a pair of pretty eyes and a beguiling smile.' He was talking of his wife but he looked sideways at her face as he spoke, as though it was important she understood what he was about to say. 'I was so infatuated that I did not properly question the trust fund that I signed upon my marriage. Of course the bride's father would regulate access to his large inheritance, one that required regular monitoring of his daughter. He knew all was not well, and worried that I would abandon her or worse when the illness took a more violent and permanent hold.' He narrowed his eyes at the memory and she saw the clench of his jaw.

Poor Marcus had been trapped, it seemed, but the visit from the clerk now made sense. By releasing his daughter's inheritance slowly, Luna's father ensured her husband wouldn't treat her cruelly or pack her off to an institution. Yet, now that he had an adequate substitute to enable him to claim the money, there was no one monitoring the real Luna's care – or lack thereof.

They came to the brow of the hill and she was met with a breathtaking view. The pale stone, foot-high walls that marked the footprint of the long-ruined abbey were clearly visible in the vibrant greens of the flat landscape below. The river continued to their right, meandering through the valley, but a sizeable settlement of houses lay before them. Little Doubton was larger than she had realised, as she'd scurried through its streets in a blind panic nearly two months previously. The scattering of stone cottages was guarded by the tall west tower of the small parish church in the centre – like a mother goose overseeing her goslings.

'No one would blame the husband of an insane woman for putting her away,' she whispered, beginning the descent, and wondering if that was what he had indeed done: slipped his deranged wife into some lunatic asylum under an assumed name, and then found a less volatile replacement.

'That's not the kind of man I am. I swore an oath before God to love, honour and obey, in sickness and in health. Luna needed... *you* needed protecting, from the villagers and from yourself, and that has been my responsibility. I have employed several women over the years to help me, but none of them lasted very long, and so I have been forced to manage alone.'

She nodded, uncomfortable that his wife's past behaviour would now be the mantle she must wear, but as they neared the village, she knew this was the downside of their deceit. If she was Luna Greybourne, then she was not only a witch, but also a violent woman lost to her own mind *and* an adulteress – according to Mr Findlay. She had no proof of that last accusation though, and wondered who Luna might have been involved with. According to Mrs Webber, her mistress had spent most of the last few years confined to the house and the woods, and they had hardly any visitors.

Perhaps it wasn't just the casting of spells and brewing of potions that had occupied Luna by the well and under the tree canopies at night.

19

Marcus and Luna walked in silence for a while, before joining a wider road, scarred with the deep grooves of carriage wheel tracks, and followed it into the bustling village. A long row of terrace cottages bled into an open square of busy shops, many with bow-fronted windows and cheery hand-painted signs on the walls. Large wooden half-barrels overflowing with purple pansies and pink petunias were dotted about, and a medieval wayside stone cross marked the junction of three intersecting roads and the village centre.

Marcus began to hastily school her as to the people and places they were about to encounter, but with so many names and facts, she was sure she would slip up somewhere. As their first port of call was to Cole's Haberdashery and Drapers, he explained that the family had been in the village for decades. They were intelligent and honest people, he said, not swayed by silly superstitions, and much respected in the village for always helping out their neighbours.

'There is a little feral girl called Penny that they pay to support. She used to run wild about the neighbourhood and was struck dumb a couple of years ago. Penny's affliction was blamed on the Ravenswood Witch, along with every other misfortune and cruel act of nature that it suited disgruntled villagers to put down to the supernatural. All nonsense, of course, but I feel it only fair to warn you of any accusations you might face. However, if there is anyone we can trust to support us in Little Doubton, it's Mrs Cole.'

Luna nodded her understanding and cast nervous eyes at the people bustling around the village square. A couple of women threw her dirty looks as she crossed to the haberdasher's and she gripped Marcus's strong arm with her free hand.

'Mr Greybourne.' A rather homely woman nodded her greeting as they entered the shop, but her eyes were edged with the fine lines that attested to a face that smiled regularly, and her demeanour was kindly. 'And who do we have here?'

'Why, Mrs Cole, this is my wife, much altered since she was last here, I grant you, largely because her health is greatly improved.'

The woman narrowed her eyes. '*Much* altered,' she agreed, looking between Marcus and Luna, confused as to what she was being told. 'How lovely to see you out and about, Mrs Greybourne.' She dipped her head. 'Although I don't think I have seen you above half a dozen times in the village since your wedding.'

'Pleased to meet you.' Luna stepped forward and put out her hand in greeting but Mrs Cole was wary of the stranger and did not take it. She realised her error. 'I mean, pleased to see you again after all this time. And how is little Sally? Much grown, I should imagine. She was only about seven the last time I saw her.'

She felt the gentle squeeze of Marcus's approving fingers and she gave him an affectionate look – one that any happily married couple might share.

'To business,' he said, not giving Mrs Cole a chance to reply and glancing at his pocket watch. 'Can you make up some clothes for my wife? She needs half a dozen day dresses, pretty but not extravagant, and one formal gown.'

'I'll need to take her measurements again.' She looked Luna up and down. 'She appears to have shrunk somewhat.' Those crinkles came out in force.

'Of course. I have other matters to attend to but I'm certain I can trust her to your care for half an hour?'

Mrs Cole nodded and called for Sally.

'Mind the shop, will you? I need to take Mrs Greybourne out the back to be measured.'

A young girl, the very spit of her mother and perhaps thirteen or fourteen years in age, stepped from the rear of the premises, as Luna was ushered through the very same doorway. The bell on the door tinkled with Marcus's departure.

'Let's get to it then. Down to your drawers and shift, if you please.'

Luna did as she was bid, trying not to mind being poked and prodded, as the dressmaker's tape measure was stretched out from its brass casing, wrapped around various parts of her body and along her slender limbs.

The first few minutes passed in silence, as Mrs Cole scribbled numbers down in a tiny notebook, occasionally licking the end of her stumpy pencil to help it write better.

'Which fabrics do you like?' she asked, waving her hand towards several bolts of patterned cloth stacked on a large cutting table.

'Oh, I really don't mind. Stick to practical colours and simple cottons that can be laundered. And no fancy trims.'

The older lady raised an eyebrow. 'You're not with him for the money then?'

Luna said nothing. This woman knew she was not who she claimed to be, but she had sworn to be Luna from the moment a kind stranger had assured the police constable she was his wife, and even Mr Findlay hadn't made her stray from that assertion.

'When my husband was a young man, Mr Greybourne gave him some money to start his business,' Mrs Cole said, as she worked. 'Even when his own fortunes declined, he would not take the money back, insisting it had always been a gift, and you don't return gifts. He's a good man.'

'I know,' Luna replied.

'Then I'll ask no more questions. He was smiling when he stepped into the shop, and is looking the most content I've seen him in years. That piece of information alone will make my husband very happy.'

They spent the next half an hour discussing fabrics and the finer details of the proposed garments. It was not long after they returned to the front of the shop that the bell tinkled again and Marcus stepped through the door.

'All done?' he asked.

'Yes, and your wife has selected some fabrics – quite modest choices. I'll get the finished articles out to Ravenswood within a couple of weeks.'

Marcus looked at his old friend and dipped his head in acknowledgement.

The bell above the door tinkled again as two young women entered. It hadn't taken long for word to spread that Marcus Greybourne and his wife were in the village, and they cast curious glances at the couple, whispering behind their gloved hands.

Luna was standing several feet away, but Marcus closed the gap and slipped his arm about her. The warmth of his touch calmed her nerves. *He is protecting me,* she thought, *like Bran,* and she was moved that he cared. She looked up to his face just as he looked down to hers and they exchanged a smile.

'After you, dear,' he said, ushering her out into the street.

Luna kept her head low and avoided looking at people as they stood beneath the stone cross.

'Is there anything else you need? Any supplies that I have not thought of?' he asked kindly.

She shook her head.

'How refreshing to be with such an undemanding woman. Quite a rarity for your sex,' he joked. 'Quite a rarity for you.'

It was absolutely not the time or the place for fanciful notions – in the middle of the day, surrounded by bustling groups of people – but she felt an intense pull between them. Her eyes locked with his again and the depth of his stare forced her chest to somersault over her stomach. This was dangerous; he was dangerous. If he could not trust her with the truth of what had happened to his wife, then the sinister possibilities would haunt her and she must remain on her guard.

And yet, even the thought that he might have committed an unspeakable crime did not stop her heart rate accelerating and wholly inappropriate thoughts of him from circling through her frantically whirling mind, beyond her control.

Not concentrating on her surroundings, she broke away from his magnetic stare and stepped back into the path of a hunched figure. Snapped out of the moment, she looked over in horror to offer an apology for her clumsiness but was spoken over.

'Don't you cast your evil eye upon me, witch,' the wizened old woman muttered, spitting on the ground.

Luna's heart began a slow thud as she realised that everyone in the street was staring at her – absolutely the last thing she wanted. A young mother protectively pulled a small child to her skirts and her husband told her not to be so silly. It seemed to Luna that the village was a mix of those who believed in malevolent forces and those who did not.

She knew her anxiety was etched across her face, as Marcus's strong arm once again pulled her close, and she took strength in that. But it had been foolhardy to come to such a public place for two very compelling reasons. Even though the locals believed her to be Luna Greybourne, she was, in reality, a wanted woman. Marcus's lies had offered her sanctuary, but there was always the risk that someone from Lowbridge was passing through Little Doubton, on their way to Manbury, and would happen upon her, know that she was a fugitive, and turn her in. The other was, of course, that Luna Greybourne was not liked in this place.

'What'ya bring the witch into the village for?' the old woman shouted, and she felt Marcus's arm tense about her waist, as he clenched his jaw.

'My wife is not, and has never been, a witch, Hilda. It's true, she was lost to her mind for a long time, but she's better now. Can't you see how quiet and rational she is?' Her husband spoke clearly and calmly to the gathering and curious gaggle, but there was an almost undetectable flare of his nostrils and she knew that he was struggling to control his temper.

'Four years of bad harvests,' someone else called out. 'Explain that.'

'Four years of unseasonable weather,' Marcus said. 'The whole country suffered.'

'How about little Penny refusing to speak, not long after she was found wandering, lost and panic-stricken on the Ravenswood road, near the jetty. I'm reckoning she saw things in them woods of yours.'

'Whatever happened to that child was not connected to my wife.'

'But Luna cast a spell on old Mother Selwood and her evil curse killed her,' came the shout of another.

'Ridiculous accusation. She believed some silly words and the genuine panic likely burst a blood vessel in her brain. There is always a rational explanation. You would just rather attribute it to mumbo jumbo.'

People were pressing in on them like the incoming tide surrounding a small island. They were totally encircled when she felt a shove from behind and fell forward, her knees hitting the stony surface of the road, as a searing pain burned hot in her neck.

'I've scored the witch!' came the gleeful cry, but Marcus had spun to face the perpetrator within a split second, finally snapping, as he held the woman he'd called Hilda by the wrists, his face a twisted glare and his voice a low snarl. His bulky frame towered above the diminutive figure.

'How dare you touch my wife?' he shouted, visibly shaking. 'How dare you hurt her? She is innocent of these crimes. You are all a bunch of small-minded superstitious people, with nothing better to do than to blame someone else for your misfortunes.' He released her and then pulled a handkerchief from his pocket and bent across Luna to apply it to the wound, his eyes concerned and his touch suddenly incredibly tender.

'There's evil magic about these parts, all right,' said Hilda, rubbing at her wrists. 'The well has been dry for decades, and even God's creatures stay away from your woods because of what goes on in there: fornication, blood sacrifices and contact with the spirit world. She's been seen, your wife, dancing around them fires that she's lit. With her pale hair, and wrapped in a linen sheet, the men say she looks like a white butterfly, flapping about, and we all know butterflies are messengers from the spirit world.' This was news to Luna who wondered, yet again, if the dead insects in her room at Ravenswood had any special significance. 'Shrieking and howling into the night, like a banshee, throwing sacrifices down the well. Everyone knows that they are gateways to the underworld, and that the Devil is being summoned and *she*...' Hilda pointed at Luna, '...is the one in league with him.'

The small crowd stepped back to give them some space and allow Luna to get to her feet. Her hand went to her neck to assess the cut. Dark red blood stained the white cotton square, and she could smell the iron-like odour, as whispers of 'witch' continued to be muttered by some.

'That woman's a sorceress, all right. She has a raven as a familiar,' a young man insisted. 'Mr Kelling's son told us. Black and evil, it follows her about and does her cursing for her.'

'We've always had ravens at Ravenswood and anyone with any ornithological knowledge knows they are intelligent creatures and clever mimics. There have been many people over the years who have trespassed on my grounds to gain access to the well. The bird could have picked that cry up from anyone. It also calls "nice bit of pie" but I'm sure no one is suggesting he is a competent cook.' There was a ripple of laughter from some, but the general mood remained antagonistic.

Mrs Cole belatedly stepped from the haberdashers to see what all the fuss was about. Her wide arms were crossed and her face was set in a manner not prepared to brook any nonsense.

'Leave Mrs Greybourne alone,' she said. 'I don't take kindly to people who are unpleasant to my friends.'

Marcus threw her a grateful look.

'Well, I for one am visiting the cunning man to get myself some charms.' The old woman remained defiant. 'Better safe than sorry... or cursed and dead on the floor.'

Without thinking her words through properly, Luna saw a way to defend herself. Findlay knew she wasn't a witch, largely because he knew she wasn't Luna, but surely he would stand up for her.

'Ask Mr Findlay,' she said, spinning to face everyone. 'Ask him if I'm a witch. He knows that I'm not a threat to you, or your precious crops. If you trust him so much to ward off evil, ask yourselves why he is so kind to me.'

It was only when she saw Marcus's reaction that she realised what she'd done.

'You've spoken to that man?' he asked, his grip on her uncomfortably tight as he pulled her closer to his face and shook her arm. 'When I expressly asked you to have nothing to do with him?' The flare of rage that he'd directed at the woman who had harmed her only moments before began to simmer up again, and she knew he was struggling not to lash out at her.

'I... I...' But there was nothing she could say because she *had* spent time with Mr Findlay.

'We're leaving,' he said, a vein throbbing across his temple. The crowd parted as the pair moved towards the Manbury road. All the good feeling between them had evaporated. Marcus wasn't just cross, he was furious, and she felt terrible then, for giving him cause to be disappointed in her.

As they left the village, Marcus striding ahead and no longer caring about her ankle, she spotted the tinker who had told her about the ferry all those weeks ago when she'd been running for her very life. He was leaning against the bakery wall and sucking on the end of a clay pipe, the tools of his trade at his feet in a little cart. He was the only person who had paid her close attention that day. To everyone else she was a scurrying figure of no interest, but he had held a conversation with her as she'd spun a tale about needing to get to London to see a dying relative, asked for directions to the ferry, and had taken the penny she had offered in grateful thanks.

He narrowed his eyes as she passed but said nothing. An uneasy feeling swirled in her stomach. What a fool she'd been to think assuming the identity of another could solve all her problems. Things were more complicated than ever, and there was a part of her that longed for her old life – before it had been cruelly destroyed by another.

20

ELOISE

Eloise spent a restless summer, unmoved by the occasional attentions of uninteresting yet wealthy young men, and contriving of ways to ensure her path crossed with the young Mr Thornbury. Not easy when he did not even attend church or indeed any other village functions. She sat through several further tedious games of cricket on the green but, although his father was often present, Daniel only appeared on one occasion and she was caught with the Fletchers again, unable to speak to him. Cricket, it appeared, was not his thing. They still had that in common, at least.

When the harvest had been gathered in, and the evenings grew darker, her spirits began to dip, much like the temperatures. There would be even fewer opportunities to bump into him now, and a long winter loomed. As if her own romantic frustrations weren't enough, it seemed that love was in the air for everyone except her. Her mother informed her that Rose had been receiving special attentions from a young man in the village called Billy Price – some character known for his shady money-making schemes, distantly related to their cook, and who flitted from one job to another. Lady Fletcher had warned Eloise's mother how difficult it was to hold on to young female staff, especially those with anything more than an ounce of common sense, because they were so often lured away by marriage and motherhood – most frustrating when you had trained them up and could see their potential.

Eloise was cross that Rose had not mentioned any such attachment to her. It wasn't as though they were friends, but she had thought of the young woman as a confidante and a valuable ally in her quest to win over Daniel. She had shared her romantic aspirations, but the maid had not trusted her enough to do the same. It might be prudent to make the most of her assistance whilst she still had her.

'Rose, I need you to do something for me.'

'Of course, miss.'

'Find out what you can about young Mr Thornbury. What time he leaves his house in the morning, the route he takes to the train station, when he returns, who his friends are, that sort of thing.'

'I shall feel ever so uneasy doing so,' her maid admitted. 'I've encountered him in the village a couple of times and he's a strange one. Quite opinionated.'

The man clearly made Rose uncomfortable and she wished to avoid him, whereas he made Eloise uncomfortable and the feeling exhilarated her. It was like reading ghost stories by candlelight, knowing you would scare yourself half to death, but doing so anyway. And Daniel was certainly preferable to the fawning gentleman who had visited the previous day, agreeing with everything she said and repeatedly assuring her that she was the most beautiful and fascinating creature he'd ever met, all the while eyeing the silverware and toadying up to her father.

However, despite her initial reluctance, and over the following week, Rose did her job well. Eloise gave the maid leave to busy herself about the village and, under the pretence of running errands, she gathered the required information: Daniel caught the six-thirty-five to Branchester, worked at one of the furniture factories on the edge of the city, and returned on the seven-twenty each day.

Rose, as a servant, could chatter and gossip with those in the village Eloise felt less comfortable engaging with, and had spoken to the Thornburys' immediate neighbour, who confirmed that the young man had a penchant for swimming in the Bran. This explained his journey through the grove on the Sunday when Eloise had followed him. Whilst everyone else was singing 'Sitting at the Feet of Jesus', he was rather to be found swimming below the drooping willows and alongside the last of the lemon-yellow goldenrod flowers. He was evidently using the sweet chestnut grove to access a part of the river that was rarely visited.

'Even now that the weather is turning?' Eloise asked, horrified to think of him in the icy river in the colder weather.

'Oh, he swims every Sunday of the year,' Rose said. 'He told the schoolmaster that it was far better for his soul than listening to some religious zealot spout nonsense to the masses.'

'Says the political zealot,' Eloise murmured, almost to herself, but a vision of the strapping factory worker powering through the water in a state of undress had derailed her train of thought.

'I think he is suspicious of me,' Rose added. 'He's been playing merry games at my expense and leading me about in circles.'

'Then talk to him,' she encouraged. 'He's not going to bite. You might even learn something. He is extremely well read. More so than most in his circumstances.'

Eloise had continued to consume books avidly, shamed by her ignorance and keen to expand her limited horizons. She struck up a friendship with Daniel's father, who she had quickly learned appreciated the odd gift of homemade cake, and borrowed a few volumes from the Thornbury bookshelves – works that touched on the theories of Engels and Marx. It wasn't that she necessarily agreed that society should share everything – some people were unfortunately beyond redemption – but more that she wanted to understand these philosophies. She could see, for example, the case for better education of the masses, and Daniel was a prime example. Here was a man who would do extremely well in life if he was given the right opportunities. Perhaps she could ensure some came his way…

'Rose?' she said, as the maid headed for the door. 'Is there anything you want to share with me?'

The young woman frowned.

'About Billy Price?'

Rose shook her head in resignation.

'Oh, miss, I don't know what you've been told, and I know Cook is excited to think I have interest from a young man, but Mr Price unnerves me even more than Mr Thornbury. He doesn't even have a steady job, turning his hand to brushing, thatching, and even hawking on the streets. He tried to kiss me on one occasion and since then, I have endeavoured not to be left alone with him.'

'So, you are not contemplating marriage?'

'No!' Her servant looked most horrified at the thought. 'I would much rather remain on the shelf than be with someone like him.'

Eloise nodded but thought her maid was overreacting somewhat. Rose was highly likely to see out her days as a spinster, if she was scandalised by an opportune kiss and too nervous to talk with Daniel. These were just men who had a bit of gumption about them.

Though, if she was honest, Rose remaining unmarried suited Eloise just fine.

* * *

'We are going for a walk,' Eloise announced. 'After the morning service. A little jaunt around the village. The fresh air and exercise will do us good. So, be sure to wrap up extra warm and wear stout boots.'

'I'll be needed at the house, miss,' Rose said. 'Mrs Banbury is serving the luncheon at two.'

'So long as you have swept the grates and set the table before church, you aren't needed. The kitchen maid and Cook always manage. Besides, I've told everyone I need your help to collect chestnuts. We can leave our baskets in the church porch to save us returning to the house.'

It was a dry early November day, although temperatures had plummeted that week. Every morning the fallen leaves of russet and gold were laced with silver crystals, and the windowpanes had intricate ferns of frost across them.

After the Sunday service, Eloise witnessed for herself the unwanted attentions that Mr Price bestowed upon poor Rose. He had the girl cornered between some gravestones and a large yew, and it was only when she intervened that he scowled and stepped away.

'Ah, you have a pretty face but no fortune, Rose, that is your sorrow,' she said, stroking her maid's arm. 'And Billy Price has neither.'

The pair shared a smile, although Rose's quickly fell away. 'I think the one thing he does have is plenty of money. Because he offered to pay me for my kind attentions.' Rose did not have to specify what these attentions might entail.

'How despicable.' Eloise was genuinely shocked. 'Let me speak to Father and forbid the man entry to the house.'

'Please don't say anything. I don't want to cause any problems for Cook.'

She had a point. Their cook was excellent, and it wouldn't do to upset the woman and lose her to another household.

They continued collecting the fallen chestnuts and Eloise was glad of her gloves as she handled the prickly casings of the nuts. Eventually, she called Rose to follow her further into the grove.

'I want to see the river,' she said, skipping under the colourful trees, swinging her half-empty basket, as the occasional fiery leaf whirligigged about their heads in the gentle autumn breeze.

Rose dutifully followed and, after a few minutes of weaving between the enormous trunks, they came to the riverbank. The water level was high, due to a thoroughly wet and miserable October, and it was flowing thick and fast.

'Let's explore the other side,' Eloise said. 'Row across and come back for our baskets later. We have plenty of time and I do feel that today is a day for adventure.'

'Really, miss, I don't think—'

'Ah, look, a boat. How fortuitous.' It certainly had been fortuitous to discover it the previous week, when she had explored this part of the river in anticipation of her planned escapade. She knew Daniel took a Sunday swim and had been delighted to stumble across an abandoned wooden rowing boat on the bank. It wasn't immediately obvious, concealed as it was by a tangle of dying weeds that had suffered in the frost, but she was certain that it was a small enough vessel for the pair of them to manage.

'It's far too cold to undertake such madness.' Rose was unusually vocal and Eloise despaired of the young woman. Where was her sense of daring?

'Shall we free it from the undergrowth?' By 'we' she meant Rose, but this was assumed by both parties. 'Oh, and we'll need oars,' she said, as her maid wrestled with the damp, brown nettle stems and wet grasses, occasionally squeaking when she was caught by a bramble.

'There are some inside,' Rose confirmed, still not looking enamoured of the proposed expedition.

Between them, they managed to drag it to the water, and Eloise waited patiently whilst Rose secured it to a post, clambered in, and set the weather-beaten oars in the rowlocks.

'I've never rowed a boat before.' Rose looked nervous. 'Will we be able to steer it?'

'I'm sure between us we can manage.' Honestly, the girl was so gloom-ridden and defeatist.

They untied the boat and Rose helped Eloise to push it away from the bank, but it was quickly apparent that rowing was far harder than she'd assumed. Sitting next to each other, they both took oars and dipped them into the murky river, swirling them about, but neither were sure what they were doing. As Eloise pushed the water away, Rose's strokes pulled it to her, and it took some time for them to coordinate, but even then, the boat stubbornly refused to head in the direction they required.

'Miss, I think I know why the boat was abandoned.' They were now drifting towards the middle of the Bran, almost equidistant from both banks. Rose pointed to the corner of the hull and both girls could see a small but growing puddle of dirty water.

Eloise felt a rising panic in her chest.

'Quick, we must get back to the shore.'

The water level started to rise at an alarming rate and soon her boots were wet. Rose was suddenly on her knees, not caring about her clothing but instead focused on the more practical task of bailing water with her cupped hands.

Eloise tried to stand and attract attention but the boat rocked alarmingly and she slipped onto her side, crying out when she smacked her elbow down hard on the edge as she fell. 'We're going to drown,' she screamed, clutching her damaged arm. 'I can't swim.'

Despair and absolute terror overwhelmed her and she could only watch as Rose valiantly continued with the impossible task of scooping out water. The poor girl was already shivering from her wet clothes and the chilly breeze.

There was a loud splash and they both turned to see the head of a man in the water surrounded by the radiating ripples from where he had jumped in.

Daniel. She offered up a thankful prayer to God. They would be saved.

Within a few seconds he'd made his way across to them and was clutching at the side of the boat.

'Take Miss Haughton,' Rose said. 'I can swim.' She had already removed her cumbersome skirts, and was now dangling her legs into the water. 'Give Mr Thornbury your hand, miss.'

Daniel helped Eloise sit on the edge, even though this tipped the small vessel alarmingly. She took his strong hands and slipped into the freezing river, giving a shocked gasp as her body reacted to the temperature. Gripping her under the armpits and keeping her head above water, he managed to kick backwards and return her safely to the shore, where she clambered out, petrified by what had just happened and shaking uncontrollably.

He sat her down and placed his dry jacket about her shoulders. The clothes he was wearing, however, were sodden; they had obviously caught him either before or after his swim. Eloise watched Daniel return to the water's edge and heave a bedraggled Rose from the water, allowing herself to revel in the lingering scent of him, as she dipped her head towards the woollen jacket. Her icy breath condensed before her face.

'You *choose* to swim in that?' she called out, pointing to the river. 'You are a madman.'

'It's a shock to the system, I'll grant you, but it certainly wakes you up, and is what my father describes as "bracing".'

'Bracing?' she squeaked. 'A quick walk down to the postbox on a crisp winter morning is bracing. This nearly killed me.'

He caught her furious expression and a gentle smile spread across his face. It didn't take her many moments to appreciate the humour of the situation. Perhaps it was indeed shock, perhaps relief, but soon the pair of them were laughing.

She had been attracted to this man from their very first meeting, and his challenging and defiant behaviour had only piqued her interest. But his strong arms about her body as he'd swum her back to the bank, and his concern for her wellbeing when he settled her on the grass, had only increased her ardour.

And when someone saves you like that, so dramatically, you are all but obliged to fall in love with them.

* * *

The village was rife with the news of the heroic rescue for days afterwards. Many of the locals, who had previously found the young man to be outspoken and opinionated, were now singing Daniel's praises and prepared to overlook his radical politics. Even the vicar begrudgingly acknowledged that it was a truly Christian act.

It was generally agreed that, had he not been close by, Eloise would certainly have drowned. No one thought to consider why the women were rowing a boat across the river, or even whether Rose might have managed to save her mistress.

The young woman had been reprimanded and embraced all at once by her tearful father, after he'd raced down through the grove, having been alerted by a dripping-wet Daniel, who had gone for help as soon as he'd established both women were safe. Eloise took full responsibility; Rose had merely done as she was asked. She found some clothes she no longer needed and a small piece of jewellery to pass to the maid as a way of expressing her thanks, and saw to it that the girl had an extra shilling in her pocket that week. And yet, the whole thing had worked out far better than she dared hope. Although nearly dying certainly had not been part of her plan, the potential gravity of the situation had won over her parents. Her father, in particular, wondered how he would ever thank the young man enough for saving his precious child. Words alone were far from adequate.

'I've been thinking about young Mr Thornbury,' he said one morning, not many days after her dramatic escapade. He was home more often than not, rarely visiting the factory now, much to his wife's delight, preferring to remain in picturesque Lowbridge than to travel to a dirty and industrial city. 'A position has come up in the sole manufacturing department and I spoke to him about the possibility of employment. It is more skilled and better paid than his current job and, if he proves his worth, I will see to it that he progresses.'

Eloise let her embroidery frame drop to her lap.

'You've visited the Thornburys?' she asked.

'He is an extraordinarily bright lad. I don't much like his politics, but had he been born to more affluent parents, he could have made something of himself. And, as you have pointed out before, the circumstances of our birth are quite beyond our control. There's something about the fellow that reminds me of my younger self, and I find I rather like him.'

Finally, her father saw his worth.

'Thank you, Daddy.' She gave her sweetest smile – the one reserved for those moments when she got her own way.

'I know that look, young lady. Don't be thinking of him as a potential suitor. I have gentlemen of much higher standing in mind for my beautiful and clever daughter.'

We shall see, she thought to herself, as she nodded earnestly at her father and returned to her needlework.

21

Walking over the brow of the hill and along the chalky river footpath back to Ravenswood, Marcus said nothing and kept his eyes on the track ahead. Luna could see a vein throbbing in his neck as he wrestled with his anger, but it all seemed so unjustified to her.

'Why do you not like Mr Findlay – the cunning man?' she was brave enough to ask, scampering to keep up with him. 'Mrs Webber says that many of the villagers go to him for remedies in their hour of need, especially when they cannot afford the doctor, as he doesn't always charge the poorest members of the community.'

Herbs and other plants had been used for thousands of years to treat the sick and injured. Why had Marcus taken against his neighbour so, when as far as she could see, the man was at best curing people of their ills, and at worst offering desperate souls a little hope?

'He is a charlatan. I grant he has a knowledge of botany, but he relies too much on hocus-pocus, and anyone who believes in such rubbish is weak-minded and gullible, in my opinion.'

She was frustrated that Marcus didn't like Mr Findlay simply because the healer believed in things that he did not, but she wasn't prepared to argue. Men always thought they were right and delighted in having the final say. They did not like being contradicted by others, most especially women. Daniel, for example, had been angry about the manipulation of the masses by the church. He was particularly adamant that belief in a non-existent God would not cure ills of the body or the mind, but she had been bold enough to argue to the contrary. She had seen people find solace, even relief, through their faith during the worst ravages of illness, and witnessed it help them through the almost unbearable burden of grief.

Did it matter whether Mr Findlay's rowan cross protected Mrs Webber from the spirits, as long as she believed it did? Or whether it had been the ointment or the incantation that had made her ankle heal exceptionally fast?

'I did not like Luna's... your friendship with him when he first came to Honeysuckle Cottage, and would request that it is not rekindled. His so-called remedies only made you worse.'

Again, there was a contrary explanation, and that was simply that the decline in Luna's mental and physical health was inevitable – not down to anything Mr Findlay had done or not done. It was easy to blame someone when no satisfactory resolution to an issue presented itself. After all, wasn't that what the accusations of witchcraft were rooted in? He stopped walking and reached out to grip both her elbows.

'I have asked very little of you. Could you not have done this one thing?'

'But I—'

He let her arms drop and shook his head. 'I was hoping that the villagers would see how you'd changed, but now I find you've been mixing with a misguided fool who thinks witches are real. He's as cuckoo as the rest of them, dressed like a court jester and trying to convince me to give him access to the well to protect us all from some unspecified evil at Ravenswood.'

She didn't try to speak a second time. Marcus clearly had a few things to get off his chest. It was interesting, however, that Findlay believed there was evil at Ravenswood and was trying to protect them from it. Whether it was the spirits of the dead floating about, the Ravenswood Witch, or even the grunting manservant who posed the greatest threat, she knew there was something very odd going on at the house.

'There was no evil,' he continued. 'Just an unstable woman clinging to silly made-up rituals as a way of channelling emotions she could not control, but once the rumours of witchcraft started to circulate, they gained momentum. Who but a witch would dance around a bonfire in the dead of night? Of course, ignorant and frightened villagers embellished the tales, and reports of the mistress of Ravenswood sailing through the night sky on a broom or summoning the spirits of the dead abounded. And then *he* appeared, with all his silly divination and hocus-pocus nonsense.'

Was this the source of his fury? The belief that poor Mr Findlay was to blame for Luna's madness, when even her own father had recognised the creeping illness consuming his daughter would never improve? Or perhaps Marcus was worried that, as one of the few people who had seen his former wife close up in recent years, the cunning man had the ability to expose them. But it was an unnecessary fear. Why couldn't Marcus see he was an ally? She felt calm and safe at Honeysuckle Cottage, which was a welcome contrast to the anxiously churning stomach and constant feeling of being watched that she felt at Ravenswood.

'I'm sorry that you feel I have betrayed you. He gave me some ointment for my ankle, that's all.' She didn't mention the incantation or her conviction that something powerful had undoubtedly flowed from the older man's hands. 'I won't see him again.' If it was a choice between Marcus and Mr Findlay, this troubled man before her would win every time. Yet there was a part of her that knew Marcus was making a huge mistake to spurn someone whose help they may need in the future.

'Taming the damn raven hasn't helped everyone's perception of you,' he muttered, still focusing intently on the path ahead. 'I'm glad one survived, but for him to have such a strange attachment to you does nothing for the case we are pleading.'

'I didn't exactly tame him,' she bristled, trying not to mind his language. '*He* attached himself to me. I think he knew I needed a friend. You have no idea what I've been through in recent months.'

Her words gave him pause, and he stopped and turned to face her again.

'I *am* unspeakably angry with you, but I must acknowledge that I am angry with myself even more. It was too soon to take you into Little Doubton. I just wanted to begin undoing the damage of the last ten years and I should never have put you in a position where you were attacked by Hilda – a bitter and gullible old woman who blames everyone and everything for her misfortunes in life, apart from herself.'

She could sense he was calmer now, the flare of his ire dying down, and she dug deep for a smile.

'It is just a scratch, even if I don't understand why I was attacked.'

'*Blood will I draw on thee, thou art a witch.* Shakespeare,' he clarified. 'Scratching a witch, especially if she is cut above the breath, is supposed to render her evil powers harmless. You're lucky she didn't get your eye.'

So, she'd been a victim of a superstitious ritual, even though she recognised it was no different from her carrying a rowan cross, albeit that was less violent. These people fervently believed that such actions would protect them.

'Then she's done what she set out to do. If they believe I really am some sort of enchantress, then surely the wound she inflicted renders me powerless. They can leave me alone.'

'If only it were that simple.' He began to walk towards home again.

'What exactly is a familiar?' she asked, daring to reach for his wide, swinging hand. She felt him tense at her touch, before moving his fingers away.

'A demon in animal form that you have tamed; a creature who will attend to you and carry out your wicked commands. How do you not know all this? Witchcraft and the accusations of such have been around for hundreds of years.'

'How do *you* know all this?' she shot back at him.

'When your wife is accused of such things, it is provident to investigate the topic as thoroughly as possible.'

'Did she... did I have a familiar before Bran? When my behaviour was more extreme? Not that he is a familiar,' she hastily added, in case he thought she had such leanings.

'No, you were never much of an animal lover. Creatures did not warm to you and you were often... unkind to them.'

This made sense because Luna had killed all the ravens, or attempted to. She thought he might expand on his comments, explain what other animals she'd had cause to harm, but he seemed reluctant to say any more.

Ravenswood came into view as they turned a corner. It still looked neglected and eerie, even though they'd made great progress with the interior. If only those oppressive trees weren't poised to throttle the very last breath from the building. They were so predatory, creeping up behind the house, ready to pounce at any moment.

'I asked in the village and may have found us some more staff,' he said, changing the subject. 'There was interest from a family who have recently moved to Little Doubton. The oldest son and one of the daughters will be coming to Ravenswood on Friday with a view to working for us. If you like her, and she presents herself satisfactorily, I will offer her a position as housemaid. The lad is wiry and his father used to grow crops for the market in Manbury, so he has experience of gardening.'

'And they are not afraid to work for a witch?' She said it with humour but Marcus was not inclined to exchange the smiles of before.

'I don't think they are in a position to be choosy. Their mother was recently widowed and has eight of them to support.' He stopped to unlatch their front gate and turned to her, hurt still apparent in his eyes. 'Perhaps if you would kindly sever relations with those who spout lies about dark magic, and Bran can refrain from shouting "curse you" at them when they arrive, they might even stay beyond the week.'

She looked for signs that he was joking, or for a softening of the eyes and upturn of the mouth, but there was nothing.

They walked through the gate and he lingered by the rose bush he'd planted back in April. She knew that the garden, and specifically the flowers, made him happy. If he was still in a sulk then she would leave him to his thoughts. The first of the buds had finally opened and it was a magnificent sight. The perfect petals were like gathered offcuts of white silk and a heady perfume danced before her in the air as she walked towards the meadow.

As she approached the house, she remembered that there was no point knocking on the front door as Mrs Webber would still be in

Manbury. Instead, she headed for the kitchens, only for a figure to dash out as she turned the corner and run in the direction of the woods.

It was a woman, of this she was certain, swathed in a long dark-green cloak with a hood covering her head, not stopping to look back. Whoever it was, she did not want to be seen – darting behind the first tree she came to. Luna could not tell her age, nor discern anything useful about her appearance, but she knew two things for sure – it was not her housekeeper and it was someone who did not want her identity revealed.

22

The young brother and sister, Hattie and Oscar Gower, walked over from the village that Friday, and Luna and Marcus interviewed the pair in the drawing room. The lad clutched at his woollen cap, turning it over and over in his restless hands, whilst his sister answered in quiet whispers, a constant look of fear across her eyes. Marcus, satisfied that they would fit the bill, took the brother out to the gardens to introduce him to Mr Webber and fill him in on his duties.

'I won't hurt you,' Luna reassured the anxious girl as the door closed behind them. She recognised that this poor child, possibly only twelve or thirteen years of age, was aware of her reputation. 'You may have heard gossip that I have a raven that follows me about, but it has only been a recent attachment, and only since I nursed him back to health. He was caught in a trap, nearly died, and is merely grateful to me.'

The girl nodded, as though she was petrified to do otherwise.

On cue, Bran tapped at the windowpane – the weather was cooler after an unexpected summer storm the night before, and it had not been prudent to leave the window open. Luna stood to let him in, all the while hoping her unpredictable companion would behave. He hopped inside and tapped his beak on the stoneware pot that held his treats.

'Would you like to feed him?' she asked.

'Nice bit of pie,' Bran said, as he waddled back and forth in front of them both, and even the nervous girl couldn't help but smile.

* * *

Things settled down for a while. Hattie and Oscar came over from the village every morning and returned together at dusk. On their second week, Mrs Cole sent them with Luna's new dresses, which were a perfect fit and, even though she had specified nothing fancy, there were subtle embellishments that lifted them above the plain garments she'd been expecting. It certainly made Marcus happier to see his wife in new clothes. Even the house was looking presentable – the ground floor, at least. And the Gower offspring had proved to be a good hire; Oscar was stronger than he looked and, though Hattie remained petrified of her own shadow, she did her work without complaint.

The Webbers were reminded to stick to the story that their new mistress was Mrs Greybourne, Marcus's wife of nearly ten years, and that nothing must get back to the village to the contrary. The housekeeper's slips when they had been the only staff could not be allowed to happen now, and Luna knew that the fantasy of it all was becoming ever more real with each passing day – for everyone concerned.

No one admitted to knowing anything about the figure she'd seen running from the house. Mrs Webber was convinced her mistress had seen a ghost, and Marcus had dismissed it. Nothing had been stolen and he thought it was most likely a gypsy girl who'd been poking around and become spooked when she'd realised the owners had returned. It took Luna a few days to realise that her broken coral necklace was missing, and for the housekeeper to notice someone had been at her medicinal brandy. Bran was blamed for the former and Mr Webber for the latter, but as nothing else untoward happened, she eventually forgot about the cloaked woman.

A whole month passed and, as they stepped into July, Luna allowed herself to believe that all her troubles might be behind her. The constable had not come for her again, seemingly convinced that she was the wife her husband claimed she was. Perhaps, like herself, he couldn't imagine any circumstances under which Marcus would willingly harbour a complete stranger, and a murderer to boot. Or was he starting to believe that she was the real Mrs Greybourne, particularly as so many of the villagers had accepted she was the Ravenswood Witch? There were no more visions in the windowpane and she was sleeping better. Perhaps they had been lingering effects of the laudanum. The attic remained silent and there were also no further threats written in the dust, although Hattie now saw to it that the bedroom was regularly cleaned.

Added to this, she and Marcus had settled back into a comfortable companionship. They often breakfasted together in the dining room, went about their own tasks in the day, and then shared their evenings together. Her misdemeanour with the cunning man was seemingly forgotten about and she found herself wondering that, should any of her siblings have survived beyond infancy, this might have been the sort of easy relationship she would have had with them. But she was fooling herself as to the true nature of her feelings towards the hard-working and driven man who, despite frequent periods of introspection, and the occasional flare of temper, had started to worm his way into her affections.

Late one morning, as Marcus stacked logs from one of the trees he and Oscar had successfully felled at the back of the house, she'd stood watching him for a while. His shirt was undone at the neck and a few dark hairs were visible where the cotton formed an open V. As he worked, she could see where the sweat from his exertions made the fabric cling to his body. It had been many weeks since she'd had thoughts of a romantic nature about a man, and the carnal knowledge that she possessed made her feel both deeply ashamed and strangely flustered, as her growing affections for Marcus inevitably danced around the edge of what being husband and wife meant. The day was cool, but the heat that crept up from the centre of her being set her cheeks aflame.

He looked up from his task and caught her staring at him. Embarrassed, she spun away and hurried to the Dutch barn, just needing a moment to gather herself. It had been built without walls and used to store straw and hay when the Greybournes kept horses, but three sides had now been boarded up to make it a more practical storage space. All the outside tools and machinery were kept there – the old gig, and an assortment of ladders and barrows. It was not a place she'd been in before and she felt the strangest chill sweep over her as she crossed the threshold.

This was a place of death – she felt it.

She looked about her, wanting to focus on anything except how Marcus made her feel, and walked to the back, where she spotted an abandoned animal trap on the top of a large wooden barrel. That's why she felt so unnerved – this barn was where those vicious jaws had held Bran captive for several days. Her hand reached out to touch the cold black metal and she shuddered.

'Come away. This is an eerie place,' Marcus's voice drifted over from the doorway, making her jump.

She hesitated, as she heard him approach. He stopped directly behind her but she couldn't bring herself to turn and face him. The warmth of his breath danced across the back of her neck before one of his large arms reached around her to lift her hand from the trap.

'I don't like Webber using these. There has been enough cruelty on these lands. If a creature must be killed, let it be outright.' His fingers lingered for far too long over hers before he let go.

Everything in her body came alive, as though his touch had sent an electric current through her. Still, she kept her back to him.

'The ravens?' she said. 'Were they all trapped like this?' She tried to focus her mind on anything other than his scent and how small she felt beneath his towering frame.

'Seven succumbed to poison in the water trough – all of which were subsequently eviscerated – two were shot, and you saw the one nailed to the gatepost. Bran was the only one caught in a trap. I remain amazed that he survived but am glad of it. Animals have astonishing instincts, sensing things we have allowed our evolution to override. He is extraordinarily fond of you...' He swallowed. 'For me, it is the reassurance I sought that you belong here.'

She turned slowly and tipped her chin up to his face. She saw his eyes dart to her mouth.

'We should—'

'Yes.'

Neither moved and an awkwardness filled the space between their bodies. He brought his face a fraction of an inch closer to hers, and his eyes flicked back to her lips, just as there was an almighty crash and a whole row of garden tools propped up along the side wall toppled, one after another, falling to the barn floor. He pulled away and the moment was lost, also falling to their feet.

She's here, Luna thought.

She's watching.

* * *

That afternoon, Luna wandered into the kitchens hoping to beg a glass of lemonade, or even offer to make up a jug herself should there not be any, but Mrs Webber was nowhere to be found, and she knew Hattie had been sent on an errand to collect milk and eggs from the neighbouring farm.

The room was totally empty but beyond the quiet of that space, she heard someone humming. The sound was coming from the tiny corridor that led out to the pantry, stillroom and scullery. With silent feet, she crept closer. The stillroom door was ajar, and she could see Mrs Webber's wide back, as she stood before the pine table, her elbows moving as she ground something with the large pestle and mortar. But it was not part of the preparations for dinner, or even a medicinal poultice, she realised with growing alarm, because to the housekeeper's left, drawn on the pine top with chalk, was a strange symbol within a circle, and she was chanting words in a language Luna did not recognise.

'She must be gone from this house.' Mrs Webber turned her head, suddenly speaking in hushed tones, clear unambiguous words, to someone else in the room who Luna could not see. 'I want her out and will do anything necessary to drive her from Ravenswood. Let's hope when the Devil comes a-calling on All Hallows' Eve, he takes the damn woman with him.'

There was a catch in Luna's throat. She had believed the housekeeper to be on her side, but the realisation that this woman was the foe masquerading as a friend that Mr Findlay had warned her about cut her deeply. Leaning forward to see who else was in the room, she finally spotted Bran and her already shaky world began to crumble. He was perched on the top of a small pine dresser and overseeing the whole ritual. She drew back immediately, wary of being discovered, and a restrictive band tightened around her chest.

She needed air.

Knowing Marcus and Mr Webber were busy in the meadow, she slipped out into the back gardens, gathering up a shawl as she left. Her head was spinning. Who could she trust? She no longer knew. Even the bird she had nursed back to health seemed to be in league with her enemies. He had always displayed his displeasure when he thought people were up to no good, like the Kelling boy or the manservant, and yet there he was standing by as the housekeeper cast a spell to drive her out. Or perhaps the pair of them were involved in darker ill-wishing? She was shaken by the prospect that the reciting of magic words and mixing potions could do her serious harm.

Outwardly, she was calm as she stood by the kitchen door, concentrating on her breathing, but inwardly she was a tangled knot of violent and uncontrollable reactions. Was this how Luna had felt? That there was no one at Ravenswood she could trust? No wonder the poor woman had spent so much time alone in the woods. By allowing herself to become part of this household, had she, as she'd suspected back in April, jumped from the frying pan into the Devil-worshipping bonfire?

The warmth and reassurance of the summer sun couldn't reach her now that she was in the shadow of the house, terrorised by the high canopies of the trees. It always felt like a house of two halves, and never more so than at that moment, as she stood there, small and friendless. Even the smells from this side of the gardens were darker: musty earthiness, damp wood and the stench of decay.

She straightened up, a slow determination building, and knew it was time to face her biggest fear: venturing into the woods. If she couldn't do this one simple thing, then she didn't deserve to remain at Ravenswood, and certainly didn't deserve to walk in the shoes of Luna Greybourne. It was a bright July day and she told herself that she had nothing to be afraid of. So many people were pulled into the depths of those trees – from Marcus's wife to Mr Webber, the fleeing woman to Old Mother

Selwood. She had to see the sacred well for herself, and set the ghost of Luna – real or imagined – to rest.

Instinctively, she reached into her pocket for the rowan cross, until she remembered with a jolt who had given it to her and wondered if it might not be of rowan after all, but some other wood that had the power to do her harm. She took it from her skirt pocket and threw it on the ground, driving her heel into the soil and snapping it, repeating that magic was only real if you believed, as she stepped from the boundary of the garden.

Before coming to Little Doubton, she'd always thought of trees as splendid and noble things. Moving from the city to the countryside had given her an appreciation of nature in all its glory. There were green parts of Branchester, it was true, but these were sparse oases in an overwhelming landscape of buildings that blocked out the light, and air saturated with dirty smoke. She recalled fondly the sweet chestnut grove of Lowbridge, and the leafy cut-through to the part of the river that Daniel had so loved. It had felt such a tranquil place, away from people, yet teeming with life. But stepping into the woods felt quite the opposite; like the barn, it felt like a place of death.

She ventured further in, thinking that the witch in *Hansel and Gretel* had built her gingerbread house deep in the woods for a reason – it was hidden from view, a place she could conduct her mischief away from prying eyes. And yet, with every step, Luna felt she was being watched. The gnarled trunks of the trees were covered in twisted faces, and the creeping branches were their wizened hands, reaching out to grab her as she passed. Gentle summer breezes toyed with the vibrant green leaves and whispered vicious threats of what would happen to her should she continue her journey.

What struck her, as she bravely strode towards the heart of the forest and, she hoped, the direction of the fabled well, was the lack of wildlife. There were no red squirrels leaping from bough to bough, no butterflies resting in the shafts of light that fell through the canopies above, and no birds at all, tweeting warnings to each other of an intruder. Now that his kin had been murdered, Bran was the only creature that this sacred place had left to protect it, but was he guarding against the forces of evil, or the forces of good?

Eventually, she stumbled into a clearing, and a patch of sunshine illuminated a stone well. A small wooden roof of overlapping timbers was supported by two posts, with the circumference of the well wider than she'd expected, perhaps four feet across. Rushing towards it, as though it could offer her sanctuary in this most eerie of places, she placed both hands on the edge, feeling the cold of the stone surround seep into her fingers, despite the warmth of the day.

She leaned forward to peer inside – a cavernous hole so deep that she could not see the bottom. It was easy to understand why people were convinced it was a portal to the underworld. Could the Devil really be summoned into this world through something constructed by man? There was a growing part of her that believed he possibly could.

'Oh,' she said, jolting backwards as she noticed strange symbols and markings carved into the stonework and scratched into the wood of the supports. The echo of her surprised exclamation swirled around those plunging walls as though there was someone or something lurking deep inside and calling back to her. She frowned and felt a cold gust rush past her face and shoulders. Something had certainly been summoned from the depths, even if it was only the stale air.

'Luna?' she called into the abyss. It came back to her not as a question but a statement, definite and taunting. 'Luna, Luna, Luna...' the echo confirmed.

And then she wondered if Marcus's wife could be lying dead at the bottom of this unused well. It was the perfect place to conceal a body. Although the whole forest whispered death, there was no unusual insect activity to indicate anything unpleasant was decomposing in the pit before her. But then the real Luna had disappeared over three months ago. Perhaps she was just bones now.

She picked up a large stone from the ground and tossed it into the well, wondering how deep the hole was. It bounced off the sides and ricocheted down the walls, until there was a thud as it hit the bottom. No water; no hope.

Luna stood upright and a small clay figure in the soil by her feet caught her eye, highlighted as it was by the sun reflecting off tiny metal pins. These pins had been deliberately driven into the limbs, heart and eyes of the miniature human form – a cruel act to get revenge on someone who had committed a perceived wrong. Even city girls knew about poppets from the silly playground games played by naive children who didn't realise what godless forces they were meddling with. She felt the wound in her neck throb, even though it had healed into a deep pink scar, as though someone was at that very instant sticking a pin into the neck of a clay figure of her.

She shuddered and shook the ridiculous notion from her head. Then she noticed another poppet, half buried in the crumbly mulch of last winter's fallen leaves. And then another, and another... Mr Findlay was right – this was a place of good and evil. No wonder half the villagers were convinced Satan himself would be summoned up on All Hallows' Eve, to prance around these woods and collect up the souls of the dead. With everything she'd found in the last few minutes, she was of a mind to accept it was entirely possible.

Having circled the well a few times, Luna decided to head back to the house, but was alarmed to realise she didn't know which way was home. If only she'd had the foresight of Hansel and Gretel and left herself a trail to follow. There was still no sign of Bran – not that she would have welcomed his arrival after his betrayal – and the midday sun was now directly above her, giving no clue as to her orientation. Panic bubbled in her chest as she turned to each tree surrounding the well in turn, but they all looked the same: towering oaks bending towards the clearing; wise old men guarding this precious watering hole – men who had been standing here for several hundred years.

There was nothing for it but to decide on a direction and continue in a straight line until she either stumbled across Ravenswood, the river, or came out into open countryside. What she could not do was remain at this unsettling place. Like a fool, she hadn't told anyone where she was going, and the thought that she might still be wandering aimlessly around in the dead of night was petrifying.

A further breeze swept across the clearing and Luna pulled her shawl tighter around her body. In the same way she had found the courage to run from the police and travel all those miles across the rugged countryside on foot, with no food or shelter, she would find the courage to get herself out of this muddle.

Picking up her pace, she started to half stride, half run away from the well, but those wizened hands were reaching for her and managed to entangle her on a couple of occasions, hooking their bony fingers into the loops of her shawl. In the end, she abandoned it when a grasping tree tugged it from her shoulders. All she wanted was to be out in the sunshine again.

After a few minutes she lurched into another, smaller clearing where she saw, to her horror, three large wooden crosses protruding from the ground. Each one had a slightly raised mound in front – undoubtedly graves.

Heart racing and mouth dry, she approached the sad line of markers for whatever was buried beneath. She could see from the way the wood had weathered that these were three separate burials over the space of several years. But why was this graveyard hidden deep in the woods? Were these resting places a secret – not meant to be found?

She approached them cautiously, her panicked mind racing with possibilities. It was still Greybourne land, so were they connected to the house or the family in some way? Or were they the bodies of sacrifices made at the well – animal or otherwise? And then she chided herself for being so dramatic. Could they be lost or stillborn babies, she considered: too young to be baptised, and therefore not allowed to be buried in consecrated ground? Mr and Mrs Greybourne had no children but that didn't mean there hadn't been pregnancies.

And then she saw something that made her heart almost stop. Each cross had an initial carved into the middle. From left to right, there was a 'C', a 'G', and the newest grave, likely only dug a few months ago because the wood had not dried out and discoloured like the previous two, was carved with an 'L'.

'Luna,' she whispered with incredulity to the trees and they laughed back at her. Surely only Marcus would have the right to give permission for burials here. Had she stumbled on the hidden grave of a woman who had perished at the hands of her husband? What if he had been *control-*

ling her? Whispering untruths into her ear to convince her she was going mad. Had she been a naive fool to let his kind eyes and gentle touch lull her into thinking she was safe with him, when she was nothing of the sort? She knew only too well that someone could present a front of compassion, yet be manipulating you with unkind motives.

And, as she suddenly heard a flapping of wings and the familiar cry of 'kiss me', she wondered if she would one day be under a fourth mound of soil, another wooden cross at her head to mark her final resting place.

23

ELOISE

Fully prepared to play the long game, Eloise sat back as winter crawled into spring, noting with satisfaction that Daniel was proving his worth. He gained a small promotion in the February, after the foreman who oversaw the sole-making passed away unexpectedly. Her father was told by the factory manager that young Mr Thornbury was popular with the workers under his supervision, and their productivity had increased considerably, as her father wryly remarked that he was expecting the man to lead a revolution to overthrow him at any moment. But the truth was, as someone not born into great wealth himself, he was listening to his new foreman and instructing his manager to do the same. The company was faring well, their reputation for high-quality footwear was growing, and plans for expansion were well underway.

Daniel began to call at the house on occasion, often tasked with delivering contracts and papers to Mr Haughton, as he lived in the same village. He always came through the tradesman's entrance at the back of the house and took the time and trouble to speak with the household staff. Aware that he was not yet the gentleman Eloise aspired for him to be, he clearly felt uncomfortable calling at the front door. But then this was his gift: he was a man able to exchange pleasantries with the poorly educated girl who worked in the scullery one minute, and discuss the benefits of installing Goodyear's welting machines with her father in their upstairs drawing room the next.

It was during one such visit that Eloise finally had cause to believe she was winning the young man over, even though the evening ended in high drama. Daniel had requested to speak to Mr Haughton about the aforementioned machine – able to stitch the sole to the upper far more efficiently than by hand. The meeting was longer than their usual brief exchanges and conducted in her father's study, but after the matters of business were concluded, Thornbury was offered a drink. Unlike her somewhat snooty mother, her father remembered his roots and was pleased with his foreman, doubtless recognising something of himself in the passionate and idealistic young man.

There was an unusually long wait for the servant bell to be answered and her mother was unable to hide her discomfort as Daniel sunk down onto the sofa next to her. He enquired politely after Mrs Haughton's health and Eloise engaged him in a short discussion about the moral messages to be found in the works of Dickens.

Eventually the flustered housekeeper entered and apologised for the delay.

'There is such a commotion in the kitchens, sir. The girls are hysterical as one of the barn cats they've formed an attachment to is outside the back door in great distress. We think it's eaten something it shouldn't have.'

Daniel leapt to his feet immediately. 'The little black one, no doubt. I know how fond your staff have become of him; he's quite the character. Do excuse me, Mrs Haughton. It's possible I can be of some help.'

Impressed by his kindness, Eloise stood up and followed him downstairs, where they were met with quite the scene. The scullery maid was in tears and Daniel briefly put his arms around the poor child and asked the cook to apprise him of the facts.

'We think it's ingested a small amount of arsenic residue from a tray the gardener was using to put rat poison into roasted apples. Stupid man left it outside the back door instead of returning it to his locked shed. Ginny gave the cat some chopped liver on it earlier today—'

'I didn't know it had been used for the rat poison,' wailed the young girl.

Daniel bent to inspect the creature who was lying limp on a blanket in front of the range.

'But he's been sick?'

The cook nodded.

'Then that's good. It's not the arsenic itself, but the quantity that kills and, hopefully, most of it is now out of his system.'

It was indeed the downfall of the rat, Eloise knew, not having the ability to vomit.

'If he has only consumed a small amount, he may yet survive. Get some water into him and time will tell.'

He stood up and walked to the sink to rinse his hands, turning to Eloise as he dried them on a piece of towel.

'Nasty stuff, arsenic. Whilst you ladies insist on swanning about in your delightful Scheele's green ball gowns, we really should be following France and banning the pigment. Workers across the country are handling it daily to produce artificial flowers, fly papers, candles and fabrics, but evidence of the sickness it causes is mounting.'

Everyone knew that it was dangerous if ingested, but she had not thought wearing it was hazardous. She made a mental note to investigate this issue and thought she might ask Rose to check her wardrobe for anything in that colour. Time and time again, he made her feel ignorant of issues that she should be aware of, but she delighted in the fact that whilst she was helping advance his social status, he was adding to her education. What a match they would be with her money and his passion.

'Thank you for coming down to look at the cat,' Rose said. 'It was a kindness.'

'I've done nothing,' he replied. 'But I know how much you girls love that little scrap.'

Cook giggled at being referred to as a girl, and Daniel nodded at them all before returning upstairs to bid his employer goodnight.

* * *

A little while later, Eloise sat contentedly with her parents in the drawing room, flicking through *Our Mutual Friend* and reflecting that whilst money had the ability to corrupt, it also had the power to breach social barriers.

'Yet again, I must own to being wrong about Mr Thornbury,' her father said, pouring himself a large brandy. 'His views are extreme but his heart is kind.'

'Perhaps his opinions will soften over time?' she offered. 'He still has things to prove but a career and a family might take the edge off his fanaticism.'

'Funnily enough, Cook is under the impression that he is forming an attraction,' he said, smiling at his daughter.

'I think so too,' she agreed. 'And you don't mind? I know that you've had reservations about him in the past.'

'Don't misunderstand me, the fellow is still trouble, but he is trouble that I can control. And you?' he asked. 'You don't mind either?'

'Of course I don't mind.' She rolled her eyes. Her father said the strangest things sometimes.

24

It was with some trepidation that Luna followed Bran back to Ravenswood. She couldn't forget seeing him in league with Mrs Webber, sitting calmly by, as she'd chanted her spell. But then she wondered if she was crediting him with an understanding that he simply didn't have. He was just a bird, sitting by the woman's side as she conducted her ritual.

'Now you show up,' she scolded, 'when I've been scared half to death.' She almost expected him to chase her from the Greybourne lands, as if the housekeeper's desire to see her gone would be manifested via the bird. But, in the end, she had no choice but to follow him, as she would never escape from the woods alone.

As she trailed behind his black swooping form, anger and fear swirled equally ferociously inside her. Staying at Ravenswood meant she would forever be labelled a witch, and the misguided woman's actions in the market square last month were only the start. It might be nearly two hundred years since the government had hanged someone accused of witchcraft, but ordinary folk still persecuted those they believed were practising the dark arts. She'd thought herself protected by Bran and Marcus but now she wasn't so sure. The bird was unreadable, seeking attention on his terms. And the man she called her husband, she knew very little about. It was entirely possible that Luna was buried in the woods and that she had died at his hand. The poor woman could hardly have buried herself.

Marcus found her in the drawing room a little while after she'd returned.

'Ah, there you are. No one seemed to know where you'd got to, and Mrs Webber is keen to serve luncheon.' He raised an eyebrow and she wondered if he suspected her of visiting Mr Findlay again. Perhaps the lack of trust went both ways.

They ate together but it was a silent affair, both focused on their own troubles. Afterwards, because a rain shower prevented her from walking about the gardens, she retreated to the library – still a sparse space but she could at least lose herself in one of the few books he'd purchased in his attempts to replace those that his wife had destroyed.

But Luna was in turmoil and found it impossible to concentrate. She was no longer sure she could continue with this farcical and possibly dangerous charade, and was completely out of her depth. Not only was she wearing the uncomfortable shoes of a woman who had completely disappeared but also a woman who was vilified by the whole village. Adding to her worries, was the possibility that the Irish tinker would realise she was the fugitive sought by the Lowbridge constable and raise the alarm.

Marcus seemed happy for her to stay indefinitely, but why? Did he plan to use her to claim the inheritance for years to come? Or was she a convenient cover for the fact he'd killed his wife? There had to be a reason he'd willingly harboured a woman wanted for murder and lied to the police about her identity. And to top it all, he would never talk about the real Luna, or address their sham marriage, as though their pretence would make the lies become real. They both had secrets and it was unrealistic for them to pretend they could continue to live like this forever and ignore their pasts.

Her ankle had healed now, and he had his money. It was time to leave, before the villagers, or the Webbers, did her serious harm. Perhaps even Marcus's friendship was as fake as their marriage, and when she was no longer of use, he would dispense with her as surely as he'd dispensed with his wife.

There was, however, the one uncomfortable truth that she'd been slow to acknowledge; she was developing feelings for him despite the possibility that he was a bad man who didn't deserve her love, or even that he was a good man but would never feel the same way about her. She couldn't possibly stay and face the devastation of either being true. Had he tried to kiss her in the barn, she knew she wouldn't have stopped him, but her heart had been shattered once and that was enough.

Finding out Mrs Webber and Bran were in league, followed by the discovery of the three graves in the woods that afternoon, reminded her how alone she was at the house. She was still the outsider – the stranger who had arrived frightened and friendless back in April. The only person remaining who she trusted was Mr Findlay, and she'd been forbidden to see him... She'd thought Marcus was the victim of his wife's outrageous behaviour but now suspected his wife might have been a victim too – of his temper. The poor woman's only friend had been Mr Findlay, and Marcus had tried to isolate her from him. Why? Had he offered the Ravenswood Witch a means of escape? He'd also offered Luna refuge and she was sorely tempted to take him up on his offer.

She didn't need any more reasons to flee, but the visitation she had later that night was the final, and most disturbing, of the straws.

* * *

It began as a dream. She knew what Luna looked like from the wedding photograph that Marcus had tossed into the flames all those weeks ago. Now those pale eyes stared at her as she slept, condemning her actions. The vision was disturbing enough to wake her from her slumbers, and as she sat up, she felt those judgemental eyes still boring into her. The prickles on her neck intensified and she shuddered, scanning the room, convinced there was someone there with her.

Not daring to move, she froze. Listening for a clue that she was not alone: a rustle or a creak of the floorboards.

There.
Breathing.
She could hear it.

'Bran?' she whispered, but the window was only open a couple of inches to allow some fresh air to circulate on that warm summer night. There was not a big enough gap for him to enter, as she had deliberately not wanted the treacherous raven to call on her.

A whisper of something? A mocking laugh?

She slid from her bed and scrabbled about for a match to light the chamberstick on her nightstand. Once she had a flame, she took it to every corner, but all she saw were dancing shadows and moving shapes.

'*Leave.*' It was almost a sigh but she could detect the definite command in that one word whispered in the air that cavorted about her body. A gentle tug of her nightgown as the half-drawn curtains swayed in the breeze. She walked to the window and the hush and hiss of the trees called her forward, only to tell her she was not wanted there.

'*Leave,*' the whisper came again.

And then she saw a reflection in the glass. Her own image stared back at her but behind her shoulder was the undisputable figure of a young woman.

Luna.

Her pale, wide eyes were unblinking, and the curl of her upper lip suggested the satisfaction of someone who had the upper hand. They stared intently at each other for a few moments in the windowpane and then she both saw and felt the reflected figure place an ice-cold hand on her shoulder. She spun around to face the woman she had so recklessly replaced.

But there was no one there.

The room was empty.

There was no rational explanation for what she'd just witnessed. She had not drunk wine that evening, nor was she particularly overtired, but she knew without any doubt that the figure standing behind her had not been a product of her imagination or a trick of the light. Luna's eyes had met her own, and she could describe the style of her hair, the cut of her dress, and even the rhythm of her breathing. And she had categorically felt her touch.

The two worlds had now collided; her very tangible reality and the spirit world that Marcus was so certain did not exist. The ghost of a bitter woman was haunting her and demanding her departure. She would not remain at Ravenswood a moment longer. It was time for her to go.

25

The house was silent, save the ticking of the clocks and scampering wind through the oppressive trees outside her window. Luna hastily changed into the dress she had arrived wearing back in April; she'd kept it, folded up at the bottom of the wardrobe, just in case. Then she bundled up a few essentials, including the shillings that she had arrived with, fetching them from their hiding place behind the chest of drawers. After opening the bedroom door as quietly as she could, in her stockinged feet she crept down the stairs and into the kitchens. There, she took a hunk of bread and a small piece of cheese, wrapping them in muslin to see her through the first day, before lacing up her boots. The journey to London would not be easy.

Slipping silently from the front door, she noticed that the pathway to the river needed scything again. The grass was long, scattered with the droopy heads of lilac foxgloves, the yellows of buttercups and the blood reds of delicate poppies. The rain of earlier had all but dried in the heat, but the glorious smell of damp earth and fragrant blooms circled around her. New beginnings, she decided. She'd done it once; she could do it again.

Shifting clouds allowed fleeting bursts of moonlight to light her way. The pale petals of the white roses guided her to the gate, and she heard the gentle gurgle of the fast-flowing river ahead. She would call on Mr Findlay first; he would offer her shelter until the ferryman started in the morning. All she knew was that she had to get away from Ravenswood and all those within it, whether they were from this world or the next.

Her hand reached for the gate latch just as Bran appeared, swooping past her, and making an almighty row. She thought for a moment he was there to attack her and instinctively protected her face by flinging her arms across her eyes. It took her a while to realise he was there to make as much noise as possible and impede her escape.

'Shhh,' she begged. 'You'll wake the household!' Although she now rather suspected that was his intention. He settled on the gatepost as she approached, flapping his wings and hopping from foot to foot. She tried again for the latch, but with deliberate and aggressive movements, he pecked violently at her fingers. His beak was strong and sharp.

'Bran!' she cried out. 'That hurt. Let me past.'

'Curse you,' he called. 'Curse you!'

The bird didn't know what he was saying, she convinced herself, although she wondered if something in the sharp tone of the noise he was mimicking matched his obvious anger.

They stared hard at each other, neither breaking their gaze. Bran's pale grey eyelids occasionally blinked at her, as she flared her nostrils in frustration. The impasse was broken by the heavy pounding of feet from behind, and she didn't need to turn to see who was running through the meadow.

'Where the hell do you think you are going at this ungodly hour?' Marcus's voice was harsh and accusatory. She turned to see his silhouette against the backdrop of the whitewashed house. A cloud drifted past the moon, allowing her to also make out his desperate expression.

It was time to face the reality of their situation.

'I'm leaving. You know this was only ever temporary. Me evading the law, and you accessing much-needed funds. The rumours of witchcraft and the attack—'

'No, I can't allow you to leave.' Was he threatening her? Her panic eased as his tone softened. 'I'm sorry the villagers treated you so badly. I will protect you better in future. I was foolish to think it would be easy to regain their trust. But you're my wife. Please don't let them drive you away.' Marcus, it seemed, was increasingly embracing the illusion that they were a married couple.

'There are ghosts at this house, Marcus – I've seen them. The ghosts of those who want me gone.' How could she stay when Luna was determined to push her out?

His face hardened. 'I had hoped you were more sensible than to get sucked into silly talk of spirits and magic. It's bad enough that Mrs Webber wards off imagined evil by carrying rowan crosses, hanging scented pomanders and scribbling powerless symbols on scraps of paper, without you joining in. I can't have Hattie and Oscar sucked into this nonsense.'

She laughed then. 'I don't think she's guarding against witchcraft; I think she's practising it. The woman was chanting an incantation to remove me. "I want her out." I heard her say it.'

In response, Marcus growled. Something she'd not heard him do before. Even in the poor light, she could see his body stiffen and his hands clench.

'That damn woman. If finding another housekeeper was easy, I would sack her. If she's been meddling in the dark arts again, I'll be furious. All week she's been saying she's seen a ghost and if I find out she's been employing dubious practices to exorcise her, there will be hell to pay.'

Her. Had Mrs Webber seen Luna too? Was the truth that the housekeeper wanted the *ghost* gone? Had she misunderstood her words? Bran's silent support would certainly make more sense in this scenario. And, to be fair, her knowledge of witchcraft was limited. A chalk circle and a handful of mystical symbols could either be summoning evil or guarding against it, and she wouldn't know the difference.

But regardless of what Marcus believed, Luna, or rather her spirit, had categorically been in that bedroom with her; she would swear this on her own life. And that meant his wife was dead.

She stared at him, wanting to question him about the woman in whose bed she slept every night, but she had struck a deal with him back in April; he would not ask about her past if she did not pry into his.

Her thoughts returned to the unpleasant discoveries of that afternoon.

'I went into the woods for the first time today. I have been so afraid to enter them, but I overcame my fear only to find upsetting things.'

'What things?' He now sounded exasperated. Here he was, begging her to stay, and she kept throwing reasons to leave at him.

'The stone well. It had poppets scattered around it, evidence of witchcraft. And then I got lost and... I stumbled across the graves.'

Marcus ran his hand through his hair in desperation. 'I tried to hide them off the beaten path; bury them where no one would find them. They are for me to visit, and me alone. I was heartbroken every single time. Taking a life is wrong under any circumstances, but these deaths were particularly brutal. You have no idea what I've been through. Every man on this earth is entitled to navigate his own way through the hardships he suffers. This is how I have managed, and my way of coping is not your concern.'

She was incredulous. What was he saying? That burying people he'd done away with, and hiding them from prying eyes, was part of his healing process, and perfectly acceptable because he'd had an awful life?

She took a step towards Bran, who was calmer now that Marcus had arrived. Would he protect her if she were to be victim number four?

'Why have you buried them in the middle of the woods? What makes you think you can get away with murder just because your life has been difficult? And am I to be next?' she wailed, all reason having fled her body with his calm explanation as to the hidden location.

'Next?' He looked confused. 'Captain, Gulliver and Lister. My dogs. Good God, Luna, who did you think was buried there?'

Dogs? She thought back to the badly scratched doorways and Mrs Webber mentioning dogs when she'd heard noises in the attics. A wave of comprehension swept over her, as he continued.

'I wish I could say they died of old age but anything I got close to... *anything I loved—*'

'Got taken from you,' she finished, suddenly realising Luna had somehow been responsible for their deaths.

'And now you're leaving me?' He looked at her bundle and the man who had undergone a whole gamut of emotions in the last few minutes – anger, frustration and disbelief – now just looked unbearably sad.

'This is hopeless,' she said, but he risked taking a step closer, looking down into her equally unhappy face. 'I've served my purpose, and in return you kindly allowed me respite. What further need can you have for me? Unless you are still holding on to me for the money? I'm not sure I can play mistress of the house year after year just for you to claim the inheritance payments.'

He'd allayed some of her fears but who were they fooling?

'To hell with the money. I want my wife beside me at Ravenswood – to see her beautiful face each morning, to walk along the river with her by my side, and to dine with her as the sun goes down. Have you any idea how lonely my life has been? How desperate? This is our second chance. We can do this, Luna. We *can* be happy.'

A bank of shifting cloud rolled in front of the moon and they briefly lost the scant light that they'd had for those first few moments. She could now hardly make out Marcus's face at all.

'Kiss me!' squawked Bran, who had been silently observing their heated exchange and decided to remind them both that he was still present. Luna's heart raced. In the darkness, did Marcus think she had uttered that request?

His shadow loomed closer and she felt his touch with a jolt, as his fingers brushed her neck. The warmth of him sent shivers up her spine and down her arms. Every hair on her body stood on end as he slid his large hand behind her shoulder and gently persuaded her closer, before dropping the most delicate of kisses on the scar from the witch scratching. The shock of this intimate gesture made her drop her bundle to the floor.

There was a pause, a seemingly inordinate amount of time when nothing happened, and then he brushed the jagged cut with his lips again and she thought she might die, there and then before the meadow path that led north back to Ravenswood, or south to the river and her freedom.

'Don't go,' he mumbled into her neck, his head bowed down, and his free arm sweeping around her back, locking her to him and preventing her stepping away. 'The ghosts are in your imagination. I promise I will protect you. Please don't leave me.'

She stood frozen, unable to rationalise a single thought careering through her head as every nerve ending focused on his touch and his heat. She took a deep breath, trying to steady her wobbly legs, but the scent of the large man before her only made her knees weaker.

'Don't go! Don't go!' Bran echoed, still behind the pair of them on the gate and bursting into life, flapping his wings and barring her exit.

But this wasn't just about Marcus and the troubles at Ravenswood. There had always been two strands to their story. He might believe he could resolve his past, but what about hers?

'I'm not a good person,' she said, dipping her head and trying to wriggle free from the man nestled against her collarbone. She knew this truth above all else. Would he want her to stay if he discovered the terrible thing she'd done? It was unlikely.

Her heart was torn. Her feelings for this sad and lonely man had been growing slowly and silently since his return from the city, and the strength of the pull between them was undeniable. Two broken people who together could be whole. And yet she had felt like this once before. She'd believed herself in love with Daniel, but perhaps he had merely offered an escape from her unsatisfactory life. How could she fall in love again so easily?

But fallen she had. By pretending that walking away from Ravenswood was in everyone's best interests, she was only deceiving herself. Her arms reached up to weave into Marcus's thick brown hair and she allowed him to share that truth with her.

Spurred on by her reaction, he traced his lips up to her ear and across her soft cheek until he found her mouth. Eager and unashamed of their feelings, there was nothing to stop them now, not even the knowledge that Bran's beady and rapidly blinking eyes were taking everything in.

Her chest heaved and her stomach rolled as their mouths engaged. She had never been kissed like this by anyone before, not even Daniel. She knew now that what she'd felt for the opinionated factory worker from Lowbridge hadn't been love, after all, because she'd never felt this all-consuming passion. She simply had to possess this man before her.

Their mouths eventually parted but their cheeks came to rest together, as their racing breaths began to slow down.

Without separating from him, her head dipped a second time.

'I'm damaged,' she said.

'And you think I'm not?'

'They are convinced I'm a witch.'

'Which means they do not doubt that you are my wife, and surely that fact alone offers you sanctuary? Anyone who claims otherwise will not be believed.'

Maybe it was better to be spat at as a witch than hanged as a murderer. She tipped her head back up to his. The clouds slid away from the moon, creating a window of light, illuminating his strong features.

'Whatever we face in the future, you must know that I am a man who stands by the commitments I make. When I promised in sickness and in health, I honoured that. When I promised not to enquire about your past, I honoured that, too. Know that I will never abandon you – not for one moment. I may have caused you to fall by the river, but I picked you up. I will *always* pick you up. You must trust me.'

She had so often been denied the things she had wanted in life. Could she possibly be allowed this one, wonderful thing?

He took a step back and put out his hand.

'Come home, Luna,' he begged, and she could see the desperation on his face. 'Where you belong.'

She reached out, and his large hand curled around her slender fingers, as she allowed him to pull her gently back to Ravenswood.

26

Luna and Marcus returned to the house after her foolish attempt to flee and walked back up the stairs together in silence. She could think of no words to say, afraid that speaking out loud would break the spell. He was still holding tightly on to her hand, like she might scamper off into the woods at any moment. And now the affection that they'd shown the outside world in their efforts to convince everyone, perhaps even themselves, that they were man and wife, had been established as real. He had kissed her and she had reciprocated.

Bran had been content when he realised she was no longer about to flee the Greybourne lands, and he flew off in the direction of the woods – the place he had been born to protect.

'Thank you for not leaving,' Marcus said as they stood in the dark corridor outside her room. 'My life and my health have improved so dramatically since April. I now wake every morning with a light heart and an eager anticipation to discover what the day holds. I should have made it clearer that you were the reason for this, and not given you cause to run.'

He paused and she wondered what would happen now. They weren't married in any legal or moral sense of the word, despite the constant pretence that they were. There was genuine affection between them, and their kisses had established this was no platonic friendship, but she didn't know whether he would act on this and take their feelings further. Could he see the fear in her eyes? Could he feel the slight tremble in her hand?

'I shall see you at breakfast.' He planted a soft kiss on the top of her head and let her fingers slide from his, before retreating down the hall. Had she been expecting him to follow her into the bedroom? And was she disappointed or relieved that he hadn't?

It took her a long time to fall asleep that night, such were her muddled emotions. So, she was to stay and he did care for her, as she cared for him. But she still couldn't shake the feeling that their time together was running out.

* * *

Love was a far simpler thing than she'd imagined. She could not understand why it had perplexed so many scholars and poets over the centuries. It was merely allowing yourself to be cared for, whilst you cared for someone in return. You did not have to declare your feelings with flowery or elegant words, nor did you have to undertake romantic gestures or let that person consume you. It was comfortable and calming, supportive and empowering. As long as they were by your side, nothing else mattered.

Luna and Marcus continued their fraudulent marriage, but they'd been playing husband and wife for so long now that the recent shift in their relationship came naturally. She had called him darling and looked at him with adoration long before their genuine affection had been established, because she believed any loving wife would have done so. Now, however, she meant every endearment and there was real love behind every adoring gaze.

The subtle change was apparent to the shrewd housekeeper. She walked into the dining room with a breakfast tray the next morning, just as her master was kissing Luna goodbye. He was off to Manbury for the day but might as well have been about to set sail for Ceylon, such was the passionate nature of their parting.

After he'd left for the ferry, Mrs Webber returned to clear the table and smiled at her mistress.

'Ah, today of all days, that you should find such happiness with each other...' Luna frowned, wondering what she meant. 'It's ten years to the day since they wed. I only know the date because she would wear black and go about the house wailing, marking it as a day to mourn, rather than celebrate.'

'Surely, the start of the marriage was happy?' Luna asked. 'Before her... my health really deteriorated?'

The housekeeper shrugged and lowered her voice.

'It weren't ever love. Lust, maybe, but the previous cook told me the woman weren't ever right. Sometimes, she appeared fine, sitting peacefully at the front of the house and watching the river. Other days she would head into the woods, screaming and crying, as brambles tore at her arms and twigs cut her feet, not even aware of her pain. A stream of doctors came and went, but nothing eased her restless mind, and she began tormenting others. Younger girls who worked at the house were scratched and clawed at when her mood were dark, and she was spiteful to the animals – whipping the horses, killing the master's dogs and drowning the feral cats from the barn. The staff gradually left and visitors stopped coming to the house.'

Marcus hadn't said anything about the day marking ten years of marriage, but then he probably didn't want to be reminded of his folly. Poor man, marrying in haste. He'd had all that time to repent at his leisure, as the old saying went.

'Please do try to remember that I am Mrs Greybourne,' Luna said, wary of being overheard. 'I don't want Hattie or Oscar thinking otherwise.'

Mrs Webber dipped her head in apology.

'It's obvious to anyone with eyes that you really care for each other,' the older woman said, picking up the tray from the table. 'I ain't seen love like this in a marriage for a long time. It certainly never existed in mine,' she added, forlornly.

'Why did you and Mr Webber marry?' It was an intrusive question but their relationship was closer than mistress and servant. She'd never felt superior to this hard-working lady and, besides, she was curious.

'It's what you do.' Mrs Webber shrugged. 'If you ain't married by twenty, there's something wrong with you. Jed had a good job at the time, before he started spending most of his wages at The Red Lion and looking to pastures new to have his fun. He was kinder to me back then, but we didn't have a lot in common, apart from our lustful yearnings. We're all driven by them, but most of us know that it ain't right, unless we've got a ring on our finger. And by the time I realised I'd picked the wrong one, and no kiddies were gonna come along, it was too late.'

This most intimate of acts was the one thing missing from Luna's marriage. Every night Marcus left her at the bedroom door like the gentleman that he was, but it was something she thought about more and more. His touch electrified her. To be honest, even a look could ignite tiny fires of desire in places that made her knees tremble. And she knew, because men could not hide the physical effect that a woman was having on them, that his reactions to her were just as powerful. But they weren't married and such an act would be wrong in the eyes of God, and He already had just cause to condemn her.

Luna hadn't thought much about not wearing a wedding ring until Mrs Webber's comments, so it was quite the coincidence that Marcus should resolve this issue when he returned that very afternoon.

'I picked something up in Manbury for you,' he said, placing himself on the sofa next to her. 'I think it's appropriate to pass it over today. We can't have strangers thinking you are unmarried and available, when you have a husband who cares for you *very* much.' He slipped a small circular leather box from his pocket and flipped open the hinged lid to reveal a simple gold band.

She took the ring from its cushioning. She needed, and had asked for, very little since arriving at the house – only her safety. They rarely had visitors, and she naturally wore gloves when they'd walked to the village, but if she was to win over the sceptical, then he was right: not having a wedding ring would look odd.

'I hope it fits,' he said, his eyes darting between her face and the box. 'Obviously, it's not as ornate as the previous one but I hope it will suffice. I was more financially secure back then.' She moved to slip it on but his hand halted hers.

'No, God witnessed me place this on my wife's finger ten years ago, and I must do so now.'

He took it from her and made sure her eyes were focused on his.

'I do,' he said.

'I do,' she repeated, as they both paused to appreciate the significance of the moment.

The sash window dropped with an almighty bang but Luna chose not to let it distract her. If this was the ghost of his wife displaying her displeasure – and it was a big *if* – then it was only because she knew she had been successfully replaced. Marcus loved her. She could see it in his eyes, feel it in the way his hand was lingering on hers.

'It's perfect. Thank you.' It was a tight fit but it would have to be cut from her finger, as far as she was concerned, because from that moment, she had no intention of ever removing it voluntarily. Whatever was coming for them, and she had no doubt something would, either from his past or hers, they would face it together. Man and wife.

She lifted her legs from the floor and curled them beneath her, leaning into his broad shoulder, delighting in the way he pulled her closer and rested his head against hers. They didn't need to fill the silence with words. They were now familiar enough with each other to enjoy the still moments, and she happily concentrated on the sensation of his warmth seeping into her skin, the familiar musky scent of him, and the steady rhythm of his breathing. In its own way, this acknowledgement of how he affected her senses was a conversation of sorts.

After a while, Luna looked up to Marcus and realised that he had fallen asleep. He'd been working so hard on the house and gardens over recent days, that she wasn't surprised that he was exhausted. Mrs Webber entered to collect the tea tray. Before she had the chance to speak, Luna nodded at the sleeping man and put a finger to her lips, and then held out her hand to the housekeeper to show off the ring. The older woman's toothless smile became even broader as she reached for Luna's hand and gave it an encouraging squeeze, before scooping up the tray and returning to the kitchens.

A distant rumble of thunder and a darkening sky persuaded her to slip from Marcus's arms and walk to the window to investigate, opening it up again to allow the air to circulate. The rain came suddenly: heavy drops relentlessly pummelling the earth and bashing down the tall grasses and delicate blooms, but the smells that drifted in from the small crack of open window were heavenly. It was still a wonder to her that their chance collision on the path by the river had led to all this. The meadow was hers to wander through, and she could gather any flowers she chose to decorate this large country house that she was now mistress of. She could call on her housekeeper to prepare a specific menu, her maid to draw a bath or light a fire. But the sleeping man on the sofa... Could she ask things of him too?

'What a shame about the weather,' Marcus said, making her jump as he came up behind her and slid his arms about her waist. The storm had woken him. 'I don't much like the rain.'

'I don't mind it. It washes the grime away, and everything smells so fresh when it's moved on.'

They stood together like that for some time, watching as the storm slunk closer, until it was overhead, lighting up the sky with dramatic white electric slashes and simultaneously rumbling in discontent.

Later, they walked up the stairs together, as they did every night, and he kissed her on the head, as was their routine. He hesitated for longer than usual, and she wondered if the giving of a ring had changed anything between them – somehow legitimised their sham marriage. She looked at him, her heart accelerating and every intimate part of her coming alive with anticipation, and tried to convey the deep longing she felt, but she would not speak the words aloud; she would not beg him to come to her. He took half a step forward and she felt her breath catch in her throat, before he froze.

'Happy anniversary,' he said, and then spun about and retreated to his room. In the end, she decided that as a God-fearing man, who knelt in the Greybourne family pews every Sunday morning and made promises to live a sinless and honest life, if he had not come to her that night, then he probably never would.

Alone in her bed, disappointed that Marcus still felt he had no right to her body, she knew the ghost of his wife, dead or not, was haunting them both. She scanned the room for signs that Luna was present – there to mock her for her failure to bed Marcus – but there was nothing.

'He's mine,' she whispered into the air. 'You had him for all those years and failed to appreciate what you had. I love him like you never did and I will treasure him. It's *you* who needs to leave.'

She waited nervously for a drop in temperature, a scampering shadow or any inexplicable and disturbing reflections in the window-panes, but there was nothing. Was this their moment of contented calm before the storm?

And then the wardrobe door swung open to remind her of the carved and jagged words within.

She is coming.
She will replace me.
She must die…

27

ELOISE

Spring had not only sprung in Lowbridge, but also done a complete cartwheel, and Eloise was happily filling her days with preparations for Easter. She made pretty cards from brightly coloured paper, blew and decorated eggs, and filled the house with elaborate floral arrangements using simple flowers and blossom cut from the meadows and hedgerows. The delicious smell of simnel cake drifted through the rooms and she heroically marched through Lent.

This most joyous of seasons was heartily welcomed by everyone as winter had been long and dreary, and Eloise, in particular, was glad to see the back of it. At least in Branchester, she had been able to visit the theatre occasionally and call on a much wider circle of friends. It was not that she hadn't been invited places – money made you delightfully popular and there were always a handful of dinner parties and other social events to attend – but the snow had been brutal that year, cutting them off for most of February. For the first time in over a decade, parts of the river had frozen over, and Rose said that even Daniel had been driven to abandon his swimming in such extreme conditions.

During this time of isolation, Eloise became increasingly close to her maid – someone she belatedly realised was a bright girl who had been hindered by unfortunate family circumstances. The pair began a friendship of sorts, where they revelled in village gossip and girlish speculation regarding the young Mr Thornbury. She was surprised to learn that Rose was also a reader, although of novels and novelettes, rather than the more serious texts she was attempting to tackle in her quest to impress Daniel.

'I attended the large girls' school in town,' Rose explained, 'and we had a particularly kindly teacher who recognised me as keen and even loaned me some of her own books, encouraging my learning. But when my mother died, my father, who was a clerk in a large shipping company, did not cope well. Eventually, he could no longer afford the fees, and I had to go into service.'

Eloise remembered something her mother had said about the man winding up a drunk, but didn't want to embarrass Rose by saying as much. Their upbringings had probably not been very different, but the fickle vagaries of fate had seen to the downward spiral of Rose's life, and the glorious advancement of her own.

Lowbridge was growing on her, and she was missing Branchester less and less, largely because the thing that made her happiest lived not two hundred yards from her front door. Daniel's intellect impressed her, his opinions excited her, his face pleased her and his refusal to make the chase easy gave her the biggest thrill of all. He became an increasingly frequent visitor at Church View, calling to see her father about work-related matters, but always happy to talk about books with her, and occasionally politics. Eloise enjoyed their lively conversation, and he delighted in both shocking her and proving her wrong. She was in love and it consumed all her waking hours. If she was not surreptitiously observing the object of her earnest affections from afar, or contriving reasons for their paths to cross in the village, she was planning their future life.

She subscribed to several ladies' periodicals, lapping up the articles on the roles of wives and mothers, and indulged in frivolous romantic novels recommended by Rose, finding them a welcome break from her more serious reading. Love was everywhere she looked: from the lambs leaping across the open fields behind their house, to the boxing hares at the fringes of the woodland. And, on that particular morning, it was flaunted before her very eyes, as her parents reminded her what a happy marriage entailed.

Everything in the Haughtons' more financially secure world continued to flourish. Her father had recently expanded his business interests, taking over a struggling shoemaker's. Without money worries, and enjoying the very best of what life had to offer, her parents were more adoring of each other than ever. Thank goodness her mother was approaching her fiftieth year and there was no danger of their family unexpectedly growing in size. The disruption would be too much to bear.

'My cousin has written to say she will be a grandmother by the autumn,' her mother said, a sheet of cream paper in her hand.

'It must be the season,' her father said, his eyes not leaving those of his wife for one moment. 'A time for new beginnings, when Mother Nature is at her most fertile.'

'I am almost certain that the schoolmaster's wife is expecting again,' she agreed. 'It's far too early for her to be announcing it, but she looked quite sickly and pale yesterday; a sure sign that she's in the family way. I blame that snow; we were all shut in with little to do.'

They exchanged a knowing look and Eloise rolled her eyes.

'I've lost at least three female workers to imminent matrimony,' he bemoaned. 'And I think even young Thornbury is preparing to embrace such a fate. He will be particularly keen to progress in the company if he is to have a wife to support.'

Eloise sat up straighter and the periodical she'd been reading fell into her lap.

'Oh?'

Her father's startled eyes met hers. 'I shouldn't have let that slip, so please forget I said anything. He spoke to me in confidence.'

Damn the young man for his smoke and mirrors games, but part of her was thrilled by his nerve. The pretence he executed that he was indifferent to her just made her all the keener, and he knew that. He was truly a match for her, with his outward display of indifference concealing the real strength of feeling underneath. Oh, what a wedding night they would have because, ever since the kiss in the sweet chestnut grove, she knew the truth. Perhaps her father would now consider him for the role of manager at the recently acquired shoemaker's. With an engagement on the horizon, Daniel must be promoted to a position of authority. Her mother certainly would not support a match to a mere foreman.

'I shall be the very soul of discretion,' she assured her father, who was now playfully kissing his wife's neck, as her mother tittered like a small girl. Eloise smiled, anticipating the day she would be so cherished.

* * *

Most of Lowbridge had been persuaded to attend a small benefit concert in the school rooms and Lady Fletcher had agreed to introduce the local quartet, so the Haughtons simply had to attend. But Eloise had never been so bored in her life... with the exception of the tedious cricket matches.

For a man imminently to propose, Daniel had been behaving most peculiarly all evening. He was not his usual outspoken self and was definitely more introspective. But then, it was a momentous occasion – asking a girl for her hand – when there was always the chance your hopes could be dashed by her refusal. But *she* would not tease or keep him guessing at her reply. She'd waited too long for the question.

Engineering an encounter during the interval, she followed him outside, and stood watching him for a moment as he rolled his cigarette, before making herself known by stepping into the pool of lamplight that surrounded him.

'You can kiss me, if you like.'

Daniel's face clouded with confusion as Eloise joined him on a wooden bench in the schoolyard, overlooking the green.

'Why would I want to kiss you?' He frowned and tucked the cigarette behind his ear, knowing it was impolite to smoke in the presence of a lady.

'You surely can't be fearful of accusations of impropriety now?' She thought back to his comments in the grove. 'I didn't have you pegged as so prudish. After all, the God that you don't believe in can hardly judge you for such an action if he doesn't exist.'

'What *are* you talking about, Miss Haughton?'

He looked at her as though she had quite lost her mind, but she just knew that he was holding back the urge to grin. Her whole body thrilled at his continuation of the charade. Perhaps, even after they were married, when they were alone in the bedroom and as a prelude to their lovemaking, she might be bold enough to suggest he still sometimes called her 'miss'. There was something inexplicably arousing about him deferring to her in this way, when they both knew that he would be in complete control sexually. *Had he already been with a woman?* she wondered to herself, a part of her rather hoping he had. How tiresome if neither of them knew what to do in that department.

'I don't know why you are being so coy.' She was cross now. Why was he still playing this silly game of indifference? 'I know you have asked my father for my hand, and my answer will be yes, so shall we dispense with the teasing? I have been so patient over the last few months, but to continue to deny me even a kiss, is beyond ridiculous.'

She bit tentatively at her bottom lip and leaned towards him. There was still the lingering smell of shoe leather emanating from him. It was a scent she remembered from when her father used to spend his days in the factory. It was masculine and intoxicating all at once.

Daniel shook his head slowly from side to side and let out a measured sigh. 'You're incredible.' She was about to thank him for the compliment but as he continued it became apparent that his words were mocking. 'I have made it abundantly clear that I have no romantic interest in you. And yet spoilt Eloise Haughton truly believes that because she desires a thing, it will be hers. Yes, I have spoken to your father about my future plans, and have even secured a modest ring, but it was not intended for you. I am in love with someone else—'

'Someone else?' She was incredulous. 'But you have few friends and rub most people up the wrong way.'

'I have a very *dear* friend, who I have spent much time with in recent months, and who has utterly and completely won my heart. A plucky girl, who is kind to others and even knows how to swim. She is bright and questioning, and admirably calm in a crisis...'

Suddenly, Eloise had the sickening realisation where this was going.

How could she have been so blind? All this time, she thought she had an ally in her quest to win over this challenging man. But she had been betrayed in the most calculated way. She did not let her eyes leave his, finding the courage to hear the truth she knew was coming.

'I am completely in love with, and fully intend to propose to, your maid, Rose.'

28

It was September. The swallows had left for warmer climes, the nights were drawing in, and everyone was needed to bring in the harvests – womenfolk and children included. It was a time for the community to pull together. Marcus, for the first time in several years, was no longer tied to the house with the care of his wife, and had offered to help out at a neighbouring farmstead. The farmer, whose wheat fields bordered Greybourne lands, had lost his oldest son to pneumonia three years ago and his wife to a tumour the summer after that. Although not friends, the man had never given Marcus any trouble, and certainly never made accusations of witchcraft against Luna for his misfortunes, as those in the village itself had been prone to do.

The man was grateful for any assistance, and even more so when Luna had turned up to help. She was young and relatively fit, and decided that sitting at home alone, missing Marcus, was serving no useful purpose. So, when anticipated bad weather threatened to spoil the harvest, she decided to be brave and offer her services. Keeping her head low and avoiding conversation with the other labourers, she joined the women who were gathering the wheat up into sheaves, not once complaining of her aching limbs or the long hours. Some people avoided her, but on the whole, everyone was too busy to indulge in gossip or name-calling.

Marcus was engaged in the much more physical task of scything, and Luna couldn't help but admire her strapping husband as he worked tirelessly to harvest the grain and beat the forecast rain. After a week of back-breaking work and very little sleep, the fields were scattered with drying sheaves, propped together in stooks, and the threatened downpours blessedly failed to arrive, much to everyone's relief.

'We have been invited to the harvest supper in Little Doubton,' Marcus announced the Sunday after the harvest moon. 'You helped to gather in the wheat so should be part of the celebrations. Despite our previous venture into the village ending in disaster, I would like to remind everyone of your face and offer further proof that you are no danger to anyone. Talk of your good work in the fields has spread, and the surprise avoidance of the storms has even been attributed to your presence.' He rolled his eyes to demonstrate what he thought of such superstitious poppycock.

'But many still think I'm a witch. Working in our neighbour's fields is one thing, but to eat, drink and make merry with these people is quite the risk.'

'I'll protect you,' he said, drawing her close. 'I promise.'

* * *

The supper was held in a large barn three miles down the road from Ravenswood and, although the evenings were getting darker earlier and the temperatures were plummeting, it was a pleasant walk. But then, anything she undertook with Marcus was a joy. Just to be near him made her heart sing.

As they approached the bustling barn, the heat of the fire and the sounds of revelry hit them. They stood in the wide doorway and she could see thick garlands of hops, dotted with corn dolls, hanging from the walls, and small candles in glass jars placed in clusters, giving a soft orange light to the space. The food smells were mouth-watering, particularly the spit-roasted pig, which had clearly been cooking for several hours. Two men were lifting it down, ready to distribute it amongst the guests, and music filled the air from the ruddy-faced chap playing a fiddle in the back corner. A woman in a white apron, who was handing around jugs of ale, beckoned them in.

Central to the scene were two long tables made by balancing boards and large doors across trestles, with rows of benches either side. A group of farm labourers shuffled up and made room for them at one end. Marcus sat himself next to the lads to shield Luna from their coarse chatter.

She looked down the length of the table before her at the platters piled high with fruits and roasted vegetables, and loaves baked into the shape of wheatsheaves sat next to pats of rich golden butter. The Greybourne lands were not arable, being largely woodland, but Mr Webber and Oscar had gathered a large basket of hazelnuts and Marcus handed them to a passing serving lad to be added to the feast.

As the fiddler played on and the chatter increased in volume, possibly due to the consumption of the ale, Luna allowed herself to relax. She belatedly noticed the Webbers were present, although not sitting together. Instead, Jed was paying an undue amount of attention to the woman sitting across from him. Perhaps she was one of the 'pastures new' Mr Webber was exploring in his reckless unfaithfulness.

Salutations were drunk to 'the maiden' – the last sheaf of corn standing – and then everyone was invited to eat. A cacophony of noise and clanking cutlery ensued. Marcus engaged with the men next to him from time to time, but spent much of the meal focused on his wife and her well-being. When everyone had eaten their fill, there was a request for help to clear and move the tables to ready the space for dancing, and Luna stood in the shadows, happy to watch the spinning revellers. The evening had passed without incident, and she didn't want to draw attention to herself by cavorting around the barn.

A small child careered into her, and Marcus told her he belonged to the woman who had so captured Webber's attentions earlier. A widow, who apparently lived out the other side of the woods, and still managed to produce offspring every couple of years, even though she remained husbandless. Luna then noticed her own husband's jaw clench as a tall man with a shock of red unruly hair and a long, thin face approached them.

'It's Doctor Gardener. You will be expected to remember him from when we first married,' he prompted.

'Mr Greybourne,' the man said, holding out his hand. 'You are looking remarkably well, dear fellow. I was quite worried about you the last time we spoke so I am heartily glad to see you much improved.'

The two gentlemen shook hands.

'And who do we have here?' He turned to Luna.

'Do you not remember my wife, Doctor? I appreciate it has been a few years since you examined her but she cannot have altered so very much.' He was challenging the man to contradict him and there were tell-tale signs of his anxiety. The men exchanged a look before the doctor turned his attention fully towards her.

There was a beat before he replied. 'Ah, yes, I understand you favour the treatments offered by Mr Findlay. Is it him we have to thank for your *remarkable* recovery? It is like looking at a new woman.' He was not fooled for a moment and she could not bring herself to answer, as the man turned back to her husband. 'Mr Findlay continues to confound me with his alternative cures and, although I am aware of the healing properties of many of his herbal remedies, he clouds the issue with his white magic. Jovial fellow for all that, and he's had remarkable success with the dairy farmer's tumour. But I'm a man of science, Mr Greybourne, as you know, and struggle with the idea that chanting a few mystical words can have any effect on a person's health.'

'That is something I wholeheartedly agree with,' her husband replied.

'Is praying to God so very different?' Luna dared to voice. She knew Mr Findlay had used magic to heal her ankle and would not have the man unfairly maligned. Despite Marcus's prejudice, she still suspected there might come a time when they would be glad of his services. Dark things were on the horizon and they would be in desperate need of the light. She was increasingly convinced that Luna Greybourne was haunting her; the face in the window, the words in the dust, the sounds in the attics – even the woman running from the house. She thought it had been a real person but all she'd seen was a flash of green cloak disappear into the woods. If the woman wished her harm – the prophecy in the wardrobe still on her mind – Mr Findlay might be the only person who could keep her safe.

'My husband insists that magic is only real if you believe in it,' she continued, 'so by that logic, I suggest that if someone tells you your malady will improve, and you truly believe them, it may indeed lead to an improvement in your condition. Is that not at the very core of our faith, after all? Something that is not tangible – God – but that has the power to make a tangible difference to our lives. We are all good Christians, I'm sure. We pray and our prayers are answered by an entity we don't understand. The power of God is magic of a sort, so surely we can't discount all magic.'

Luna saw the vein in Marcus's neck throb as he narrowed his eyes, becoming agitated. 'Now is hardly the time to have a philosophical debate, my dear. Apologies, Doctor. My wife is not used to ale and we should be returning home. Darling, please fetch your shawl.'

Marcus gripped her elbow and gently propelled her towards the barn doors, remaining to finish his conversation with the doctor. Luna had not drunk ale, but didn't mind. He was saving face and she had overstepped the mark. As she sifted through the pile of abandoned coats, she caught the end of their conversation. It was not an angry exchange, but both men were quite definite in their assertions.

'Look here, Greybourne, you must be aware that as a man of science, I know that a twenty-eight-year-old woman cannot shrink several inches, nor can she change her eye colour. I am not one to seek out mischief, and you have been a good friend to me in years gone by, but as your so-called wife pointed out, I am also a man of God,' the doctor continued. 'I like and respect you enormously. I don't know how you have managed over the last few years, and I admire the sacrifices you've made, but if I am asked to swear an oath on the Good Book, know that I will not commit perjury for you.'

'I understand and would not ask otherwise. Equally, I will stand in a court of law and willingly proclaim that she is my wife of ten years, and only God will know the truth. Do excuse me. Luna is waiting.'

Marcus walked over to her and looped his arm through hers, waltzing her out of the barn. As she stepped into the night, a blinding pain shot through her eye to the back of her head. It only lasted a moment but it was enough to unsettle her, and was probably just a result of the tension with the doctor.

Although the evening had largely been a success, it was perfectly obvious that the villagers were split in their beliefs; the uneducated and more superstitious amongst them were convinced she was the Ravenswood Witch, responsible for all their misfortunes, from the failure of their butter to churn to the baby born with a withered arm. The more educated members of Little Doubton knew damn well she wasn't who she claimed to be, and these were the people she worried about. How long before the tinker spoke up, or Doctor Gardener had words with the constable and rumours of her true identity began to circulate?

29

Every evening Luna parted from Marcus in the corridor, and every night she lay awake hoping to hear his approaching footsteps, for the door handle to turn and her husband to come to her bed. But she remained disappointed. That slender band of precious metal had, however, given her a courage she hadn't felt before. Even speaking up in front of the doctor was something she would not have considered doing a few short weeks ago, despite Marcus's ensuing, if short-lived, sulk.

It was she who suggested that they start to attend the services at St Mary's on a Sunday together – something she understood his real wife had never done, not so much as stepping foot in the churchyard once after her wedding day. He was delighted with her proposal, convinced that it would further add to the villagers' acceptance of her, especially should she stand on hallowed ground and not immediately shrivel up and die. The vicar would rejoice in the godless Luna returning to the fold and celebrate her salvation.

Mrs Webber walked to Little Doubton with them on the Sunday morning, delighted her mistress was now a churchgoer. Interestingly, the older woman had no problem squaring her faith in God with her belief in the supernatural, much as Doctor Gardener happily reconciled his religion with his scientific beliefs.

There was a gasp from some of the congregation as Luna stepped through the lychgate, walked up the gravel path and entered the south door, without bursting into flame. The irony, of course, was that as she knelt penitently on her knees, with her head bowed, and prayed for forgiveness for her own unspeakable acts, she secretly longed for Marcus to transgress and commit sins of the flesh with her.

'Perhaps folk will be more friendly now that we are seen to be a Christian household. The vicar does look at me queer sometimes, as though your previous outrageous behaviour might be contagious.' Mrs Webber rolled her eyes. 'It's bad enough being judged for Jed's sins.'

'Does he not attend?' Luna asked.

'You'd think he'd be here every week to atone for what he did, wouldn't you? Reckons he paid his price with his gaol time, but it's not like that's his only transgression.'

Luna wondered if she was referring to the beatings he gave his wife, or his immoral sexual behaviour. Probably both.

'He says stepping into the church makes him feel funny.' She shrugged. 'Won't so much as put his foot in the churchyard.'

Was there more to it than that, though? Perhaps the man couldn't step on hallowed ground in case *he* burst into flames. Maybe he was the one leaving the poppets at the well and invoking the Devil?

Over the next couple of weeks, the face of the woman she'd replaced occasionally appeared in the window or the mirror, but she didn't mention it to anyone, worried they might think she was going mad. Added to which, her mysterious headaches returned intermittently – a shooting pain that lasted a few seconds and then dwindled to nothing. She didn't want to worry Marcus or consult Dr Gardener, so she initially kept it to herself, but after spotting Mr Webber creep across the back gardens and enter the woods in the middle of the night again, she decided to confront the man, wondering if her strange heads were the result of him sticking pins into some effigy of her.

'I've seen you leaving the house in the early hours and should like to know where you go.'

'Well now, that ain't your business, to my mind. You ain't my wife and

I don't have to account for myself when I'm off duty. Besides, you're not really the mistress of Ravenswood and we both know it.'

'I am Luna Greybourne and if you wish to keep your job, I strongly suggest you speak to me with more respect.'

She was getting braver at standing up for herself, but the surly manservant grunted in response. 'You've got no idea of the power of that well, 'ave you?' he said, leaning closer, a snarl across his lips. 'There's all sorts happening in them woods, stuff that would make your hair curl. My foolish wife thinks she can protect herself from it all with a few silly charms, but the evil that's out there won't be stopped by a twig wrapped in red thread. You need to leave Ravenswood, young lady, because you'll either end up sucked into it all and be dancing round bonfires before you know it, or become a victim, and I honestly couldn't say which is worse.'

His rough face loomed large and she felt threatened. What she didn't know was whether the man was giving her some friendly advice – run while you can – or telling her, that if she insisted on staying, he would see to it that she suffered.

She regretted confronting Webber and increasingly suspected him of being behind her headaches – something that was confirmed in her mind when Bran came to her room one night, and dropped a poppet on the bed. The crude clay figure was female, with a pin driven into the very place on her head that was causing her so much pain, but the most disturbing thing about it was that 'Luna' was scratched across the torso; there was no ambiguity over who this doll represented. One thing was certain: someone wished her ill and, as Bran never left the Ravenswood lands, the person responsible was highly likely to be someone close to home.

For the first time, she considered that Mr Webber might be in contact with the spirit world. He'd admitted to seeing strange things in the woods. What if he was the one conjuring up the souls of the dead? If he'd had a physical relationship with Mrs Greybourne when she'd been alive, then he would have a motive to drive her imposter out. Luna now felt certain Marcus's wife was dead – the missing woman's presence in the house was too real for her to be safely tucked away in an asylum. The manservant, maybe still in love with his former mistress, was in league with her ghost and they'd been conducting a campaign of terror against her since she'd first arrived. She knew him to be capable of violence, but was her life in danger?

Despite everything in her body telling her that Marcus would not forgive her, she knew that there was only one person who would understand how terrified this discovery made her, and who might be able to offer advice regarding the odious Mr Webber.

* * *

Luna decided to pay Findlay another visit, but deliberately waited until Bran was in the woods before she slipped from the house. Marcus was shut in the study, which so far was just a large desk and small pile of books on the floor, to attend to business correspondence. Now that he was able to focus his attentions on his financial affairs, his investments were proving incredibly lucrative. She told him that she wanted to visit St Mary's for quiet prayer and would not be gone long. He was cursing his inability to locate an important document, and, preoccupied, merely nodded his acknowledgement.

As she walked down to the pretty whitewashed cottage, there was a small part of her that felt guilty for disobeying her husband, but if he would not accept that the supernatural was at play here, she would speak to someone who did. The bright red hips and haws were a portend of a harsh winter, but September had been mild and the trees were unusually late to display their fiery sunset of leaves. Within a few weeks they would fall and the only colour would be from the evergreens.

Mr Findlay answered the door wearing a deep-purple waistcoat and with his hair sticking up in tufts. Now that the weather was cooler, he had a bright blue knitted scarf wrapped several times around his neck.

'Luna! What a surprise. I didn't think you'd be allowed to visit once Mr Greybourne had returned.' He ushered her inside, clearly delighted to find her on his doorstep.

'He doesn't know I'm here,' she was forced to admit. 'He thinks I've headed to St Mary's.'

The cunning man raised a white, bushy eyebrow and grinned. 'A delightfully clever move, my dear. Let them see Luna repents her sins and is embracing the church. Win the vicar round and the congregation will surely follow. Unfortunately, the reverend and I do not see eye to eye over my use of divination through the tarot and my unorthodox communications with the spirits of those who have moved on. To his mind, it is one step away from summoning the Devil, but he fails to understand that it is merely the departed wishing to reassure their loved ones that they are at peace.' He pointed to a small crucifix on the wall. 'I worship in my own way, and am not convinced you need to be in a centuries-old stone building to have a relationship with the Lord. Ultimately, it is the good deeds that we perform and the honest and unselfish ways that we live our lives that are the best way to honour Him.'

She agreed completely. Mr Findlay had kept her secrets and been kind to her from the beginning. Mrs Webber told her how desperate people came to him when the vicar had condemned their moral lapses or the doctor failed to heal their ailments, and how he eased their troubled minds when they were genuinely afraid of things relating to the spirit world.

As she entered his cosy home, the same sharp pain pierced her head. She groaned and placed her palm across one eye, as Mr Findlay rushed to her side and helped her to a seat.

'What on earth is wrong, dear lady?'

She explained about the repeated episodes and he nodded, before busying himself by mixing up a selection of herbs to make a tea that he assured her would help.

'We cannot be certain it is ill-wishing, but I suspect someone is sticking a pin into a likeness of you as we speak. I'd hoped you would win the local people round. Mrs Cole spoke very highly of you and your help with the harvest when I was last in the village. Your presence at the celebration was welcomed, so they are surely reassessing their unjust vilification of the Ravenswood Witch.'

'I think it might be someone closer to home and that Mr Webber is the person you warned me about. He's been practising witchcraft by the well at night, and summoning the ghost of the Ravenswood Witch. Summoning Luna Greybourne,' she clarified.

'You've seen her?' he asked, and she nodded.

'She wants me gone from Ravenswood, or possibly even dead.' She cast her eyes to the floor. 'Of course she does; I've been trying to convince everyone that I am her.'

Mr Findlay came over to her and reached for her hand. He gave it a squeeze, passing no judgement on her actions.

'I told you that she had passed on. She has visited me, too, and is trying to tell me the truth of her passing, but she never was a woman who made much sense in life, and I fear she is even more confused in death.' He gave half a smile. 'It worries me that her rage will be unjustly directed at you when you are an entirely innocent party in all of this.'

He walked back to his shelves and began to rummage amongst the bottles and jars, tipping a quantity of something into a small cotton bag.

'I will send you home with some dried sage to throw on your fire and dispel the evil in the house. Placing small piles of salt in the corners of your bedroom will help to protect you at night. I'm concerned that Mr Greybourne was responsible for her demise and we know he has a temper, so you must keep this all to yourself.'

'But he is wrong about you,' she pointed out. 'Especially when all you have ever done is help me. In many ways he is a very stubborn man, and his refusal to accept there are things in this world that defy explanation is one of them.' She paused. 'But I think, equally, you are wrong about him. I think he did his best for Luna and cared for her, in his way, as I care for him.'

Mr Findlay looked up from stirring the teapot.

'Ah. I thought I sensed a change in you.' He poured her a small mug of the fragrant tea and placed it on the table next to her. She took a few sips and immediately felt calmer.

'The cards have told me many things, and that there will be an increased affection between the two of you is one of them.' He smiled. 'That you truly care for him is good news, indeed. Perhaps I am wrong about Luna's death. It has been known to happen on occasion,' he joked. His blue eyes twinkled. 'She was my friend but, of course, I only ever heard her side of the story. It is not impossible that she was manipulating the truth. If you are happy with Marcus, then I am happy.'

There was something about his crinkled eyes and soft smile that invited honesty.

'More than I have a right to be,' she admitted.

'I noticed the wedding band when you removed your gloves,' the astute man said. 'And from the pink across your cheeks and breathlessness when you speak his name, do I detect an improvement in relations between yourself and your husband? Has this companionship developed into something more... intimate?'

'We are not living *truly* as man and wife,' she said, wriggling in her seat as her cheeks grew even hotter. She wasn't prepared to admit the frequent carnal thoughts of Marcus that consumed her days and interrupted her dreams. She had been slow to admit her feelings to herself. 'There is a fondness there, to be sure, but perhaps more akin to brother and sister.'

Their shared kisses and racing heartbeats were no one's business but theirs, yet Mr Findlay's delight at this piece of information was plain to see. He even dug out some biscuits from a tin on a low table near the fire.

'I dearly hope that will change with time. If she died at his hand, then perhaps he was forced by her actions. I do not say that he is a bad man, but suggest he might be someone who has done a bad thing. He deserves to find love. I don't think he ever had that with her.'

She was keen to move the conversation away from any possible future relations between her and Marcus and back to the threat she felt from her manservant.

'Could Mr Webber have been responsible for Mother Selwood's death? We only have his word that she was cursed by the Ravenswood Witch.'

Mr Findlay took the seat opposite her.

'The man was undoubtedly there when it happened, lurking about the woods doing goodness knows what. He carried her back to Ravenswood and his wife sought my help. She had, without doubt, been struck down with a terrible apoplexy. But let us remember that Mother Selwood fancied herself a witch, so was not an innocent in this story. People forget that she went around cursing people herself, and was rather put out that a younger, more... exotic woman was stealing her thunder. I understand she confronted her about it at the well that night. There was an argument and Luna cursed her. She was forever cursing people – even me on occasion.'

This explained how Bran had picked the phrase up. Was he also clever enough to associate it with anger? He'd certainly been mad at the Kelling boy for stealing the spoon.

'But the apoplexy could have equally been brought on by the very agitated nature of their confrontation,' Luna pointed out, trying to find a rational explanation for the whole thing, and Mr Findlay shrugged.

'In the end, it was all rumour and guesswork. The constable didn't trust Webber as he had form, and Luna was taking opiates and remembered none of it, although happily claimed the cursing. She wanted people to believe she was a real threat, and a dead woman certainly enhanced her reputation as a witch. Everyone gave the Greybournes an even wider berth after that, and they'd hardly been neighbourly with them beforehand.'

Luna frowned. So, Mr Webber had been the only witness and Luna had been so drugged that she couldn't remember the incident. Was it just Luna that Mrs Webber carried her amulets and charms to protect herself from? Hadn't Mr Findlay told her that men could be witches, too?

Conscious of the time, Luna drank her tea. She should be returning to Ravenswood.

'I meant it when I said that you are welcome here any time – day or night – if you ever feel in danger. Please trust no one, and I do mean *no one* at the house. There is undoubtedly great peril ahead for you, and I know that there is still a malevolent presence that wishes you harm; I saw it in the cards. It is my experience that evil can be very cunning, dressing itself up in the guise of a friend. Stay alert.'

Luna felt a shiver run through her. There was no doubting that Mr Webber was a bad man and, after all she had learned at Honeysuckle Cottage that afternoon, she wondered whether he could actually be in league with the Devil Himself.

They walked together through the front garden, many of the flowers over now, but hardier shrubs and herbs were still thriving, and the smell of woodsmoke was in the air. She slipped through the white-painted gate and latched it behind her.

'Thank you.'

'Not at all. Here is the sage I spoke of, and I have another gift for you.'

'Oh?'

He passed over the cotton bag, along with a small glass bottle containing a pale pink liquid, with a matching silk ribbon around the neck.

'Should you decide your husband needs a helping hand to act on any amorous feelings he might have towards his wife, put two drops of this in his cocoa and leave the bedroom door unlocked.'

He gave a cheeky wink and Luna couldn't help but smile.

30

ELOISE

Eloise was consumed by anger. Her first thought had been to dismiss the maid without references and see the duplicitous girl suffer for her betrayal. But logic and reason won out. She wanted to know the truth of the matter; how had the romance developed and to what extent had Rose encouraged the man she had so clearly marked out for herself?

None of it made sense. Rose, a relatively quiet girl, had always been nervous of Daniel, someone she thought rude and intimidating. It was hard for Eloise to admit her own stupidity. There had been an arrogance in her assumptions that he couldn't possibly be looking at her maid, when she was the wealthy, better-educated and more fragrant alternative. His very job depended on the goodwill of her father, for goodness' sake. Did the silly man have no ambition? Because marrying a maid, even though Rose had been born to a higher social standing than her present circumstances suggested, would not further his career prospects, and insulting his employer's daughter would put paid to any further benevolence on her own part.

Rose, she had to begrudgingly admit, had a pleasant face and a kindly demeanour. She was embarrassingly honest and rather too trusting. Eloise considered this for a moment. Perhaps her maid hadn't actually encouraged the young Mr Thornbury and had no idea about his romantic aspirations? Eloise should at least ascertain the truth before she considered revenge.

Unsure how to broach the subject, she was surprised when it was Rose who spoke of it the very next day.

'Oh, miss. The most dreadful and unexpected thing has happened.'

Eloise looked up from her toilette and caught sight of her maid in the dressing table mirror. The girl's face was streaked with tears and she was repeatedly wringing her hands together in front of her cotton apron. Rose took a few steps towards her mistress and then fell to the floor, like a penitent sinner.

'Oh?' Eloise slowed her movements down, carefully replacing her small jar of cold cream onto the green glass tray, interested to hear what the girl had to say for herself. She slid it forward a quarter of an inch to align it perfectly with her hairbrush.

'Daniel Thornbury says he loves me. Oh, miss, I swear I did nothing to encourage him. I had absolutely no idea he felt this way. You kept asking me to spend all this time with him, and all I did was talk about you, I promise. Pressing your case and extolling your virtues...'

This was why he had been visiting the house so frequently, Eloise realised. Always downstairs talking to the servants before calling on her father. He had entered through the kitchens so that he could contrive reasons to see Rose. What was it about this girl that had the men so hypnotised? Even that Billy Price was still hanging about like an eager tomcat.

And yet the stupid girl wittered on. Eloise removed a tortoiseshell hairclip and squeezed it so hard in her anger than she nearly snapped it in two.

'...I did nothing to encourage his feelings, nor did I ever reveal that I felt the same...'

Gabbling in her desperation, the truth of the situation had slipped out. Eloise turned her head slowly, her flared nostrils the only outward indication of the rage that was bubbling up inside her.

'You feel the same?'

Rose's mouth fell open and her cheeks coloured up the instant she realised what she'd inadvertently admitted. 'Well, yes, but there has been no encouragement on my part. I knew you were in love with him and I had no designs on him whatsoever. I didn't even like him at first. I told you I didn't particularly want to talk to him, but I couldn't help but admire how he came to our rescue in the river, and be touched by his concern when Ginny accidentally poisoned the cat.'

Eloise's eyes narrowed briefly. Was this snivelling girl trying to place the blame for this deceitful attachment back on her? She took a calming breath and glanced at her own reflection, checking that her rising anger was not apparent on her face. She allowed her brow to relax, knowing rage would not serve her well in that moment.

'He said he'd been biding his time, not sure whether his affections were reciprocated. Honestly, I have no idea what I did to make him think this was the case. Oh, miss, what shall we do?'

The girl nervously toyed with the coral pendant Eloise had given her after the incident at the river. She was of a mind to tear it from Rose's neck, but restrained herself. It was worth very little and, besides, she wanted the maid to think of her as a friend for as long as possible.

'He has proposed,' Eloise said. It was not a question.

'And I said no. This whole thing is upside down. I thought he was going to ask for *your* hand. We both did.'

Did she take her mistress for a fool? They would both pay for this: Rose and Daniel. She stood from the low stool and walked past the distraught maid, stroking her head as she passed, and cupping the girl's chin to tilt her head upwards.

'Don't worry. I do not blame you. You did right to refuse him. Say nothing of this to anyone and let's see if we can't sort this dreadful mess out.'

And she stepped into the hallway, her fists clenched so tightly that her nails were digging into the palms of her hands, as she kicked at the balustrades and then calmly descended the stairs.

* * *

As spring continued to scamper along the tangly hedgerows and through the purple carpet of bluebells in the woodlands of Lowbridge, Eloise bided her time.

Rose was repentant and remained entirely trustworthy. She said nothing of the situation to anyone else, hoping her mistress would find a way to resolve the misunderstandings. Daniel Thornbury, according to Eloise's mother, who had overheard village gossip after church, was heartbroken after being spurned by some local girl – although the woman at the centre of this intrigue was unknown. Even her father, who was an honourable man, would not reveal the identity of Daniel's proposed, much to the frustration of her mother. He would do anything for his wife, but not betray another man's confidences, it appeared. Eloise was tempted to share the revelation herself, if only to see the reaction on her mother's face, but instinctively felt to do so might not be to her advantage, so remained silent.

'I told you that young Mr Thornbury was not worthy of your attentions,' her father said. 'He's handed in his notice because of this romantic disappointment, and after all the trouble you went to securing the position. The man is a damn fool. I had great plans for him.'

So did I, she thought forlornly.

Despite her protestations of innocence, Eloise had now decided that Rose had clearly been encouraging Daniel. No one buys a wedding ring unless they truly believe that the object of their affections will say yes. She must have been making eyes at him and playing her for a patsy. They would both be humiliated for their betrayal.

Her mind began to race with ideas for revenge. To sack the maid and send her away would be far too quick and simple. She wanted to make the punishment last. Perhaps she could spread some unsavoury rumours about Daniel. She considered accusing him of ungentlemanly behaviour, but couldn't be sure he wouldn't twist it all against her. She had to be subtler, cleverer. Make sure any actions could not be traced back to her.

And then she had a simply splendid idea; she would do something that injured both parties. Exact revenge on Daniel but point the finger at Rose. She clapped her dainty hands together in delight.

And she knew just what she was going to do...

31

Luna placed the rose-scented potion underneath a pile of linens in her chest of drawers. Not long after Marcus had bought her the new dresses, he'd placed another order for a selection of necessary undergarments, and Mrs Cole had provided everything she could possibly need. Her modest wardrobe was growing.

The gift was kind of Mr Findlay, who meant well, but she would not use magic to force her husband to come to her, nor would she give him anything to drink that she had not prepared herself, even though him coming to her bed was the thing she desired above all else.

Later that afternoon, Marcus came to find her after the arrival of the second post.

'This is not good,' he said, waving a letter at her. 'Great-Aunt Elspeth. A formidable and shrewd woman.'

Luna looked up from the floor where she was kneeling in front of the linen cupboard, sorting the household napery with Hattie. She got to her feet, curious as to the significance of the correspondence.

'She is coming to Ravenswood.'

'Oh?'

He looked back at the piece of paper. 'Tomorrow. This letter must have been held up in the post, for it was written three days ago. We do not have time to prepare.' He let out a groan and anxiously ran his hand through his hair. 'She has already embarked on her journey, and is stopping at a halfway house this evening.'

'And the purpose of her visit?'

He shrugged. 'I honestly have no idea. As you know, I tried to visit her back in May but she wasn't in London. She hasn't been here for several years, partly because it is such an arduous journey, but largely because she did not take to you, nor you to her.' Both were conscious that Hattie remained in the room. 'You'll remember that I tended to visit her by myself during the first few years of our marriage, when I was able to leave you unsupervised. You have not met above three times, but she was at our wedding.'

She was now quite used to Marcus referring to his wife's past as though she really was the woman herself, even though sometimes it made her uncomfortable to have the crazed actions of another attributed to her. He knew she wasn't Luna as much as she did, but what a glorious thing if they could live out the fantasy. If only everyone would just leave them alone.

'Hattie, you may return to the kitchens to help Mrs Webber.' The girl nodded and exited, as Luna wrestled with the knotty problem her husband had just presented. 'Maybe she is coming to congratulate us on being married for ten years?'

'I fear that is not a cause for celebration in her eyes. My choice of bride did not go down well.' His expression remained anxious as he returned his focus to the details of his great-aunt's communication. 'She is quite elderly, so we can only hope her memory has dimmed with the years. Or even her eyesight. I suspect, however, her tongue remains unaffected.'

Marcus gave a little snort but she knew he was clutching at slippery straws. He raised his eyes from the page and looked at her.

'Regardless, she wishes to stay for two nights. Mrs Webber and Hattie must prepare a room for her.' His worried expression betrayed the true reason for his anxiety. 'She must have my room; there is no other yet suitable, and Oscar can help me bring one of the sofas upstairs.'

There were only two beds upstairs at the house, and insufficient time to order another. He could hardly squeeze in with the Webbers. But the absence of the appropriate furniture aside, it was hardly scandalous for a husband and wife to share the same room. Why was he so worried?

'If you wish to present a happy couple to your aunt, and demonstrate the true extent of our reconciliation, then wouldn't it be perfectly natural for us to be together in the master bedroom, and for her to witness this? We can manage. It's fine.'

Ever practical, this was the obvious solution. It wasn't as though they were strangers any more. There was genuine affection between them, and an undeniable attraction. It was his decision not to act on this beyond their passionate kisses and gentle, often subconscious, caresses. Was his real concern that the desire that swirled between them might suck them down the eye of some carnal tornado and leave only destruction in its wake?

She walked over to him and rested her hand on his shoulder. He leaned his cheek towards it and gave her fingers a soft kiss, but she felt certain that his heart rate had accelerated almost as much as hers.

'Very well. It would appear I have no choice,' he said, and swallowed hard.

* * *

Great-Aunt Elspeth was not quite what Luna had expected. For a start, she had silk violets threaded through her loose, wavy hair and, when she removed her oversized mink coat, she was wearing a pale green loose-fitting cotton smock, heavily embroidered with a twisting ivy motif, which floated about her thin frame, almost swallowing her up. She resembled some kind of picture-book sprite – if sprites looked a hundred years old and carried walking sticks.

She was helped down from her carriage by Oscar and tottered up the meadow path with Marcus's arm linked through hers. Her man would stay in the village for the duration of her visit, where the horse could be better stabled and, as the carriage pulled away, a small trunk was left behind for the young boy to bring inside.

Luna could hear the old woman and her great-nephew's chatter as they approached.

'I've been worried about you, dear boy, and was sorry to miss you back in the spring. I've been particularly keen to visit, having heard rumours that have caused me great concern. Your letters may be cheery and give the impression that everything is fine, but I am adept at reading between the lines and had to see the current situation for myself.'

'Life is good, Aunt,' he reassured her, as they approached the front door where Luna was lurking. 'Better than it's been in a long time. And, look, here is my wife to greet us.'

Disarmed by her kindly appearance and obvious love for Marcus, Luna put out her hand and half-curtsied. The old woman sniffed and then looked at her as though she was something bobbing about in a chamber pot, before walking straight past her and into the house.

Luna blinked in surprise and her husband turned his head back and threw her an apologetic glance. Most people who had come across Luna Greybourne disliked her and Great-Aunt Elspeth was no exception. It would take some time to win this woman over, assuming they could successfully pull the wool over her rapidly dimming eyes.

* * *

'I like the paper in here. Dahlias,' Great-Aunt Elspeth said, as the three of them took their seats in the sparse, but thankfully now damage-free, dining room. 'A symbol of devotion and love.'

Luna looked across at Marcus, who had the faintest tinge of pink showing across his cheeks, even though his brows were furrowed and his jaw was set. She knew very little about flowers generally, even less so of the sentiments they supposedly represented. It had not occurred to her that his recent choice of wallpaper might be a coded message.

'I remember you had a delightful mulberry-coloured variety in your garden, Aunt,' he said, avoiding Luna's eye. 'I've been establishing new borders at the front of the house and will plant more bulbs out next spring. A favourite bloom of our queen – such an array of colours. I lost my dahlias to the frosts a few years ago but my man managed to grow some marigolds and sweet peas from seed this year and the last of the flowers remain.'

The loss of the blooms was unlikely to be due to adverse weather conditions and more likely one of his wife's spiteful acts of destruction. The meadow had probably survived because she could hardly destroy a whole field, but if she had killed her husband's dogs, she'd have had no compunction destroying his dahlias. Ravenswood had certainly been devoid of any formal flower beds until Marcus had started earnestly tackling the garden and replanting back in April.

Hattie arrived with a large tureen, her tongue half out of her mouth as she concentrated on keeping the dish level and not spilling the contents. She remained jumpy around Luna, as though her mistress might turn her into a toad at any given moment, but was getting better.

The old lady peered into the bowl set before her and scooped up a spoonful of the soup, taking a hesitant mouthful. She pulled an unimpressed face.

'What happened to the cook who worked for your father? Frightful-looking woman but at least she knew how to season the meals.' Her face said it all.

'I've had difficulty keeping staff.' His answer was guarded, as Hattie was still in the room. 'Mrs Webber has been very loyal. She does her best,' he finished.

The soup wasn't terrible, but with its overwhelming odour of cabbage and greyish appearance, it resembled something a peasant family might eat, not something to be served in the house of a gentleman.

'Employ a new cook,' his aunt ordered and he nodded his compliance. 'This one will likely kill you all before Christmas, if your wife doesn't get to you first.'

There followed an awkward silence before Luna was brave enough to speak. 'I do so admire the delicate embroidery on your dress. Ivy is such a hardy plant, if somewhat invasive. It has grown all up the back of the house.'

She was trying to win the old lady over but Elspeth was having none of it and merely huffed. 'It's *supposed* to guard against evil but it has spectacularly failed on that account. I also recall it being in the flower arrangements at your wedding, as it symbolises everlasting life, devotion and fidelity.' She snorted.

Luna tried again. 'It's lovely to have you here and I look forward to getting to know you a little better.'

Great-Aunt Elspeth looked across at Luna through her wire-rimmed spectacles.

'A most unlikely sentiment. You, dear girl, have some explaining to do. I have been informed that you prance around the woods, either naked or wrapped in bed linen, shout obscenities at passers-by, and occasionally attempt to summon up the Devil.'

Hattie gasped and dropped the tureen she'd been returning to the kitchens. It crashed to the ground and soup sprayed everywhere – up the table legs and across the wooden floorboards. The incident immediately shifted attention away from Luna's response and towards the calamity.

'Honestly, child, what is wrong with you?' Aunt Elspeth snapped, but Luna looked kindly on the girl, jumping to her feet to help deal with the dreadful mess.

'Luna.' Marcus's tone was sharp. 'Hattie is capable of cleaning up the mess. It's not your concern.' She had embarrassed him by behaving like staff when all he wanted to do was appease this judgemental old lady.

Luna slid back onto her chair and nodded, her eyes cast down into the soup before her, as Great-Aunt Elspeth returned to her earlier accusations. 'I correspond occasionally with the reverend at St Mary's,' their guest explained, as she waved an imperious hand. 'He is a personal friend of my parish priest. I met him several years ago in London and he keeps me updated as to the comings and goings of Little Doubton. It transpires your nocturnal activities draw a substantial amount of attention hereabouts.'

Why, Luna wondered, should her behaviour, which had been much improved since the spring, suddenly be of concern to this elderly lady? There had been no nudity in the woods since April – not from her, at any rate.

'I have not been out at night for many months, and have quite got the desire to run around unclothed out of my system.'

'It is not the nudity I object to,' the aunt clarified. 'After all, it is how we all came into the world. I'm not averse to being at one with Mother Nature myself, in the confines of my own home. But it is your ungodly attempts to engage in the dark arts that disgust me. I think you have put your husband through quite enough.'

Luna sighed and rolled out their usual response. 'I was under the influence of opiates, which mercifully no longer have such a hold on me.' She tried to look suitably contrite for a crime she had not committed. 'With Marcus's love and support I am faring much better. I hope the reverend also told you I now attend St Mary's and was well enough to help with the harvest back in September?'

Great-Aunt Elspeth sniffed. 'He also informed me that several years ago you cursed an old lady from the village and the unfortunate soul passed away not long afterwards.'

Marcus leaned forward to intervene on her behalf, repeating the explanation he'd given to the villagers. 'The woman was a self-proclaimed witch and quite the troublemaker. I am certain that her fear of my wife's meaningless words frightened her so much that it led to her apoplexy. As I have said to others in the past, physical symptoms can originate from mental stress. *People can die from fear,*' he explained. 'When you are so petrified that your heart races out of control, all it takes is a weak constitution and you have a sudden death. Something similar no doubt happened to her brain. Luna's curse was no more real than talk of dragons or unicorns and I am surprised at you, Aunt, for thinking otherwise.'

Aunt Elspeth narrowed her eyes. 'My journey has been long and I wish to retire. Marcus,' she commanded, 'escort me to my room. I will need assistance with the stairs.'

He got to his feet. 'Of course.' He slipped his arm through hers and helped her from the seat, with Luna convinced it was merely an excuse to talk to her great-nephew alone, and possibly demand that he immediately commit his mentally unstable wife to an asylum.

32

Marcus and Luna put off retiring to bed for as long as they could, both painfully aware of the imminent sleeping arrangements. But in the end, as the clock struck ten, they climbed the stairs together.

They were in the habit of taking a lamp each, knowing they would part outside the master bedroom, but this night, there was just one lamp between them. He opened the door for her as she carried it carefully across the room and placed it on the mantelpiece, whilst he lit the chamberstick by the bed.

'What did your aunt say about me?' she asked, no longer able to hide her curiosity.

'She asked me what was going on.'

'In what way?' That was not the response she'd expected, rather that the old lady had proclaimed her not to be Luna, or demanded her immediate removal from the house.

'In the way that she knows something isn't right but can't put her finger on what. We can try to win her around again tomorrow.'

'She clearly made her mind up about me a long time ago. But she's worried about you. Your face is a permanent frown.'

'I have a lot of things on my mind right now, not least of which is my desperate desire for her to like you, because whilst I love her dearly I can't have her spoiling things.' By this she understood that he meant exposing her for the fraud that she was.

She shrugged. 'There's nothing we can do except show her that I am better.' All afternoon they had played their parts, and whatever suspicions Great-Aunt Elspeth might have, she surely could not doubt the affection between them.

There was a moment of silence as they stood opposite each other, neither knowing what to do next.

'I can take the floor,' he said.

'Don't be ridiculous. There is a perfectly good bed here; we can share. It's what husbands and wives do.'

Surely, two people could lie alongside each other without having to be intimate, she reasoned. Just because she desperately wanted something more to happen, didn't mean that it must. Unfortunately.

'I have slept alone for many years.' His brows knitted together. 'I am not used to sharing.'

'Then I promise not to wriggle or steal the counterpane,' she said, hoping humour would ease the tension. 'I'm sure we can be sensible about this.'

She picked up a silver-backed hairbrush from the dressing table and heard him lump down on the bed as she began to pull it through her hair. Risking a quick glance in the oval mirror before her, she could see a million troubles scored into the lines and contortions of his face. After tugging the last of the knots out, she placed the brush on the glass tray and turned back to him. He smiled, pretending all was well.

'Thank you. For everything these past few months. You've made a very difficult time for me more bearable.'

'We have both helped each other.' She shrugged. 'And I appreciate that you've never once asked me any questions about my—'

Marcus stood back up and raised his hand to stop her saying anything further.

'Leave the past where it belongs. It's not our truth. I want to live in the world where Marcus and Luna Greybourne are happily married and their future is full of unwritten possibilities.'

This was the closest he'd come in a while to acknowledging the lie they were perpetuating. She also wanted this to be their truth more than anything, but was not unrealistic enough to believe that the past would not catch them up and cleave them apart. Even if his great-aunt failed to recognise Luna was an imposter, there were others who knew: the tinker, Mrs Cole, the doctor...

'Then Marcus and Luna Greybourne will have no problems sharing a bed without making a fuss.' She tipped her head to one side to make her point.

'Of course.' He nodded.

'And remember, darling,' Luna said, unable to resist teasing him again. 'I sleep on the right.'

'As do I. This will be interesting.'

His eyes twinkled and they exchanged a smile until, without taking his eyes from hers, his face became more serious. She noticed his Adam's apple bob down as he swallowed hard.

They were going to do this, she realised; they were actually going to sleep alongside each other, with both of them carrying the knowledge that there was a romantic attraction.

He unknotted the white bow tie from his winged collar. Luna watched mesmerised as he tugged at one end, and the other slid up his shirtfront and disappeared around his neck. He threw it onto the covers and began to tackle the row of small mother-of-pearl buttons on his shirt with his thick fingers. Embarrassed, she turned away. There was nowhere to hide; no folding draught screen to duck behind, or dressing room to slink into, reappearing moments later in her nightgown. In for a penny, she decided, and began to unbutton the bodice of her dress. If he wanted the fiction to be real, then she would do her best to follow suit. Didn't he deserve some happiness? She had allowed herself to become his wife in nearly every way possible. There was nothing untoward about them undressing in the same room. And she could hardly fall pregnant from a covetous look.

She shrugged off the bodice and turned her attention to the hooks and eyes of her skirt, conscious that he'd stopped moving behind her, and suspected that he was watching her disrobe. She took a determined breath and continued to remove her layers, until all that remained was her linen shift. When she turned back to the bed, he spun quickly away, knowing he'd been caught. In turn, she assessed his broad back, noticing for the first time a deep jagged scar across his left shoulder blade. She thought back to the day they had met and his discomfort with that arm. He had never talked of the injury, but it appeared to have healed well enough.

Ever-practical, and knowing herself how a thoughtless mistress could make extra work for staff, she gathered up her dress and took it to the wardrobe. Delaying the moment when she would have to climb into bed beside him, she fiddled about, placing the garments on hangers, aware of his frantic scrabble to remove the remainder of his clothing. When she turned back, he was once again sitting on the foot of the bed, this time in just his long cotton drawers, his nightshirt folded beside him. She glanced at his broad chest and the scatter of dark hairs across it, feeling a flip of her stomach.

'When did your magic become so powerful?' he asked, looking up at her.

Her quizzical expression invited further explanation.

'This spell you have cast on me,' he said. Despite his great size and thirty years, he suddenly looked like a child, asking what kept the moon from falling out of the sky.

'You don't believe in any of that,' she said, walking over to the bed and coming to a halt directly in front of him, looking down at his troubled face. 'You've repeatedly insisted that magic – good or bad – isn't real.'

'Then what is this unfathomable thing consuming me? Making me unable to eat, sleep and barely even remember to breathe?'

He put his hands on the bed, either side of his wide hips, and pushed himself up. Their gazes held as he rose from being level with her stomach, to towering over her so that she had to tilt her head up to his. It was both exhilarating and frightening being so close to his naked torso. She felt so small in that moment, so vulnerable. Her own chest was constricting and her heartbeat racing, much like the day she had tumbled into him. But this was not from the fear he would hand her over to the police. This was from the fear that he would be able to read her thoughts and know that she longed for his touch and ached for his body.

'Perhaps it is simply that, after ten long years...' he began to answer his own question, '...I have finally fallen in love with my wife?' His low voice and raised vein pulsing noticeably in his neck suggested he was as nervous as she.

He had taken the bravest step – spoken openly of the feelings they both knew were there. The night he prevented her from fleeing Ravenswood had proved that. His courage gave her courage. She knew he would make no further move without her consent, and belatedly suspected this was why there had been nothing other than passionate kisses between them. It had to come from her, so what was she stalling for? They were alone and he had laid his heart on the Persian rug between them. She could either trample on it or admit these were the words she'd been hoping to hear. The silence of the room, save the ticking of the clock, was as voltaic as the atmosphere every time they locked eyes.

She reached up for his cheek, rough where his whiskers were growing.

'Then know that she is equally in love with you. And she wants nothing more than for you to be her husband – in every sense of the word.' She swallowed. 'Make love to me?' It was the boldest sentence she'd ever uttered, and the most reckless. Her hopes rose in her chest like a hot air balloon.

'No.' He shook his head and everything crashed to the floor as her head dropped. He didn't want her. He was playing some game she was too naive to understand. Reaching out, he cupped her chin and tipped it back to his face. 'Not until you are perfectly clear that whatever name you go by and even though everyone understands you to be Luna, I do know you are not her and I do not want you to be her. I *never* loved her but I have fallen utterly and completely for you.'

He gripped her by the shoulders and his stare went deeper than she thought possible. She nodded and he leaned down to her to let his forehead rest against her own.

'She was always a rough bed mate, and the things she enjoyed only frightened me and caused me pain. This will be different. I will lead and I will be gentle.'

Luna had destroyed this poor man before her in every possible way, and yet he still had the capacity to trust and to hope. Her heart had been his for longer than she cared to admit, but now she knew it would never belong to anyone else. Between them they would find a way to heal each other.

'I'm so sorry for all the pain you went through in the past.' Her voice was now a shaky whisper. 'I only want to bring you pleasure...'

A deep groan rose up from his throat as he anticipated her honouring this statement.

He pulled back to engage her eyes and then tucked a long strand of her loose hair behind her ear, before bending back down towards her mouth as their lips bumped together. It was different from the urgency of their kiss by the gate, or their recently exchanged kisses – it was a prelude to something far more monumental. There was no hurry; they had the whole night ahead of them.

A sudden gust of wind moved the curtains. Was Luna somehow aware of what was about to take place in this room? Marcus may be dismissive of his wife's magic but she could not shake her belief in the woman's supernatural powers. The intimacy between them had unsettled the Ravenswood Witch – she felt it as surely as she felt the desperate and fierce longing of the man before her. He moved to the window and pulled the sash down. Neither Bran nor anyone from the spirit world would be floating through the open window and joining them that night.

Before returning to her, he blew out the lamp that she'd stood on the mantel, leaving just a smaller dancing flame from the chamberstick by her side of the bed. The reduced light made the whole situation even more intimate, and when he stood before her this time, his hesitancy and shyness had dissolved into the dark shadowy corners of the room. But the guilt of her past tapped on her shoulder and she knew they could not commit to each other in this most intimate of ways if she was not honest with him.

'There's something I have to—'

He raised his hand to silence her a second time.

'We've talked for long enough.' He stifled her admission by swooping down on her mouth and easing her gently back onto the bed. She tumbled onto the pillows and allowed her arms to fall above her head. He paused for a moment, his whole body hovering above hers, as his eyes focused on her wedding band. Manoeuvring to free his left hand, his thumb briefly caressed the ring, before he returned his gaze to her face. He released her fingers and then slid his large hand from her knee to her thigh, taking the hem of the shift with it. Finally he spoke, never once breaking eye contact.

'With this ring I thee wed, with my body I thee worship, with all my worldly goods I thee endow.'

And barely a moment later, with swift and definite movements, the two lost and broken people lying across the shared bed in a house haunted by shadow, made their own light, as they became man and wife in the eyes of God.

33

ROSE

Rose was crying as she ran into her mistress's room, pausing only to knock out of courtesy, but the door was open and she was in such a blind panic, she didn't wait for a reply. Eloise was sitting before her dressing table, still in her day dress, and had begun to unpin her hair as she waited for her maid to attend to her.

'What on earth are you in such a flap about, Rose?'

'Oh, miss. I can hardly believe what I'm about to tell you. Daniel Thornbury is dead.' Her distraught squeak became a wail. 'How can that be?'

It was her mistress's turn to look pale, and her hands dropped to the stool and her fingers gripped the edge of the seat.

'Dead? Not sick? Are you sure?'

'The doctor was called but he was already stone cold, eyes wide and had no pulse. His poor father found him this morning, and thinks he passed away several hours ago. I was in the kitchens when their neighbour burst in to tell us all.'

In her confused state, she'd run straight upstairs to share the news with Miss Haughton.

'If he believed himself unwell, why did he not seek medical

assistance?' Eloise's voice was shaky and Rose could only assume her mistress was as upset as she.

'Mr Thornbury senior had gone out for the evening, having left his son in bed. He'd been complaining of a headache, painful limbs and giddiness. They both believed he was coming down with a nasty cold, but the doctor, having examined him, obviously found something amiss. He wants to test for poisons but I can't think why he is even considering such a thing.'

Rose couldn't understand. Surely, he had not been so distressed by her refusal that he'd taken his own life? How else could he have consumed poison? It could hardly be an accident.

Eloise stood up and began to pace the room in her stockinged feet, with her half-unpinned hair trailing down her back. Her expression was one of intense concentration until she finally came to a standstill. 'Can you not? And yet you gave Daniel a bottle of cordial. Had he drunk your gift, I wonder? And what exactly did it contain?' Her mistress narrowed her eyes in thought. 'You did tell him it was a *cordial*, I trust? A syrup to be diluted?'

'But the gift was from you.' Rose was confused. 'And you didn't give me any special instructions to pass on.'

Eloise clenched her fists but continued to speak as though she were an irrelevance, not bothering to acknowledge her statement. There was colour back in her mistress's face now, and she wore a look of grim determination rather than the utter horror of moments before. Prickles of unease crept up Rose's arms and across her shoulder blades. There was something very wrong about this whole situation, and she was starting to suspect what that might be.

'How curious, also, that you bought those flypapers from the chemist not four days ago. Nasty things which, as we know, contain arsenic.'

'But I purchased them on your instruction.' Rose was now utterly terrified as her world began to crack and splinter before her very eyes.

'Me? Don't be so ridiculous. I have no need of flypapers. I understand the housekeeper keeps a supply in her locked stores, and I do not get involved in the ordering of domestic items. Why would anyone need papers in April? Really, Rose, the answer is disturbingly obvious. If arsenic is found in the cordial, you will have quite some explaining to do. It will not take the rumour mill long to turn in a small village like this, and for it to become common knowledge that you turned down his proposal. I'm afraid, if I am made to swear under oath, I will have to admit that you were heartily sick of his advances, that you confided to me that he had even tried to take you by force, and how angry that made you. Don't forget, you came to me the other night in great distress and said you sincerely wished him dead.'

Rose looked at her mistress, mouth agape, as the truth finally hit her. Every word that was coming from her pretty pink mouth was a vile lie. Eloise had done this evil thing: poisoned a man simply because he did not want her, and framed the girl he loved. Perhaps she had not intended to kill him; her shock at the news was genuine enough and she was irritated with Rose for not telling Daniel to dilute the cordial, but she was behind his death – of this, she was certain.

The two women locked eyes and she knew her assumption was correct by Miss Haughton's smug expression. Rose took a step backwards. She'd always known Eloise to be a spoilt girl. It had been apparent from her first day in service at this house; she had demanded the largest bedroom, facing the green, and her parents had acquiesced. David Haughton adored his daughter and would believe anything she told him: truth or lie. A slow churning began in Rose's already constricting stomach. To be so calculated. This woman had decided if she couldn't have something, then no one else would have it either – it was beyond madness.

'I feel so utterly wretched for you, really I do.' Eloise finally broke the silence. 'Men can be such beasts. I'll tell you what, how about we pretend this conversation never took place? I shall turn my back and allow you to leave this house without raising the alarm. In half an hour, I will ring the bell and ask where you are. There, now.' She walked over to Rose and gently placed her hand on the maid's cheek. 'I really can't say fairer than that. You always struck me as a bright girl, able to read and write, when many in your position can't. You are well presented and resourceful; I'm sure you can start again somewhere. They will want someone to hang for this heinous deed but it won't be me, and if you are a sensible girl, it won't be you either.'

Frozen to the spot, as though her mistress's touch had turned her to stone, Rose's mind was racing. Everything she had done for this overindulged and entitled woman over the past few months had been their secret. She hadn't talked about any of it with her fellow servants. Yes, people hereabouts would say she was of sensible character, a hard worker and a good Christian girl, but if it was Eloise's word against hers, she would not be believed. Whispers of Daniel's proposal and her subsequent refusal had already made it into the kitchens. Cook had even confronted her about it two days ago after dinner but she had given vague answers and made excuses to leave the room.

But to run away – surely that would only confirm her guilt?

'Twenty-eight minutes…'

What else could she do? She had no real friends in Lowbridge and, whilst she rubbed along with the rest of the staff, there was always the barrier of her education, the other girls resenting her slightly. She had no family left alive and the one person she had grown close to at the house had betrayed her in the most heinous way. Her mother had always told her she was too trusting.

Miss Haughton's duplicity was alarming, but the most distressing thing about this whole situation was that the man she had developed feelings for now lay dead. He had been the first person in so many years to look at her as an equal, to encourage her learning and praise her accomplishments. And when he had proposed, she knew that he was in earnest. Had Eloise not staked her claim and been in every way superior to her, she would have accepted him in a heartbeat. But Rose was loyal and honourable. She had stepped aside.

Daniel Thornbury was an innocent, killed by a woman scorned. Whichever way she looked at this, she knew the odds were not in her favour. She had no one to turn to, but Eloise had everyone, from her devoted parents to the most upstanding members of their small village community.

'Twenty-seven…'

And Rose felt she had no option but to run.

34

ROSE

Rose did not dare return to her rooms. She couldn't trust her mistress not to ring the bell the second she stepped into the corridor, despite her promise. Instead, she headed down the servant stairs and out the side door into the kitchen gardens, leaving with only the clothes she was wearing. The light was already draining from the sky and she suspected there was to be a frost that night from the sharp nip in the air.

Keeping to the shadows, she crept up the driveway and ducked behind a cherry tree, billowy with pink blossom, and could see people popping in and out of the Thornburys' cottage. Curious but kind neighbours checking in on the grief-stricken father, no doubt.

Her practical side came to the fore. No one had reason to suspect her of anything at this point; the body had only been removed that afternoon, and the coroner was not yet involved. She pulled her shoulders back and walked at a steady pace around the opposite side of the green and down the track that ran between the church and the schoolhouse. She decided to follow the river Bran the twenty miles or so up to Manbury, where she could catch a train to London. It was much further away than Branchester, and only a branch line with a more intermittent service, but because it was not the obvious choice, it was less risky. Everyone would assume she'd head to Branchester, where she had grown up and still knew people.

Only when she was out of sight did she start running again. Her only thought was to get out of Lowbridge, but as she forced one shaking foot in front of the other, occasionally stumbling in her panic, and her breath raspy in her throat, she realised she had no money. How would she purchase her ticket? Or pay for lodgings upon her arrival?

She suddenly remembered that Billy Price lived at the bottom of School Lane. Might he be kind and lend her a few shillings? He was always boasting about his dodgy dealings and had once told her that if ever there was anything she wanted, all she had to do was ask.

'...Because you certainly have something I want,' he'd said in his oily voice, looking deliberately at her chest, and she'd known exactly what he'd been referring to. Rumour had it that Lady Fletcher's dairymaid had been known to give him the things he wanted and was suitably recompensed on every occasion.

The notion had horrified her, and she'd held on to the morals of her good Christian upbringing. Many a time, those she was in service with had joked about their escapades with young men, but she had not joined in, determined to save herself for marriage. However, now all she could see was her own swollen blue face with a hangman's noose around her neck. She had no doubt she would pay for Eloise's crimes. Those with money and influence were often able to buy themselves out of trouble.

Unsure whether she had the correct house, she rapped cautiously on the back door and moments later Billy's face appeared. He was rolling a cigarette and looked surprised but delighted to see her, kicking the door open wider with his foot and inviting her in.

'I'm in trouble. I need money. Can you lend me some and I'll pay you back? I swear it.' She slipped into his tiny kitchen and could smell the meaty aromas of a recently cooked stew, noticing the clutter of the room. She was holding out the hope that he might trust her enough to offer a loan. She would happily pay a bit of interest and post the money back to him as soon as she had work. He must know that she was an honest girl. There was absolutely no one else she could ask and she would need to be out of Lowbridge before daybreak, because her absence would imminently be noticed at Church View, if it hadn't been already.

He studied her briefly – dishevelled and likely with tear stains down her pale cheeks – then he tucked the cigarette behind his ear and closed the door.

'My, my, my.' He stood with his back to her only exit, stroking his chin and looking down at her. 'Not so la-di-dah all of a sudden, are we, missy? Prancing around cocking a snook at me because you believe yourself to be better 'an me. But you come a-knocking at this hour *now* that you want something, when there's only one thing I want from you and you ain't ever been willing to give it.'

'I need money to get to London.' She repeated her plea, not wanting to get drawn into a conversation that sickened her.

He slipped his pocket watch from his woollen waistcoat and glanced at the time.

'Nearest station is Branchester but I'm reckoning you've missed the last train. So, I'm wondering where you'll be spending the night, especially having no money and everything.'

It suited Rose for him to think she was headed to the city, even though she knew full well it would take her two days to walk the twenty miles to Manbury. It wouldn't be long before word got out and everyone started looking for the fugitive, so let him send them in the wrong direction.

If she could only get to London and find work, everything would be all right. Why, oh why, had she run? But it was too late now for regret. She swallowed, hardly able to believe the words she was about to say.

'How much?'

'What?'

'How much will you pay me?' She understood now how desperate people could be driven to do desperate things.

Billy was incredulous. 'So, you've gone from all high and mighty to a common whore in the blink of an eye.' He slithered towards her like a curious snake and met her watery eyes. 'Jesus, Rose, what kinda trouble you in?'

This was stupid. What was she doing? Debasing herself in such an abhorrent way. The gallows would be preferable. She took a step to pass him but felt a rough hand grip her shoulder.

'Wait up, young lady, I didn't say I wouldn't consider your interesting... proposal.'

And so Rose Turner did a wicked thing on a bleak Tuesday evening in April, something neither God nor her dead parents would ever forgive her for; she sold her soul to Billy Price for a handful of shillings and the promise he would swear blind he'd not seen her pass by that night.

35

It didn't matter that she had not stood before a vicar in a fine dress, clutching a small posy of flowers, and signed the parish register. As far as Luna was concerned, she was a married woman, with all the carnal knowledge and domestic responsibilities that came with the title. Her truth was that the giant but gentle man sharing her bed was her husband. This she would maintain until her dying breath, even if they were physically torn apart. Their union was complete, and she hadn't even needed Mr Findlay's well-meaning potion to persuade him to come to her.

Their lovemaking had lasted quite some time, a powerful coupling that hadn't required words. They'd communicated with the intensity of a look or the persuasiveness of a touch, both recognising that this coming-together had been inevitable.

Not long afterwards, there had been the most almighty crack in the room and Marcus had scrambled out of bed to light the lamp on the mantel. The dressing mirror had split clean across the middle. It was, he said, just one of those things. A weakness in the glass that had finally given way. He looked at her with an expression that defied her to offer another, less palatable, other-worldly explanation. But she knew who was responsible and why.

She had invited him to claim her body a second time, almost in defiance of her ghostly foe. As the flame of the dying chamberstick candle flickered out, they had fallen together, exhausted and complete. When her heavy eyelids finally closed, she knew if she were to be hanged tomorrow, she would be content to know she had been loved and had loved in return. She would rather die young than live a long life without experiencing the happiness of that night.

Bran tapped on the windowpane in the early hours and Luna woke in the half-light to find Marcus's heavy limbs draped across her naked body, his head on the pillows facing hers, and his brow unfurrowed and smooth. The smell of him, the smell of *them*, was overpowering and addictive.

She slid from his proprietorial arm, grabbed a robe from the back of the door, and walked to the window. To her horror, she saw four words written in the condensation that had formed on the inside of the glass, the moonlight from outside allowing her to read them.

The time has come...

Luna felt each painful thud of her panicked heart pound in her chest. This had been done in the last few moments, as water was running from the bottom of the letters towards the sill. Marcus had not moved from her side and no one had entered the room. The spirit of his dead wife was warning her that she was imminently to make good on the threat scratched into the wardrobe. She wiped the warning away with the flat of her hand, wondering if their actions of the night before had been the tipping point, or if the witch was waiting for All Hallows' Eve to enact her revenge. Regardless, Luna knew that her reckoning was rapidly approaching.

Her shaking hands fumbled with the sash as she let the impatient raven in. Amongst his many quirks, he was a jealous bird and, had he not been shut out of the room that night, she might even have suspected him of breaking the glass. He gave a deep, throaty kraa-kraa and Marcus stirred.

'Come back to bed, Luna. I need more sleep, especially if I'm to face my suspicious great-aunt at breakfast.' He shuffled onto his elbows, sensing movement from where the raven was now perching on a chair-back. 'Is there someone else in the room?'

'Bran often visits me at night,' she explained. 'He is my not-so-silent guardian and likes to check that I am safe.' She no longer doubted the bird's loyalty.

'Ah, so I have competition.' Marcus smiled and tapped the counterpane. 'Should I train Bran to attack any man who so much as looks at my beautiful wife? I will not share her.'

She climbed back into the bed and nestled into his wide arms, looking up at him, hoping that he would assume her quivering body was due to the temperature. 'You have nothing to fear. There is no one else,' she said, hoping her tone conveyed her sincerity.

He must know, however, that he had not been her first. There was no blood and she understood that men instinctively knew if you had been with another. She had tried to tell him the previous night but he had silenced her. He simply would not allow anything outside their fairy tale to exist, but it was important to her that he understood that her night with Billy had not been an act of love, but of desperation.

'Once, before I met you, when my life was at its blackest, I did a wretched thing in order to survive. I will never forgive myself but I cannot undo it.' It was the only explanation she could offer, allowing him an opportunity to condemn, or even question her further, but he did neither.

'I am not here to judge you because I have been in a black place, too. A place with no light and so very little hope, but we have left those dark corners now so let's not speak of them and instead walk towards the sunshine.'

He gave her a soft smile but she thought she could read a desolate sadness in his eyes and wondered what might be curled up in the dark corner he had walked away from. She desperately hoped it wasn't the body of his dead wife.

* * *

It was obvious, to her at least, how relaxed Marcus was at the breakfast table, compared to his anxious demeanour of the previous day. She hoped it wasn't as simple as the flooding of his sexual desert, and more that the certainty of their commitment to each other had given him peace.

Great-Aunt Elspeth was late to rise but when she entered the drawing room, the pair of them lay intertwined on the long upholstered sofa, Marcus half asleep after his repeated physical exertions of the previous night, and Luna resting across his large thigh with a small volume of Dickens in her hand. She still revelled in the luxury of reading for pleasure during the day. Marcus was looking to build the library up again and had recently purchased some of his favourite novels and reference works from the auction house in Manbury, where big houses sometimes sold off their contents to pay estate debts.

It took Luna a while to realise they were being observed from the doorway, and she sat upright when she spotted the old lady, jolting Marcus awake as she did.

'Aunt, do join us,' he said. 'Did you have a pleasant night?'

He got to his feet and helped her to settle in a high-backed chair near the crackling fire.

'Clearly not as good as some.' Her shrewd eyes looked between the pair of them and Luna felt a creeping heat rise from her toes. Their night-time activities had been overheard.

'I'll ring for some refreshments,' Marcus said. The bells had finally been repaired – a task that had taken Mr Webber and young Oscar two days. 'You have missed breakfast but it is the perfect time for tea and cake.'

'Hattie made a fruit loaf,' Luna added. 'In fact, I think we should consider training her up as a cook and finding another housemaid. She is quiet but extremely bright.'

That she should be in the position of choosing staff when she had once been staff herself had taken her a long time to get used to. It might make her a more understanding mistress; she hoped so. Hattie was becoming increasingly efficient, as was Oscar, and this had taken a huge burden from Marcus's broad shoulders.

Great-Aunt Elspeth tutted. 'Bright, maybe, but clumsy. And she's only a girl. She can hardly be thirteen and has no kitchen experience.'

Perhaps it was the thought that she had nothing left to lose now that made her defend herself. Perhaps she just felt safe at that moment, knowing Marcus loved her. Or perhaps she was finally accepting that she was mistress of this house and she only had to answer to her husband. Whatever it was, Luna felt emboldened enough to take the old lady on.

'I choose not to judge her on age, but on her actions. She is punctual, efficient and knows her way around the range. Cooking is not a strength of Mrs Webber's, but if I have someone who is capable of doing that job in my household, then I would be a fool not to employ her as such, just because she is deemed too young. Women, in particular, are given so few opportunities in life and goodness knows the Gowers could do with the extra money.'

The old lady narrowed her eyes and Luna knew she had piqued her interest with her talk of women's subordination.

'A consideration for another day,' Marcus said, trying to head off a confrontation. 'In the meantime, cake.'

He rang the bell and it wasn't many minutes later that they were treated to tea and fruit loaf, but the conversation was stilted and the atmosphere frosty.

The silence was broken by a sharp tap at the windowpane that made Great-Aunt Elspeth jump. Luna's heart sank as Bran's black outline appeared on the sill.

'What the devil?' the old lady muttered.

Luna stood up and opened the window, knowing she would get no peace if she ignored him, and he hopped into the room as the old woman's mouth dropped open in horror.

'Get that abhorrent creature out, Marcus. Having them in your woods is one thing, but they are harbingers of death and allowing them inside is madness.' She was visibly shaken and looked to her nephew for support.

'Bran is Luna's raven and he does no harm.' His tone was firm.

The bird flew to the jardinière stand and Luna petted him before taking her seat. She was thrilled her husband had stood up for her and hoped Bran would behave. That he had not attacked the elderly stranger was a good sign; he was an excellent judge of character.

'You really aren't your usual self today, Aunt,' Marcus commented. 'But I suspect I know just the thing to bring you cheer. Please try to be civil to each other whilst I am absent. I won't be gone long.'

He looked at the pair in turn before departing, and the two women chose to quietly sip their tea, rather than engage in conversation, both hoping he would be true to his word.

* * *

'Oh, madam, come quickly! Mr Greybourne has had a terrible accident.'

It was barely ten minutes later when Hattie appeared at the drawing room door, breathless and tearful, frantically gesturing for her mistress to follow her.

Luna had moved to a side table to deal with some correspondence at a small writing slope, and Great-Aunt Elspeth had quickly fallen asleep in her chair. The old woman's garland had slipped across her eyes, making her look like a drunken wood nymph.

Luna threw a look at their house guest, who was still dead to the world, immediately abandoned her letter and ran through the kitchens and out to the side of the house.

Marcus was lying on the ground with his eyes closed and at first she thought he was dead. Blood, so much blood, pouring from a deep gash on his forehead. She rushed over to him, trying to remain calm but tears streamed down her face. She could not lose him like this. Was God punishing them for their lies? Or had the words on the glass been for him? He had been in the room with her last night, after all.

'What happened?' she cried, glancing up at Oscar, who was standing over his master, his face pale and his hands restless.

'He was picking the last of the marigolds and one of the roof tiles flew at his head. Knocked him clean off his feet. I couldn't get no answer from him, nor could Mr Webber when he got off the ladder. So Hattie came for you.'

'Mr Webber was up the ladder?' She looked over to the manservant, slinking around behind the cold frames, laying the ladder down and avoiding her eye. She'd found a pulse on Marcus now and was calmer. Her husband was not dead.

'Replacing the tiles, like I was told,' Webber grunted. 'I was throwing them broken ones down to the lad and this one just leapt from my hand... Reckon it was caught by a gust of wind, coz I weren't chucking it this way. I swear.'

Luna turned to Oscar to corroborate Webber's story but he just shrugged.

'Heavy slate tiles don't get whisked up by a gust of wind,' she said. The list of reasons she had to dislike this man was growing longer.

'I never threw it at him, if that's what you're thinking.'

This was not the time for an argument and she instead focused on Marcus's welfare.

'Oscar, go to the village and fetch Doctor Gardener. Hattie, find Mrs Webber and ask what we should do in the meantime. It will take Oscar easily half an hour with no horse.'

The housekeeper, who had been upstairs dealing with the bedlinen, appeared in the gardens within moments. She'd treated the real Luna's injuries for several years, albeit under Mr Findlay's guidance, so the woman had a good knowledge of basic medical care.

'Send the girl for the cunning man,' Mrs Webber said, hurrying towards them all. 'He has a poultice for bleeding and a medicine for the head. I'm afraid I used the last bottle up and haven't got round to getting no more.' She looked to her husband who narrowed his eyes but said nothing.

'Oscar has set off for the doctor,' Luna explained. 'You know Mr Greybourne won't want us dealing with that man.'

'But he's unconscious and don't know what's happening. We needn't tell the master where the medicine came from. I've been using him for years to stock our medicine chest and guide me regarding the care of those at Ravenswood. The master just never knew.'

The young girl waited for her mistress's resigned nod of approval and then scampered to the front of the house, whilst Mrs Webber went to the kitchens and got a wet piece of flannel to press on the wound. They made Marcus as comfortable as they could without moving him, both women knowing full well that head injuries were potentially very serious. Hattie returned within a quarter of an hour with a small bottle of yellow liquid and a poultice of yarrow and comfrey root.

'The cunning man said to get four drops of this into him immediately, and to make him rest for the remainder of the day. Watch that he's not sick and don't let him eat anything for a few hours.'

Almost as soon as Luna had dribbled the liquid into her husband's parted lips, he opened his eyes and, after a few minutes, was gently helped to a sitting position. He insisted he was well enough to get to his feet but Mr Webber took his arm and guided him inside, where they waited for Doctor Gardener. Everyone was under strict instructions to say nothing of Findlay's help. Luna told Marcus that Mrs Webber had sorted the poultice, which, in a way, she had.

Great-Aunt Elspeth had been woken by the commotion and was quite alarmed to hear of her great-nephew's accident but there was nothing useful she could do. The doctor duly arrived and thought there would be no permanent damage. Like Findlay, he prescribed bed rest and, with Mr Webber's help, Marcus was taken upstairs. Her husband, he reiterated, had had a lucky escape.

'A young boy died in Manbury this summer, after being hit by a cricket bat,' he said. 'Head injuries are tricky, so send for me if Mr Greybourne starts vomiting or has convulsions.'

Luna paid him in the entrance hall, expressing her thanks, but not wanting to engage in conversation, knowing how he felt about their deception. The doctor, however, was very complimentary about the house, remarking that the last time he had been to Ravenswood – and this was several years ago – it had been in quite a sorry state.

'We're trying to rebuild our shattered lives,' she said, showing him the door. 'And want nothing more than to be left in peace to do just that.'

He paused at her words and then nodded. 'Take good care of him,' he said, as he doffed his hat, and made his way to the waiting gig.

* * *

'Please, madam, may I speak to you?'

Hattie intercepted her mistress in the hallway as she returned to apprise Great-Aunt Elspeth of Marcus's condition.

'Of course.'

'This morning, when I asked Mr Findlay to come back to Ravenswood, not knowing that the master had forbidden it, he said that his life would be in danger should he step on Greybourne lands.' The young girl's eyes betrayed her fear. 'Is there really someone at the house who would see him dead?'

'I'm afraid that the work he does to keep us all safe from the spirit world and those who practise dark magic, means that there might be bad people in this world who would wish him ill. But I can assure you that I would never cause him harm. On the contrary, I think the time is coming when I will be very glad of his assistance.'

She could not answer Hattie's question directly because she could not promise there were no witches at Ravenswood. Mr Findlay had warned her that evil could dress itself up as a friend and this worried her more than she cared to admit.

'He insisted I told everyone at Ravenswood to stay at home on All Hallows' Eve,' Hattie said. 'His cards have warned him of evil summonings and the shedding of blood. He's genuinely worried for the safety of everyone here.'

Luna nodded, grateful that he had got word to her. She knew All Hallows' Eve was a dangerous time. The thin veil between this world and the spiritual world might allow the real Luna to do more than write threats in the dust or on the window, to appear in a reflection or to crack a mirror.

'I'll admit that I was very scared of you when I started here,' the maid said. 'But you don't seem anything like the tales I've heard, and the cunning man reassured me. He said not to listen to the village gossip, because it wasn't you I needed to fear. But the stories of the well and the things that go on in them woods at night… I can't lie, madam, it makes me very uneasy.'

Luna appreciated her honesty and didn't want to lose her, especially as she was proving such a good little worker.

'Mr Findlay is quite right, Hattie. I can promise you that I am not involved in such practices. My husband will tell you it is all nonsense, but I understand that the woods have a fearsome reputation. They are used by the villagers as a cut-through and we can't always control who enters them. If you and your brother were given All Hallows' Eve and All Saints' off, allowing you both to remain safely in Little Doubton with your family, would you please try to overcome your fear?'

The young girl nodded and slipped a small rowan cross from her pocket.

'I'll try. Mr Findlay gave me this. He said it will keep me safe.'

Luna smiled at her conviction, and regretted destroying her own charm. Even though the Gowers didn't sleep at the house, she didn't want them in danger. Not every threat was mortal. Even though *she* wasn't the Ravenswood Witch, that didn't mean the woman who claimed to be such wasn't still a risk to the household.

Luna returned to the drawing room to sit with Great-Aunt Elspeth and gather her thoughts. Her bottom had barely touched the seat before the old woman spoke. There was no preamble to her words, and no kindness in her eyes.

'The housekeeper assures me that Marcus will be fine but I am glad we find ourselves alone again, as there are things I wish to say and I don't want my great-nephew party to the conversation. I love him very much – he is one of the few people I truly care for in this world – but I do not, and never did, care for you. Whilst I appreciate it has been many years since I saw you last, the change in you has been bothering me ever since I arrived.'

Luna swallowed. She had a feeling she knew where this was heading.

'Your care for him over this accident has been somewhat a surprise to say the least because, even at the wedding, I found you dismissive and cold towards him. The foolish boy was barely twenty and found himself swept up by the attentions of an attractive young woman. Like every red-blooded male, he was not able to think clearly because of it, marrying you with the most undue haste. You never looked at him with anything but indifference and yet, suddenly, I find the pair of you skipping around like newlyweds. Why could that possibly be, I wonder?'

She tipped her head to one side, waiting for an explanation but Luna gave nothing away.

'Do you not think it possible for people to fall in love years after being together? I regret my previous behaviour, but Marcus has explained how the opioids affected my reasoning. Now, with the support of my patient husband, I am happily free of such an addiction and we have grown closer because of it. There is no mystery.'

Great-Aunt Elspeth tutted and narrowed her eyes. 'The last time I was here you drank laudanum like tea and that was years ago. No one recovers from such a dependence. I'm afraid I do not believe you are who you claim to be.'

The pair locked eyes but Luna would not allow herself to be intimidated. She had something worth fighting for: Marcus.

'Do you remember the colour of the gown I wore to your wedding?' the old lady persisted.

'Of course not. It was the most monumental day of my life. I had far too many other things to concern myself with.'

'And the name of Marcus's dog as a boy? The one his father bought in Manbury when he was six years old?'

'Again, please forgive me if my memory is inadequate. The drugs often left me in a fuddled state. There is much I struggle to remember, but I do know that his last three dogs were Captain, Gulliver and Lister, and he loved them all dearly. Tell me, Great-Aunt,' she said, leaning forward in challenge as something occurred to her. 'How did your beloved nephew nearly come to die when he was just six years old? What was he up to, that no one knew about that could have killed him?'

Great-Aunt Elspeth looked momentarily thrown, caught out by Luna turning the tables on her, but was unable to answer. After a pause that confirmed she did not know of the near-accident, the old lady shrugged.

'You say you love him but know nothing of his dangerous escapades in the hayloft? Forgive me, but as I generally find one grey-haired elderly lady looks much like another and, like you say, it has been many years since we last met. How can I be sure that *you* are who you say you are?'

'This is ridiculous,' Elspeth scoffed. 'Whether you remember me or not, Marcus knows I am his great-aunt and his word should be sufficient.'

'And Marcus has told you that I am Luna, his wife.' She let the implication hang in the air between them.

'Enough with this nonsense. I'm old but I'm no fool. If you are Luna Greybourne, then I am a creature from the planet Mars.' She thumped her bony hands down on the arms of her chair. 'My vision may not be as sharp as it once was, but there is nothing wrong with my mind. This happy domestic scene has been bothering me ever since I arrived, something nudging at the back of my atrophied mind, and now I remember: her pale eyes – part of the reason my poor nephew was so bewitched in the first place. You are not who you claim to be, young lady, and are executing an unkind deception – one I'm furious that my great-nephew would even attempt. Because, whoever else you might have hoodwinked, you have failed to convince me.'

Luna swallowed. She had put up a good fight but those haunting pale eyes of the Ravenswood Witch, eyes she'd seen herself reflected in the windowpanes of her room, would be her downfall. Yet, still she clung to the fiction she so desperately wished was fact.

'I *am* Luna Greybourne and I love your great-nephew with every fibre of my being. You can proclaim it otherwise, but I would stand in a court of law, lay my hand upon the Bible, and swear it to be the truth.' Whether she could truly commit such a sin was debateable but for the purposes of this argument, she would state it as fact.

Elspeth shook her head from side to side, world-weary and disappointed. 'And yet all I am asking of you, young lady, is your honesty. *Who are you?*'

But Luna had sworn an oath to herself and was not prepared to break it. To admit her real identity to anyone would be tugging at the first loose thread of their life together and would inevitably lead to the unravelling of the rest. She had not spoken her real name aloud for half a year, not even to Marcus whom she loved completely, and she had no intention of doing so to someone who disliked her. 'Luna Greybourne,' she replied, defiantly.

'Then it is time to get the law involved. Tomorrow, I shall see about contacting the local constabulary. I will not have my nephew hoodwinked a second time.' There was a look of grim determination across her wrinkled face, and both women stared at each other like warriors about to do battle. 'Now, if you would be so kind as to ring for the girl, I would like to sit somewhere else – the library, perhaps. The unbearable stench of deception in here has made me feel quite unwell.'

* * *

Luna had become a much stronger person since arriving at the house back in April and would not be bullied by Great-Aunt Elspeth. Nor would she sit by and let bad people hurt those she cared for. She'd been walked over all her life, but Marcus had put her in a position of trust and responsibility. He believed in her. It was about time she believed in herself.

Elspeth had retired early for the night and Luna chose to do the same. She wanted to be with her husband, even though she would have to be mindful of his current fragile state.

'Please get rid of Mr Webber,' she begged. 'He tried to kill you.'

Marcus was propped up in bed, three cushions behind him and a cross expression on his face, not because his wife was requesting the immediate dismissal of the manservant, but more likely because he felt like a fraud and resented being told to rest.

'No, he didn't. Even Webber isn't that stupid,' he replied. 'He's served time for killing one man, he's hardly going to attempt to murder another. I don't much like him but he does what he's asked, and I don't have grounds to sack him. No one could have thrown a slate tile with that degree of accuracy; I was twenty yards away. It was an accident. Let's leave it at that. Besides, you wouldn't want to lose Mrs Webber, and you know she'd have to leave if her husband went.'

Whilst this was true, Luna was determined to keep a closer eye on the man. However, she didn't want to push the matter when Marcus was recuperating so left it to battle out another day.

Sighing, she rose to her feet and begin to undress, surprised how self-conscious she felt considering their activities of the previous night.

'Well, I say, this is a jolly fine affair,' he huffed. 'A man's wife all but naked in front of him, and he under doctor's orders not to do a damn thing about it.'

She smiled and slipped on her nightgown, leaning across the bed to kiss his cheek. A thousand worries were coursing around her head, and the most immediate of these was trying not to worry what havoc Great-Aunt Elspeth might wreak in the morning.

36

Great-Aunt Elspeth was not present at breakfast, even though Hattie had been up to attend to her on a couple of occasions. The meal had been a muted affair, with Marcus now downstairs but being fussed over by Mrs Webber, like a mother hen. Luna was sure their housekeeper felt guilty by association, as his injury had been the fault of her husband, accidental or not. It was likely she had a degree of sympathy with her master, having suffered herself at Webber's hand – the loss of her teeth, Luna had subsequently learned, testament to this.

With no sign of their house guest by midmorning, Luna took it upon herself to visit her bedchamber. The feisty woman appeared even smaller and frailer in the huge bed than she did with her great-nephew towering over her. Without a garland of silk flowers on her head and a colourful smock she looked like any other elderly person. With them, she was a magical woodland imp: mischievous and powerful.

Luna sat on the edge of the bed not sure what to say. All the fight seemed to have evaporated from the older woman overnight and she looked quite pale.

'The thing of it is, I'm dying,' Elspeth said. Again, there was no greeting or preamble to her words. When she had something to say, she simply came out and said it.

'I'm so very sorry,' Luna said, realising this was the reason behind her visit and overwhelming concern for her great-nephew. She would want to know that he was happy before she took her last breath.

'I don't see why. It's not your fault.' Her lips were pinched and her eyes narrow.

'Marcus will be bereft.'

'But not you.' It was a statement, not a question. 'You will be pleased to be rid of the judgemental and interfering old woman.'

'Not at all. You say what you think, instead of hiding behind pleasantries and good manners. Most of all, I understand that whatever you say or do is because you love my husband and want the best for him.'

This was the conclusion she had come to the previous night, tossing and turning in bed, gazing at the sleeping man she would happily lay down her life for. This was the nub, after all: loving someone so much that you would defy God Himself to see them happy.

'And that is why I asked for your honesty,' the old woman said. 'I know that you are not who you claim and I have come to a decision.'

Luna prepared herself for a request to summon the constable.

'As I made perfectly clear to you yesterday, I did not like Luna Greybourne and, much to my surprise, I find that I rather like you. Of course, I have questions: what has happened to her? And who exactly you might be, not to be missed in your previous life and prepared to live this frankly outrageous lie with my great-nephew. But I will likely be dead within the month, and probing around in your lives to extract these answers will not prolong my time on this earth or bring me any comfort – in fact, I rather suspect it will do exactly the opposite. What *will* be of comfort to me in my final days, however, is that Marcus is finally happy after a decade of misery. He is in love with you and I am persuaded that you are in love with him, too. That is enough for me.'

Luna stared at the woman in disbelief. So, that was it? No announcement to the world that she was a fraud? No insistence that she reveal her true identity? And no inquisition into the whereabouts of his real wife?

Tears began to build in Luna's eyes, as she struggled to reply. Despite her resolution never to stray from their fantasy, this dying woman deserved the truth, or what little of the truth she knew. She reached out for the old woman's hands and met her equally watery eyes. 'You may be surprised to learn that I have very few of those answers myself. I turned up at Ravenswood, lost and alone, and your great-nephew took me in for reasons that I still don't understand to this day. He does not talk of her, nor does he complain about what she put him through, but instead looks to the future with a determined defiance that I rather admire. We may yet be undone, but I have left my past behind and will happily take on anyone who tries to prevent him from being my future.'

'Thank you for sharing that.' There was a reciprocal squeeze from Elspeth's surprisingly strong bony fingers. 'And know that I shall not be the one to unravel your life. I may not approve of the deception but then I will not be the one answering to God for my actions. To see my great-nephew laugh, and talk again of flowers and replanting, and hear his plans for the future, is everything to me.' She patted Luna's hand. 'And now, would you ask that rather jumpy young maid of yours to fetch me a jug of warm water? I will heave my failing body from this bed and spend some time with my great-nephew before I leave.'

Their shared love of the same man, and Luna and Marcus's obvious affection, had averted disaster.

The three of them had an enjoyable luncheon, followed by a gentle turn about the grounds. Great-Aunt Elspeth delighted in hearing of Marcus's planting plans, and offered suggestions of her own. If he was aware that the two ladies had somehow reached a truce, he made no comment. Instead, Luna caught him looking adoringly between her face and his great-aunt's when he thought she wasn't looking, as possibly the two people he loved most in the world.

Later that afternoon, they saw Elspeth off in her open carriage, watching in silence as she disappeared into the distance with the widest smile across her thin, pale face, clutching a huge bouquet of slightly wilted marigolds, and with a crown of freshly picked white asters threaded through her long grey hair.

37

A week later, Marcus received the sad news that Great-Aunt Elspeth had passed away. Her death had been expected but they had both hoped she would not be taken from them quite so soon. He attended the funeral alone, as the graveside was most certainly not a place suitable for a woman, and returned home astonished to learn that, apart from some charitable bequests, he was to inherit the majority of her wealth. Along with the promising return he was receiving from his investments, it seemed life was finally being kind to the Greybournes.

Luna and Marcus sat side by side on the bench overlooking the meadow. It was a crisp October evening and she was wrapped in a thick shawl that Mrs Webber had knitted her. One of her husband's wide arms pulled her close, as they watched the racing gilt-edged clouds glide across an indigo sky.

'All Hallows' Eve is nearly upon us,' he said. 'The villagers are already building themselves up into a ridiculous hysteria but at least this year I will not have the worry of what my wife is up to.' He kissed the top of her head and a contented sigh escaped his lips.

A shiver rippled across her skin as Mr Findlay's warning came back to her. If only Marcus could be made to see how the cunning man could help protect them. Could she broach the subject and get him to understand they would shortly be needing Findlay's help? Luna's ghost had been quiet of late, but if there was any day that she would make a reappearance and cause her harm, then that would be the day. They needed all the protection they could get, but she had to tread gently.

'Perhaps we could embrace some of the simple traditions associated with the day? Even though I appreciate you don't believe in such things, where I grew up there was always a bonfire in the neighbourhood to ward off the spirits, and there are various plants that will bring us good luck and prosperity: lavender and rosemary?' She could see his nostrils flare and his arm about her stiffened slightly.

'I know Mrs Webber secretes birch around the house and I turn a blind eye to it, but please don't become one of those who believes that nailing a horseshoe to your door will keep the people inside the house safe from harm, or drinking nettle tea will help a barren woman conceive.'

'I know you think that those who mix up herbs and potions are doing so for nefarious ends, but monks have long since known how to harness the bounty that nature offers. Even God tells us in the psalms that herbs are there for the service of man. Mr Findlay prepares medicines that help people. He's a folk healer, who offers peace of mind, if nothing else.'

If he could be made to see the man was friend and not foe, and she had Marcus's permission to visit Honeysuckle Cottage, then she could get the cunning man's advice over this forthcoming festival. He could help her to keep those at Ravenswood safe from the wrath of Luna's vengeful spirit and the dark magic that would invariably be undertaken at their well, whether Marcus approved of such things or not.

'I don't want you within fifty paces of that man,' Marcus said. 'He is a quack and a fraud, whose interfering, however well meant, has only caused me greater problems in the past. Do not disobey me over this, Luna. I have promised to keep you safe and you must trust me to do just that.'

His face was stern but she knew that he meant what he said, both about keeping away from Findlay, and that he would protect her. Theirs was a love that she had not thought to find again in her lifetime, and she must guard it and, if necessary, make sacrifices in order to keep it. It would always be something they would disagree over: his conviction that magic was nonsense, and her conviction that it was real. The reflection of Luna standing behind her that day had not been in her imagination, the crack in the mirror was not the fault of some imperfection in the glass, and she felt instinctively that the words on the window were her final warning.

The light had all but gone now so they returned inside the house. Hattie had lit a fire and they warmed themselves in front of it for a while as they waited for Mrs Webber to announce dinner. Instead, the maid entered with a worried look on her face.

'Begging your pardon, sir, but the parish constable is at the door asking to see you.'

Marcus stood up from his chair with a puzzled look and Luna wondered what the police wanted with her husband so late into the evening.

'See him in.'

A minute later, Constable Jones walked into the room, and nodded at the Greybournes.

'I apologise for the lateness of the hour...'

Marcus nodded, clearly as anxious as she was to hear of the reason for his visit.

'This is somewhat awkward, sir.' He removed his helmet and spun it nervously around in his hands. 'I know we've had this conversation before, and I'm not usually one to challenge the word of a gentleman, but new evidence has come to light, and I have reason to believe this woman is the runaway I sought six months ago.'

The man looked genuinely troubled. He cleared his throat as Luna and Marcus avoided each other's eyes.

'It is my duty to investigate such a claim, especially as Rose Turner is still at large. We believe she poisoned a certain Daniel Thornbury from Lowbridge, a man whose proposal of marriage she had turned down only a few days previously.'

Marcus's face as the details of the case were announced gave nothing away, but Luna saw the whites of his knuckles as he gripped the back of the fireside chair. 'We have been through this before and, frankly, I am somewhat insulted that you are standing before me and my wife implying we are liars.'

The constable cleared his throat.

'If you had some proof of the young lady's identity?'

'You may check the St Mary's church register at your leisure. You'll find we were married in the summer of 1875.'

'With respect, sir, that proves you have been married ten years, but it does not prove that *this* woman is your wife. Do you have a wedding photograph or even a formal portrait taken of you together before this spring?'

Luna was not as composed as her husband and, in fear of saying the wrong thing, let him handle the matter.

'When my wife was at her most distressed, she destroyed many of our possessions – photographs and documents amongst them. Ask the Kellings what state this house was in when they came to hang wallpapers. Only a few rooms were habitable, for goodness' sake, man; she really was not of sound mind back then.' He turned to Luna. 'Forgive me for talking of these things, darling.'

The constable looked unconvinced. 'Thing is, sir, an Irish tinker who travels about these parts, swears that this is the lady who stopped to ask him the way to the ferry back in April, the day before we came across you both on the path by the river. He saw her with you in the village a while back, but it was only when he was in Lowbridge and heard talk of the unfortunate death of the shoe factory foreman and the maid who ran away shortly after his body was discovered that he made the connection.'

'And I have people who would swear that this is my wife of ten years – Mrs Cole for a start. Honestly, man, who do you trust? An Irish tinker or a respectable woman of business?'

'I can't see that the fellow has anything to gain from making this claim, but I've found people can be persuaded to say anything for money,' the constable pointed out. 'And that could apply to the tinker or Mrs Cole.'

Marcus's cool reserve started to slip. 'Are you suggesting I would bribe a local shopkeeper? Perhaps you should ask the opinion of Hilda, the old woman who called my wife a witch and stabbed her in the street? And arrest her for doing so, while you are about it.'

The policeman rubbed at his long whiskers and tried to keep his tone placatory. 'Mr Greybourne, I am obliged to investigate this accusation. An innocent man was murdered, a young woman fled the village the very next day, and his father seeks justice. But there must be a way to settle this before it becomes a matter for the courts. Unfortunately, the local magistrate is now involved and you are required to meet with him to discuss the matter. I've been asked to request that you and your good lady wife attend his offices in Manbury, a week on Monday, at ten o'clock prompt. If you would kindly provide proof of her identity, we can resolve the matter to the satisfaction of all.'

For the first time since the constable had stepped into the room, Luna's eyes met those of her husband. They had survived Great-Aunt Elspeth, but a magistrate would hardly overlook their deception just because they were a young couple in love, as she had done. 'Please inform the magistrate that we will be there,' Marcus said. 'The sooner this nonsense is put to bed, the better. We have absolutely nothing to hide.'

He walked over to the bell and rang for Mrs Webber. 'My housekeeper will see you out.'

Luna, amazed by her husband's audacity, still had not uttered a single word and could not bring herself to even wish the man a good evening.

For the truth was, they had *everything* to hide and everything to lose.

38

Historically, All Hallows' Eve marked the start of the winter period – the date when herds returned from pasture and land tenures were renewed. It was also a time for honouring the saints and remembering those who had passed away. The Celts believed the veil between the living and the dead was at its thinnest on this day, allowing the departed to walk this earth again. These spirits were expected and, in many cases, actively welcomed. Communities set bonfires on hilltops to relight their hearth fires for the winter and to frighten away any who would do them harm – because there were certainly some ghosts you didn't want visiting. But, unlike the genuine dread that those in Little Doubton felt, most people viewed it as a festival of fun and celebration.

The particularly frivolous saw this night as a favourable time for foretelling the future, and young ladies took the opportunity to divine their marriage prospects with nonsense parlour games. Carved turnip and pumpkin jack-o'-lanterns hung about the villages and towns, where people made merry and danced into the night. Even the queen was known for her extravagant parties in Balmoral, where a witch effigy was carried through the estate and tossed into a bonfire. Little Doubton, however, had lived for generations with the legend telling of the Devil being summoned up through the Ravenswood well and dancing through the streets, gathering the souls of those destined for the underworld. There would be no All Hallows' Eve parties held there, unlike the coming together for the harvest celebrations. No one of sound mind would be seen outside after dark, even those who claimed not to believe in the legend. Instead, gifts of food were left on the doorsteps for the souls that passed by, and everyone remained behind their firmly bolted doors.

It was rather surprising therefore when Marcus told her that he was going to the well that morning, with all its associations with witchcraft, and asked if Luna would like to accompany him.

'But you know I find the woods disconcerting.' She suspected her anxiety was etched across her face.

'And equally, you know how much I love them. Nature brings me so much joy; from my love of flowers, with their exquisite beauty, fragility and heavenly scents, to my admiration of the sturdy oak, which embodies strength, longevity and renewal. I always find that wandering amongst the ancient trunks of the trees makes me feel calmer and more at peace. Too long have my woods been used for dark practices, and the creatures within it vilified for unjust reasons. My ravens were protectors of the well, and yet are associated with death purely because they are scavengers.'

Luna knew that people were wary of Bran for just this reason; even Great-Aunt Elspeth had not been enamoured of the bird. But he was no omen of ill, instead a loyal friend who guarded against evil. If Marcus could see the good in him, could she revise her opinion of the woods?

'Bats are similarly feared, frightening us at night with their swooping dives,' he continued. 'But they are only after insects attracted by the light. There are always two ways of looking at things; some people choose to see the dark side of our flora and fauna, whereas I choose to see the light. Today, of all days, let me show you the beauty and wonder of our woods, and let us dispel those silly notions that you carry.'

She hesitated. It was the one day she wanted to remain safely within the walls of her home, but she could sense her husband's building irritation.

He put out his hand. 'I can't allow your misguided superstitions to haunt you. Let me show you that there is nothing to be afraid of.'

The low October sun was strong but it had little heat to impart. The ground was dry as they crunched through curled leaves and fallen nuts, and there was a dusty smell in the air, not dissimilar to the hymn books of church. Most of the trees were bare now; a few stubborn leaves remained, clinging on until the next gust of wind took them on their final journey to join the scattered yellows, oranges and reds of the woodland floor. Only the oaks and beech trees clung to their brittle umber leaves.

They stopped at the animal graves and Marcus was silent, kneeling down before every cross and placing a small hand-knotted bunch of teasels on each one, collected from the meadow before their departure. Luna stood back to let him honour his dead and his memories. Perhaps they could consider another dog now, although it would almost certainly put Bran's beak out of joint.

They wandered in and out of the dappled light, as he told her the names of the various mosses and fungi they encountered. He talked about the harmony of the woodland, and explained how nature dealt so efficiently with the cycles of life and death. Most of these trees had been here before he'd been born, he said, and it was a comfort to know that they would likely be standing long after he had died.

Finally, they came to the clearing and a strange feeling swept over her.

'It's sinister here, Marcus. I don't like it.'

'That's because the sun struggles to reach the forest floor for much of the year. You naturally associate it with the dark, and therefore the nonsense practices of those who come out at night. But centuries ago, this was a hallowed and healing place.' He spread his arms wide and grinned. 'On such a splendid morning as this, how can you think of it as a place of evil? I have been cursed in these woods a hundred times and yet I stand before you, alive and unharmed. The magic is not real and you have simply been manipulated by storybooks and rumour.'

Perhaps she could see the beauty in the grand oaks: wise and wonderful old men guarding the water source. But the thick carpet of acorns scattered around her feet reminded her that there were no squirrels or other small mammals to feed on them. She walked to the well and trailed her hand around the cold stones of its construction.

'Do you think it will ever flow again?'

He shrugged. 'That is down to the vagaries of nature and certainly not dependent on some ridiculous legend proclaiming new life must be created here in order to bring the well back to life – utter hogwash. This is a place of joy, Luna. Be joyous.' Could she embrace the love that Marcus so clearly had for this place? She walked into a patch of dappled light and lifted her face to the heavens, feeling his eyes upon her.

'You are so beautiful,' he said. 'Chosen by the sun.' He moved to stand in front of her and reached for her cheek. 'I forget sometimes what you have been through in the last six months, and I don't think I have always been very understanding.'

'You have been *everything*,' she replied.

He bent down to find her lips with his own. Still new to their emotions, and both with an inability to rein them in, what started as a gentle kiss became an unstoppable avalanche of longing that neither of them could control. The companionship had come first, and in some ways it had been enough. But now that they had discovered their intense physical connection, they took every opportunity to explore it. Within moments of his kiss, her hands were clawing at his hair and he manoeuvred her backwards until she bumped into the trunk of one of those ancient guardians.

'Let's make this place somewhere you associate with happy memories,' he whispered into her ear. It wasn't a question, and he fumbled to hitch up her layers of skirts, before lifting her from the ground and supporting her weight. She instinctively wrapped her legs around his waist and draped her arms about his neck.

She nodded her consent.

'Hold on to me,' he instructed, as he moved his hands beneath her to deal with his trouser buttons, before returning them to her slender waist.

She tipped her head backwards with that first thrust, looking up through the tracery of thin branches to the blue sky beyond. Only when the intensity of everything overwhelmed her, did she close her eyes and allow all rational thoughts to float to the leaves at his feet.

A few minutes later, she was gently lowered to the ground. Marcus held her close as his racing heart and jagged breaths began to slow, and she considered how utterly reckless they had been to make love in the open air, where anyone could have stumbled across them, but then that had been part of the thrill. Finally, he took a step back and she smoothed down her dress, her legs still trembling but her love for him stronger than ever.

'There now, we've made our own magic,' he said. 'How can you not think of the woods fondly after this?' He smiled and put out his hand to guide her home.

* * *

The house was quiet upon their return, partly because Luna had honoured her promise to Hattie that she and her brother need not come to Ravenswood on All Hallows' Eve. It was surprising how much their youth and bustling presence added to the energy of the house, and now that they were absent it felt empty.

She desperately wanted to talk to Marcus about their impending visit to the magistrate, but how could she ask him what they could do to convince the man of her legitimacy when he would not discuss the truth? He stuck to the fantasy that she was his wife of ten years, and not a fugitive from justice.

Disconcerted by the unusually noiseless house, she called for Bran. He hadn't come to them in the woods, nor had he eaten the food scraps Mrs Webber had left outside the back door. She searched for him in the gardens and even rattled his treats, but Marcus reminded her that he was a wild bird with an exceedingly strong will, and not her docile pet. He would show up when it suited him and not a moment before.

Later, they walked together with Mrs Webber to the All Hallows' Eve church service, where the vicar talked of those who had passed away in the community over the past twelve months, and they lit candles to remember the dead. Marcus, she noticed, lit two, but she made no comment. Fully aware of the legend, and the sensitivities of this congregation, the vicar finished the service early enough for people to return to the sanctuary of their homes in daylight.

Once back at Ravenswood, Mrs Webber repeatedly stressed the need for Luna to remain safely inside, and made a big show of bolting all the doors and discreetly slipping sprigs of rosemary where her master wouldn't notice them. Marcus insisted that his wife took a mug of cocoa upstairs to help her sleep, but it tasted strange and she wondered if he had added a sleeping draught to the drink. In the end, she tipped half of it into the chamber pot under the bed when he wasn't looking.

'Sleep tight, little one,' he said, kissing her on the forehead before blowing out the candle. A part of her had hoped for him to come to her again, but she also knew he'd been distracted since returning from church, and wondered if, despite his denials, there was not a small part of him mourning his great-aunt, or even his wife. Because tonight was dedicated to remembering the dead and she strongly suspected he was doing exactly that.

39

She wasn't sure of the hour but Luna stirred and reached her arm out to Marcus's side of the bed. Although the sheets were still warm, he was absent. Sitting upright, she focused on the shapes in the shadows, but there was no moment to suggest he remained in the room with her. Where had he gone to in the middle of the night, on All Hallows' Eve, the one night he knew she would not want to be left alone?

Bran had still not appeared and she went to the window, lifting the sash and hoping he would fly down to greet her. But all that came in through the open gap was a chill breeze and the faint aroma of woodsmoke.

As she looked out, she saw someone crossing from the house to the woods. It was definitely a man judging by the length of his stride, but the figure was of slim build and far more likely to be Mr Webber than Marcus. Could he be connected to Bran's disappearance or her husband's night-time wanderings? Luna wondered if he was heading to the well; she would not be at all surprised if he had made the clay figures of her. Although Webber had not shown much outward interest in his wife's supernatural leanings, the cursing of Mother Selwood still sat uneasily with Luna. Had *he* cursed the old woman? Her heart started to thud alarmingly. She wondered, not for the first time, if their manservant could be the witch.

It was only then that it struck her that Bran and Marcus might be in danger. Was tonight the night Luna would finally wreak her ghostly revenge? And if the Ravenswood Witch was in league with Webber, what might the two of them be capable of? Findlay had warned her there would be people at the well, and that blood would be shed. A cold fear started to seep from her chest and spread to all areas of her body, rendering her arms and legs numb. Her fears of being exposed as Rose were superseded by this much more immediate concern, and she couldn't stand by and do nothing.

'*The magic is only real if you believe,*' she reiterated to herself, as she quickly pulled on a woollen skirt over her nightgown and grabbed a shawl from her wardrobe. It was interesting how her deep love and concern for another gave her the courage to overcome her fears. The woods were not evil; they were simply a place of quiet solitude and wisdom. Marcus had shown her that she did not need to be afraid of the trees or the shadows. But she had long suspected there was cause to be frightened of Mr Webber and what he might do.

Five minutes later, she was downstairs and peering in every room in her attempt to locate her husband, desperately hoping he had popped into the drawing room for a nightcap, or, unable to sleep, and taken himself to the library with a hot cocoa. But when she eventually got to the boot room, she saw that his boots and warm woollen coat were missing. It meant Marcus had left the house, so she collected a hurricane lamp and slipped outside, noting that the back door through the kitchens was unbolted. As a last-minute thought, she scooped some salt from the salt box, in a feeble attempt to protect herself from evil spirits.

She was done with all the secrets and lies. Marcus must know what had happened to his wife and she could no longer pretend it didn't matter. Their life together was a fabrication and they would invariably be found out. She may not have been responsible for Daniel's death but, by running away, she had let the real culprit escape justice. And Mr Webber was a bad man, cruel to his wife and up to no good in the night. It suited him for everyone to stay locked up on All Hallows' Eve because then he would not be followed into the woods. But she no longer thought he was turning his hand to something innocuous, like a bit of poaching, and now genuinely believed he was practising the dark arts.

The lamp cast long shadows as the chill in the night air bit into her skin. There was a low mist floating about her feet and she wondered at her bravery. But then she was a different person to the nervous maidservant who had turned up at Ravenswood six months ago. She pulled the shawl tighter around her shoulders and set off with determined steps, towards the smell of woodsmoke and faint glow she could see between the trunks of the skeletal trees, wishing Bran would appear, his prolonged absence now causing her real concern.

The handle of the lamp gave an eerie squeak as it swung in her raised hand, but she kept striding deeper into the wood that had been so welcoming only a few hours before, trying not to think of the spirits of the dead, until the bonfire was within sight.

She stepped into the clearing, looking for whoever was responsible. The mist was patchy here, where the heat from the fire had dispelled it, and she could see a selection of puzzling objects on the ground next to a small hessian sack. A large area of soil had been swept bare of leaves, and a pentagram was scratched into the dirt within a larger circle. She had no idea what the shapes and symbols meant, but suspected necromancy was at work here. This was no bonfire lit in remembrance of those who had passed away over the previous year, but something far more sinister. This fire was symbolic of creation and destruction, a way to harness transformative powers. Someone was trying to summon the dead, or perhaps even the Devil.

She hurried over to the well and had the unnerving sensation she was being watched, but by a physical presence or a spiritual one she wasn't sure. A lantern stood on the well's edge, and its flickering light illuminated several new poppets that certainly hadn't been at the site that morning.

'Well, well, what do we have here?' a voice came from behind.

A rough hand gripped her shoulder and her blood froze in her pulsing veins, because she knew exactly who was standing behind her.

'I've been expecting you.'

40

That cheery voice had lost its friendly edge. The sense of calm Luna had always felt in his presence was now a searing terror. She had been such a fool.

Luna spun to face Mr Findlay, surprised to find him shrouded in a light brown cloak and hood. Those blue eyes of his no longer looked twinkly and friendly but had taken on a more sinister edge. There was a snide curl of the lip and a haunting solemnity about his gaze.

'I trust the rest of your household have heeded my warning to remain inside, as I really do not want to be disturbed, tonight of all nights.'

Luna said nothing. At that moment in time, the only person safely inside the house was Mrs Webber.

'The dark one will be joining us soon and I am certain you will find it a truly magnificent spectacle.'

It took her a few seconds to understand what he meant by the dark one. He certainly wasn't referring to a grumpy Marcus. He noticed her confusion and clearly delighted in explaining.

'You must surely be aware of the properties of the water from the Ravenswood well. They have been referenced in numerous demonology texts since the Middle Ages, and I moved halfway across the county to have access to it because I believe there may be even more power here than at my beloved Stonehenge. I have tired of waiting for Mr Greybourne to do his part and get the well flowing. It is up to me, my dear, to realise the legend, and then you shall witness the horrifying yet transcendent pageantry of All Hallows' Eve. I'm afraid I need your assistance though, which was why I cast a summoning spell. And here you are.' He looked inordinately pleased with himself.

She thought about what had made her enter the woods but felt strongly that the decision had been hers and hers alone. There had been no inexplicable force dragging her reluctant feet outside. He may have ground up powders and muttered magical words, but the fact she was at the well was coincidence, and linked purely to her desire to find Marcus, not his use of sorcery.

'I don't understand; you counteract dark magic, you don't practise it.'

Mr Findlay looked disappointed and opened up a small leather pouch hanging at his waist to scatter the dried contents onto the fire. Revived by the highly combustible offering, it swelled and roared – a dragon woken from its slumbers and showing its anger by expelling deep orange flames that reached out into the blackness that surrounded it. A heady exotic fragrance with sickly sweet undertones filled the air. He inhaled deeply before turning his attention back to her.

'I thought you were brighter than that, *Rose*.'

She felt a jolt as he said the name out loud. No one, except Constable Jones, had spoken it in months, but she gave nothing away. Ravenswood was her home and Marcus was her husband. She would not acknowledge anything from before that time.

'The constable was round a few days ago asking questions,' he continued, feeling the need to explain how he had come by his knowledge. 'Some housemaid from Lowbridge poisoned a young lad who was sweet on her. Ran from the village the day his body was discovered and was tracked to Little Doubton, where the trail went cold. How strange, I thought to myself, that it should be around the time you arrived at Ravenswood.'

He smiled but his cheeks no longer looked rosy. Instead, he looked jowly and the roundness of his face only served to highlight how small and sinister his eyes were.

'But worry not, dear child, I said nothing. I simply could not have you arrested and taken to Branchester gaol when I need you here. You may not be who you claim to be, but you are certainly the woman Marcus Greybourne loves, and that means you are the one I've been seeking.'

Seeking? The word made her shiver. It was bad enough that the constable was hunting her, but that Findlay had also been pursuing her made her blood run cold in her veins.

'I don't know what you're talking about. I'm Luna Greybourne,' she said, even though they both knew it to be a lie. Her heart started pumping faster and her eyes darted about. Planning to make a run for it, she wondered which path was her best option, but Findlay was inching closer, blocking her escape. She began to back away but her body came into contact with the cold stone well. He had her pinned.

'We can play that game, if you wish, my dear, but I am running out of time now, so I'd rather we focused on the matters at hand. Shall we begin?'

He reached forward and took the lamp from her shaking hands, resting it on the edge of the well next to his own lantern.

Luna's mind raced to make sense of what was happening, as he studied her confused expression. A small shrieking black bat swooped past her face, making her jump, especially as there were so few creatures in these woods. Then she remembered Marcus had told her that the insects were attracted by the firelight, and the bats were here for the insects. There was nothing to be afraid of – apart from Mr Findlay it would suddenly seem.

'Oh dear, are you now only realising that I am not what I have led you to believe? Perhaps you should have listened to Mr Greybourne, but women always think they know best.' He shook his head. 'I need the well to flow again, if not for tonight, then soon, because I waited far too long for Luna to break the spell to no avail. I consider myself a patient man, but the time has come for action. "When new life is created at the well, so shall the well come back to life".'

But surely this was just a silly superstition. Marcus was undoubtedly right about that, too. Only an act of nature could cause it to flow again.

'I don't understand what that has to do with me.'

'I thought it was Luna, you see? The rumours of the well's power were legendary, especially in the circles I move in. These woods are special – the purity of the water, the depth of the shaft, the presence of such ancient oaks. Before the persecution of my kind, and the drying out of the sacred water source, this was a truly magical site and it was foretold that one day it would become so again. When I arrived in Little Doubton, the tarot told me that the woman to fulfil the prophecy would be the mistress of Ravenswood, and it was the creation of her child that would cause the spring to flow.'

Luna felt a shiver run through her. Was that why he'd given her the rose-scented potion? What she'd thought was genuine concern for her happiness was a manipulative attempt to get her and Marcus to have a physical relationship, in the hope that a child would come from the union.

'Two years I waited and nothing.' He sighed. 'She believed herself barren, perhaps she was, and it only served to contribute to her madness and despair. However, I considered what she had not, that it might be her husband who was at fault, and so decided there was more than one way to skin the proverbial cat. I had only divined the truth of the mother, not necessarily the father.'

Findlay's gaze was dreamy and unfocused. 'She was utterly beguiling; those pale eyes had me hypnotised from the first time we met,' he continued. 'I had not touched her, as I thought it was her husband who must fulfil the prophecy – but when we finally came together in that way, she was by the well, twirling about totally naked in a beam of moonlight, waving a long thread of scarlet ribbon in the air. She pretended not to notice me and continued to leap and writhe in time with her mystical chanting, until I slipped off my cloak and she saw that I, too, was unclothed...'

'I don't want to—' But Findlay would not be silenced. He wanted to relive this memory and wanted her to hear him do so. How wrong she had been to think Mr Webber was Luna's lover, when all the time it was Mr Findlay.

'I remember how she tipped her head back, stretching her arms to the sky, as though she could sweep her fingers through the stars, and allowed me to reach out and trace a line from her wrist, down her arm to circle under one of her breasts. We both knew why I was there and revelled in one moment of perfect stillness before she became a wild beast, pulling me to her with a roughness that took even me by surprise. Her husky laugh was cruel and self-satisfied, as though it was she who had orchestrated events – perhaps she had. And then the savage hunger in both of us was allowed to explore its violent and unfettered recklessness. We were so alike, you see?'

Luna most definitely did *not* see, nor did she want to hear any more, but he was determined she would listen to his tale.

'Her desires were even more disturbing than mine, and when she had finished, and rose from me, the moonlight highlighted the deep scratches and smears of blood that covered her thin, pale body. She had enjoyed every moment, and the pain and brutality of it all had been part of the thrill.

'Our encounters, though, proved unfruitful and I suspected she was barren, after all. The prophecy made no sense. And then you appeared and I began to wonder if I'd interpreted the cards incorrectly. But I should have known that the honourable Marcus Greybourne would not touch you.' He sneered. 'And it would seem the love philtre I passed to you has failed me.'

'I never used it,' she said, defiantly. 'And I'm glad now, for anything could be in it.'

'You drank my teas though.' He gave a sly smile. 'And were all the more suggestible because of them.'

Revelations were tumbling out at an alarming rate. What had he put in those infusions when she'd visited Honeysuckle Cottage? Had he been drugging her? *Had he been drugging Luna?* She was thankful not to have relied on the laudanum. But as the sickly scent in the woodsmoke grew stronger, she suspected he had put something equally intoxicating on the fire.

He caught her alarmed expression.

'Devil worship is so often misunderstood; we merely desire to indulge in a lifestyle others might consider immoral or sinful.' He shrugged. 'Often, it is at the expense of weaker individuals, but I do not lose sleep over that. We shun abstinence and advocate an eye for an eye. I do not think we are so very terrible just because we have the backbone to grab what we want from the world. My happiness is greater and my life more colourful than yours. I am not confined by your rules. I make my own.'

'But you have healed so many villagers, even protected them from witchcraft.' She was still struggling with how she'd been duped.

'What better way to win people over? It certainly worked with you. Besides, it's not that I wish people ill, just that I wish *specific* people ill. I do not desire to be persecuted as a witch, so it is rather fortunate that the accoutrements one needs to practise good magic can equally be used to practise bad. There are a few things I keep out of sight...' She thought back to the locked trunk at Honeysuckle Cottage that he'd told her contained poisons and valuable spices. 'Things it would not be wise for me to have on display, but I generally find people are more helpful when they consider you an ally. And, because I believe in giving even the hunted fox a fighting chance – it rather adds to the game, don't you think? – I even tried to warn you.'

How stupid she had been. Findlay had said it over and over again: not everyone could be trusted, even those she thought of as friends.

'But you said the evil was at Ravenswood.'

'And you don't think she is? You have admitted to seeing her. She visits me too. Marcus killed her, you know. She finally told me this and begged me to take his life, but I thought I needed him, like I need you, to get the well to flow.' He shrugged. 'It was clear to me that you loved him, but I had not counted on his faith. He is a man who does not condone sexual immorality – quite the mystery to me because it is such an inordinate amount of fun. Luna and I often laughed at how he had even saved himself for their wedding night.'

How dare they mock Marcus, she thought, rubbing her temples as she tried to focus on everything she was being told. But her head was feeling woolly and her senses were fighting for clarity.

'I'm a desperate man, Rose, and have waited long enough. If new life must be created at the well, then let us create it...' he grabbed her wrists and jerked her horrified face closer, '...tonight.'

The bumpy stones embedded in the well walls dug painfully into her back as he pinned her down with his surprisingly strong right arm, bending her backwards so that her head hovered above the deep shaft behind her. He used his free hand to wrestle with the buttons of the purple trousers he wore under the cloak, but she was not having this and fought back. If this was to be her fate, she would not make it easy for him.

'Feisty little thing, aren't you? I think I like your angry spirit even more. Luna was always a willing, if violent, participant, and yet your genuine struggle is surprisingly arousing.'

It was no use. Even had he not been physically stronger and taller, the way he had his body across hers and her vulnerable position, bent backwards across the well, meant she was never going to throw him off. She began to cry out in the hope that someone, anyone, would hear, determined to break free, even though she knew it was impossible. Where were they? Bran and Marcus, her protectors?

The scent from the fire was snaking around them, more concentrated now as the herbs and powders intensified in the heat, floating about their heads like a creeping and ominous fog. She felt alone and suddenly very foolish; she had trusted the enemy for the second time in her life, and failed to spot his duplicity until it was too late.

Her head was starting to spin, thoughts wriggling out of her control as everything became blurry and distant, but she would not let this man win. Standing in front of the persuasive Eloise, she had buckled at her mistress's strength and allowed herself to be manipulated. The decision to flee had been the wrong one; she knew that now. It would have been better to stand up for herself – to fight. And now that she finally had a life she wanted to fight for, she would do exactly that.

Twisting her pinned hands towards each other, she was able to slip one slender wrist free of his tight grasp. As she liberated it, it flew behind her head and caught the nearest of the lamps, sending it tumbling into the well. There was a cracking of glass as it ricocheted off the sides of the deep shaft on its way down, the light immediately extinguished, and then an unexpected splash as it eventually hit the bottom.

The well held water, which meant the spring was flowing once more.

'How can this be?' he asked, frowning as he peered over the edge and into the dark chasm below. He turned back to look at Luna, before both sets of wide eyes fell to her flat belly.

41

Just as she'd begun to convince herself that the magic was nonsense, a small part of her wondered if what she and Marcus had done in these very woods that afternoon could possibly have any bearing on this startling revelation. If so, it meant that she was now carrying his child, although with their recent and reckless intimacy, maybe it was inevitable.

Mr Findlay's eyebrows rose in surprise.

'So, you have lain with the foolish man who took you in, after all. And presumably in these very woods. How very daring. I must own to be wrong-footed... and even a little disappointed that I'll not have the pleasure. Not tonight at any rate.'

Her anger at his smug satisfaction began to bubble like the very spring that was surely now feeding the well. She lifted her head and spat in his face, but Findlay didn't so much as blink as he let his arms fall from her clothing and released her remaining hand.

'This All Hallows' Eve,' he smiled, 'the possibilities are endless. A simple summoning for Him to gather all the departed souls of the year can now have even more majestic results. He will be so pleased with me. The water will give me greater powers and add to my strength. But, as I can't have you running off, I must first perform a binding spell.'

Still blocking her escape by his proximity, her inability to move at that moment was also partly due to the shock revelation that she couldn't even begin to deal with properly. Findlay fixed his eyes on her face as he uttered an incomprehensible incantation to the background of the building scent. It was getting harder to focus and a kaleidoscope of colours blurred the edges of her view, but she managed to push herself into an upright position. Whatever he had thrown on to the fire was affecting her on so many levels: her vision, her balance, her ability to think clearly.

As Findlay's words drifted in the air between them, Luna felt her legs grow heavy and almost physically anchor to the soil – as if invisible roots had snaked from the soles of her feet and twisted into the ground. She attempted to take a step but was welded to the woodland floor as surely as the farrier nails a horseshoe to the hoof. How was this even possible?

Marcus's often repeated words were first and foremost in her mind, and she clung to the image of his uncompromising face to give her strength. She was being tricked by a master manipulator into believing that she was under his power, when none of it was real – just suggestion and the influence of powerful drugs.

Confident that she couldn't move, Findlay turned his back on her and walked over to the assortment of candles, jars and strange implements abandoned on the ground. The hood fell from his head as he began to place curious objects around the large circle on the woodland floor. A chant in that strange and indecipherable language that he so often used came from his mouth. Happy with the final arrangement, he held his arms out to the fire, palms upwards as twisting shapes appeared, and pale grey streaks of hazy nothingness were pulled towards the flames. They resembled trails of smoke but instead of drifting away from the heat, they were being sucked towards it.

'She wanted to kill you but I asked her to wait, although I can quite believe she's causing mischief in the house – the odd visitation, perhaps a slammed door or a chill breeze? And now she joins us tonight,' Findlay said, turning to her. 'Watching all this.'

Luna swallowed hard. She twisted her head, even though her body was largely immobile, but she couldn't see anyone with them in the clearing.

'She came to me not long after you appeared at Ravenswood. I hadn't seen her for days and wondered if Greybourne had put her in some asylum, but it was then that I knew the truth. Her spirit was angry and bitter. And now the master of All Hallows' Eve calls her, along with all the dead souls he is entitled to collect. She is walking these woods in her misery and has confirmed what I suspected all along: Marcus killed her.'

'No.' Luna shook her head, unable to believe this of her husband. She knew him to be a good man, but nagging doubts started to swim in her watery mind, thrashing against waves of uncertainty. He had always been so sure that their deception was not in danger of discovery. Was that because he knew of his wife's demise? And then she thought back to the morning after they had first made love and how he had tacitly acknowledged that he, too, had done wicked things.

Luna looked to the trees and it was as though the whole wood was coming alive; her surroundings were still swirling incomprehensibly, but the murky smudges had more definition now. She could make out contours and limbs. The whispers of a host of voices echoed in her ears, and the eyes of a hundred creatures fell upon her face. She could swear there was a cackle as one of the ambiguous bands of shadow whooshed past her face and into the fire, causing it to swell even more; the mass of it was now over four foot wide and spreading. Findlay was adding souls, not wood, to the bonfire.

'And here she is!' Findlay announced, with all the excitement of a small child. 'Look how she dances in the flames. Always drawn to the fire, was Luna.'

The dizziness was threatening to destroy her tenuous grip on conscious thought, but there was, without doubt, a dancing woman, writhing and twisting in the building orange inferno. The figure was naked, with long hair falling around her body like a cloak and her arms high, waving in ecstasy.

'The light from the fire guides them here, and then holds them until He can come from the depths to gather them together and lead them on a merry dance through the streets of Little Doubton. Anyone foolish enough to be in his path is swept up and dragged back to the biggest blaze of all – the raging inferno that is the underworld.'

As more of the floating figures were pulled into the clearing, she tried to focus on them: staggering men emerging from the gnarled trunks of the trees, grimacing old women floating down from the bare branches above, and the occasional young child – part smoky illusion and part human. She thought for the smallest moment of time she even saw Webber in the shadows of the dense trunks, which made no sense because as far as she knew he was alive and well.

Satisfied with his work, Findlay walked back to those objects not in the circle. Luna had abandoned her calls for help. She felt weak and muddled, but she was also gripped by a morbid fascination with everything that was unfolding before her.

He was not looking at her, instead busying himself with his ritual, and continued with a steady stream of chatter and elucidation, occasionally humming to himself.

'Of the ten commandments, I do believe I have broken every single one,' he said with glee. 'I despised my parents and even hastened my own mother's departure from this world – sanctimonious bitch. I have stolen since I was old enough to crawl, worshipped many gods, and have no special reverence for the Sabbath. But of all my transgressions, coveting Luna and committing adultery with her, time and time again, gave me the most satisfaction. She had to come to me at the cottage after we were spotted by those damn ravens, as they would no longer let me in the woods, but with her help I made them pay for their actions. Yes, undoubtedly my preferred sin is adultery,' he said. 'But the taking of a life, human or otherwise, comes a pleasing second. Tell me, my dear, what did it feel like when you poisoned the poor man in Lowbridge? Did you feel a secret thrill? A moment of power and triumph?'

Luna didn't respond, merely narrowed her eyes and tried to give nothing away. She would not protest her innocence to him, especially as it occurred to her that if he believed she was capable of murder, it might be in her favour. He walked to the other side of the well and took a large grimoire from the medicine bag that she belatedly realised was tucked out of sight. He placed the book on the flat stone edge to the side of her; she could still turn her head enough to see what he was up to. Mystical symbols were embossed into the cover of the leather in gold, and the edges were protected by brass corners.

'And now he calls for blood, my master, to enable him to claim the damaged as his own. Those whose thoughts and desires are far from pure: the selfish, the tainted and the duplicitous; the non-believers and heretics.'

He opened the pages, his finger running along the jagged, inky words. 'Ah, yes, the blood of a sacrifice, a handful of crushed deadly nightshade berries and water of the purest origins – all to be stirred anti-clockwise with a black feather.'

At the word *sacrifice*, the colour drained from her face and an icy chill crept across her skin. Was he now to kill her so that she might be an ingredient in this spell?

'Luckily for me, I can kill two birds with one stone, or rather procure two necessary elements of this ritual with one bird.'

He walked over to collect the sack, untied the neck and pulled out a limp Bran. His beak was bound shut and a rag wrapped around his body to disable his wings.

'No!' she screamed, and still her legs would not cooperate.

'This is why the water is so important,' he explained. 'The fresh blood of an innocent – and you are sadly no longer that – and the water from the well combine to increase my powers. I have not been able to summon him since those damn ravens attacked me every time I approached the boundary, but this year... *this year* I shall fulfil my destiny. And to have the water flowing again is beyond my wildest imaginings.'

He rubbed his chubby hands together in unconcealed glee and drew a long blade from the folds of his cloak. The fire was now barely fifteen yards from them, and was beginning to roar, almost as if the dancing souls within were creeping closer in expectation. As the flames leapt higher, their colours changed from deep reds and oranges to a more intense yellow and white.

Placing Bran onto the flat stone edge with one hand, Findlay lifted the blade with the other. The bound raven jerked his head and tried to peck at his captor, but it was useless.

'No last-minute deliverance for you this time,' he said to the bird. 'I really was terribly frustrated that you'd survived the cull I had been so many months encouraging Luna to execute, but with all of your kind gone, I shall at last be free to come and go.'

The anger within Luna was building. Findlay was behind everything. But was his magic real or imagined? Whatever he'd thrown onto the fire was clearly affecting her mind. Could the binding spell be entirely in her head? She had to fight this. Marcus was right.

Focusing every ounce of strength she had on the muscles in her legs, she managed to lift her right leg and shunt it forward, combining it with the most primal growl that escalated to a victorious crescendo as she felt this strength grow. Findlay was momentarily distracted from whatever incantation he was reciting and looked over to see what all the noise was about.

He opened his mouth to speak but instead his jaw dropped as he realised she was lurching towards him. Dragging her other leg to the front, her slow stumble became a drunken stagger, until she rushed at him, shoving him to the ground. They landed in a heap with her body over his, as the knife and the bird fell from his hands. With one swift movement, she pulled at the twine restricting the raven's beak and Bran shook his head free, before tugging the cloth from his body and finally stretching out his liberated wings. He flapped them furiously as he called into the night air, 'Curse you! Curse you!'

'Do your worst, Bran,' she cried. This man deserved no sympathy.

The bird turned his head to look at her and, fearful of what was to come, she grabbed the knife to protect herself, but neither bird nor man were interested in her. Findlay scrabbled to his feet and lurched for the raven, who flew at him with all the frenzy of a rabid dog. Again and again, the wrathful creature attacked, as his prey waved his arms ineffectually in the air. Luna knew from experience how strong and sharp that lethal beak was. She also suspected that the cunning man's own senses were as dulled as her own from inhaling the potent fumes from the fire. The scene before her was a mass of black, furiously flapping feathers and the sickening shrieks of both hunter and victim.

'My eyes! Not my eyes!'

She was forced to turn her head away as she witnessed the streaks of blood where the beak was inflicting its damage, and scrunched up her own eyes, as if not watching would make all the horror disappear. If only she could shut out the sounds of agonised screams and frantic beating wings as the bird attacked.

'You bitch!' Findlay screamed. 'Call off your familiar. What kind of witch are you?'

She gripped the knife tighter between her shaking hands, expecting the man to come at her again now that her guard was down, but when she turned to face him, two bloodied eye sockets confronted her, and he was swinging his head wildly from side to side. The sight of him, his face hardly even recognisable *as* a face, made her retch into the rotting leaves.

The brief silence that followed was interrupted by a loud shout.

'What the hell?' A pounding of feet and Marcus's shocked voice pulled her back to the moment. Findlay lurched to the left as Marcus rushed over to her, and Bran flew up onto the roof of the well, clearly feeling he'd done enough.

'The waters... I need the healing waters...' Findlay started to zigzag aimlessly around, waving his arms in front of him and moaning in pain.

'My God, if you have laid a hand on my wife, Findlay... Luna? Are you okay. What the hell is going on?'

He fell to his knees beside her and placed both arms around her shaking body, drawing her close. They both watched as Findlay spun in circles, with no idea where he was, and then blundered blindly towards the bonfire. The beast had grown even greater, as the ferocious flames came dangerously close to overhanging branches, and fingers of flame seemed to reach out and grab the man. Could he not feel the intense heat licking at his cloak? The cloth caught and Luna realised he was on fire.

Again, she was forced to turn her head away as an almighty roar of flame was followed by blood-curdling shrieks, and she buried her head in Marcus's broad chest. There was an intense wave of heat and every square inch of her skin felt afire, before a final roar and then an eerie flickering and crackle of burning wood. She turned back to the bonfire to find it had inexplicably damped down to almost nothing.

'Did he touch you? Are you hurt?' Marcus gripped Luna's shoulders to look at her face and she shook her head.

Relieved that she was unharmed, he let her fall into him again and stroked her hair, holding her close as she sobbed into his coat and explained how she'd come looking for him but instead found Findlay, who had talked of summoning the Devil and tried to murder Bran.

'That damned man was so much more dangerous than I thought. And, also, completely unhinged. I hope you were sensible enough to know that whatever you think you saw, you were being manipulated?'

She nodded and decided to say nothing of the spirits. Yes, her reality had been warped with opiates or some other mind-altering substance, but she was in no doubt that Mr Findlay had possessed dark powers that were not of this world.

'I called for help,' she said. 'Where were you?'

'I came as soon as I realised there was activity in the woods; firelight and shouts carried in the night air. I thought you were in the house. I thought you were safe. I put something in your cocoa. You were supposed to sleep through the night.'

He hadn't answered her question but she didn't pursue it. He was here now and, for the moment, that was enough.

They huddled together on the woodland floor for a while, both shaken by the what-ifs and what-had-beens, until the distant sound of voices caused them both to turn their heads towards the house.

It made no sense but as the babble of chatter got nearer, it was apparent that a huge crowd of people were heading for the well. Marcus helped her to her feet and stood slightly in front of her, protecting her from whatever was coming, but it was a sight neither of them could have anticipated.

Streaming into the clearing came half the village, some shouting and angry, holding pitchforks and sticks; others, like Mrs Cole and the doctor, were unarmed and trying to pacify the baying masses.

'There she is!' Hilda, the old woman who had scored her in the village pointed at Luna, as everyone fell silent.

'There's the witch.'

42

'What's all this about?' Marcus asked, directing his question to Dr Gardener, who was at the front of the crowd.

'We were summoned by your manservant, Webber, who called around the village shortly before dusk, telling us to assemble by the well at midnight if we wanted to know the truth of who was behind all the witchcraft and dark things that have been happening. Many wouldn't leave their houses on All Hallows' Eve but some of us were curious enough to band together.'

'Safety in numbers, and all that,' said Constable Jones, although the policeman was not in uniform and Luna thought she could see the wooden grip of a revolver tucked into the band of his trousers.

Where *was* Webber? Luna scanned the faces. Perhaps she really had seen him earlier in the trees – not as a spirit summoned like the others, but as a mortal, causing mischief and mayhem.

'And we've seen the truth now, with our own eyes,' one of the men brandishing a spade shouted. 'The Ravenswood Witch in the clearing at the witching hour. It's quite obvious she's been Devil-worshipping. Look at the marks in the soil, the candles, the grimoire.'

Luna was horrified.

'These aren't my—'

'Burn her!' Hilda screamed, as the doctor turned to the old lady with an incredulous look on his face. 'She's too powerful for my poppets. Seven of 'em I've made of her and nothing.' So *she* was behind the clay figures and the blinding pains – this sad old woman who was so convinced that Luna was a witch. 'Burn her, I say.'

'Really, madam, contain yourself. We have moved on since those barbaric times.' The doctor was quite indignant and swung back to Marcus. 'But I do think the woman claiming to be your wife has questions to answer, Greybourne. Something unsavoury has certainly happened here tonight and I have fears for her sanity and, if you are supporting such ritualistic nonsense, perhaps even your own.'

'It's not what it looks like...' Marcus began but was shouted down by the crowd, just as a young man sprang out of the rabble and grabbed Luna, pushing her away from the protection of her husband and holding a knife to her throat.

'Stop this nonsense at once!' Mrs Cole stepped forward. 'Freddie, put the knife down.'

Luna felt the cold of the blade against her skin and wondered if this was how it would all end. Would this lad see to it that she never left the woods alive? One quick slice across her throat and it would all be over. With her swimming head and thudding heart, she half-believed it would be the merciful option.

Marcus lunged to snatch her back, but the man growled and his weapon-bearing arm went rigid. Not prepared to risk her safety, her husband stepped away.

'Leave her be.' Mr Webber came rushing from the depths of the trees. 'She ain't a witch. She ain't even Luna Greybourne. You've got this all wrong but I saw everything.' He shook his head and shuddered. '*Everything*. It's that Mr Findlay I called you all here to see. I'm pretty sure he's behind it all: the animals, the ill-wishing, even the muteness of the little feral girl.'

Luna felt the knife drop away as the young lad's hand fell to his side, but his grip on her arm remained tight.

'Findlay's our friend,' Mrs Cole said, gently. 'I don't believe in the supernatural, but I do know him to be a kind man and a healer of sorts, even if the doctor doubts his methods. He has helped so many in the village and passed over thoughtful gifts and money to support Penny. He's not responsible for her being struck dumb.'

'I know many of you don't have cause to trust my word, but I know what I saw,' Mr Webber insisted. 'I've been passing through these woods at night since I started working here – the reasons ain't no one's business but my own – and I saw the cunning man with Mrs Greybourne, just before the birds wouldn't let him enter the woods no more. I never said nothing because I'm largely of a mind that if I stay out of other people's business, they'll stay out of mine. But him and her were casting spells, dancing naked and fornicating together—'

'Harlot!' screamed Hilda, running up to Luna and spitting in her face. 'Spawn of Beelzebub. Pagan whore. Kill her for her carnal wantonness!' It appeared she was determined to condemn Luna for something – anything – and being a fallen woman was as good a reason as being a Devil-worshipping one.

'Findlay?' Marcus's eyes widened in disbelief. *'It was Findlay?'*

He had known then, as the cunning man had implied, of his wife's indiscretions, even if not who they were with. But was it enough to drive him to murder?

The constable gently guided Luna away from Freddie. She returned to her husband's side and he drew her close once more.

'Go to Honeysuckle Cottage,' Mr Webber insisted, addressing the horde. 'All of you. Findlay ain't gonna stop you. He's dead in that fire and you need to be thankful for it. I knew things were brewing, coz I've been watching him these past few days and broke into his house tonight, after he left for the well. What I found there would make a grown man weep. I ain't saying too much coz there's women here, but he had some pretty grotesque books upstairs, with pictures in 'em showing wicked things with children. There were evil instruments, stuff in jars that'd turn your stomach, and a journal under his pillows. I can't read the words but I'm betting it ain't his thoughts on the reverend's weekly sermon.'

He slipped a slim leather notebook from his coat and handed it to the doctor, who moved to stand closer to one of the lamp holders and started to flick through the pages.

'I know I've slapped my wife about a bit in my time, but I ain't never done the unholy evil things he did.'

'Merciful Father,' the doctor whispered, as his eyes rapidly scanned Findlay's words. 'Penny. No wonder the poor girl stopped speaking.'

For a moment, the woods were silent as people absorbed the magnitude of the cunning man's depravity. They started to cast nervous glances at each other and shuffle from foot to foot. Luna thought back to when Findlay had talked to her about looking into the eyes of a monster who had ill-used little children, and she realised he was undoubtedly talking about himself. The evil that had so frightened him had stared back at him from his own mirror.

'Take some of the men, Constable, see for yourselves. And then tell me he wasn't practically the Devil Himself. I may not be a good man, and God knows one day I shall pay for my sins, but the things I saw in his trunk and kept around his bed will haunt me until the day I die. Findlay fooled us all but I saw him summoning the dead tonight, assaulting this woman, trying to murder her raven—'

'Her familiar, more like,' the old woman shouted but was largely ignored by those around her, who were losing interest in her accusations against Luna, too shocked by Webber's words and their implications.

'To my mind, we should be thanking her and that bird,' the manservant said. 'They've saved us.'

And with the impeccable timing that Bran always seemed to possess, he swooped down from the tallest oak and flew past Luna's face, with something dangling from his beak. She felt the cool rush of air as he swept past, and realised with horror what the small, white sphere swinging from a cord was, as Findlay looked into her soul one last time.

Her legs buckled and she felt the strong arms of Marcus catch her as everything faded to black.

43

Luna opened her eyes to a softly creeping dawn and found herself across the chaise longue in the drawing room, a blanket across her legs, and the housekeeper holding a cold wet cloth to her forehead. Her head was throbbing and she thought that if she moved too quickly, she might be sick.

'Poor lamb. With everything she's been through, it's not surprising that she passed out.'

'Is she awake?' Marcus's voice came from the back of the room. 'Let me sit with her. I want to be with my wife.'

Mrs Webber reached for Luna's hand, squeezed it and muttered something about her being the daughter she'd never had. As she stepped away and returned to her duties, Marcus slid into her seat and his concerned eyes bored into those of his wife.

'Oh, my darling girl. I'm so sorry for everything I've put you through from the moment we met on the path back in April. I broke your ankle, scooped you up and promised to keep you safe, but in reality, all I have done is cause you more harm. I wasn't there for you tonight and can't forgive myself. I have kept you in the dark and, in so doing, I placed you in greater danger.'

The threatened nausea slowly subsided and she shuffled into a sitting position. Fragmented memories of earlier began to drift back. Findlay was the witch, he had fooled them all, and now he was dead, so what was Marcus still keeping from her?

'Then tell me everything.'

He rubbed his hand back and forth across his mouth and shook his head. The pause stretched out between them and his silence began to worry her.

'I lose you either way.'

'Try me.'

He sighed and briefly closed his eyes, as if to sort things in his own head, before he began his tale, taking himself back in time, and finally addressing the question that had troubled Luna since her arrival at Ravenswood. Where was the woman she'd replaced?

'A storm was on its way; I could smell it. The trees were restless and there was an icy chill in the air. My wife had been hiding out in the woods for days, hysterical and violent. Sometimes my efforts to calm her only distressed her further and so I'd let her be and taken the opportunity to go into Manbury. My finances were at crisis point and I suspect she was hiding partly because she knew how much I was relying on the inheritance payment, and was determined I should not receive it...'

He took in a long breath and then slowly exhaled. Secrets once spoken aloud were no longer secrets.

'I returned that afternoon to find one of my precious ravens nailed to the gate. There was a stillness about Ravenswood that unsettled me, and as I walked about the gardens I found dead bird after dead bird. Mrs Webber had heard noises from behind the barn earlier but was too frightened to investigate, so I headed out the back and found my wife standing in the doorway, a knife in her hand and covered in blood.'

Luna did not like where this was leading but remained silent. She had asked him to tell the truth and she must listen to it, however unpalatable it proved to be.

'She told me that she was done with the damn birds,' he said. 'That she was sick of their beady eyes watching her from the treetops, mocking her existence and judging her actions, and that they deserved to die. That I deserved to die... That she was sick of me, that I was a pathetic excuse for a man and that she'd found someone else.' He shook his head again. 'That screwing a bad man was so much more thrilling than bedding a good one...'

She blushed at his choice of words, as Marcus got to his feet and walked over to the window, looking out across the meadow, and down to the river. It was as if he couldn't face her as he relayed the next part of his story.

'And for me that was the ultimate betrayal. I was broken and couldn't do it any more. The storm finally arrived as the rain began pattering out a gentle tattoo on the shed roof and the light was all but gone. I told her that I was done with her. She was on a path that would only lead to her destruction, and I no longer had any desire to prevent it. I simply turned and walked out of the barn and into the rain. The lesson being never turn your back on a madwoman with a knife in her hand...'

Luna saw the truth of it all in that moment. The shoulder injury on the day they met.

Swinging her legs to the floor, she rose slowly to her feet and walked over to him. It seemed he had run out of adequate words. She placed the flat of her left hand on his broad back, gently sweeping up to the wound he'd been nursing in April. He reached across his chest to meet her fingers. Still, he would not turn to face her and they stood in silence for a few moments.

Bran appeared at the window before them and tapped for it to be opened. Marcus released her hand and stepped forward to slide the sash upwards, but the raven did not hop across the threshold, and instead bird and man had one of those silent conversations her husband was so adept at having, before he finally turned to face her.

'I was with her last night, when I should have been with you. We had unfinished business and I had to say goodbye. I think Bran wants me to take you to her.'

Luna frowned. Was he talking about his wife? Or someone else? And why had he not finished his tale? His wife had stabbed him and then what? She'd been so certain that the real Luna Greybourne was dead, because she'd seen her ghost on several occasions with her own eyes – including last night in the bonfire. His words made no sense. Had Marcus put her in an asylum? Or kept her closer to home? He reached out his hand and she took it, as he guided her through the house and out into the meadow – now a yellowing carpet of dying flowers and grassy tussocks. Bran flew alongside them as the morning dew hung heavy on the vegetation, soaking into her skirts and boots, and a chill wind whipped across her face.

They came to a halt at the gate, and Marcus stood before the last of the white blooms on the rose bush, visible in the dawn as they reflected what little light was available. Bran landed on the gatepost and there was an expectant silence as they both looked at her. It took her a few moments to realise that they had reached their destination.

He had brought her to see the woman who had beguiled him and then bedevilled him.

He had brought her to Luna.

This bush was not simply part of the replanting, she realised, but a marker for what was buried beneath. Findlay had been right to claim Mrs Greybourne was dead. It all made sense now: why Marcus had been so certain their charade would not be exposed by a returning wife, and his words when he'd admitted he too had been driven to commit desperate acts.

The white rose symbolised forgiveness, and that was what he was asking for. She, naturally, had a love of the blooms that were her namesake, and had even looked up their meaning after his aunt had talked of the language of flowers. This bush was now past its best; the remaining petals had brown edges and many were scattered on the soil beneath, but the plant was strong and had established nicely. She reached out to touch a flowerhead and several further petals floated gently to the ground.

Luna met Marcus's eyes and saw the burden he carried, and would carry with him always. He had come to his wife on All Hallows' Eve to say a final goodbye. The second candle in the church had been for her. She didn't ask how the woman had died, and instead gave the smallest nod of her head to confirm she understood what he was showing her, thinking how strange it was that the shrub that bore her real name, Rose, now guarded his wife.

'We shall leave the past where it belongs,' she said, quoting his words from their first night together back at him. 'It's not our truth. Let us live in a world where Marcus and Luna Greybourne are happily married and their future is full of unwritten possibilities.' They still had to face the magistrate, and there was a very real risk that her identity would be revealed, but if this was to be their last few days together, she would embrace them.

She heard him exhale a slow sigh of relief. There was no judgement from her; she was going nowhere. Had he killed Luna in fear of his own life? Had he killed her because he simply couldn't take any more? Or had she turned the knife upon herself because of something he'd said or done? She would never make him speak the truth of that night. In fact, she would ask no questions at all, because she wasn't certain she could cope with the answers. It was enough that he was telling her, without the need for words, that she could be Luna if she chose. There would be no vengeful wife returning to dethrone her.

She looked across at the river, rippling streaks of gold shimmering across the surface, as that rising globe of fire bestowed colour once more on a world that had been so very black.

Finally, he spoke. 'I have always preferred the front of the house: the wildflower meadow, open landscape and view across the river. I think you are happier here too, are you not?'

'Yes,' she said, not sure which Luna he was asking. He was after reassurance, and she was happy to give it to him.

The truth was that, despite the unpleasant memories this house held for them both, she was content at Ravenswood. She had all the family she would ever need: a loving and devoted husband, and, if the well was to be believed, a baby on the way. All she hoped for now was that they were able to make new memories and that they would be happy ones.

'You took a huge risk, that day by the river when I broke my ankle,' she said. 'I was not guilty of the crime they were hunting me down for, but you were not to know that.'

Marcus studied her for some time before answering.

'One look at your face and I knew you were a good person; your concern for both my pocket watch and my well-being completely astonished me. There was something in your eyes I recognised, something I could not pin down, but it spoke of desperation, loneliness and a desire to be loved. I think you could see that in me, too.' She nodded. 'I promised myself in that moment that I would never ask you anything beyond your name. My reality would be that the beautiful girl in my arms was my wife. Her kindness was all I ever hoped for; her love I had never anticipated.'

He reached out and pulled her close, wrapping the sides of his thick wool coat around them both, so that they were as one. She could smell the lingering woodsmoke and buried her head into his cotton shirt, until she found the smell of him – overpowering and addictive.

'I have repeatedly asserted that I do not believe in witchcraft,' he whispered into her hair. 'Even though I'm not sure I will ever be able to adequately explain everything that has happened on my lands, but it is undeniable that real magic exists in this mysterious universe of ours.'

'Oh?' She looked up at his serious face.

'Haven't I always insisted that it is only real when you believe it? And from the moment I scooped you up from the bank, and considered that a woman could show me kindness and compassion, I realised that I deserved a little happiness. Everything I wanted was in my arms, and I have never allowed myself to stop believing you could be mine, even though it was an impossible dream—'

She interrupted him with a gentle kiss, rising up on her toes to reach his mouth with her own.

'I love you with a passion that burns brighter than any sun,' he said, as they broke apart.

'I know.'

She looked down at the rose bed and thought of the morning they'd collided. Marcus had climbed up to the path, returning to a spade lying on the ground, after washing his hands in the river and she suddenly realised why he had been so preoccupied, and not seen her racing for the ferry.

In all likelihood, moments before she had barrelled into him, Marcus Greybourne had buried his wife.

44

As they stood together under a breaking dawn, Constable Jones came staggering up the track that led to the ferry, and beyond that, Honeysuckle Cottage. The man's face was grey and his eyes glassy and unfocused, as he called out to them. He came to a halt by the gate and Marcus reached for Luna's hand and held it tight. They would fight whatever was thrown at them as man and wife, and she would go to the grave declaring herself to be Luna Greybourne. They knew each other's darkest secrets now, and if that had not torn them apart, then nothing could.

'I took a small party of villagers to Findlay's place,' the constable said, his head shaking slowly from side to side as if to dislodge the things he'd seen. 'And we now know Mr Webber's words to be true. The whole thing has disturbed everyone beyond measure and some of the men returned to deal with the woods for you, sir.' By this, he could only mean that all evidence of what had happened at the well was currently being tidied up or disposed of. 'Your man even talked a bit about what he'd witnessed with your wife over the last few years, *before* she was able to wean herself from the laudanum. He says it's like she's a different woman now she's free of the opiates and deserves a second chance.' The men exchanged a look. 'Let's just say, the villagers who mistook your wife for a witch now realise that she is not guilty of any of the unjust accusations of dabbling in the supernatural.'

Marcus nodded.

Yes, thought Luna, *because Webber told them I'm not her.* In their gratitude for ridding them of Findlay, the community were prepared to accept her as his wife of ten years, even though many knew this to be a lie. Luna could just imagine Mrs Cole taking the lead and telling everyone of the hell that Marcus had lived through, and asking if he didn't deserve a little happiness.

'Little Doubton owes you a great deal, Mrs Greybourne. I shall be informing the magistrate that I have no doubt of your identity, and several upstanding members of the community are prepared to swear on the Bible, if necessary, that you are who you say you are. And that includes Doctor Gardener – whose testimony alone should put the matter to bed. The young lady who made the accusation against her maid has no reason to suppose Rose Turner is in Little Doubton, and the tinker can be persuaded to keep quiet.'

Luna and Marcus looked at each other in surprise. Dear God – what had the cunning man been responsible for that God-fearing men would perjure themselves? The mutilated animals, summoning the dead... and Penny. It didn't bear thinking about.

But Luna didn't want to spend her life looking over her shoulder, worrying about who might stroll through their front meadow looking for her, or who she might meet when she popped into the village for supplies. She was done with running.

'I have no right to ask this, Constable Jones, but if the magistrate can be made to accept that I am Marcus's wife, perhaps he could also be persuaded to look further into the murder of Daniel Thornbury. I would be eternally grateful,' Luna said.

'I think you have every right to ask for our help, Mrs Greybourne. If you asked for the moon, I've a feeling the people of Little Doubton would cast a fishing line into the night sky and hook it down for you. If you tell me all that you know, I will certainly do my best.'

'Then please ask him to consider that Rose Turner may well be innocent. A woman fleeing because she was framed by another? Miss Eloise

Haughton was in love with Daniel and was not best pleased when he proposed to her servant girl. It was she who asked Rose to buy the flypapers, and who made the cordial that Daniel drank. Why would a maid purchase such a thing for the household, unless she had been asked to by her mistress? The maid was not stupid; she would have gone to a chemist where she was not known, if she intended to use them to kill.'

'Then Rose should return to Lowbridge and defend herself. It was beyond madness to run.'

'I believe she panicked because her mistress was prepared to tell wicked lies, and she didn't think she would be believed.'

The constable nodded and she felt Marcus's arm pull her even closer.

'Then I will do my best. Although I should like to know how you have come by all this information?' he asked, but he knew; she could see it in his eyes.

'Let's just say that once, what feels like a lifetime ago, I knew Rose Turner very well.'

'Then please pass my regards on to her, should you see her,' he said, and nodded.

'Oh, that poor woman is long gone. I doubt anyone will *ever* see her again...'

* * *

Luna left Marcus by the front gate, talking to the constable, and returned to the house. He promised not to be long but she needed to rest.

She passed Mrs Webber bustling about in the kitchens so stopped to speak to her.

'Goodness, where have you been?' the housekeeper said. 'Woke up to find myself alone in an empty house and the doors unlocked. I thought witches had got the lot of you.'

'We're all fine but I am exhausted and must sleep. I'll tell you all about it another time. Please inform the master I'm upstairs when he returns. My head still feels very wobbly and the shock of everything hasn't hit me yet.'

Although it had been colder outside than it was in, she was starting to shake. It would take a long time to work through everything that had happened to her in the last six months but much of it she would shut behind a solid door and padlock from the outside, never to be opened.

With the constable promising to investigate Miss Haughton's involvement in Daniel's death, was it possible that Mr and Mrs Greybourne could now walk into the sunlight together and not give a backwards glance to the shadows left behind?

Mrs Webber looked concerned but didn't question her further.

'Of course. Get some rest, my dear, and I'll prepare a special dinner for this evening when you're feeling a bit perkier. I thought I might try something new. I've seen a recipe for quite an exotic soufflé and you look like you could do with cheering up.' Luna took a deep breath and forced out a smile. Mrs Webber and exotic did not go hand in hand and she was looking forward to Hattie's return the following day. 'And let me know if you see that husband of mine. I haven't set eyes on him since yesterday evening, but I know he's been home because he's taken some fresh clothes from the drawer.'

Luna nodded, climbed the stairs and headed for the bedroom, but when she got to her doorway, she froze. There were footsteps in the attic again, she could hear them as plain as day, yet she had seen the ghosts pass over to the other side in Findlay's bizarre ritual – Marcus's wife, amongst them.

Ever-practical, she knew she would not be able to sleep if she didn't investigate, and this time, she was not laid up in bed with a broken ankle preventing her from doing so. She walked to the end of the corridor and opened the small door that led up to the top floor. It had not been locked since her arrival in the spring, when Marcus had finally known it was safe to retrieve those possessions and heirlooms that he had kept away from his wife's violent temper.

Cautiously, she pulled the door towards her and, with silent feet, crept up the narrow wooden stairs. She had not been to this part of the house before, having been told by Marcus to stay away from it when she'd first arrived. As her head peered over the top step, she could see it was dotted with tea chests. A few fragile ornaments and lamps stood about, and four very small windows gave her enough light to make out the hunched figure of Mr Webber bending over a small crate. A carpet bag was by his feet and he was filling it with selected items. He heard her before he saw her and jumped up.

'Now look 'ere—'

She knew exactly what he was up to but was too weary to care. He'd probably been taking the occasional small trinket since Marcus had ordered the attics unlocked, she realised, and it was undoubtedly him she'd heard when she'd been laid up with a broken ankle. But his thieving wasn't what she wanted to address. She stepped up into the room and faced him.

'I'm not sure why or how you managed to gather the village together, particularly on a night when so many were petrified to leave their houses, but I am forever in your debt.'

His head jolted backwards; he'd not been expecting praise. His eyes narrowed but he detected the sincerity in her voice.

'Well...' He shrugged, 'Like I said, I'd seen things and, although I don't like you much, I liked her even less. I'm pretty certain she weren't no witch,' he scoffed. 'She was out of her wits, a vicious little bitch when riled, and her dancing and singing were all a load of mumbo jumbo. But when I finally worked out that bastard was behind it all, I was worried for everyone's safety – 'specially my own. It was only when the doctor started reading out bits of that journal that we realised how wicked he truly was. Them birds knew though – that was why they never let him into the woods and why Bran made such a fuss that day he came here to help with your foot.'

Of course, she'd assumed the raven was agitated by being near Mr Webber – which he probably was; he was a desperately unpleasant man who treated his wife like a punchbag. But Findlay had been a whole other level of evil, and the raven had sensed the cunning man downstairs that day. Their visitor had believed all the birds dead. No wonder he never returned to Ravenswood after that first occasion; Bran would have pecked him to pieces.

'There's been evil about these parts for a long time,' he continued. 'I guess it was easy to pin it all on a madwoman but, it turns out, even the most pious amongst that lot would happily perjure themselves for the woman who removed the very Devil from our lives.'

'Like I said, thank you.' There was an awkward pause and her eyes fell to the carpet bag. 'Your wife is looking for you.' But Luna knew he was preparing to leave Ravenswood for good and she'd worked out why.

Webber's nightly expeditions had been to visit the widow she'd seen him with at the harvest supper. The woman lived over the hill, on the other side of the woods, and she suspected the manservant had been seeing her for years. The figure she'd seen running from the house the day they returned from the village had been his visiting mistress. With his wife away, the cat had played. It was possible that the man was even father to some of the smaller children.

'Look, the missus didn't see me creep back in this morning, and things here have got... complicated, so consider this me handing in my notice. That young Oscar can do twice my work and I know you don't much like me. I'm sure you'll be glad I'm out your hair.' He paused. 'I didn't do it, you know, throw the tile at the master. I swear I dropped it down to the lad and it shot sideways like magic. Never seen anything like it.'

She nodded, knowing that there were things she had also witnessed since arriving at Ravenswood that defied explanation. Perhaps the real Luna *had* been responsible; it wouldn't be the first time a jealous woman had harmed the man she loved. Would Eloise ever be made to pay for her crime? Luna didn't know, but there was a whole village who would swear that she was not Rose Turner. It was unlikely Miss Haughton would be seeking her out; a guilty missing maid would suit her just fine. A found and innocent one might not.

'I'll be leaving now, if you don't mind.' Webber bent down to retrieve his bag, before hoisting it over his shoulder, the contents within clanging as metal hit metal. 'Tell the wife I'm sorry for everything. It's the drink, see? I just can't stop m'self.'

He didn't need to say anything further. Life was not black and white. Both herself and Marcus understood that only too well. Good people could be driven to do bad deeds, and occasionally bad people could do good.

The manservant walked towards her, but she was blocking his exit and stood firm.

'I don't want to hurt you, but if you try to stop me, I will.'

If she cried thief, Marcus might hear her and come to her rescue, but she didn't want her husband involved in a fight, particularly as she had no idea if Mr Webber was armed. Material possessions meant nothing to her. Her life here meant everything.

She stepped to the side and let him pass.

His one good deed – the kindness he had shown by rallying the village and clearing her name – was worth every last silver spoon.

* * *

When she entered her bedroom, Bran was sitting outside the window, waiting for her. She opened the sash, expecting him to hop over the sill, but he stayed outside. Too tired to play his games, she crawled under the counterpane and left the window as it was, for him to come and go.

There was the sound of beating wings approaching, and Luna turned back to see two black silhouettes against the morning sky.

'Kiss me,' squawked Bran.

The smaller bird hopped from foot to foot, before settling and tipping her head to preen his feathers. And Luna smiled to herself as she allowed her eyes to close and her mind to float off into a dreamworld, far from the nightmare she had just been through.

Luna had found her magic, collided with it on a riverside path early one April morning, when she truly believed her life was at an end, and now it appeared her beloved Bran had found his own magic, too.

ACKNOWLEDGEMENTS

Once again, there are a whole host of people to thank for their help in getting this book written, polished and out there, because no woman is an island, and all that...

In no particular order, my grateful thanks go to Isobel Akenhead, my genius editor, who persuaded me witches were the way to go. Big thanks to the wider Boldwood team, but especially Marcela Torres, for whom nothing is ever too much trouble, my delightful copy editor, Helena Newton, eagle-eyed Em Schone for her excellent proofreading and the biggest high five to Alexandra Allden for the cover – you totally nailed it. Working with such a fabulous publisher just gets better and better.

Thank you, as always, to my agent, the formidable Hannah Schofield. You don't buy a guard dog who whimpers in the cupboard. You buy one that means business. She means business.

I must give a special mention to the few days I had Chez Swain when I was dealing with a particularly tough round of edits. Thank you for the peace and quiet, plot wrangling, and the distinct lack of people who were related to me, H. J.

Thanks also to my office buddy, Clare, who frequently looked things up for me in her *Culpeper's Complete Herbal*, and for her support when I scared myself silly with some of the research. Apparently, it's not wise to google how to summon the Devil, in case he pops by...

And talking of research, *Cursed Britain – A History of Witchcraft and Black Magic in Modern Times* by Thomas Waters was the book that reassured me that the accusations against, and fervent belief in, witches was still prevalent in nineteenth-century Britain. It was an invaluable resource.

As always, my real-life author friends, who are many, but particularly Ian Wilfred, Heidi Swain, Clare Marchant, Rosie Hendry, Kate Hardy, Claire Wade, Kate Smith, Mick Arnold, Glynis Peters, Jessica Redland, Laura Pearson and Morton Gray – for all keeping me sane at different times and in different ways. And to Dena Green for reading the book very early on when I was having doubts.

To Sue Baker, Lynsey Bessent, Grace Power, Diss Bookshop, Eye Library, Park Radio and all the lovely readers, bookshop owners, librarians, book bloggers and event organisers.

And finally, the famalam. You guys are the best.

Jenni x

ABOUT THE AUTHOR

Jenni Keer is the well-reviewed author of historical romances, often with a mystery at their heart. Most recently published by Headline and shortlisted for the 2023 RNA Historical Romantic Novel of the Year.

Sign up to Jenni Keer's newsletter to get a free short story

Visit Jenni's website: www.jennikeer.co.uk

Follow Jenni on social media here:

- facebook.com/jennikeerwriter
- x.com/JenniKeer
- instagram.com/jennikeer
- bookbub.com/authors/jenni-keer

ALSO BY JENNI KEER

No. 23 Burlington Square

At the Stroke of Midnight

The Ravenswood Witch

Letters from *the past*

Discover page-turning historical novels from your favourite authors and be transported back in time

Join our book club Facebook group

https://bit.ly/SixpenceGroup

Sign up to our newsletter

https://bit.ly/LettersFromPastNews

Boldwood

Boldwood Books is an award-winning fiction publishing company seeking out the best stories from around the world.

Find out more at www.boldwoodbooks.com

Join our reader community for brilliant books, competitions and offers!

Follow us
@BoldwoodBooks
@TheBoldBookClub

Sign up to our weekly deals newsletter

https://bit.ly/BoldwoodBNewsletter